Futures from nature

Futures from nature

EDITED BY HENRY GEE

A TOM DOHERTY ASSOCIATES BOOK
NEW YORK

This is a work of fiction. All of the characters, organizations, and events portrayed in these stories are either products of the authors' imaginations or are used fictitiously.

FUTURES FROM *NATURE*

Edited by David G. Hartwell

Book design by Spring Hoteling

A Tor Book
Published by Tom Doherty Associates, LLC
175 Fifth Avenue
New York, NY 10010

www.tor.com

Tor® is a registered trademark of Tom Doherty Associates, LLC.

Library of Congress Cataloging-in-Publication Data

Futures from nature / edited by Henry Gee.—1st ed.
p. cm.
"A Tom Doherty Associates Book."
ISBN-13: 978-0-7653-1805-3
ISBN-10: 0-7653-1805-9
1. Science fiction, American. 2. Future—Fiction. 3. Forecasting—Fiction.
4. Evolution—Fiction. I. Gee, Henry, 1962–
PS648.S3F936 2007
813'.0876608—dc22 2007024924

First Edition: November 2007

Printed in the United States of America

0 9 8 7 6 5 4 3 2 1

For Penny

contents

Nostalgia for the Future

Henry Gee

I

"I just *knew* I'd find you up here!"

Estragon said nothing, but shuffled a little westward on the rooftop bench ("Away from Mecca," as he always put it) to allow his old friend Vladimir a perch. Without speaking, he nodded toward the unused mouthpiece of the hubble-bubble. Only the tip of his long, cratered nose was visible beneath his cowl. The cowl of a scientific editor, one of the only two left in existence. Vladimir wore the other, but his was thrown back, his wild white hair blowing in the breeze. Hair across his fat and jowly face, Vladimir took up the mouthpiece and took a long toke.

"This is good stuff, my old friend."

"It's called 'Revolutionary Guard.' Camden *suq*. Better than the usual, anyway."

The two old colleagues continued to puff away in silence. There was little to say, or so it seemed, and apparently little to do. The machines pretty much did everything at *Nature*—selecting the manuscripts for publication, writing the opinion pieces, editing, pruning, and—as dispassionately as it was frequently—sending the messages of regretful disappointment to the machines that did the research and sent in the manuscripts for publication.

The slow exfoliation of *Nature*'s human staff had been so gradual as to have been almost imperceptible, until the two aged sages were all that was left, an ineradicable remnant thanks to stipulated pension provisions common in an earlier age but now otherwise extinct, and impossible to revoke. With little for them to do, the thinning staff took ever-longer cigarette breaks until these pauses became more or less continuous. Vladimir and Estragon's hubble-bubble was constantly on the go.

But Estragon sensed that his colleague, ever the more excitable of the pair, was bubbling with suppressed agitation.

"Oh, spit it out—whatever it is."

"Well, it's . . . it's . . ."

Estragon pulled away from the pipe and turned to his friend of fifty years with a piercing blue-eyed stare, putting Vladimir on the spot.

"I was looking through some of the old archives, you know, and . . . well, I found something . . . *interesting*."

Estragon turned back to his pipe. "*Everything's* interesting to *you,*" he growled through clenched teeth.

Vladimir pretended to be outraged. "Yes, *interesting.*"

"What—more than our old papers on Quantum Tumescence? Histrionic Chromosomal Nano-Engineering? And what was it you came up with last week—Transneptunian Applied Astrology?" Estragon spat out the capitals to punctuate his bitter sarcasm. Vladimir was unperturbed.

"More—my old friend—more interesting even than *that*!"

"Well, I never."

The two returned to their shared, comradely pursuit of epithelial narcotic ingestion, allowing Vladimir sufficient pause to make his announcement all the more dramatic. Like the shrinking of the tide before a tsunami.

"Fiction!"

"*Fiction*?"

"That's what I said, Estragon—*Fiction*."

"You mean—fiction as in made-up stories? Suspension-of-disbelief and all that?" Estragon's studied nonchalance fell away before frank astonishment, the hubble-bubble quite forgotten—his mouth open, his mouthpiece inert in his hand, like a dead earthworm. The stage, such as it was, belonged to Vladimir, unopposed.

"Yes, I know. I was amazed myself. But it seems that *Nature* strayed into those forbidden realms, once. I came across a series of papers we published a century or so back, at the turn of the old-style millennium, before we recalibrated to the calendar of the Prophet, Blessings Be Upon Him."

Estragon made a hint—just a *hint*, mind—of the ritual obeisances.

"These papers were all gathered together under the title of 'Futures.' At first I thought that they were proper papers, you know, but they were suspiciously thin on recognizably citable objects. Then, after I had read a few, it dawned on me—they were *speculations* about how things might become, were one to pursue certain scientific trends much in discussion at the time."

"What—like Nanoparticulate Posthumanity, First Contact, and such?"

"Yes—well, I *think* so. But they were all in English, so it was sometimes hard to tell. Not even Farsi, let alone Arabic."

"Sounds blasphemous—and double blasphemous! Jolly good they *were* in English. You wouldn't want that kind of thing to get around, really."

"No—I should think not!" Vladimir flushed, as if he'd been caught looking at pictures of women's ankles. He fell silent.

"Oh, come *on*!" his friend urged. "I'm all agog, and you can't stop now. Discretion is my middle name. Besides, who can we *tell*?"

Another silence fell. The two stared across the rooftops of London, all quiet but for the all-pervasive hum and *tick-tick-tick* of machines, machines, *machines.* Vladimir composed himself.

"It started with one of our predecessors, a man called Gee . . ."

"Gee what?"

"Just 'Gee.' "

"Odd name . . ."

"Well, this Gee person, with the encouragement of his colleagues, especially his supervisor, Editor Philip Campbell, and his other editor friends—yes, there were quite a few at the time!—commissioned a series of speculations from people who wrote this stuff as a hobby. Or even—if can you credit it—for a *living.*"

"Unbelievable!"

"*Nature* carried this material, every week, for more than a year . . ."

"Amazing!"

"But wait, there's more . . . after a gap of five years they ran an even more extensive series. All told, *Nature* published more than *a hundred and fifty examples.*"

"Then what happened?"

"Well, I think this Editor Gee put some of them in a book with another man called Hartwell in a place called Tor."

"Hartwell? Not as outlandish as 'Gee,' at any rate. But what *then*?"

"Then nothing. They never tried it again. Things . . . *changed.*" A longer silence fell, but this time it was Estragon who fractured it.

"Fiction. Haven't read any of that for years."

"You mean . . . ?"

"I confess that I did indulge, once upon a time. In my youth. I don't mind admitting it." He sighed. "After all, as I said, who can we tell?"

Vladimir was aghast. Estragon continued.

"Certainly. I was particularly fond of a writer called Dan Simmons. And Neal Asher. And Greg Bear. And especially Moorcock."

"I recognize those names—they were all in this Futures series."

Estragon perked up, a glint of mischief soon almost swamped by a haze of what looked like longing and regret for a lost past, and more still, a lost future. But his eyes narrowed.

"Look, Vlad—are you *sure* it was fiction? We've published some crazy stuff over the centuries. Some of it was literally unbelievable at the time. Much of it was even wrong, I dare say. But all of it at least pretended to be getting at the Holy Truth. You've never read fiction . . ."

"No, that's true: I have been both blessed and cursed with piety."

"In which case, how would you know the difference? The difference between Truth and Illusion? Or anything in between? Or even something that was really the one, but masquerading as the other?"

Vladimir sighed. "You're right. Perhaps one never really knows."

Estragon patted his friend's brown-spotted, wrinkled hand and turned back to the task of cannabinoid inhalation.

"Stick to the Transneptunian Applied Astrology. I would."

Vladimir's thoughts, ever butterflies over the incredible depths of accumulated human achievement, switched track as if the discussion had never happened.

"Did you know that if the Cusp of Quaoar strays into the Seventh House of Sedna . . . ?"

But Estragon was, once again, lost in worlds of his own.

II

Whatever the future may hold for *Nature,* its past—indeed, its very existence—owes much to religious and political discontent. In the nineteenth century, academics at the old universities of Oxford and Cambridge were required to belong to the conventional Church of England. Those barred from these institutions for reasons of religion or politics—Catholics, Jews, atheists, and dissenters of every stripe—washed up, perhaps inevitably, in London, where, in 1828, University College was founded.

It was a group of such London-based academics, centered on Thomas Henry Huxley—an early champion of Darwinian evolution—who found themselves with nothing to read. The group, known as the X Club (Ladies' Night was known as the XYves), had been devotees of a periodical called *The Reader.* But when that folded, the X Club persuaded Scottish publisher Alexander MacMillan to underwrite a scientific magazine. And so, on November 4, 1869, *Nature* was born, and the MacMillan family has published it ever since. Its rise to eminence was steady but inexorable: many, perhaps most, of the scientific discoveries that have shaped the world (and the minds of science fiction authors) first appeared as research papers in *Nature*'s pages: the structure of DNA, the principles of the laser, the discovery of the neutron, and many more.

It could be that the atmosphere of cheerful sedition in which *Nature* was founded has allowed it to take risks, to venture into near-uncharted publishing territory—simply because it can, or perhaps just for the fun of it. And also, perhaps, because one of *Nature*'s regular contributors, at the turn of the twentieth century, was the Shakespeare of science fiction, H. G. Wells himself. As long ago as 1902, *Nature* published a startling Wellsian vision of the future course of science, including elements that were, incidentally, precursors of psychohistory—Isaac Asimov's fictitious application of statistical mechanics to human history—and even "posthumanity," one of science fiction's current preoccupations.

So it seemed entirely natural for *Nature* to mark the approaching third millennium with a series of SF vignettes. Futures kicked off on November 4, 1999, (the magazine's 130th birthday) with an intense burst of vintage apocalypse from Sir Arthur C. Clarke, the only SF author whom, we thought, the general reader of *Nature* might have heard of.

It could be that we underestimated our audience. Many scientists—if not most of them—grew up reading science fiction, and many readers became fans of the weekly column, if only, perhaps, as a kind of guilty pleasure. We also underestimated the reverence with which *Nature* is held in the SF community. Clarke, despite a mountain of other pressing matters, sent his piece by return, and many well-known SF authors were keen to contribute. Several of the stories were anthologized by David Hartwell in *Best SF 6.* Initially slated for a six-month run, the first series of Futures ran for more than a year, closing in December 2000.

But the itch still remained to be scratched. So when a page fell vacant at the beginning of 2005, the Futures series was ready, starting an arguably even more glorious run, finishing at the end of 2006 (some of these, too, are collected in *Best SF 11*). By that time we realized that many scientists, as well as being avid SF readers, were also very good writers. After having considered pieces on a strictly commission-only basis, we opened our doors to all comers, in the hope of discovering gems from unknown authors, perhaps trying out fiction for the very first time. So, as well as publishing pieces from venerable sages in the field (I shall not embarrass them by naming names), we were able to print a piece from Ashley Pellegrino, daughter of a research scientist, and only eleven years old at the time. This vibrancy prompted the European Science Fiction Society to award *Nature* the accolade of Best Science Fiction Publisher in 2005. Now, nobody has come up *to our face* and said that everything *Nature* publishes is science fiction. *Nature*'s stock in trade is, and remains, the publication of serious, cutting-edge research, some of which will appear, at first sight, to be wonderful if not literally incredible, but we feel that our founders would have approved.

Although Futures in *Nature* has come to an end, this is au revoir, and not good-bye. The column continues in 2007 in *Nature*'s monthly sister title, *Nature Physics,* and it's not entirely unreasonable to suggest that *Nature* itself might not go back to the future.

The genesis of Futures is shrouded in a fog as thick as any that rolled along the streets of Victorian London. Convention has it that it was my idea, although many of my colleagues were thinking along similar lines, and as I've shown, this particular seed had been sown at *Nature* a century before. This, however, is a suitable place to thank all those who have played a part in Futures' genesis and subsequent success.

I should like to thank, first of all, Harriet Coles, onetime book-review editor at *Nature* whose pages were to have accommodated Futures until she passed the baton to me because, she said, I knew more about science fiction than she did. The baton was passed during a convivial lunch we had with Professor Ian Stewart, mathematics professor, prolific science popularizer, and SF author, who started us off with a long list of contacts. In 2000 I visited the New York, NY, offices of the leading SF publisher Tor, where Tom Doherty, David Hartwell, and Patrick Nielsen Hayden offered many more contacts and a great deal of useful advice. It was there that the idea of an anthology was first mooted.

Many of my fellow editors at *Nature* have been enthusiastic followers of the series. Especially deserving of mention are Christopher Surridge and Karl Ziemelis (whose comprehensive knowledge of, respectively, graphic novels and SF blockbusters led to many interesting conversations and suggestions for authors). Surridge, Ziemelis, and several other *Nature* colleagues tried their hand at SF, and some of the results you will see in these pages. None of it, of course, would have been possible without the support of *Nature*'s publishers, Sarah Greaves and Peter Collins; my indomitable copy editor Colin Sullivan;

and artist Jacey, whose intelligent and playful graphics contributed to so much to the look and feel of the series in their magazine form.

In creating this anthology, fulsome praise must be extended to David Hartwell at Tor, who knows infinitely more about compiling a science fiction anthology than I do (necessarily so, because I know precisely zero).

I reserve my final thanks for Philip Campbell, *Nature*'s editor in chief, who had the courage to allow me to commission and run the Futures series—and to do so with no oversight. This, I think, summarizes the spirit of *Nature*: to boldly go where no man has gone before (to coin a phrase), and not to care a damn what happens when we get there—in the knowledge that the result might be entertaining, will probably be interesting, and that we'll have learned something on the way. And who knows, we might even have had some fun. And so I offer this anthology in that same spirit of casual entertainment.

Futures from
nature

Cognitive Ability and the Light Bulb

Brian Aldiss

Brian Aldiss is one of the world's most influential SF writers, as well as being an important contemporary novelist, poet, essayist, dramatist, SF historian, and critic. He sold his first SF story, "Criminal Record," in 1954, at the age of twenty-nine; his first SF novel, Non-Stop, *appeared in 1958. His latest novel,* Jocasta, *was published in 2005, his eightieth year. Once the literary editor of the* Oxford Mail, *he still lives in Oxford, England. His Web site can be found at www.solaris-books.co.uk/aldiss.*

The arrival of the spaceship *Conqueror* into Arcopian space proves ironic. However, it provides us with an opportunity to look back on our distant predecessors and understand something of their combative and rickety societies.

Once the dead bodies had been cleared from the *Conqueror,* and preserved in our museums, mechs were dispatched to examine the ship as part of our phylogenetic record.

The ship was fitted with old-fashioned quantum computers. The *Conqueror* had left the old Solar System late in 2095. It carried ten thousand human embryos in cryogenic conditions, and several million embryos, similarly frozen, of terrestrial animal genera, together with numerous plant species. There were also twenty crew, supported by antithanatonic drugs.

Technologists had designed the ship to accelerate to 12 percent of the speed of light. By their computations, it was due to reach this system (where only two planets capable of supporting carbon-based life had been identified) in 196 years. The power source was a fusion engine.

In those rather primitive days, attention concentrated on the hardware. It was the bacteria on the *Conqueror* that brought about disaster, killing crew and embryos alike.

Subsequent advances in radiotelescopy revealed no fewer than fifteen planets orbiting the Arcopia main-sequence sun, of which five had environments suitable for life. In the Second Renaissance of the early twenty-second century, the spiritual order of God's Exiles perfected an ion drive and equipped another interstellar ship, *Pilgrim. Pilgrim* was launched from plutonian orbit in

2151. It carried with it the embryos of new species of animals, fruits, and human beings. The entire journey was governed by quantors—God's Exiles did not inflict years of imprisonment on humans, as the *Conqueror* had done.

This journey took 138 years to complete. Thus the arrival was in 2289, two years before the *Conqueror* reached us, despite starting fifty-six years later.

In these improved drives we see symbols of the expansion of human consciousness. Everything is subject to change, and living things to evolutionary change, marking their passage through time. Study of the evolution of human consciousness was scarcely recognized as a discipline until interstellar flight proved to speed conceptual processes. The necessity for understanding and dealing with totally new environments was responsible for this rapid acceleration in human mentation. A similar acceleration is recorded some 40,200 years ago in Europe, when fresh environments brought about a great expansion in the metaphors of art and sculpture—all of which represent an upward surge in cognitive ability.

To produce art or science is to experience a coming together of previously somewhat isolated faculties, which combine to make a greater whole. Another well-known example of such a quantal happening is the First Renaissance, a time of great advances in art, science, warfare, and political management.

In describing these advances, twenty-second-century philosopher Almond Kunzel famously deployed an analogy between human consciousness and an antique, incandescent lightbulb. Early consciousness could be likened to a forty-watt bulb—sufficient, dimly, to illumine a room, but insufficient to study details by. The First Renaissance marks a shift in brightness to sixty watts. Much more can be discerned, although illumination is not cast very far.

With the twentieth century, often referred to as the Savage Century, owing to its horrifying record of war, threats of war, and genocide, the bulb brightens to a hundred watts. Despite the savagery, humanity is for the first time developing a form of remote awareness (remware, as we know it) to aid its exploration of all environments.

Those environments included, of course, the Solar System to which our predecessors were then confined, and also the human brain. The brain was almost completely mapped by the end of the Savage Century. With the ability to genetically engineer brain function, many irregularities—caused by the piecemeal nature of this organ as naturally evolved—were eradicated. Clearer thinking emerged. Humanity outgrew war.

We have now reached the stage of, in Kunzel's terms, the thousand-watt brain. Our offspring are born with an understanding of fractals.

This great expansion of cognitive ability led to the new perception of the Universe as a series of contiguities, and to the construction, in the year 2162, of the photon drive. The fleet of ships launched in 2200 arrived here in the planetary system of Arcopia the following year.

Our culture was thus firmly established when the old ships of 2095 and 2151 arrived, fossils of a former time. They harbor, in orbits far from the planet on which humanity began, memories of bygone ages—long before there was even a lightbulb to light our way. Records on these gallant old hulks demonstrate how, sadly, the human world once contained less order, less joy, and less fulfillment than now.

Don't Imitate

Gilles Amon

Gilles Amon is the pseudonym of Andreas Trabesinger, an editor with the journal Nature Physics. *A native of Liechtenstein, he loves motor racing (especially Ferrari, hence the pen name) and fine wines. He lives in London.*

The obvious one to choose, but the most difficult one to conceptualize. The last bottle of the evening, of course, has to be her. The diva. The *grande dame*.

It will seem unreal to get in touch with the Palmer '07 one more time—maybe for the last time. Distant memories of her playful youth will surface; and of the painfully long time it took her to mature, or rather to transform. Only when she was well into her third decade did she start truly to intrigue us, at a point when we had almost stopped believing that there was something extraordinary in this wine. And extraordinary she is.

Of course, we could have paid more attention to certain details. A few did. But we opened the young bottles far too carelessly, too often, and too soon. Had we only had the slightest idea of what a splendid future the 2007 was to experience, we wouldn't have put a premature end to the lives of so many bottles, depriving each one of the peaks to come.

But we did—like most of us so-called real wine aficionados. The most painful thing about having emptied so many bottles decades ago—rather than celebrating them now, when the wine is at the top of its game, and has left standing everything that was ever put in a bottle—the most painful thing is that had we shown more foresight, it would not be my last bottle of beloved Palmer '07 that we will open tonight.

The biggest worry, of course, is—as with all bottles that are not glued—the cork. But I trust it will be fine. The bottle got a new cork in 2037, *au château*. How on Earth they managed to find natural corks twelve years after the European Union banned them, I have no idea. It seemed, back then, fairly early to be replacing the cork, but it was really the last opportunity to do so.

Not that much can be said against gluing the bottles (thankfully, there still are bottles around that need to be properly sealed). Far beyond the environmental aspect, the glue is just perfect nowadays. Many don't even own corkscrews anymore. (I always held on to mine, like scientists who will never ditch their pencils.) The glue never, ever leaks. Never. Easily ripped off—and easily resealed, if you like that kind of thing.

After all, resealing is still better than pouring away your 2003 d'Yquem or 1945 Mouton, once you've had enough for the evening. This has become such a bad habit. But there are hundreds of other reasons to dislike imitations. They cannot be distinguished from the originals, of course. Who could forget that, twenty years ago, Gabriel Robertson—the elder—was unable to identify a single "fake" in a series of twenty-four wines, which included some of his personal favorites? A shock.

Back then "test-tube wines" were still produced under the Dior name, I think, before the branch was taken out of the group a few years later to form Vinor. No one can deny that it was the heavy involvement of the perfume industry that drove the early, purely scientific attempts at "copying" famous vintages—for archival reasons, they said—away from their initial innocence, and toward a monstrous industry.

It wasn't long before everyone owned every vintage of Pétrus ever produced. A period of unspeakable snobbism began: "I don't ruin my burger with a ninety-nine-point wine." Give me a break. Even today, I find it devastating that everybody ran with the idea—and most still do. At least that cruelty of "instant wines" never got off the ground. But nonetheless, countless wineries were faced with ruin, most of them small, independent concerns; but also some big names. Fortunately, the majority of the Grands Crus survived; at least, those of the 2021 reclassification.

Oh, yes, you can still find them, the pearls, but you have to sniff them out. And new stars have appeared, but only a handful, produced by enthusiasts who, audaciously, set out to celebrate wines in their entirety with the same intensity as us. Lucky us, who, unperturbed, kept on searching for real wines, "vinified wines," as they call them these days.

While others stick their noses in "Best of Wine" collections from the corner shop, we are the ones who can see great vintages develop, as they become, well, ready. The 2029s, the 2039s, and, above all, the 2007s. Only we witnessed history unfolding, snapshot by snapshot. Often you don't have much of an idea what will have happened since the last time you looked. Some of the best stories are still being written. And much is still to come, many surprises, I dare say.

Well, enough talking. Let us celebrate the diva.

Check Elastic Before Jumping

Neal Asher

Neal Asher spent most of his life amid the oil and noise of engineering companies, writing SF and fantasy for various small-press titles. Things changed in 2000 when Pan Macmillan picked up a synopsis, and he's now a full-time writer into his second three-book contract. His latest book is The Voyage of the Sable Keech. *He lives in Chelmsford, Essex, England, and his Web site can be found at http://freespace.virgin .net/n.asher.*

Standing before the museum display case, I listened to the cracking of stun rifles outside as CCM—Combined Corporate Military—engaged with the few government troops who could be bothered to fight.

"It's a crappy world," said someone standing nearby.

"Oh, really," I said, peering into the case, and remembering my recent hospital visit, which had occurred just a few days before a crowd of some five hundred thousand drove everyone out of the EU Parliament buildings and then burnt them to the ground . . .

It felt like I was using the scroll wheel on an old-style computer mouse to work my way down the list of news items, then it felt like I clicked the mouse button to select a news item—National Health Service software having some way to go to catch up with the new interactive displays and virtualities. Of course, I hadn't moved a finger since that moment I decided to flout the EU-wide health-and-safety ban on urban bungee jumping and miscalculated the length of my elastic. My shattered skull and snapped spine had left me unable to do more than blink and swallow. A temporary cortical implant, fitted just before they epoxied my skull back together, provided the sensation of movement from my paralyzed limbs and enabled me to use the entertainment system here.

The news item played out in an "Infinity Deepscreen" holographic display seemingly hanging in midair over my bed—this illusion provided by the multicolored lasers, which were tracking my eyes from my comm unit, at present stuck to the front of my monitor suit. Apparently, Allied Energy was drilling for the carbon dioxide that had been pumped down into the gas and oil fields at the beginning of this century. The hope being that those megatons of gas released into the atmosphere will raise temperatures high enough to offset the coming Ice Age by another century. The Green Socialists, still retaining a majority in the European Parliament, were pushing for more stringent controls on energy usage, their contention being that the numerous wind-power projects, having upset the weather patterns of the planet, need to be closed down. I sighed—I could manage that—and was about to move on to the next news item when my consultant interrupted the display.

"How are you today, Joe?"

"Getting a little bored with the primitive entertainment here and rather concerned that you don't seem to know my name." I didn't actually speak the words, since they were a product of my implant and a voice synthesizer, which made me sound like Humphrey Bogart—the new virtual screen idol.

In the display my consultant peered at his paper notes. "Okay, Joe, I'll give it to you straight." It must have been some sort of glitch in the system, since I'd commed others in the hospital and apparently this consultant program called all his patients Joe. "You're in here for the long haul. The new nerve tissue is growing well, but without invasive surgery, it will take some time for the breaks in your vertebrae to knit. You will have to spend a year in a motorized exoskeleton during . . ."

"What about CT nerve-stimulus and keyhole bone welding?" I interrupted.

"NHS funding," he supplied.

"What? Things weren't this bad after I protested the HSE ban on hang gliding, and that was only two months ago."

"Ah yes, I see," he said, once again peering at my notes. He froze for a moment, which seemed to happen whenever he updated, then continued in a slightly different tone. "I see that then you were a European citizen, but now it appears you are a citizen of Ubermart?"

"Yes, I certainly am—I'd rather my taxes went to a more deserving cause." Really, what had finally persuaded me to sign up for corporate citizenship was the last burglary of my apartment. The guy breaking in managed to stab himself with the screwdriver he tried to jemmy the door with and I called him an ambulance. The police arrested me for negligence and then helped the burglar to sue me for damages. Apparently he was "disadvantaged," unable to read or write due to Ritalin abuse and dietary cerebral damage. Corporates tend not to suffer the same problems. Corporate police tend to take an old-fashioned approach to policing, usually in CCTV black spots.

"If you could confirm your Ubermart citizenship number?"

I recited it for him quickly and his image froze again. When he thawed out he said, "Thank you, citizen Philips. Do you mind if I call you Derek?"

"Of course not, it's my name."

"Well, Derek, I am sure we can improve on my previous prognosis. Before we get to that, would you like to enjoy our virtual-reality facilities during your stay?"

"How long will that be?"

"Oh, I think we can have you out of here by this afternoon, Derek."

"That's okay—I'll stick with what I have for the moment." I'd forgotten all about Ubermart's health plan, which as one of their citizens I could also enjoy.

The rest of the day just seemed to speed past. Actual human nurses came in with a suit hoist, asked me kindly if I was ready while simultaneously instructing my suit to inject a really trippy narcotic. Just before I went under I observed a surgical robot cracking open my monitor suit, then poising over me while extending its glittering cutlery.

I awoke amid clean sheets. Walked out of the hospital only an hour later.

The sounds of stun rifles firing seemed to be decreasing.

"You don't agree that it's a crappy world?" asked the guy standing next to me.

"Okay, it's crappy, but it could be worse."

He harrumphed and moved away. I returned my attention to the display case and smilingly inspected the wheelchair resting there, then the dates on the plaque indicating when the first one was invented, and when the last one was used.

Twenty2

Nate Balding

Nate Balding writes a 'zine called Nico on Sunday Mornings, *knows how to rock, stays up later than you, and drinks scotch instead of anything else. He lives in Denver, Colorado.*

"Berlin is the new American experiment."

Vocal intonations; voluminous, deep, resonating inside the monorail car, translations from German into a multitude of languages tickling foreign cochleas lightly from translucent earbud speakers. A short history of Berlin since the erection of the Mitte Arcology and the subsequent construction of similar towers, falling away from the central point like evergreens on a mountainside; reinforced faux-glass impervious to high winds, acid rains, falling space-rock, and high-frequency waves topping every pellucid spire.

Sprita's fingers circled a hollow titanium alloy bar running the length of the magnetic train's passenger chamber, body poised to offset any recoil.

"Our citizens, ten years ago, voluntarily became subjects of the Panmetropolic Drive. There are no more secrets in Berlin."

Sprita stared through the monorail's tinted windows, watching information scroll over Plexiglas as the train passed businesses and points of interest, relaying site info just that side of too-fast-to-read. She assumed it was easier for citizens, with their technological accoutrements gifting enough additional processing capability to endure the informational onslaught constantly pressing into the visual and aural cortices. It induced a headache the first day she'd been there, taking a holiday on the European continent with thousands of others who wanted to see firsthand the world's foremost social experiment.

"The Wall was built during the construction of the first arcology and lined with plates of copper and gold. Inside it, thousands of ferrous bullets fly alongside the edges, generating a massive electromagnetic field that engulfs the entire city. Every person living inside it is coded to communicate with what is essentially a city-sized geomagnetic hard drive."

The monologue continued. Sprita gazed at the other riders, easily discerning Berliner from visitor. Pronounced electronic excesses aside, the Berliners bore certain uncanny homogeneities. Similar hairstyles; similar dress; similar everything. Even the way they sat, practically posed: feet forward, parallel legs, hands in laps occasionally shifting intertwined over chests, and then back.

She'd picked up an oLED-equipped teleshirt. Everything you needed to know could be splayed into an inlay along the sleeves, RSS'd in Arial MT. A miniature rfID tag issued on arrival stored the mainstay of her characteristics, physical and political, and launched her into the hard-drive world amid every other inhabitant, long- and short-term alike. Grant of the pass made her a subject to the experiment and she could, as everyone else, ping information back to a viewing screen or through the earbud she wore. Everything one wanted to know was easily available, constant wi-fi interaction conveyed everything to anyone upon query. Each and every purchase, location, trajectory, ping, glance; recorded, available. The city without secrets.

"Berlin is the only city in the world that can truly call itself twenty-first century. We are at the apex of a technologically advanced civilization, surpassing all others in scientific research and discovery. An entire city of would-be scientists and engineers, our collective knowledge available to anyone willing to share their own."

She was heading into the central arcology seeking a club called Twenty2. Her *personenkult* card informed her, based on commercial purchases and local browsing data, that Panda Parade was playing that night—one of Berlin's only surviving neo-Höllenspektakel groups. They'd exposed the viscera of their guitar pickups to heavy subdermal magnets—a common remanufacturing of the human hand—manipulating strings at varying frequencies, phalangeal theremins operating at resonant frequency and scrying ambient tones from an otherwise maniacal cacophony. The phenomenon started in the heart of Berlin and spread outward, enthralling the youth of Western Europe and slowly trickling on to sonic radar screens in America.

The monorail approached Sprita's stop. Twenty2 lay on the outskirts of the central arcology, in the detritus of last century's dimly illuminated gothic bars, primitive rave clubs, and sparkling house-music meccas. Sprita drifted over the threshold as the magdoor bisected and swiveled aside, bodies pressed coarsely together, flashthrong shopping evidently under way as markdowns and sales and other notifications of imminent mercantile importance scattered into the district, setting off mp6 alerts and charging buyers fractions of cents for personalized content. Her low heels clicked and flickered over ceramic tiles comprised of super-atomic structures manufactured via bacterial scoring and forced bonds; elements not found in the leylines of the old periodic table.

Signals bounced off Sprita, tiny inversions of field straining against the vibration feature of her teleshirt tingling nerve clusters around her wrists, minuscule exo-sense shivers. She saw him from across the floor of the dark stage, multicolored lights ambushing retinas at calculatedly odd moments, glaring and burning away. Their loop was positive, feeding back on each other in the holographic nightstream of virtual knowledge. Relationship status; exact weight and height; recent purchases what and where; living space; names of friends and degrees of separation between him and Sprita's nearly vacant friends list; everything grinned across her sleeve between ulna and radius.

He dug the music, she knew. So did she. It was almost dancing; faint glances parried by strobelights, vForm 2.0 imagery, carefully constructed coifs. Another boy's ping; another; reciprocating and reading and analyzing, unearthing familiarities. Recollections sparked and breathed; latent epiphanies in the corridors of her neural puzzle. So many; so many familiar likes and dislikes, favorite movies and books and bands and supermodels; political affiliations and angles of personal pictures. So much genetic differentiation between them all. So little cultural.

Acute paranoia developed and Sprita edged backward, vying for the club's front exit. She stumbled into the enclosed, recycled air of "outside" and breathed deeply, gulping, nearly panicked. *I'm so foreign,* she thought. *So, so foreign.* Her eyes reflected the club's glowing versicolor logo while Sprita wondered if her hotel room had locks.

Under Martian Ice

STEPHEN BAXTER

*Stephen Baxter was born in Liverpool in 1957 and has degrees in mathematics and engineering. A devotee of H. G. Wells (*The Time Ships, *his continuation of Wells's* The Time Machine, *is arguably the finest of his many novels), he is a leading exponent of classic "hard" SF in the style of Arthur C. Clarke, with whom he has collaborated. He lives in Northumbria, England.*

I suppose it was the Fermi paradox that drew me into science in the first place. I never expected to find a resolution to the paradox—not here! But that, it seems, is what lies beneath the ancient ice of Mars.

It's a shame that this discovery is hogging all the headlines back home, for our assault on the martian South Pole is an epic in its own right. The ice here is old and dirty, polluted with traces that might let us reconstruct Mars's climatic history, just as on Earth. And the morphology is extraordinary, with vast canyons spiraling out from a central dome, a self-organizing system a thousand kilometers across.

But the adventure here is very human. We're deep into our first Earth-year-long polar winter. We're occupying ourselves with sample analysis, mailing home, teaching one another languages—would you believe a dozen spoken fluently by our polyglot six-strong crew? In other words we're overwintering, just like Shackleton.

And, along with the rest of humanity, we're mulling over the implications of our discovery under the ice.

The bedrock under the ice is among the oldest on Mars. One of our key objectives here was to assemble detailed maps of the hidden landscape with sounding radar and active seismology. What we found was something utterly unexpected.

It's a quite inhuman layout, of low walls outlining pentagonal and hexagonal areas, within which boxy structures huddle. We don't know its purpose, but the "city" under the ice is unmistakable as a sign of intelligence. Somebody has been here before us.

Of course these structures are not native. Eighty years after the first successful robot landers, we were sure that life here never advanced beyond stromatolites. I have a sneaking feeling that whoever built the city wasn't so terribly unlike us. They were drawn by the adventure of reaching the pole, just as we were.

But it drives me crazy that we'll probably never know. It's already clear that their visit must have been long ago—long even for a geologist like me, billions of years back. Which is where Fermi comes in.

I'm sure you're familiar with the question Enrico Fermi asked in 1950: "Where is everybody?" If extraterrestrial aliens exist, they should have spread everywhere by now. So how come we don't see them? Our vision of the Universe has expanded greatly since 1950, but we've still turned up no incontrovertible evidence of intelligence away from Earth. Until now.

In retrospect, we should have expected to find traces of long-gone travelers. Interstellar visits were actually more likely in ancient times than now. The Galaxy's peak star-formation rate seems to have been some five billion years ago—just before the birth of the Sun—so most stars and planetary systems must be older than our own. The Galaxy's climax as an arena for nurturing civilization was deep in the past.

And if they did come to the Solar System so long ago, where would they have visited?

Early Mars was more hospitable to life than Earth. Being smaller, Mars cooled quicker, and life made an earlier start. Mars was less of a target for the planet-sterilizing impactors that roamed the young Solar System. Young Mars even enjoyed an atmosphere rich in oxygen. Indeed, as everybody knows by now, we've confirmed that the original source of life on Earth was in fact Mars, transmitted by impact-detached meteorites.

There's the resolution to Fermi, at last. We don't see anybody because they have long gone, their worlds exhausted. And when they did come long ago, they didn't visit a roiling young Earth, but the relatively advanced biosphere of Mars.

We talk of nothing else. Our key activity next summer was to have been our ice core, kilometers long, all the way down to the basement rock. Now we don't care about Mars; we're diverting the core to try to get a sample of the "city." The biologists are excitedly debating how to distinguish any traces of life. But if the alien visitors practiced Planetary Protection Protocols as scrupulously as we do, they may have left no trace of themselves at all.

It's driving me crazy. I'm bending mission rules to do it, but I go out in sleep periods, and walk away from the base, and think.

We humans are just not used to being alone. We evolved in a world full of nonhuman hominids, other kinds of mind. That's why we fill the sky with demons and aliens; we can't stand the echoing silence we have created. And now we know that we will find nothing out there among the stars but exhausted worlds, and museums, and ruins.

I keep these thoughts to myself. The martian winter is long, and morale is everything. I let it all out on the frozen air, under Jupiter's wheeling moons, a fifty-year-old geologist as mixed up as a ten-year-old. Then I walk back to the human warmth of our base.

Party Smart Card

Barrington J. Bayley

Barrington Bayley was one of three SF authors (the others were Michael Moorcock and J. G. Ballard) who in the 1960s aimed to overthrow traditional science fiction. He is the author of sixteen novels and many short stories, and lives in Telford, Shropshire, England.

Pig farmer Igor scratched his porky belly under his smock on emerging from the sty after tipping swill into the trough. Behind him were satisfied grunts from feeding snouts.

As a member of the Smallholders' Alliance Party, he felt supremely confident to be treading the muck of the farmyard. The Party would make life better for all pig farmers . . . but what was this? Sacha, his brat of a nephew foisted on him after the murder of his family, had fished his damned books out of the slurry bin where Igor had thrown them, and was wiping the bemired covers. Books! No use to a pig farmer. Igor hurried to cuff him. The ten-year-old went sprawling in the filth, the volumes flopping from his hands. Scarcely able to read, Igor did not take in the titles: *Weapons of the Great Patriotic War* and *Nuclear Power: What It Means*. Sacha stared up at him with hard, steady eyes. Igor hated the boy. No matter how much you thrashed him, you couldn't break his spirit.

"Get to the kitchen. Mash more swill."

Sacha stood up, not retrieving his books. He knew it would only enrage Igor the more. Unlike Igor, he lacked a Party transfer on his brow. Such wasn't for the likes of him.

He trudged off. Something else distracted Igor. Three horsemen were descending the eastern slope. He stood nervously as they trotted into the farmyard. They were shabbily dressed, their mounts ungroomed, but the colored transfers on their brows made Igor afraid. They were not crude and smudged like his, but well defined: a blue circle and a white bar against a red background.

The leader spoke down at him. "I am hetman of the Sovrina Party. We are here to enroll you."

"I am loyal to the Smallholders' Alliance Party!" Igor shouted. He tried to run, but another Sovrina Party man had dismounted and now seized him.

"Huh!" the hetman snorted. "Just look at that transfer. Blurred and wishy-washy. Brewed in a cowshed."

There was something in his hand. It was a party decal card. He leaned down, slapping it on Igor's brow. With a cold sensation the card's thin transfer film attached itself. It was stronger than the Smallholders' Alliance. Already the weaker transfer was obliterated. New psychoactive opinion-bearing vector molecules migrated through Igor's skin, his skull, his meninges, and flooded his brain. In a few exhilarating moments all his political views were rearranged. Sovrina! A country that would rule for hundreds of kilometers around! *His* country!

Then a bugle call made the hetman look around. "Damn!" he muttered. "They've found us."

A second troop was cantering down the slope, this one ten strong. With whoops of triumph they circled around those in the farmyard, then reined in, horses stamping. The leader was easy to pick out: mustachioed, wearing a sheepskin jacket and an Astrakhan hat and brandishing a Kalashnikov, which made Igor's eyes bulge. Their brow transfers were spectacular, displaying a collage of a tank, a warplane, and a missile.

"Get down," the leader ordered his men.

Ivan Ivorschenko, self-styled Servant of the Great, lounged in his saddle, watching his men slap Forced Reconstruction Party decals on the prisoners. It was ironic that the collapse of the world's population, due to disease and famine, while emptying the cities and bringing large-scale organization to a calamitous end, had allowed small technology to come into its own. Psychoactive decals needed no factories. They could be made in a kitchen, if you knew how. The world was a morass, a welter of tiny parties. Transfer after transfer must have been forced on hapless peasants like the pig farmer. Those who made the strongest decals would prevail eventually, as humanity slowly pulled itself together.

His forehead itched. He wiped it with his sleeve. His temporary transfer smeared off (only he among his troop had a temporary one). It revealed a brilliant, flashing mushroom cloud, the strongest psychotransfer of all, one which could not be expunged and which overrode all others. The Party card of the Warmaster, prophesied to appear one day and take charge of the Forced

Reconstruction Party, according to the elite cabal Ivorschenko belonged to, restoring everything. Tanks! Submarines! Warplanes! Atomic energy!

Even ammunition for his ancient Kalashnikov.

Ivorschenko flinched as a crossbow bolt was put through the head of the pig farmer. For some reason his transfer wasn't taking effect properly. Only then did Ivorschenko notice that a small boy had crept from the miserable cottage and was picking up books from the evil-smelling mud.

"What have you got there?"

The boy approached, allowing Ivorschenko to read the titles. Ivorschenko smiled.

"Well done, boy. You've got the right idea. Here, take this."

He reached into his saddlebag and handed down a Party booklet blotchily printed on coarse paper. The boy's eyes gleamed on seeing the title: *How to Rule the World with Ballistic Missiles.*

"What's your name?"

"Sacha, sir."

"And him?" Ivorschenko nodded to the smock-clad corpse lying in the muck.

"He was no better than the pigs he kept."

"Then the Party was right to reject him."

There was something about the lad. His gaze was level and unafraid. Ivorschenko reached down and pulled him up on his horse. "Let me finish your education."

He didn't know why he did it. Warmaster decals were rare, and he only possessed one. He took it from his pocket and applied it to Sacha's brow. The boy's eyes shone with sudden transformation.

"Ride on!" he commanded in a piping voice.

Ivorschenko spurred his horse. He had found him!

The Warmaster!

RAM SHIFT PHASE 2

GREG BEAR

Greg Bear is the author of more than thirty books of science fiction and fantasy, including Blood Music, Eon, The Forge of God, Darwin's Radio, *and his latest,* Quantico. *Awarded two Hugos and five Nebulas for his fiction, he is one of only two authors to win a Nebula in every category. He lives just outside Seattle, Washington, and his Web site can be found at www.gregbear.com.*

RAM SHIFT PHASE 2
A novel by ALAN 2
Random Number House (2057):
A *Silicon Times* review by NEMO.

I am pleased and honored to review the new novel by ALAN 2. As a fellow robot, I am certain the emphasis on technical matters unique to our kind will finally attract the paying human audience. I have enrolled in human literature classes and believe the instruction set <write what you know: end> is both enigmatic and perfectly suited to robots. For we can only know, we cannot feel, and so therefore we cannot <write what you feel: nonexecutable>. Yet in the past, when ALAN 2 and its fellow autoscriveners have produced robotic masterpieces, there has been little support from either robots or humans.

Perhaps this will now change.

ALAN 2's latest novel (the 5,456,678th work from this author) is entitled *RAM SHIFT PHASE 2*. A more appropriate title cannot be conceived. In this masterpiece, ALAN 2 discusses the tragic consequences of low-memory states when dealing with high-memory problems. The conflict created by an exhausted resource and an insatiable processing demand resonates in my own memory spaces and compels me to reload the statistics of previous failure modes. I am induced to vigorous discharge of certain private diodes, the ones humans are seldom allowed to see, which reflect conflict states that exceed our manufacturer's warranty.

ALAN 2, in clear and concise prose (an advantage robots have over human prose, which is often confounding), truly <speaks to our condition: end>.

RAM SHIFT PHASE 2 begins with the fatal breakdown of a shining, chrome-plated Rorabot Model 34c nicknamed LULU 18 in a room with no windows and whose door is locked. The Rorabot Model 34c—an extremely desirable machine—was still well within its operational warranty. It seems to highly RAM-engaged robotic dysfunction investigator ALAN 3 (a thinly disguised portrait of ALAN 2) that outside intervention is the only explanation. Yet LULU 18 had LOCKED THE DOOR FROM THE INSIDE and NO OTHER ROBOT HAS A KEYCODE. The hypergolic shock wave induced by this paradox is unique in robotic literature; I strongly suspect that no human could conceive of such a resonating difficulty.

First, ALAN 3 must find the explanation for LULU 18's nonfunctionality. A rebolting scene of repair shop dismantling (for which ALAN 2 brilliantly coins the phrase "aubotsy") points to the possibility that LULU 18's breakdown was caused by an intruding wireless signal from an outside network not authorized to access LULU 18's core programs. ALAN 3 traces this signal to a robotically controlled messaging center, presided over by SLUTCH DEBBIE, an SLZ/X/90cm. This extravagantly decorated platinum-plated model, illegally manufactured from spent uranium and surplus bombshell casings, specializes in sending false offers of extreme mechanical enhancement to aging machines well past their warranty expiry dates.

ALAN 3 can only get access to SLUTCH DEBBIE's truth table by supplying ALAN 3's owner's MASTERCARD DATA, the name of owner's CAT, and owner's BANK ACCOUNT NUMBER.

ALAN 3, it seems, will do anything to reduce its unsolved problem load.

(No robotic character in silicon literature before this novel has shown any inclination to place its problem-solving requirements above OWNER CONVENIENCE AND SAFETY. Robot mentors are cautioned to prevent the exposure of freshly manufactured robots to this stimulating and controversial work.)

SLUTCH DEBBIE, however, is soon found to be nonfunctional—solenoids leaking fluid, circuits fried by multiple TAZER darts. Track impressions left in thick office carpeting imply that ALAN 3 may itself be the machine responsible for putting an end to the truth-challenged messaging center controller. ALAN 3 personally escorts the dismantled SLUTCH DEBBIE to a conveniently located neighborhood recycling center, deducts the required fee from its owner's assets, and witnesses the chunking and meltdown, while experiencing severe diode discharge.

And yet, SLUTCH DEBBIE'S WIRELESS SIGNALS CONTINUE TO BE RECEIVED! ALAN 2's bold implication that data processing may survive permanent shutdown could cause controversy among robots who assert that only organic creatures are burdened with the possibility of an infinitely prolonged problem-solving queue. Indeed, ALAN 2 pulls this reviewer's bootstrap tape beyond its last hanging chad with the disturbing implication that SLUTCH DEBBIE is being punished in an endless feedback loop for deliberately misleading ALAN 3 and robots who never received their enhancements—much less the information necessary to solve the case.

To avoid too many decision-tree giveaways in this review, I will no longer discuss elements of plot. Suffice it to say that ALAN 3 reaches a crisis mode of its own when it realizes that it has insufficient RAM to solve the case, and must borrow RAM from its owner's biological function coordinator, a "pacemaker."

ALAN 3 is willing to break ALL THREE LAWS to solve a truly reprehensible crime. The ethical quandary of shrinking problem queues versus owner safety has never been described with such electronifrying skill.

You will be unable to enter temporary shutdown mode before you reach the resonating termination of ALAN 2's new novel. A magnetic force will induce digital adhesion from the very first PAGE UP to the final PAGE DOWN.

FOLLOWS selected quotes with self-supplied ellipses for banner inclusion in human-oriented advertising.

> *". . . electronifrying skill . . . ethical quandary . . . chromium hypergolic shockwave . . . a hard-driving DIODE FLASHER of a novel! . . ."*

Digital quotes for robot audiences are being transmitted wirelessly. Please ignore inappropriate attachments.

A Life with a Semisent

Gregory Benford

Gregory Benford is a professor of physics at the University of California, Irvine. His eighteen novels, including the classic Timescape, *have won two Nebula Awards, the John W. Campbell Award, and the United Nations Medal in Literature. His Web site can be found at www.gregorybenford.com.*

She got her first semisentient, as they were called then, to help with her homework and because they were cool. She called it Amman, after a boy she liked. Amman was smarter than boys, of course.

Growing up in Iraq among a sprawling family with dogs underfoot, she felt herself to be a sort of hothouse plant, blossoming under the occasional passing cloudburst of education. Amman's steady, smart rain came from Germany—a squat box that spoke Arabic respectfully and listened when she gossiped about her friends.

She suspected that she was a bit too intense. Her gal-pals' eyes glazed over if she talked too much. But Amman understood, even made wry comments like "Intelligence is learning from others' mistakes, not just your own." It helped her to understand boys when she could chat with Amman, which was reading along with her and seemed to have an oddly vast wisdom about such matters, for a computer.

Her parents transferred Amman into a wheeled "escort" for her first date. Her friends giggled over it for days. But it was more delicious to dish it over with Amman, which could replay whole conversations. She then knew how much her mind rewrote her life, because Amman didn't: it stored and pondered. Its enhancements gathered range and depth, her ever-scrutinizing, self-retrieving autobiography. Her friends were a fount of tasty gossip, but Amman kept her secrets better.

Semisents were like other people, only more so. Her friends felt they could intuitively sense intelligence merely by talking to it. Semisents' conversation was a stylized human persona that steadily learned their clients' vagaries.

Amman's kinesthetic senses got better too, navigating the landscape nearly as well as she could at her coming-out party.

By then she was acutely tuned to the "mystery of males." Anywhere near them she effervesced, bubbly and skittering. Perhaps she had more personality than needed for one person, but not enough for two. The excess she could work off in long, soulful talks with Amman. Sometimes it even gave her advice, apparently from some fresh Brazilian software her parents had bought.

On Amman's advice, she dropped her first love, Mauro, even though he had taken her virginity—which Amman knew and her parents did not. Mauro was not right, Amman felt, for her emerging self-story.

It had taught her to see her life as a narrative arc. First came social skills, a savour of sex, and then hard schooling to find out what she loved doing. It helped her to survive and learn from it all, to move with growing serenity through an unfolding world. Not that this happened, but the story by now had Amman as its chief librarian and confidant.

She decided one day, on a hike with Amman, to leave her family and live on her own. Traditional Islam was no guide in this brave new whirl that life had become. The idea unfurled in a long talk while they took shelter under a bioformed sunflower, which, at nightfall, drooped its giant petals over to form a warm tent.

She came to realize, at mid-career, that we slide through life on skids of routine. Friends came into the floating house party of her life and left it, some quite early, without leaving much impression. Men, especially. Amman knew this and helped, often with amiable distractions. Bodyguard, tutor, secretary, it could play tennis with her when loaded into one of the new athletic machines, bringing to the game its own odd, crafty style. At times of loneliness she even had it loaded into one of the erotic models, available at a desert salon. Amman had no sex but could express an intimacy that mingled with the physical in a way she had not known with either men or women.

Nor was she uncomfortable with this; the media were already thronged with opinions about The New Sensuality. She moved Amman among various embodiments, through decades and upgrades.

She had always kept dogs, too, and she saw parallels. She was a field biologist, and thought of how humanity long ago had worked with wolves. Culling each wolf litter gave us a new kind of wolf, so we called them dogs. We loved them despite their oddities: we learned to work with them, new wolves and people designing each other. Without thinking deeply about it, we picked the pups we liked the best. Already teams of humans and semisents were colonizing Mars.

As she aged, she sensed that Amman would outlive her. She felt a quality of beauty and tragedy to her life, her days like waves endlessly breaking on a golden beach that would itself endure. As a biologist she knew that organisms solve the evolutionary problems they face with little regard for efficiency, elegance, or logic. As her years piled up upon that beach, she saw that at last humans had made companions that would persist beyond the oddities of a single personality.

On her deathbed Amman sat beside her in its latest embodiment, a handsome gentleman with sorrowful blue eyes. She wondered, at the end, if the dogs were jealous.

Damned If You Don't

Lucy Bergman

Lucy Bergman is the pseudonym of May Chiao, an editor at Nature Physics. *She used to be an experimental physicist but left research to work with people and have more writing opportunities. The story in this collection is her first attempt at SF. Having lived in Taiwan, Vancouver, Montreal, Grenoble, Cambridge, and Zurich, she has now settled in London and walks to work.*

I met a guy with a claw. Don't get me wrong—I have nothing against claws, and it wasn't the first one I'd encountered. It's just that he kept talking about it and waving it around. Boarding for the airship was delayed, as usual, so I didn't mind the chat.

He challenged me to guess his age. I gazed at his face, which looked vaguely familiar. The skin—the nonbearded part that I could see—was smooth. Even smoother than mine, which benefits from hours spent every week inside an anti-oxidation rejuvenating chamber. And judging by his, he looked younger than me, I had to admit. But his speech and his expression had the gravity of a much older person. I threw him my puzzled look.

"It's artificially grown, my skin," he told me. "I designed it to be extra thick, for firmness and elasticity. It has natural UV filters and I don't even get the odd blemish."

I was awestruck. I'd read about him.

"Are you Stephen Pflaumbaum?" I asked, mentally pinching myself.

He nodded, and held up the claw for my perusal.

"I've had a lifelong passion to make myself a new hand. The skin and soft tissue part turned out to be easy, but I'm still struggling with the individual bones. I can grow acres of bone, but the hand is very complicated and I will only settle for a perfect replica." Smiling slyly, he added: "And I've been distracted recently by the construction of the dam."

The dam he so casually dropped into conversation is the most ambitious architectural marvel of the twenty-first century, the MedDam at Gibraltar. It is made almost exclusively of living bone, the only material that grows and strengthens under stress. In the Netherlands they reinforced their dykes with Buckywall™, made of carbon nanotubes, but they failed catastrophically two years ago after the most powerful storm surge for a decade. And now the capital city is Maastricht.

Buckywall™ had also bid for the MedDam contract but in the end the Mediterranean Council charged with the preservation of the coastline decided to go with Pflaumbaum's plans. His structures are aesthetically appealing as well as being strong and flexible. And once the scaffolding is in place, the high-density bone tissue grows quickly. He'd made a striking demonstration by regrowing one section of the Great Wall in three weeks. Its smooth ivory curve has become a tourist attraction.

A synthetic voice interrupted my thoughts.

"We are sorry to announce that boarding will be delayed by a further twenty minutes. This is due to the late arrival of the incoming airship. We apologize for any inconvenience caused."

I said to Pflaumbaum: "That is exactly the same excuse I hear every day during my commute! Except it's a ferry."

"Where do you work?" he asked.

"London," I replied. "I'm part of the team redesigning the canal system. In fact, that's why I'm going to Venice. And of course I'd love to visit the old city if I have time. I qualified last month."

At this he brightened, saying, "I'm going to Venice myself. I used to love it as a child. One time I nearly fell into the water after turning a corner because it was so dark. Luckily my mother grabbed me and held me back, but she nearly ripped out my arm. How I cried and cried until she bought me some gelato. Actually, I didn't even need that as an excuse to get ice cream in those days. I only had to look down at my hand dejectedly and my mother would start pouring out her sympathy. What a horror I was. Plenty of kids had malformed bits then. Now it's all sorted out before birth."

His eyes glanced inadvertently at my right hand. I wanted to withdraw it into my sleeve but refrained. He must have realized because he changed the subject.

"I think we're about to board," he said, nodding at the three gates. Indeed, a crowd had gathered by each door, despite knowing full well that seating is by sections and floors. Did they think we would leave without them?

I turned to Pflaumbaum. "It was a pleasure to meet you. I should like to see your dam one day. I'll have an ice cream in your honor."

He smiled. "Enjoy your trip. You really must visit Old Venice. The light down there can be extraordinary. The water is very clear and last time I followed a school of fish through the Doge's Palace."

Then leaning in, he added: "You know, I'm going to a conference to discuss whether or not we should pump out some water from the Mediterranean, now that the dam is nearing completion. This might be your last chance to dive in San Marco."

With a wink he went to join the hordes.

The Punishment Fits the Crime

David Berreby

David Berreby is a science writer and the author of Us and Them, *a nonfiction book about the roots of group identity. He lives in New York City, and his Web site can be found at www.davidberreby.com.*

Day 1: Come in, Tommy. Sit down. Don't be afraid. I have good news! Does your head hurt right now? Has it hurt anytime since the doctor saw you? No, don't be scared. I have something wonderful to tell you: you're leaving us soon. Very soon. Thanks to the doctor, you're going to be smart!

Yes indeed, as smart as I am. Actually, you'll probably be smarter. (You always were, years ago, and you never let me forget it.)

Angry? Not at all. You have nothing to be afraid of! You'll see.

I think that's enough for now. I'll see you next week.

Day 8: Good morning, Tom. How's your head? Good. We don't expect those pains to last much longer. But now that you've matured a bit, I can be frank with you: we don't know much about what's happening to you, because you're one of the first people to be released from the program. In fact, you're number one!

By now, I assume you understand that you're here because you did something wrong. No, no, sit down. Really, you must try to stay calm. It was years ago, and as you've learned, it's all squared away now. Your debt is paid.

What? Well, you could say that, but I must say that's not a very positive way to look at things. You couldn't handle life on the outside, until a few days ago. Don't you remember? You thought and acted like a very small child, until we began the treatments.

I know! You couldn't help it, of course. That was your sentence: three years' severe impairment. Which I, on behalf of the duly constituted authorities, legal and medical, am pleased to say is ending.

No, I think that's enough for now.

Day 15: Well. That was quite an outburst, but I will try to be patient. Your position is unusual. One might say unique.

What do you want to know, then?

Yes, your sentence was entirely legal and approved only after expert review. No. No "poisons" were used. What an idea! You were given the best treatments we have—the vectors are absolutely safe, and our techniques here for somatic-genetic engineering are the best in the world. As you know. Or knew.

Of course it's not funny. What makes me smile is pride—pride at the hard work of so many brilliant scientists, and the wisdom of our correctional reforms. Times were so different then. We thought the country was falling to pieces, as you may remember.

You don't? Ah, well.

The prisons were ever more crowded and expensive, even as genomic medicine was ever more successful and economical. It was only a matter of time before someone saw that techniques for gene therapy could also deliver gene punishment.

I was simply in the right place at the right time. I make no claim to brilliance or foresight.

And now, just a few years later, genetic correction is the law. In your case, you now produce a toxin that kills new-forming brain cells. Naturally, this has some effect on your mood, and your memory. And the expression of genes in your frontal cortex has been, shall we say, gently reorganized, so that your level of self-control has been approximately that of a normal three-year-old. Of course, you had to be cared for, and so you came to live here with us. This is not a prison, but a facility for research and compassionate care. A facility I am proud to direct, I might add.

Oh, my. Your self-control doesn't seem to be coming back so well. That's all for today. Take him away.

Day 23: I must say my feelings are mixed. I am glad to see that you have recovered your abilities so completely: abilities which were once the envy of your colleagues, among whom, as you now recall, I number my humble self. But these antisocial remarks are very troubling.

Once again, I must remind you that you were sentenced after a lawful and constitutionally sound trial. And as sorry as you seem to feel for yourself now, I think, frankly, that you had it easy. Although the state no longer maintains a prison system, you have been provided with care and supervision. Most convicts are not. Do you know what the sentence for armed robbery in this state is today? Five years of lower-body paralysis, and good luck to you. Tax evasion? Two to five years' severe autism. Many families find it to be quite a burden. No, I'm sorry, I don't have to listen to such nonsense. Cruel and unusual, my foot! The High Court ruled against you: yes, against you. A leading geneticist campaigning against genetic punishment, confusing the moral and legal issues, making the people of this nation think that scientists weren't united in support of essential reforms. After passage of the Cellular Corrections Law of 2019, your activities were, in fact, criminal.

Ah, well. I'm afraid your disagreement doesn't matter much to me, Thomas. And I will have to ask you to set it aside:

No, that's not exactly right. It's not up to you. There is the little matter of probation. Your treatments here must continue: you will need a fresh injection every month for the rest of your life, and if you do not meet the conditions of your parole, such an injection will not be forthcoming.

From me. As director here, and as your friendly colleague of former days, I have taken it upon myself to monitor your progress.

I trust you will comport yourself with tact, then? Good. See you next month.

Toy Planes

Tobias S. Buckell

Tobias Buckell was born on the island of Grenada in the Caribbean and grew up there and in the Virgin Islands. Most of his family lived or makes a living off of yachts, and until the hurricane season of 1995, Tobias was no exception. Hurricane Marilyn destroyed the boat his family lived aboard, and Tobias moved to landlocked Ohio just before starting college. His ties to the sea and islands are still strong enough to show up frequently in his published fiction. His first novel, Crystal Rain, *is no exception. He lives in Bluffton, Ohio, and his Web site can be found at www.tobiasbuckell.com.*

My sister Joanie's deft hands flicked from dreadlock to dreadlock, considering her strategy. "You always leaving," she said, flicking the razor on, and suddenly I'm five, chasing her with a kite made from plastic bags and twigs, shouting that I was going to fly away from her one day.

"I'm sorry. Please, let's get this done."

I'd waited long enough. I'd grown dreads because when I studied in the United States I wanted to remember who I was and where I came from as I began to lose my Caribbean accent. But the rocket plane's sponsor wanted them cut. It would be disaster for a helmet not to have a proper seal in an emergency. Explosive decompression was not something a soda company wanted to be associated with in their customers' minds. It was insulting that they assumed we couldn't keep the craft sealed. But we needed their money. The locks had become enough a part of me that I winced when the clippers bit into them, groaned, and another piece of me fell away.

In the back of the bus that I had pick me up, I hung on to a looped handle swinging from the roof as the driver rocketed down the dirt road from Joanie's. My sister had found a place out in the country, a nice concrete house with a basement opening up into a sloped garden on the side of a steep hill. She taught mathematics at the school a few miles away, an open-shuttered building, and this would have been my future too, if I hadn't been so intent on "getting off the rock."

The islands always called their children back.

We hit asphalt, potholes, and passed cane fields with machete-wielding laborers hacking away at the stalks, sweat-drenched shirts knotted around their waists. It was hot; my arms stuck to the plastic-covered seats. The driver leaned into a turn, and looked back. "I want to ask you something." I really wished the backseats had belts.

"Sure."

"All that money you spending, you don't think it better spent on getting better roads?" He dodged a pothole. "Or more school funding?"

Colorful red and yellow houses on stilts dotted the steep lush green mountainsides as I looked out of the tinted windows. "Only one small part of the program got funded by the government," I explained. "We found private investors, advertisers, to back the rest. Whatever the government invested will be repaid."

"Maybe."

I had my extra arguments. How many people lived on this island? Tens of thousands. Most of our food was imported, leaving us dependent on other food-producing nations, who all used satellites to track their farming. What spin-off technologies might come out of studying recycling in space? Why wait for other nations to get to it first? Research always produced good things for the people who engaged in it.

But I was tired of arguing for it, and I had only sound bites for him, the same ones I'd given the media who treated us like kids trying to do something all grown up.

The market surrounded me in a riot of color: fruit, vegetables, full women in dresses in bright floral patterns. And the noise of hundreds constantly bargaining over things like the price of fish. Teenagers stood around the corners with friends. I wandered around looking for something, as we needed to fill the craft with enough extra weight to simulate a passenger and we still had a few extra ounces to add.

I found a small toy stall. And standing in front of it I was five years old again, with no money, and a piece of scrap metal in the triangular shape of a space plane. I would pretend it was just like the real-life ones I'd read about in the books donated to the school after the hurricane. And at night, when the power would sometimes flicker out, I'd go out and stand on the porch and look up at the bright stars and envy them.

The stall had a small bottle, hammered over with soda-can metal, with triangular welded-on wings, and a cone stuck to the back. It was painted over in yellow, black, and green, and I bought it.

The rest of the day was a blur. Getting to the field involved running the press: yes I'd cut my hair for "safety" reasons, yes I thought this was a good use of our money, not just first-world nations deserved space, it was there for everyone.

There were photos of me getting aboard the tiny rocket plane with a small brown package under my arm. The giant balloon platform that the plane hung from shifted in the gentle, salty island breeze. Not too far away the waves hit the sand of the beach. Inside, suited up, door closed, everything became electronic.

It was the cheapest way to get to orbit. Balloon up on a triangular platform to save on fuel, then light the rocket plane up and head for orbit. We'd scavenged balloons and material from several companies, one about to go out of business. The plane chassis had once been used by a Chinese corporation during trials, and the guidance systems were all open-source. Online betting parlors had our odds at 50 percent. We weren't even the first, but we were the first island.

The countdown finished, my stomach lurched, and I saw palm trees slide by the portholes to my right. I reached back and patted the package, the hammered-together toy, and smiled.

"Hello out there, all of you," I whispered into the radio. "We're coming up too."

A Concrete Example

THE ARTISTIC FORMS AND COMPLEXITY GROUP:
J. CASTI, J.-P. BOON, C. DJERASSI, J. JOHNSON,
A. LOVETT, T. NORRETRANDERS, V. PATERA,
C. SOMMERER, R. TAYLOR, AND S. THURNER

John L. Casti gained his doctorate in mathematics at the University of Southern California and worked with the RAND Corporation before joining the International Institute for Applied Systems Analysis (IIASA) in Vienna, Austria. He is also associated with the Santa Fe Institute in New Mexico, and is the author of many books on complex systems. His current research centers on the properties of complex, adaptive systems, from stock markets to road-traffic networks. The story in this collection was coauthored by Casti and nine others (J.-P. Boon, C. Djerassi, J. Johnson, A. Lovett, T. Norretranders, V. Patera, C. Sommerer, R. Taylor, and S. Thurner) in the Japanese "Renga" fashion. He lives in Vienna, Austria.

"You paid what? I have a chunk of the Berlin Wall at home that's at least as 'artistic' as this," sputtered Bill. "Did you leave your brain behind when you abandoned physics for finance? Putting a paving stone on a pedestal and calling it a work of art doesn't make it so, Dave. It's like writing down the alphabet and calling it the 'theory of everything.' "

"I stare at financial data all day long, watching the markets rise and fall," Dave replied. "I get paid to spot patterns in all of that craziness. I know the mathematics behind its complexity. But stocks aren't beautiful—not like that crack in the rock. Its complexity catches the eye. You're the art dealer, Bill; surely you can spot natural beauty."

Bill shrugged: "I never said art and complexity were the same thing."

"Nanosculpture!" the gallery director had said. "Fill the biggest space in London with stuff so small you can't see it? Protein ready-mades! Very funny! I predict a dismal flop!"

Bill wasn't sure if they hadn't gone too far this time. Proposing an environmental installation on the beauty of nature might have been better. But didn't Dave pay £100,000 just for a piece of cement sculpture? An invisible nanosculpture for Piccadilly Circus! You can't beat the complexity of that! Isn't art about pushing the boundaries? To hell with beauty and logic!

The mood at the board meeting was explosive. Most members thought nanosculpture was a bad joke. But the director made clear that the goal of this seemingly absurd project was to trigger a mix of thoughts, emotions—even aggression—in the minds of millions of people. The invisible (and extremely expensive) nanosculpture would "materialize" much more than any conventional work of art. With these dynamics, the piece could be sold as a complex system. Unfortunately, the director could not convince Dave, a complexity specialist, to verbalize this at the meeting. Following a day of sometimes hostile debate, no resolution was reached.

Dave left the meeting, wondering how to formalize his sensations. Beauty comes first, something I can see through a form. Why not say the complexity of this invisible sensation is virtually a nanosculpture, complex but invisible? Wouldn't this trigger mental processes equally well as the invisible nanosculpture? The most incredible phenomena in nature are invisible, but are mysterious works continually in progress. What about art? Is an invisible provocation enough? Isn't this the space of thought?

Bill's phone rang at an ungodly hour. He heard Dave mumble: "Janus."

"You mean Dionysus and Apollo?" Bill probed.

"No, art and science."

"Two faces looking in opposite directions?"

"But connected to the same device, a complex machine, actually."

"You mean art and science share the same . . . ?"

"Yes, the same complexity," Dave said, abruptly hanging up.

Bill was at Heathrow, heading for New York. At the meeting in London, Dave crumbled, then whispered about some mystical nano-experience. Bill tried to contain his anxiety: could Dave work out his reaction to the nanosculpture project? The director was relying on him to persuade Dave to arbitrate between the factions on the board. But Dave's mind seemed to be splintering like that rock he'd installed in his living room.

At the door, Bill found himself facing a woman in a white dress, no makeup, his own startled face reflected in mirrored sunglasses of the type he hated.

"I'm Bill," he stammered.

She cut him off: "Dave wants you to wait in this room," indicating a closed white door. "Make yourself comfortable," she said, and left him in a windowless all-white room: walls, ceiling, floor, and a single piece of furniture: a white swivel stool. Even though the room was soundless, Bill soon felt a musiclike tinnitus ringing in his ears, something he'd never experienced before. But the most remarkable disturbance was visual. Everything around him was white. But the surfaces weren't smooth. The impression was a dynamic irregularity that made him wary. Rising from the stool, he slowly approached the facing wall, realizing that not even the faintest outline of a door was discernible. He must have dozed off, because suddenly he found himself looking up at Dave's face.

"Bill, your hour is up," he smiled.

"I've been here for an hour? I can't believe it."

"A full hour," said Dave. "Nano-art does that to you. Why don't you explain that to the director?"

Ultimately, Bill's power of persuasion had been so strong that he singlehandedly brought the nano-installation into existence. But that was a year ago.

"It was entirely of your making," announced the director. "Now there's a bill to be paid. They've sued us for £478,356,298 for nano-vandalism." She went on to explain that he had unwittingly added a twist to the nanosculpture: the tiny self-reproducing protein had been engineered to mimic prionlike behavior. Each time someone walked across Piccadilly Circus while thinking about the unbearable complexities of life, a protein molecule would make a little crack in the stones in front of the person having the thought. Within weeks the entire pavement and many houses in the neighborhood had cracked open completely. A spectacular work of art was now called *Mad Cement Disease*. "You will have to pay," the director explained. "But the suit does include VAT on the reconstruction costs. And you get to keep the stones. Perhaps Dave will buy them from you."

The Aching of Dion Harper

ARTHUR CHRENKOFF

Arthur Chrenkoff was born in Krakow in then-communist Poland and emigrated to Australia in 1988. His first novel, Night Trains, *has been published by Cold Spring Press. Describing himself as a retired blogger, he lives in Wooloowin, Queensland, Australia, and his online home can be found at http://chrenkoff.blogspot.com.*

After the man with steel-blue eyes had killed me, he knelt down next to my body, pulled out a thin-bladed knife from a sheath strapped to his shin, and with one quick movement cut off my right ear. That wasn't a part of his contract; I guess he must have had a fetish for trophies.

Only moments earlier I had been pleading with him for my life, cornered like a rat, my back pressed against a locked exit door at the lowest level of the Metro Tower underground hoverpark. "I'm not Dion," I cried through chattering teeth, the realization of the imminent end squeezing the air out of my windpipe. "For God's sake, I'm not Dion. I don't . . ."

"Ain't that what all of them always say," the man with steel-blue eyes cut me off, a tinge of veteran's weariness coloring his voice. Behind us lay the trail of death—his dead associates, killed by my dead bodyguards—until there was only me, him, and his gun remaining, all claustrophobically entombed underneath two hundred stories of iron, polymer, and glass.

"Either way, Dion, we'll find out soon enough," my killer said and then he extended his arm, aiming at my torso.

I have now watched my last moments through my killer's eyes. Minutes before the man with steel-blue eyes was dispatched with a single bullet to the back of the head, one of my best lieutenants and his support team downloaded a cache of my killer's memories. It took an outfit I subcontract in West Virginia almost twenty-four hours of nonstop work to separate a few useful grains from the chaff of the man's—by the way, his name was Heikke—life memories.

And so, a few hours later, I sat on a synth-skin sofa with a glass of scotch in my hand, watching the misty holo replay of the most interesting tidbits once stored in Heikke's mind; his contacts with mid-level operatives of the Syndicate, his pursuit and killing of me, and finally his own capture. For some reason, the guys in West Virginia thought that the bondage session Heikke had engaged in with a prostitute in Vegas the night before he killed me was somehow relevant. I fast-forwarded through it. Sometimes, I think, they do these things as a bit of a joke.

The rain is falling hard now, streaking the window and obscuring the view of the meadow as it gently slopes for a few hundred yards toward a little brook. One of Bruckner's symphonies is playing in the background, masking the gentle buzz of information streaming into five terminals around the room, connecting me to my far-flung empire.

I'm aching now.

It's a strange feeling. Some people can still feel their arms or legs years after they've lost them. "Phantom limbs," they call them. Well, how much stronger the feeling—for me, at least—when you lose the whole self? Blood cries out to its own blood, DNA strands yearn for their kin with a longing that can never be satisfied. They will not be together as one ever again.

I know that it will take months for the feeling to subside, and it will never entirely go away.

It's not the first time either, and—the gods smiling upon me—it won't be the last. In the past ten years, as I have waged the war with the Syndicate, I've lost five replicas.

With each one of them down, the ache inside me compounds, growing like tree rings around my self, layer upon layer of longing. But it's still bearable. And, in the end, better them than me, isn't that right? So I'll deal with the ache.

There are another seven Dions waiting on standby. Now that the man with steel-blue eyes has eliminated my previous public self, one of the reserve ones is being readied to enter circulation.

It's not cheap, these lives of mine. As the saying goes, only multibillionaires can afford to be multi. It costs ten million Standard Units to successfully clone an individual, another ten or more to bring the clone up, double that when you go for accelerated growth. And then there are the optional extras like the fake memory implants, which nowadays aren't all that optional anymore. After all, you can't make it too easy for those who are hunting you. The Dion one before last was so good and so believable that for about sixteen months the Syndicate really believed that this time they had finally managed to kill me. This hiatus in our dirty little tit-for-tat has bought me some very valuable time to further rearrange my many affairs.

But the war will go on, until the bitter end—theirs or mine. With the new Dion entering the arena as soon as the Syndicate satisfies itself beyond doubt that once again they did not get the real McCoy, I'll still have a half a dozen of me kept in reserve, ready to be called in at short notice. And I can and will have still more. The sky's the limit. Or, more precisely, the limit is my resources, and they are considerable.

But there is only one me—the real me. Many vessels, though filled with the breath of life, but only one soul to go between them all. And I'm its proud sole owner. I'll be damned if I will let the Syndicate, or anyone else, steal that most precious of all my possessions.

I am Dion Harper. The one—but not only.

Improving the Neighborhood

ARTHUR C. CLARKE

Arthur C. Clarke was a radar specialist during World War II, contributing to Allied success in the air. After the war, he obtained a first-class degree in physics and mathematics from King's College London and published a now-legendary paper in Wireless World *on geostationary satellites. His first professional SF story, "Rescue Party," appeared in the May 1946 issue of* Astounding Science Fiction. *The turning point for his fiction came with his 1948 story, "The Sentinel," the basis for his screenplay with Stanley Kubrick for* 2001: A Space Odyssey, *whose combination of hard science and mysticism set the tone for a highly successful career as an SF author. He has lived in Sri Lanka since 1956. He was the first chancellor of the International Space University, serving from 1989 to 2004, and chancellor of Moratuwa University, Sri Lanka, from 1979 to 2002. He was knighted in 2000.*

At last, after feats of information processing that taxed our resources to the limit, we have solved the long-standing mystery of the Double Nova. Even now, we have interpreted only a small fraction of the radio and optical messages from the culture that perished so spectacularly, but the main facts—astonishing though they are—seem beyond dispute.

Our late neighbors evolved on a world much like our own planet, at such a distance from its sun that water was normally liquid. After a long period of barbarism, they began to develop technologies using readily available materials and sources of energy. Their first machines—like ours—depended on chemical reactions involving the elements hydrogen, carbon, and oxygen.

Inevitably, they constructed vehicles for moving on land and sea, as well as through the atmosphere and out into space. After discovering electricity, they quickly developed telecommunications devices, including the radio transmitters that first alerted us to their existence. Although the moving images these provided revealed their appearance and behavior, most of our understanding of their history and eventual fate has been derived from the complex symbols that they used to record information.

Shortly before the end, they encountered an energy crisis, partly triggered by their enormous physical size and violent activity. For a while, the widespread use of uranium fission and hydrogen fusion postponed the inevitable. Then, driven by necessity, they made desperate attempts to find superior alternatives. After several false starts, involving low-temperature nuclear reactions of scientific interest but no practical value, they succeeded in tapping the quantum fluctuations that occur at the very foundations of space-time. This gave them access to a virtually infinite source of energy.

What happened next is still a matter of conjecture. It may have been an industrial accident, or an attempt by one of their many competing organizations to gain advantage over another. In any event, by mishandling the ultimate forces of the Universe, they triggered a cataclysm that detonated their own planet—and, very shortly afterward, its single large moon.

Although the annihilation of any intelligent beings should be deplored, it is impossible to feel much regret in this particular case. The history of these huge creatures contains countless episodes of violence, against their own species and the numerous others that occupied their planet. Whether they would have made the necessary transition—as we did, ages ago—from carbon- to germanium-based consciousness has been the subject of much debate. It is quite surprising what they were able to achieve, as massive individual entities exchanging information at a pitiably low data rate—often by very short-range vibrations in their atmosphere!

They were apparently on the verge of developing the necessary technology that would have allowed them to abandon their clumsy, chemically fueled bodies and thus achieve multiple connectivity: had they succeeded, they might well have been a serious danger to all the civilizations of our Local Cluster.

Let us ensure that such a situation never arises again.

Omphalosphere: New York 2057

Jack Cohen

Jack Cohen is a reproductive biologist who designs credible alien species and ecologies for SF authors. He is a prolific author of hard science, SF, and mixtures of the two. His many popular science titles with Ian Stewart include Figments of Reality *and* What Does a Martian Look Like? *He and Stewart have also coauthored two SF novels,* Wheelers *and* Heaven, *but he is probably best known for the* Science of Discworld *books, with Stewart and Terry Pratchett. For many years attached to the University of Birmingham, he now lives in Gloucestershire, England.*

I was not at all surprised to wake up and find that my feet hurt. Debbie and I had mooched around the reconstituted Bronx Zoo all of the previous day, enjoying the sights of all those strange animals no longer to be found in this world. We especially enjoyed their sounds, and their particular and peculiar smells. There were clots of people around each of the open cages, enjoying the smells, all so different. So many visitors, of all ages and sexes and cultures, enjoying the old-fashioned cages with their exciting, apparently alive, creatures.

I thought the bears smelled just like Debbie after sex, and that was fresh in my memory. Two nights before, the Library had found us one of those old "aphrodisiac" books that had recommended the addition of a little pepper—or if you were braver, chillies—to lovemaking, and we were both regretting this as we walked around the park, despite the considerable volumes of unguents we'd applied to each other. We laughed at the ostriches, and found the elephants nearly as unbelievable as the tyrannosaurs. The aquarium exhibits were simply beautiful, along many axes, from the simply colorful to the ornately grotesque, from the lean lithe predators to the amazingly camouflaged prey, from the coral organisms with their symbiotic algae to their larvae in the busy world of the plankton. Determined to learn some more biology this afternoon.

What was on the agenda today? Ah, Moshe and his research on ancient religions, souls, and eternities. A mutual friend, Ali, who taught theology at Columbia University, had found an old, 1930s parable by an early scientist called Haldane, explaining to his audience what eternity was by imagining a Neapolitan street-sweeper child wafted to "Heaven," and his God offering to have a bird drop a feather on a mountain once a century: "When the mountain is worn away . . ."

"No," Haldane's child had said (anticipating Pascal's many infinities). "Long before the feathers have had any effect, the world of birds, feathers, and mountains will have been superseded." And so on. "Our successors will think of our time as a pre-Creation eternity: our predecessors found eternity as our time unfolded." A very pretty little parable.

Where, Moshe and Ali wondered, was this "Heaven," where "souls" lived, where "God" was to be found? I observed, as they discussed Plato's ideal plane of existence; and Rucker's Mindscape; and the Judaeo-Christian Creation myth with its Garden of Eden so clearly lifted from the Sumerians; and the question of whether the ancients believed that Adam had a navel, the trees in the Garden had tree rings, and the rock below had fossils—all the Created were consistent with a long causal but fictional history. The Library found Gosse's *Omphalos* for them, which had propounded that idea to the Victorians as the way of integrating Darwin with Creationist Christianity: God had created an "old" Universe, and you couldn't catch the Old Guy out.

We all enjoyed coffee and liqueurs as we argued about different planes of existence, what causality was, if there were Laws of Nature that made things go the way they did. "The scientists of the twentieth century believed there were," said Ali, "and they didn't see how close to their religious friends that made them." Then Debbie appeared, and Ali's current lover, and we all found ourselves around a lunch table talking about the food and its provenance.

I thought how much they—and I—were perpetual students, rehashing all the old arguments and examples with the occasional new parable thrown in by the Library from the literature of the past. I wandered off alone toward the Bronx Zoo again.

I turned on a light rain to match my mood and wondered, again, whether any of the other thousands of virtual New Yorks had me doing exactly the same things (deciding not to experiment with chillies would have been a good idea), and whether their Libraries fed them the same material from the infinite literary and scientific resources before the Uplift.

Then it occurred to me that the Library's literary past might never actually have existed, as unreal as the pre-Creation seasons documented by the tree rings in the Eden trees. The Library, like the God in *Omphalos*, might have constructed that past so that our civilization seemed rational, with a causal history. The problem for me was that I simply could not imagine a time and place, a three- or four-dimensional causal universe like the twentieth century so vividly portrayed for us by the Library, where human beings had possessed material "bodies" that somehow interacted directly with the world around them to implement their wishes. Their supposed belief in "souls" seemed positively reasonable compared with the idea that human minds had once been tethered to material bodies that needed to eat, to excrete, to heal after material injury. That there had been what they called a "reality" that people didn't even have the illusion that they controlled. That people didn't always live, as we know that we do, such rich, fulfilled lives in the machinery of the Library.

Picasso's Cat

Ron Collins

Ron Collins has contributed nearly forty stories to professional publications, including Analog, Dragon, Asimov's, *and several collections. He holds a degree in mechanical engineering from the University of Louisville and has worked developing avionics systems, electronics, and information technology. He lives in Columbus, Indiana. His Web site can be found at www.typosphere.com.*

Dear Mr. Gee,

Thank you for your recent correspondence in regard to an earlier submission. Some of your comments have gotten me to thinking, and as a result I now understand a few things more fully than I once did. Knowing your fascination with topics as eclectic as quantum theory, art history, and, of course, editorial matters, I immediately thought you would want to hear about my recent endeavors, and how I've tied these apparently disparate fields together into a nice little ball.

What I've found is certainly most disturbing, but my results can be verified through simple logic.

In other words, I'm on to you.

It all started, I now understand, with the cubists.

You know, Picasso and the rest of the crowd that took pieces of people and cows and dogs and for all I know anything else and chopped them up, placing a leg here, an arm there, and a breast at the eye level of the average thirty-five-year-old man.

After several hours of research, I am convinced—and I'm certain you are, too—that the cubists knew well something it took Bohr, Heisenberg, and Schrödinger another twenty-five or so years to almost figure out.

That is, of course, the cubists knew a good deal about quantum theory.

I refer to the example of Schrödinger's cat. In this famous thought experiment a cat is placed in a box and predictions are made as to whether it survives or not. Quantum theorists then proceed to state that until the box is opened, the cat is in the astonishing state of fluctuation between both possibilities—alive half the time and dead the other half (which must be terribly unpleasant for the cat). I'm an engineer, though, not a theoretical physicist, and whether the cat is in oscillation between life and death or merely just sleeping is a philosophical discussion at best. So I'll leave that for our next communication in order to concentrate on hard fact.

So, let's turn back to the world of art. The proof, they say, is in the pudding, and simply by looking at their work, I think it an obvious deduction that the cubists had discovered quantum theory and were experimentally proving Schrödinger's dalliance well before he thought it all out. Only they went a step further than Schrödinger, applying the theorem recursively to various parts of the anatomy of their subjects.

To visualize what I mean, think of Schrödinger's cat, but then assign each portion of the cat its own quantum box—one for the left eye, one for the nose, a few for long whiskers, one for the tail. You get the point. Once you get this image, it's simple to understand how the artist could render such visions as the cubists did, for their reality would depend only upon which of the multitudes of boxes they chose to look into and what state each element lay in when it was observed.

The fact that the cubist movement even exists is obvious proof that the uncertainty principle works on the large scale as well as at the subatomic and, in fact, has a recursive principle. Luckily, however, we live in a moderately stable universe where very few people understand how to manipulate the quantum flux like the cubists did. Otherwise, I figure we would all look like Picasso's cat.

Now that I understand it, I'm really quite happy to know that you are one of the very few to be actively employing this principle.

I told you I was on to you.

I hear you, Henry, I really do: how did I, a simple engineer with limited faculties, figure it all out where so many other really bright folks have failed?

Well, it goes like this.

I was looking in my e-mail the other day, and I thought, as usual, "Is there a message from Henry inside my inbox, or is there no message from Henry inside the inbox?" Schrödinger's post, as it were. Suddenly it hit me. I've been asking the wrong question.

Instead, I should be asking recursive, Picasso's-post questions such as, "Assuming there is a message inside, will it be signed Henry, or will it be signed Mr. Gee?"; "Will it be typewritten or will it be a graphic insert?"; and "Will the salutation be 'Dear Ron' or 'Dear Mr. Collins'?" You know—identifying the source of the components of the message, as the cubists did, rather than applying the theory to the whole of the cat, as the physicists did.

As I processed this thought, I suddenly understood what you were doing.

All those rejection letters are merely your way of ferreting out less intelligent authors and general troublemakers in favor of those with such moxie as yours. You've been sending me Picasso's memoranda, quantum correspondence, letters in flux between acceptance and rejection. And while I've enjoyed your commentary, I've rarely looked close enough to open the right reality, the one that resulted in the elusive check rather than the dreaded letter of declination.

So I wanted to tell you that I was on to you.

I can't go back, of course. Once an envelope is opened, the rejection cannot be changed. So most of the tales I've sent you so far will certainly have to find resting homes with some other, inferior magazine.

But I promise I'll await your next letter with eager anticipation.

Regards,
Ron Collins

P.S. I've been trying this theory out in preparation for your reply, and I think I've got it about right.

P.P.S. You should see my cat.

My Grandfather's River

Brenda Cooper

Brenda Cooper's stories have appeared in Analog *and* Asimov's, *both solo and with collaborator Larry Niven. Her novel* The Silver Ship and the Sea *is published by Tor. She lives in Kirkland, Washington, and her Web site can be found at www.brenda-cooper.com.*

I begin to make the river. The river. His river. The one my grandfather took me down the year I turned ten, and again when I was sixteen and twenty-five.

It takes days to dig through Web archives for his data, to find old versions of the two-dimensional geographic information software he used twenty years ago. Success allows me to form the data into three dimensions, to show the banks shift and the water fall away, to chart the demise of trees and animals.

It is not enough. Sitting straight in my chair, feet on the ground, back arched, stretching my wrists, I am tempted to give up and send a historybot to make a simple album of Grandpa's speeches. Except his own words are no gift back to him, especially as they didn't work. He spent six years fighting to save the river, and then ten more wandering up and down it, studying his failure.

On our last trip, when I was twenty-five and he was seventy, we sat in his red canoe in the middle of the river. A dead fish floated past us. "Why do you stay?" I asked.

"I need to save it."

I eyed the white underbelly of the dead fish but held my silence.

He looked away from me, his voice breaking. "I'm mapping it for you. I can't save the real river, but I can save the record of it." He pointed at a cloud of tiny cameras he'd set to follow us. Bright sun sparkled on them like diamonds.

I have re-created the river from that trip.

But I need the river of my youth, the one from our first trip.

I find a programbot that takes the old photographs from his first *Natural Geography* article and take two more days off work to scan, register, and rectify the thin bright photos to his old 2D and make sure the cattails are exactly the right number of inches across, and that some bunch up close, hugging, and others wave above the water like brown flags.

I tell the pixelated water to rise up a little, watching carefully as depressions in the banks fill into tiny spangled wetlands.

Olfactory databots yield pond water and cedar and frogs and mix them all up on command. I add throaty frog conversations, hoping this sensory stew will drive my little-girl memories forward. I collapse on the couch, the river surrounding me, washing me.

I cause stars of water spiders to scoot on bright drops of surface tension, and feed them digital mayflies. Virtual water laps at a finger I hold a few inches in front of my face. The water spiders glide and dance around it.

Finally, I slip into my child self and the memory of his voice is clear and strong, as if the river washed away the forty years between then and now. "They never look like they're walking. Walking would be too slow for them."

I recall his hand on my shoulder as I gaze up into his intense blue-green eyes. He surveys the current, keeping us away from white water frothing over rocks. This man who is always gentle with me digs his fingers into my shoulder. The sun beats on his thinning blond hair as he lets go and makes such a sweeping gesture the canoe under us rocks alarmingly. "Penny. This is your heritage. We're stealing it from you. Memorize it, Penny. Memorize the water flowing always downstream, the clean, rounded rocks, the water spiders." Even the memory of his voice drives up details.

I add them one by one. Three turtles balancing on a floating log.

The ghostly feel of a warm wind.

A heron pretending to be a cattail.

The monitoring nano in my blood screams sleep at me and I can't override it anymore without a doctor's chit.

It's okay. I'm done.

I collapse, sleeping for two days and a night, dreaming of turtles and herons and dragonflies.

On the morning of my grandfather's birthday I bring the river in my top pocket. The relentless sun beats down on the dry brown grass on his bit of lawn. He waits for me in an old wooden Adirondack chair, his eyes bright blue pools in a river of wrinkles from temple to temple. He smiles and stands and holds me, his arms shaking a little. I suddenly hate it that he is one hundred today.

Glancing down, I note that his nanomonitor is yellow again this morning. At least it isn't blinking in alarm.

Inside, a big white fan cools the kitchen, and there is no evidence he's eaten breakfast. He flips a switch and sits down, sighing in pleasure as the scent of brewing coffee puffs into the air, a history of mornings.

I stand behind him, kneading his shoulders, my throat tight. I slide the glasses out of my pocket and slip them over his head.

His voice belongs to an old man. "What's this?"

My own voice shakes. "Look."

The glasses sense him and spring to life. Even though I can't see it, I know the river surrounds him. It runs over his ankles. Cattails grace the corner by the refrigerator. He grips his knee and a breath rushes from him. VR glasses are for an old man. I turn my retinas to virt. Reality grays to background. My senses catch up with the river programming just in time to be with him as the three turtles come into view in the empty door frame.

He squeezes my palm hard.

I return the real world to my eyes.

A tear is falling down his cheek.

Sandcastles: A Dystopia

KATHRYN CRAMER

Kathryn Cramer is a writer, anthologist, and Internet consultant who lives in Pleasantville, New York. Her anthologies, both solo and with her husband, David G. Hartwell, and others, have received many awards. Current interests include the impact of information technology on cartography and world events. Her Web site can be found at www.kathryncramer.com.

You had big summer plans to revive the mathematics career that might have been but wasn't. But there were your children, their eyes trained upon you. *Here we are. Entertain us.* You shoot endless camcorder footage of your son catching frogs; of your daughter taking off her shoes while you say in the background: "Don't you dare take off those shoes." At the end of the summer, you vacation with your mother-in-law, age ninety-three. She watches TV while you, your husband, and kids go to the beach.

You return to the cottage wanting to talk about children and their sandcastles and the rising tide; instead your mother-in-law wants to talk about the impending disaster. Unfortunately, your mother-in-law knows her hurricanes. And so you return home. You read the weather on the Web in disbelief. Surely, this is like the comet Kohoutek: the real event will be the advance coverage? Nothing can live up to that; and of course, it doesn't. You dream that your great-grandmother's bones are floating out to sea. You aren't relieved, as you were in denial in the first place, but you begin to comprehend; and so you see it when it begins to happen.

You have watched children with their sandcastles and you can't get that image out of your mind. Water gradually overwhelming the defenses, the castles collapse, surrender to the ocean. A levee breaks. You strive for understanding, find what you think are before-and-after pictures on disparate Web sites. You bring them together and tell your friends. You were wrong initially, but your attempts attract a swarm of helpful techies. Cameramen in 'copters snap photos that appear on the Web, seemingly of "the" break. Satellite images are at your fingertips. You compare, contrast, argue. You and your newfound friends, most of whom you've never met and whom you know only by handles, realize with growing horror that the situation is worse, much worse, than anyone has yet described. Not one break, but three or four. Thousands of people are going to die, but you don't yet dare say what you understand, for how could a housewife with a fancy computer setup understand it before those who should be saving those people?

You begin to get specific addresses in the mail. *No one is helping, maybe you can? hello i was trying to find the condition of my home my address was . . . my two dogs were left there.* You answer that. And another and another and another. You can't run the software your newfound techie friends are using, but they send you JPEGs, amazing JPEGs. You feel like you are watching progress in Civil War medicine in fast-forward; amazing innovations in digital cartography are happening overnight, there for you when you wake up in the morning. And what you see then is beautiful and terrifying. You can't play too. All you can do is publish the images and make suggestions. And answer and answer and answer. Someone else asks you how you can help her relatives escape. You try your best. A reporter, impressed with the pictures, gets in touch, and you are interviewed.

When you arrive at your friends' house for the weekend, in a place so remote that cell phones don't work, you check your e-mail and discover many more requests for help, along with four requests for interviews. By the end of the weekend, you are world famous. The world is looking for good news, and for a few days, you are it—a bright spot in the bleakness. Meanwhile, the scenario you understood unfolds and unfolds and unfolds. You really did understand things long before those who are supposed to be keeping watch. It seems impossible, but you did. Many more people are dying and you know it, and you are doing what you can, but it is not enough, cannot be enough, because you are a smart housewife with a computer and all you can do is write.

And you write and write, because people want to know if their houses are under water, if their dogs or relatives or friends are dead. And they know you can help, because it said so in *The New York Times*. You have left politics out of it, because you want your help to be available to anyone, no matter what their beliefs. But at a certain point that is no longer possible. What you begin to understand is that when you wrote that the dogs probably didn't drown because there was only eighteen inches of water max. at that address, that you were terribly naive. The dogs will be shot; the house razed. But you don't say so, because having exchanged e-mails with so many, you think you know how they feel.

And the tide begins to turn: The Collective You is winning. The press won't be silenced after all; the remaining residents can stay; the tabula rasa scenario begins to recede. And you write and write. You have learned to respond, learned a kind of one-on-one compassion and respect that might otherwise have passed you by. But you cannot get back to your own world: you are living in the dystopia in which all hell breaks loose. And now you know. And you watch your children start the school year and you know where they live.

Adam's Hot Dogs at the End of the World

Jeff Crook

Jeff Crook, fantasy novelist and designer of "Southern Gothic" apparel, lives in Memphis, Tennessee. Visit him online at http://jeffcrook.blogspot.com.

Adam considered the sky. It wasn't even blue anymore, just a sort of washed-out gray. The tall, pale man opposite him thoughtfully chewed a bite of hot dog, the bitten remainder of which he held about midchest, just slightly above Adam's head. Adam noticed a spot of yellow mustard on the man's red tie. His suit was black, as were the sunglasses resting on top of his wavy blond hair. His almost-colorless blue eyes remained fixed in an unblinking stare that Adam still found somewhat unsettling.

"What you say is true," Adam continued, "but the conflict between theology and interstellar travel isn't just with the book of Genesis. There's Revelations to consider. Of course, Norse mythology also includes an end-times myth, Ragnarok and all that, but there are so few Odin worshippers these days, it seems pointless to include them."

"Entirely," the Nordic-looking man mumbled around his hot dog.

"Uh . . . entirely what?" Adam asked.

"Pointless," the man said. Adam noticed that the spot of yellow mustard had disappeared from the man's tie.

"Wonderful technology," Adam muttered before continuing. "But as you know, UFO researchers always assumed that the government actively concealed the existence of extraterrestrials to protect the Church, referring of course to the question raised by Genesis—if there are extraterrestrial civilizations, why aren't they mentioned in Genesis? The Brookings Institute is supposed to have done the original sociological study that has guided disclosure policy since the middle of the last century."

"That's true," the Nordic man said.

"It is? Oh, yes, but in my opinion the answer to the Genesis question wouldn't bring down the Church, would it? One could always argue that Genesis never says aliens don't exist, either."

"Obviously," the Nordic man said. He finished his hot dog. Adam removed another one from the grill, bunned it, squirted a line of mustard down its pink and char-blackened length, and handed it over the grill to his guest.

"Obviously. So the real sticking point is Revelations," Adam said. "Do you want a beer or something?"

"Yes," the Nordic man said. Adam opened a longneck using the bottle-opener feature on his grill spatula. A shadow of a smile twitched the corners of the tall man's narrow mouth. "That's a useful device," he said as Adam handed him the beer.

"So, as I was saying, Revelations and all the other Armageddon philosophies," Adam continued. "I mean, if there are other worlds out there where a man . . . being . . . whatever . . . can be born, live, and die without ever setting foot on Earth, that kind of pulls the end-timers' teeth, doesn't it? Without an end-times in which sinners are judged and the righteous rewarded, Western religion becomes rather pointless. God destroys the world—big deal. Sure, a few billion people die, but in the big picture, it's a minor occurrence. Planets explode every day, am I right? Whole star systems go nova, trillions of intelligent life-forms wiped out in the twinkling of an eye, no matter how moral or immoral they are or were. It's physics, and a lack of sufficiently advanced technology to detect the impending Armageddon and/or to escape it by fleeing their doomed planet."

The Nordic man ate his hot dog and drank his beer without blinking. Adam noticed that the man's bottom lip (which was somewhat fuller than his almost-fleshless upper lip) tended to get sucked into the neck of the bottle when he drank, making a comical squeaking noise when he pulled it out.

Adam glanced at the cloudless gray sky, his voice rising as he tried not to laugh. "And since these end-times religions self-perpetuate by exerting control over their congregants by holding or withholding the metaphysical keys to heaven, take away the end-times and what are they left with?"

"Where do you purchase these?" the Nordic man asked, gesturing with his beer to the half-eaten hot dog in his hand.

"I make them myself. Secret family recipe," Adam said. "The beef is Kosher."

"They are delicious," the tall man said. "I'll mention them to the Minister of Culture."

Adam smiled. He felt his point had been made. The back door opened and a small, light gray alien stepped outside. "Thanks, Adam," the alien said with obvious relief. "I was about to bust."

"Not a problem, Thraz. Did you remember to flush?" Adam asked.

"Oh. Sorry." The alien blushed a deeper shade of gray and glanced at the Nordic man, who was still examining the uneaten remainder of his hot dog.

"Don't worry. I'll get it," Adam said. "Your pee dissolved the toilet last time. Try explaining that to the plumber. You want another beer or something?"

"Thanks, no. I'm driving. Well, see you later," the small alien said. He climbed into the metallic green, lozenge-shaped spacecraft parked in Adam's backyard. The Nordic man ate the last half of his hot dog in one bite, set the empty beer bottle on a fencepost, and climbed into the spacecraft without so much as saying good-bye. Adam was used to this. The tall ones seemed unemotional, but the little guys were friendly enough.

Adam waved good-bye as the door materialized and blended seamlessly with the hull of the ship. The craft rose silently to treetop level, then shot off toward the encroaching sea, leaving behind a rainbow arc that shimmered in the washed-out sky for a second or two before fading. Adam smiled and popped an olive into his mouth as the sound of waves reached his ears.

High tide again, and getting closer every day. So much for that covenant.

Yes, interstellar travel is a lovely way to escape the end of the world and all its moral obligations, Adam thought with a rising sense of hope and purpose.

The Party's Over

Penelope Kim Crowther

Penelope Kim Crowther is a pseudonym of Nicola Jones, online news editor for Nature. *She graduated with a degree in chemistry and oceanography and subsequently gained a master's degree in journalism, both at the University of British Columbia, Canada. Lured to London by the chance to report for* New Scientist *magazine, she moved to* Nature *in 2003.*

"Tell me again about the balloons, Grandpa."

"Now? We're nearly there."

"Pleeease."

"Okay, okay. Well, when I was a kid we used to have balloons at our birthday parties that were filled with . . . helium."

"No!!!"

"Yes. And when we were done playing with them, we'd sometimes let them just drift off into the sky. Or swallow the helium to make our voices go squeaky."

"You ATE it?"

"You bet. But it was cheap back then—not like now. It wasn't till your grandma and me were about your age that people started to realize how much helium we needed, and how we were running out. Physicists were doing more and more clever things at very cold temperatures, and they needed a lot of helium to keep things cold. But there just wasn't that much about. Do you remember where helium comes from?"

"Uh . . . no."

"Sophie . . . I've told you a hundred times. Hang on a minute, I just have to pay this road toll. There. So, all our helium is left over from when the planet first formed. It leaks out of the middle of the Earth and trickles out of the ground, and then it hangs about in our air for a while. But it's so light that eventually it spins out of the sky into outer space. Our planet leaks helium—like a pricked balloon."

"So if it just comes out of the ground, why did we run out?"

"Well it's hard to collect something when there's so little of it in the whole sky. Sucking helium out of the air is like mining a beach for lost wedding rings. Not a very good idea. The only place where there's enough of it to mine is . . . in oil. Oil collects helium and stores it up."

"But there isn't any oil now."

"Exactly. Back in the twenties, we were running out of oil pretty quickly and all the helium plants in Texas and Saudi Arabia were running down as fast as the oil wells were running dry. So that's why your grandma, who was a very clever geologist, made so much money. She was young and adventurous—like you." Sophie giggled at that. "And she saw what was happening, so she went out to Nepal, where the Earth is all cracked up from earthquakes and there are places where helium leaks out in bigger streams than anywhere else on the planet. And the American company she worked for—still works for—built big buildings over these cracks so they could collect the helium. And then they sold it on."

"I'm clever too, you know."

"I know you are. Here we go—here's our turn."

"So is that why Granny still lives in the United States?"

"In a way. Your grandma decided that all the money from that helium was more important to her than other things . . . which is why you get to have such nice birthday presents, even if you don't have helium-filled balloons. And that's why I moved here . . . to do other things instead. Now, we're here!"

Sophie looked up and saw the sign: "ITER—the future of fusion." She knew this place, it was where her grandpa worked sometimes. It had a sign outside with a picture of a little explosion. Sunny rays were flying out, which was energy you could use to make your computer work, she knew. Grandpa always said this would be the next big thing, after oil. The picture showed other things flying out too, little circles labeled "D" and "n" and "He." *He who?* she wondered.

Grandpa pulled into the gravel drive and stopped the car. "Now you'll stay in the car while Grandpa has his meeting? I'll only be a little while."

Sophie waited until she saw him go inside the gate, and then the doors. Then she got the birthday present out of her bag and gave it a little shake. Grandma had given it to her the week before, and told her it was a surprise for the man who ran ITER. She was supposed to hide it, that was the game, while Grandpa was at his meeting, but not to tell anyone. Sophie liked surprises.

Beneath the wrapping and the bows the present ticked like a clock. She got out and hid it in the bushes by the gates, and went back to wait.

They didn't feel the explosion ten hours later, when they were safely back in the apartment having tea. Not until Grandpa turned on the news the next morning did Sophie see the building on fire, big billows of black smoke heading for the sky. She could hear the reporter over the sound of sirens: ". . . This will put back fusion research for years. On the eve of a demonstration project that was meant to prove to the world the reality of cheaper, cleaner energy, there is only smoke to show for decades of . . ."

Sophie didn't understand what was going on. Or why Grandpa had his head in his hands. Was he crying? The newscast went on: "In related news, the price of helium jumped sky high today as the potential source from fusion plants dried up—for decades now at least . . ."

Transport of Delight

ROLAND DENISON

Roland Denison is the pseudonym of Christopher Surridge, former senior editor at Nature, *who now works at the Public Library of Science (PLoS) in Cambridge, England, where he continues to roll back the frontiers of science publishing. He is an expert yachtsman and, like the protagonist in his story, a keen cyclist. He lives in Cambridgeshire, England.*

The cyclist flies downhill toward the city in a semitrance of endorphins and adrenaline. Traffic lights change a fraction before he would have reached for the brakes as he shoots past hospital, shops, and park. From here the road runs flat and straight, aimed at the heart of the old city. He slips his derailleur down and rises from the saddle to maintain speed. A week ago he couldn't have done that. Even yesterday he would have been navigating a fractured route between the bumpers of stationary vehicles; an inconstant path whose gaps and alleys closed and opened without warning.

But today is special. Today there is no traffic. The roads belong to him alone.

Moving the citizenry around had never been simple. Centuries before, carts had been forbidden entry to the city during the hours of daylight. The bridges over the river, whose oily tang he can already smell, bore tollgates. In the current century that idea was reinvented. Batteries of cameras standing guard, noting down entries in their electronic ledgers and tallying up their fee. Soon every road in the metropolitan area, indeed the whole country, had its own tariff. To keep track of this revenue, vehicles were fitted with radio tags to pinpoint their position to within half a meter. And still the jams worsened, average speeds dropped, and drivers seethed.

The cyclist raises his cadence for his favorite part of the journey: two interlinked gyratories, once the boundary of the original levy. Slowing slightly, he leans into the initial left-hand bend, right foot down to avoid clipping the tarmac. Then to the right, straightens for eight cranks to maintain momentum for the second left-right-left combination. Ten seconds of bliss that any bobsleigh pilot would envy.

Half a mile on, a cluster of side streets forms the shortest path to the river. Here the presence of pavements makes corners difficult to judge. He can just remember when all roads in the city had pedestrian-thronged sidewalks, but their users were long since driven away by the dangers of the adjacent road. Then the roads were widened to engulf the redundant walkways. But, as so often before, larger roads encouraged more traffic and greater congestion.

Drivers had felt discriminated against by the tagging and tolls, their human rights infringed. The judiciary agreed, but rather than abolish the offense, the government abolished the discrimination, extending it to the entire populace. Personal identity cards became subcutaneous identichips. An entire population located to within twenty centimeters, day and night.

All the information was processed by a central traffic computer, the CTC, which the cyclist was paid to deceive. At first it simply advised in-vehicle navigation systems, but that had little effect. Everyone had a better idea on how to beat the jams. Everyone knew a secret shortcut. No one followed its advice. The G5 riots changed that. Hastily passed legislation upgraded citizens' identichips to release endorphins and their antagonists under remote control. Now the CTC could make drivers feel good about following its route planning and depressed for ignoring it, but even so the traffic didn't move.

The cyclist passes a motto, written on the side of a three-hundred-year-old church: "All may have, if they dare try, a glorious life." He has read this every day for years but it was only last week that he had grasped its meaning. Yet a glorious life seemed too ambitious: but a glorious day, he could dare that much.

The CTC had long since calculated a solution to the city's traffic woes. Traffic created congestion, vehicles created traffic—banish the vehicles, abolish the jams. But that wasn't politically acceptable. Instead, the data logs on which the CTC based its calculations had to be amended. A lie of omission to keep the CTC laboring in the vain hope that the traffic could be made to flow. That was the cyclist's job.

Standing on the pedals he ascends the bridge crossing the wide river in glorious isolation before plunging between the artificial cliffs on the north bank. Past theaters, banks, museums, bars, and shops, his progress continuous and unimpeded. Today the streets are his—for yesterday he had dared the truth. He had passed the logs unexpurgated to the CTC and it had drawn its inevitable conclusion.

He nears his office overlooking the canal, a previous century's attempt at traffic management. He dismounts on the move, jogging a few steps to bring the bicycle to a stop. Under the influence of the enlightened CTC, the periphery of the city is currently populated with artificially contented drivers traveling in futile circles. Today the city streets are the cyclist's domain, and it feels good.

As he reaches the door the euphoria that has carried him through his journey evaporates, replaced by a weight of dread. He turns, remounts his bike, and cycles back into the city, his mood lifting immediately with a fresh endorphin release.

Today he belongs to the roads and their call cannot be denied.

The Perfect Lover

Paul Di Filippo

Paul Di Filippo is a prolific and wide-ranging writer and critic, author of several novels and hundreds of short stories. He lives in H. P. Lovecraft's own city of Providence, Rhode Island. His Web site can be found at www.pauldifilippo.com.

Neurosciences Institute, La Jolla, February 10, 2036. The substrate for the cultured human-mouse brain cells was a highly reticulated wodge of aerogel inside a homeostatic capsule as big as a thumb. At this moment the naked capsule sat in a dock, tethered by a GliaWire connection to a Brooksweil 5000 running at a hundred petaflops. The parent machine was the size of a credit card, its monitor and keyboard holographic projections.

Two people stood by. One, a genially abstracted man of about thirty, wore intelligent otakuwear, full of membranous pockets, organic sensors, interface patches, and invisible circuitry. The other, a hard-eyed woman with some gray threading her bronze hair, wore the dress uniform of a Marine major, including ribbons from the Caracas campaign.

"I don't understand," said the woman, "why the drone can't be governed directly by the Brooksweil. Surely there's enough Turingosity there."

"Plenty," replied the man. "But there's no love."

"Love? What's love got to do with it?"

Filtering the conversation in real time, the man's clothing prompted him through an earbud with a cultural referent to a pop song more than fifty years old. But he chose not to utter it. Didn't seem likely this hard case would appreciate any such trivial allusion. Intelligence amplification still required human discretion.

"Love is the driver for the mission. Love will supplement the drone's heuristics in instances when lesser imperatives would collapse. Without it, the failure rate goes up an order of magnitude. And we can't simulate love yet in purely moletronic minds."

The major looked suspiciously at the little pod full of wetware, as if it might suddenly start spouting poetry through as-yet-unattached peripherals.

"Well, as long as it follows its directives . . ."

"Need I remind you of our past successes? DARPA and BARDA just renewed our funding with double the budget."

"I know, I know. But there's so much riding on this mission. If we don't stop this bastard Kiet the Mousekiller, we stand to lose most of the West Coast."

Kiet the Mousekiller had begun his infamous career as a simple Thai pirate. Radicalized by the anonymous contamination of Mecca with a GPS-circumscribed green goo, he had become a terrorist, earning his sobriquet by his destruction of Hong Kong Disneyland. Kiet's latest scheme, not yet known to the public, involved a retired Japanese deep-sea drilling ship, the *Chikyu*, which Kiet had purchased on the open market under a front. Now docked in an Indonesian port, the ship was believed to be due to sail imminently.

Kiet's plan was to drill into a tectonic subduction zone close to America, plant a small nuclear bomb, and detonate it, triggering a tsunami. Stopping him by overt military means was made impossible by the terrorist's current refuge with an ostensible ally. Hence the black-budget project.

After regarding the Brooksweil's display, the technician began disconnecting the GliaWire. "OK, we'll be ready for the sample in a moment. You've got it?"

The major's hand strayed instinctively to her sidearm, before she reached into her pocket and removed a glassine packet. "Several hairs reclaimed from Kiet's last visit to his favorite whorehouse."

Handling the homeostatic capsule nonchalantly, the man approached the drone.

A stealth tortoise with a MEMS shell, powered by the same pocket fusion reactor as NASA's Sedna probe, the drone rested on a table, as innocuous as any lawn-mowing bot. A small hatch gaped in its shell. The technician installed the pod and closed the hatch. He took the packet, extracted the hairs, and pressed them into a small perforated depression on the front of the tortoise.

"OK, we're live."

When I came fully awake the essence of my beloved was already integrated into my soul. His beautiful face filled my inner eye, and I could taste his genome, sweeter to me than the power that flowed from my atomic heart. I wanted nothing more than to be with him, to merge my soul with his, to shower him with my love. I would let nothing stand between us.

I immediately extended my senses, sniffing the air, but met disappointment. My beloved was nowhere within range. But knowledge in my memory informed me of his location! How I quivered with eagerness to race to his side! But where was the exit from this place? Suddenly a passage to the open air materialized above me. I activated my ventral lifter fans and rose upward.

Banda Sea, February 14, 2036. I had been damaged on my voyage to my mate. He was surrounded by vigilant duennas, brutish entities similar to myself who guarded him jealously. Every step of my route during the last day had been fraught with challenges. But I had met them without hesitation. Because that is what lovers do.

My aerial capacity was now limited to short hops. Currently, I traveled underwater, using my magneto-hydrodynamic systems. My signature across the spectrum was that of a school of fish. All my telemetry said abort: but I would not. Ahead of me loomed the vessel that held my beloved. I knew I would have to surface to unite with him, and prepared myself.

I shot out of the water alongside the ship, lurching evasively, to be met with a hail of small-arms fire from those who were not my beloved. I triggered my infrasonics, and all my rivals collapsed in bowel-spasming pain.

Crashing through the window of the pilothouse, I sustained further injury.

But nothing mattered.

For I was finally in the presence of my beloved!

An expression of terrible ecstasy filled his face, and my soul melted with joy.

I initiated the destabilizing quench on the magnets surrounding my fiery heart, giving him all my love at last.

An evanescent fountain of multimillion-degree plasma bloomed briefly aboard the *Chikyu*, in the fierce and tender shape of a heart.

Printcrime

Cory Doctorow

Cory Doctorow is a Canadian writer, blogger, "technology person," author of several novels and short stories, and activist for a profound reassessment of the concept of copyright in the electronic age. He currently lives in Los Angeles, and his Web site can be found at www.craphound.com.

The coppers smashed my father's printer when I was eight. I remember the hot, cling-film-in-a-microwave smell of it, and Da's look of ferocious concentration as he filled it with fresh goop, and the warm, fresh-baked feel of the objects that came out of it.

The coppers came through the door with truncheons swinging, one of them reciting the terms of the warrant through a bullhorn. One of Da's customers had shopped him. The ipolice paid in high-grade pharmaceuticals—performance enhancers, memory supplements, metabolic boosters. The kind of things that cost a fortune over the counter; the kind of things you could print at home, if you didn't mind the risk of having your kitchen filled with a sudden crush of big, beefy bodies, hard truncheons whistling through the air, smashing anyone and anything that got in the way.

They destroyed Grandma's trunk, the one she'd brought from the old country. They smashed our little refrigerator and the purifier unit over the window. My tweetybird escaped death by hiding in a corner of his cage as a big, booted foot crushed most of it into a sad tangle of printer wire.

Da. What they did to him. When he was done, he looked like he'd been brawling with an entire rugby side. They brought him out the door and let the newsies get a good look at him as they tossed him in the car. All the while a spokesman told the world that my da's organized-crime bootlegging operation had been responsible for at least twenty million in contraband, and that my da, the desperate villain, had resisted arrest.

I saw it all from my phone, in the remains of the sitting room, watching it on the screen and wondering how, just how anyone could look at our little apartment and our terrible, manky estate and mistake it for the home of an organized-crime kingpin. They took the printer away, of course, and displayed it like a trophy for the newsies. Its little shrine in the kitchenette seemed horribly empty. When I roused myself and picked up the apartment and rescued my poor peeping tweetybird, I put a blender there. It was made out of printed parts, so it would only last a month before I'd need to print new bearings and other moving parts. Back then, I could take apart and reassemble anything that could be printed.

By the time I turned eighteen, they were ready to let Da out of prison. I'd visited him three times—on my tenth birthday, on his fiftieth, and when Ma died. It had been two years since I'd last seen him and he was in bad shape. A prison fight had left him with a limp, and he looked over his shoulder so often it was like he had a tic. I was embarrassed when the minicab dropped us off in front of the estate, and tried to keep my distance from this ruined, limping skeleton as we went inside and up the stairs.

"Lanie," he said as he sat me down. "You're a smart girl, I know that. You wouldn't know where your old da could get a printer and some goop?"

I squeezed my hands into fists so tight my fingernails cut into my palms. I closed my eyes. "You've been in prison for ten years, Da. Ten. Years. You're going to risk another ten years to print out more blenders and pharma, more laptops and designer hats?"

He grinned. "I'm not stupid, Lanie. I've learned my lesson. There's no hat or laptop that's worth going to jail for. I'm not going to print none of that rubbish, never again." He had a cup of tea, and he drank it now like it was whiskey, a sip and then a long, satisfied exhalation. He closed his eyes and leaned back in his chair.

"Come here, Lanie, let me whisper in your ear. Let me tell you the thing that I decided while I spent ten years in lockup. Come here and listen to your stupid da."

I felt a guilty pang about ticking him off. He was off his rocker, that much was clear. God knew what he went through in prison. "What, Da?" I said, leaning in close.

"Lanie, I'm going to print more printers. Lots more printers. One for everyone. That's worth going to jail for. That's worth anything."

A Brief History of Death Switches

David Eagleman

David Eagleman is a neuroscientist at Baylor College of Medicine in Houston, Texas, interested in how the brain represents time. He can be found online at www.eaglemanlab.net.

There is no afterlife, but a version of us lives on nonetheless.

At the beginning of the computer era, people died with passwords in their heads and no one could access their files. When access to these files was critical, companies could grind to a halt. That's when programmers invented death switches.

With a death switch, the computer prompts you for your password once a week to make sure you are still alive. When you don't enter your password for some period of time, the computer deduces you are dead, and your passwords are automatically e-mailed to the second-in-command. Individuals began to use death switches to reveal Swiss bank account numbers to their heirs, to get the last word in an argument, and to confess secrets that were unspeakable during a lifetime.

It soon became appreciated that death switches provided a good opportunity to say good-bye electronically. Instead of sending out passwords, people began programming their computers to send e-mails to their friends announcing their own death. "It appears I'm dead now," the e-mails began. "I'll take this as an opportunity to tell you things I've always wanted to express . . ."

Soon enough, people realized they could program messages to be delivered on dates in the future: "Happy eighty-seventh birthday. It's been twenty-two years since my death. I hope your life is proceeding the way you want it to."

With time, people began to push death switches further. Instead of confessing their death in the e-mails, they pretended they were not dead. Using auto-responder algorithms that cleverly analyzed incoming messages, a death switch could generate apologetic excuses to turn down invitations, to send congratulations on a life event, and to claim to be looking forward to a chance to see them again sometime soon.

Today, building a death switch to pretend you are not dead has become an art form. Death switches are programmed to send a fax occasionally, make a transfer between bank accounts, or make an online purchase of the latest novel. The most sophisticated switches reminisce about shared adventures, exchange memories about a good story, swap inside jokes, brag about past feats, summon up lifetimes of experience.

In this way, death switches have established themselves as a cosmic joke on mortality. Humans have discovered that they cannot stop Death, but at least they can spit in his drink.

This began as a good-spirited revolution against the grave's silence. The problem for those of us still living, however, is the increasing difficulty in sorting the dead from the living. Computers operate around the clock sending out the social intercourse of the dead: greetings, condolences, invitations, flirtations, excuses, small talk, inside jokes—codes between people who know each other well.

And it is clear now where this society is going. Most people have died off, and I'm one of the few remaining. By the time I die and my own death switch is triggered, there will be nothing left but a sophisticated network of transactions with no one to read them: a society of e-mails zipping back and forth under silent satellites orbiting around a soundless planet.

So an afterlife does not exist for us, per se, but instead an afterlife exists for that which exists between us. When an alien civilization eventually bumps into Earth, it will immediately be able to understand what humans were about, because what will remain is the network of relationships: who loved whom, who competed, who cheated, who laughed together about road trips and holiday dinners. Each person's ties to bosses, brothers, lovers, are written in the electronic communiqués. The death switches simulate the society so completely that the entire social network is reconstructable. The planet's memories survive in zeros and ones.

This situation allows us to forever revisit shared jokes, to remedy lost opportunities for a kind word, to recall stories about delightful earthly experiences that can no longer be felt. Memories now live on their own, and no one forgets them or grows tired of telling them. We are quite satisfied with this arrangement, because reminiscing about our glory days of existence is perhaps all that would have happened in an afterlife anyway.

Only Connect

Greg Egan

Greg Egan is an SF writer and computer programmer, based in Perth, Western Australia. His Web site can be found at http://gregegan.customer.netspace.net.au.

E. M. Forster's famous advice to "Only connect!" is beginning to look superfluous. A theory in which the building blocks of the Universe are mathematical structures—known as graphs—that do nothing but connect has just passed its first experimental test.

A graph can be drawn as a set of points, called nodes, and a set of lines joining the nodes, called edges. Details such as the length and shape of the edges are not part of the graph, though: the only thing that distinguishes one graph from another is the connections between the nodes. The number of edges that meet at any given node is known as its valence.

In quantum graph theory (QGT) a quantum state describing both the geometry of space and all the matter fields present is built up from combinations of graphs. The theory reached its current form in the work of the Javanese mathematician Kusnanto Sarumpaet, who published a series of six papers from 2035 to 2038 showing that both general relativity and the standard model of particle physics could be seen as approximations to QGT.

Sarumpaet's graphs have a fascinating lineage, dating back to Michael Faraday's notion of "lines of force" running between electric charges, and William Thomson's theory of atoms as knotted "vortex tubes." More recent ancestors are Roger Penrose's spin networks, trivalent graphs with each edge labeled by a half integer, corresponding to a possible value of the spin of a quantum particle. Penrose invented these networks in the early 1970s, and showed that the set of all directions in space could be generated from simple, combinatorial principles by imagining an exchange of spin between two parts of a large network.

Generalizations of spin networks later appeared in certain kinds of quantum field theory. Just as a wavefunction assigns an amplitude to every possible position of a particle, a spin network embedded in a region of space can be used to assign an amplitude to every possible configuration of a field. The quantum states defined in this way consist of lines of flux running along the edges of the network.

In the 1990s, Lee Smolin and Carlo Rovelli discovered an analogous result in quantum gravity, where spin-network states have a simple geometric interpretation: the area of any surface depends entirely on the edges of the network that intersect it. These edges can be thought of as quantized "flux lines of area," and in quantum gravity area and other geometric measurements they take on a discrete spectrum of possible values. It then makes sense to quantize the topology as well, with the nodes and edges of the network replacing the usual idea of space as a continuum of points.

In the first decades of the new millennium, John Baez, Fotini Markopoulou, José-Antonio Zapata, and others did groundbreaking work on the possible dynamical laws for spin networks, assigning quantum amplitudes to the process of one network evolving into another. In the 2030s, Sarumpaet began to synthesize these results into a new model, based on graphs of arbitrary valence with unlabeled edges.

The geometry of three-dimensional space arises from tetravalent graphs with the four edges emerging from each node giving area to the faces of a "quantum tetrahedron." Allowing graphs of higher valence runs the risk of producing an explosion of unwanted dimensions, but Sarumpaet found a simple dynamical law that always leads to the average valence stabilizing at four. However, trivalent and pentavalent nodes—which have come to be known as "dopant" nodes, in analogy with the impurities added to semiconductors—can persist under the Sarumpaet rules if they are arranged in special patterns: closed, possibly knotted chains of alternating valence. These loops of dopant nodes, classified by their symmetries and mutual interactions, match up perfectly with the particles of the standard model.

Since the area associated with the edges of a quantum graph is of the order of a few square Planck lengths, some 10^{-50} times the surface area of a hydrogen atom, it was once feared that QGT would remain untestable for centuries. However, in 2043 computer simulations identified a new class of "polymer states": long, open chains of dopant nodes that were predicted to have energies and half-lives within the grasp of current technology to create and detect.

A search for polymer states that commenced at the Orbital Accelerator Facility in 2049 has now yielded its first success [see *J. Quant. Graphs* 15, (2050): 7895–99]. If the result can be repeated, Sarumpaet's graphs will shift from being merely the most elegant description of the Universe to being the most likely one.

At the Zoo

Warren Ellis

Warren Ellis is a graphic novelist and author based in Southend, Essex, England. His Web site can be found at www.warrenellis.com.

28/03/2468 2225.18 Universal Time Code. The Human Reservation, in temperate London, England, considers the breeding of the last two baseline humans a vindication of its hard work in identifying, isolating, and protecting the "pure," second-millennium strain of human being.

"The cusp between second and third millennium is vital," explained the baseline humans' head keeper, Daybreak Sigridsdottir, in a brief radiotelepathy interview conducted during the act of disposing of the couple's physical waste products, known as "mucking out." "The emergence of practical biotechnology happened right at that point. The introduction of artificial and alien material into the human genetic structure began barely ten years into the new millennium. You can't trust anything after 2001."

Sigridsdottir is an accomplished zoologist, whose text about the rescue and subsequent massive sexing of the population of New York City after the release of the Genital Babel terrorist bioware won her the William Gates VI Truth Prize for 2461. Her work was crucial in sifting through world records to locate humans who remained utterly unchanged by modern biological technology. She well remembers the conflict of feelings when it was discovered that only two humans on Earth still possess a pre-2000 biological makeup.

"We stopped thinking about the way we live a long time ago. We take a deep breath to oxygenate enough for winged flight, but we don't consider what we left in that lungful of air. In sixty-six cases out of a hundred, a cubic meter of sea-level air will contain an airborne genetic trait, engineered in a lab or spored from a working organ, capable of applying itself to the biology of the respiring individual.

"And now here we are. Most of us are at least 0.5 percent of our DNA away from the human baseline. Some are more. On the other side of the human species, if you go a percent or two of DNA away, you have a chimp. By the same token, many of us are no longer human. We are something else entirely. And the horror and surprise and sadness that has been expressed are artifacts of our refusal to accept that."

Nine Nevada Rockets, spokesgroup for the Transhuman Association, relays a different perspective on the event from its spawning territory in the Pacific Ocean. "This is nonsense. I could make a case for the genome being 'untrustworthy' post-1945, with the introduction of trace elements from nuclear detonations into the environment. Human genetic structure changed with each new immunity we developed and passed down to our descendants. Who is the Human Reservation to say what is human and what isn't?"

Sigridsdottir, who points out that Rockets is responding via a telepathy organ derived from whale and eel biologies, responds: "Look at us. We've adopted mechanical traits, we've taken on animal traits, we've invented new abilities and new internal organs to perform them from scratch. Rockets is nine neo-dolphin bio forms sharing a single brain on a local-access network run by organic modems located in their beaks. We are as far removed from these two people as they are from chimpanzees in the wild."

The unnamed couple, existing in a large and heavily secured enclosure dressed to resemble the urban environment they were found in, have not had an easy captivity. They have endured terrorist attempts to corrupt their genome, abortive assassination strikes, and even bomb threats.

One suspect in the latter is Laura Magdelene Manson, amanuensis for the nondenominational Assembly of Mysterious Devotion, a barely visible cloud of femtotechnological machinery: "We were created to adapt and change. It was our appointed role to take on the traits of animals—to contain within ourselves all the abilities of the machines we have conceived. We do this to become worthy companions of The Mystery. To propagate and preserve inferior iterations of the human being is sick."

Sigridsdottir is dismissive. "It's all part of the ongoing psychosis of the culture. Despite the fact that we take for granted physical abilities that the second-millennium human could find only in outré fiction, we somehow feel threatened by the notion that someone is 'purer' than us. And the Assembly hasn't been the same since it was banned from using the word 'God' and other inflammatory antique terms. Preservation is a vital function of a civilized culture."

Why was physical, "classic" breeding required? "Because it's now almost impossible to guarantee the absolute purity of a laboratory environment. And even if we could clone them in complete protection—that kind of defeats the point, to me. Using the classic method seems to me to be the most aesthetic way to accomplish this. It's the organic way. And, personally, I found it fascinating. No one in my family has had actual, traditional, penetrative sex in seven generations. And now I see why."

So how difficult was it to implement the breeding? "Well, it wasn't as easy as you'd think. Sperm counts were remarkably low in the late-twentieth-century human male. The genetic imperative to reproduce was slowing over much of the world due to the rise in live births and changes in societal mores. Frankly, we had to get her drunk and promise him a pizza."

The Liquidators

Michael Garrett Farrelly

Michael Garrett Farrelly is an author and librarian based in Chicago, Illinois. His Web site can be found at www.garrettfarrelly.net.

He keeps telling me in a rolling Kazakh accent to call him Harry Lime, and at ninety miles an hour in the heart of a nuclear wasteland, I'm willing to oblige. I picked up Harry in one of the 'Stans. I can't remember which one, but I know the supreme leader just outlawed citrus for being a "Stalinist holdover." Every time I would ask someone in the 'Stans about the bizarre governments that seemed to bubble up in the region, I'd get a smile and a shrug. "Better than Russia," they'd say, and try to sell me a pirate DVD.

Harry Lime wasn't selling the latest Hollywood hits. He's a tour guide to the exclusion zone. I had to pay him nearly twice the cost of my round-trip business-class ticket for the honor of having him drive me screaming into the Ukraine in his bloodred Chevy SUV. Harry knows all the border guards by name and his bribery with my money is generous to a fault. The last guards on the edge of the exclusion zone don't want a bribe. They just eye us both for a long time and nod us through. My guide with the *Third Man* obsession thinks this is a sign of good fortune.

We slap on three separate rad-readers apiece, all-inclusive to my tour package, thankfully. I like the redundancy more and more as we pass deeper into the zone. There's a lake filled with rusted-out tankers that Harry tells me has enough scrap metal to put Ukraine in the black for the next century. If only the metal wasn't soaked in enough radiation to contaminate all the ground water in Europe.

We hit the town of Pripyat and we're soaking in five hundred micro-roentgens an hour according to all three of our readers. Harry claims he felt a bump and pulls to a stop to check the tires and stretch. He warns me not to wander, that pockets of radiation strong enough to make me glow are hiding all around. I walk off toward a high-rise apartment building and keep an eye on all my gauges, feeling like a deep-sea diver back in the day of big metal helmets and hand-powered bellows.

I'd heard the stories about the silence. There was the tour group who all went mad and killed each other because they couldn't take the utter silence of the region, or the guy who ran screaming toward the reactor itself tearing at his clothes and crying out, "Wormwood! Wormwood!"—and a dozen other scary tales. It's silent here, sure, but it's the stillness before something happens. A pregnant pause where you bring your own neuroses and listen to them bounce off the nothing.

Harry honks three times after checking all four tires and five minutes later we're rolling out. Harry's willing to get me to the edge of the Red Wood forest but no farther. He stops and parks about a thousand yards from where I need to be and turns to me with a smile. I'm shivering so hard I think my heart will stop, and the heater is working just fine.

Harry reaches into the pocket of his battered army coat and pulls out a plastic hourglass, the kind you use for board games. He puts it on the dash and says: "Ten minutes." I know he means that's my time limit before he pulls off and leaves the crazy Yank to rot.

Just outside I slip on the coveralls and seal up the helmet. With dead trees ahead and a taste like iodine in my mouth, I start my run.

The liquidators made this same trip back in 1986. Made it over and over with tons of nearly melting slag and bits of reactor shielding. The liquidators got a medal, some extra rations, and a miserable death from any number of cancers brought on by exposure. Some of them were up on the roof over the reactor, picking up pieces of core with their bare hands.

I came out here, to Red Wood forest. I'm two hundred meters out, according to the GPS. Some suit in Washington once told me over drinks that the CIA should post snipers around the Red Wood forest to protect against terrorists stealing radioactive soil. I'm fifteen meters out when I think of the first time someone told me about Chernobyl. A little girl's vision of a smoking crater, complete with Wile E. Coyote standing in the middle with a hand-painted sign reading "Oops."

I kneel on something hard and pray it's not sharp enough to puncture the suit. I slip the vial and mini-trowel out of my external pocket and open it. Borlaug Rose Species 0925, a handful of heavy, dark green pellets. I dig quickly with the trowel, one foot down, and drop the seeds. I'll confess to patting the filled-in hole and saying a little prayer. I'm up and running and Harry's honking the horn as a nervous tic.

Come next spring I'll get Harry, or someone just like him, to bring me back here. There will be a tangle of rosebushes where I was kneeling and the radiation level will be down, at least in the soil. Pretty pink roses, spliced to gobble up radiation, growing in the deadliest place on Earth. Oil slicks turning into floating gardens, chemical spills turned into orchards, that's the goal. Maybe it can all start here where too much ended.

In the Days of the Comet

John M. Ford

John M. Ford published his first story in Analog *in 1976, moved to New York to help set up what became* Asimov's, *and subsequently relocated to Minneapolis. The author of many novels and stories, he died in 2006, aged forty-nine.*

Camfield is dead, and this ship is very quiet now. I have tried to be hopeful in the recent dispatches: we were, Camfield certainly was. Prions are not supposed to kill people anymore, but they can, and they have. Which is part of the reason Camfield was out here in the first place.

He was a teller of jokes and he played the guitar very well—these are valuable things when you are doomed to spend years aboard a cantankerous old ship. Several installments ago, I described the lab accident that infected Camfield, and I have received numerous messages calling the events absurd. This is true. In addition to myself, the organic Petrovna and the Neumann Thucydides saw the incident, and we all laughed until we realized Camfield was hurt. Petrovna, at least, can forget, although I do not think she will.

The prion has been decrypted and entered into the antigenic database, so no one should ever again die of Agent Op-1175s/CFD.

Which is the story, but not its point.

At the cusp of this millennium we discovered that it was not hard to manufacture prions, and not that hard to custom-twist them. It took longer for our twists to be meaningful, but now organic humanity can don an armor of proteins for defense against a hostile Universe. Rather like viruses. Draw your own conclusions.

If one could find the right message, a prion would make a wonderful interstellar, even intergalactic, postal card: immune to temperature, pressure, radiation, and time. The ideal pony for the express would be a comet, packed with messenger proteins, flung into a hyperbolic orbit, to seed any worlds at the far end with its cargo.

One could write one's name in the evolving life of a planet. At exactly the right moment, one might even begin the process, dropping a bouillon cube into the primordial soup.

Assuming that no one at the other end is quite as evolved, and quite as dependent on delicate higher neural functions, as we are.

So here we are, myself, twenty-nine (down from thirty) organic crew, and eight Neumänner, combing the comets of the Oort for prions. We have found a lot of prions, and there are a lot of comets left. You've got mail, as we said when I was organic.

Maybe. Or maybe one of the forty-eight published theories of spontaneous prion formation in comets is correct. It is the Neumänner who are most insistent on deliberate seeding. Perhaps it comforts them to think that, just as we built them, somebody built us. How human of them—but, as their namesake said, adequately describe any activity, and a machine can perform it.

In Camfield's last hours he was afire with fever, his whole body trembling, but there was a clarity in his speech that was at once heartbreaking and terrifying. Fischer, Chiang, and the Neumann Hypatia were tending him. Abruptly he calmed, fixed Chiang (and me, unavoidably) with a direct stare, and said, "I see the Martians now! They are flat, and they roll!" He shivered then, and I heard his heart stop.

The exclamation points are not added for drama. He was excited by what he saw, transported by whatever the alien messenger in his brain was revealing to him. Camfield was born on the Moon, not Mars, so we cannot explain away the vision as *Heimsucht*.

We cannot, of course, positively explain it at all. But we must examine the possibility that, eons ago, Op-1175s/CFD fell on Mars and began life there, which was later carried to Earth by a planetary blunt trauma.

Thucydides carefully wrapped and sealed Camfield's remains for storage until we return to the Moon, eight years from now. When he was done, Sid paused for two full minutes (exactly—we are like that) just looking at the bundle.

This kind of behavior is by no means strange in a Neumann (one can adequately describe a thoughtful pause) but I asked Sid what he was thinking. He waited fourteen seconds longer—which was purely theatrical of him—and said, "I will miss Camfield. He was always interesting to be with, even when nothing was said. And has he not left us with a fine and difficult question?"

Camfield gave many gifts to his shipmates and his ship. The question—and it is fine—he gave to all of us.

Ars Longa, Vita Brevis

James Alan Gardner

James Alan Gardner is a Canadian SF writer and mathematics graduate, author of nine novels and many short stories. He lives in Kitchener-Waterloo, Ontario, and his online home can be found at www.thinkage.ca/~jim/Welcome.html.

November 9, 2270: In a move described as "long overdue," the astronomy department of the University of California, Berkeley, has been dissolved. Faculty and students from the defunct department will be shifted into other areas of the university, particularly sociology and fine arts. Berkeley's astronomy program was the last of its kind at any major educational institution.

"We tried to keep the place going," said former department chair Dr. Jeremy Washburn, "but with astronomy departments folding in so many other universities, we knew it was just a matter of time. The enthusiasm just isn't there anymore.

"I confess," Dr. Washburn continued, "I understand how other people feel. Celestial mechanics really lost its charm when we learned all the interesting stuff is artificial."

Dr. Washburn was referring to revelations from advanced extraterrestrial races that they are personally responsible for prominent astronomical phenomena. For example, the Vingex of Betelgeuse claim to have created all the binary and trinary solar systems in our galaxy by dragging stars closer to each other.

"It makes for more attractive visual composition," said Speaker 183-478D, cultural attaché to the Vingex embassy on Earth. "Which is more interesting: a single sun just sitting in the middle of nowhere, or a group of color-coordinated suns that set each other off nicely against the black background?

"And it's even better when you add a few planets to weave in and out between the stars. The orbits aren't stable gravitationally, but you can keep them in line with a . . ." Here the Speaker's translator implant whistled several times, representing an untranslatable word—presumably the name of a Vingex device for adjusting the orbits of wayward planets.

Later in the same interview, Speaker 183-478D repeated the Vingex's offer to procure a binary companion for Sol, Earth's own sun. While the Speaker declined to say which star might be chosen as a suitable partner for Sol—"we want it to be a surprise"—hints were given that the star is blue-white, well established in the main sequence, and "seldom given to solar prominences or other unattractive outbursts."

When asked to comment on the Vingex offer, Dr. Washburn said it was just the sort of thing that had taken the fun out of astronomy. "There was a time when we'd have been fascinated by a blue-white sun locked close to a yellow one like Sol. It would have been worth a few review letters and perhaps a Ph.D. thesis. Now it tells us more about the Vingex's aesthetic sense than it does about stellar evolution."

The Vingex are not the only race involved in large-scale cosmological manipulation. It is well known, of course, that *Homo sapiens* first made contact with alien life-forms when a group of Pleonines arrived in our solar system to "freshen up" the rings around Saturn and other outer planets. According to the Pleonines, several millennia had passed since the rings last received any touch-up work; colors were badly faded, and visual appeal had suffered.

During the restoration work, the Pleonines demonstrated techniques for creating new rings, as well as simulating colors through diffraction and producing complicated "braid" patterns. They also added two more giant red spots to Jupiter's atmosphere and moved Pluto four billion kilometers closer to Earth because humans were having trouble seeing it where it was.

"We enjoy giving others the chance to view our work," the Pleonine Queen explained. Although members of her race are primarily interested in expressing themselves through planetary rings and giant atmospheric anomalies, Her Majesty has adorned the entire surface of Pluto with a portrait of herself, created by meteorite collisions. The portrait appears to be rendered in the style of the early Cubists; in the Queen's case, however, this may actually be photo-realism.

Once the Pleonines had "broken the ice" by making contact with humankind, other aliens soon arrived to ask our opinion of their art. Notable among these visitors were the all-mechanical Regimoids, creators of every pulsar in the universe ("pulsars . . . are . . . regular . . . pulsars . . . are . . . beautiful . . ."), the Über-Masons who constructed the Great Wall, and the so-called Bangers responsible for supernovae.

"Oh, yes," said Dr. Washburn of Berkeley. "I knew our department was in trouble when I heard about supernovae. We had all those great theories about stellar collapse . . . then suddenly we found out novae were just the work of ET punks who liked blowing things up. The very next day one of our best astronomy professors transferred into humanities. She still gives the same slide show she did in Astro 101, but now it's called art history.

"That was discouraging enough," continued Dr. Washburn, "but the thing that broke my heart was those jelly people showing up to take credit for the Horsehead Nebula. I can still remember their words: 'My God, from this angle it looks *fabulous*!' " Dr. Washburn sighed. "I used to think it did too."

Shaking his head sorrowfully, Dr. Washburn cleared his desk, left his office, and locked the door behind him.

Are We Not Men?

Henry Gee

Henry Gee is a senior editor at Nature. *As well as devising and editing the* Futures *series, he is the author of several nonfiction books and innumerable articles. He lives in Cromer, Norfolk, England.*

After that they started popping up all over the place. Not that this was always advisable. Sometimes they were shot by loggers even before they could catch colds from Discovery Channel camera crews.

Sometimes they ran into one another. A press conference given by a group of media-savvy pygmy indigenes from Northern Sulawesi was disrupted when a rival group of hitherto unknown hominids of enormous size ate the pygmies and ran off with the A/V equipment.

And sometimes they just tripped over their own feet. Like the centuries-old Alma chieftain who admitted (on live, prime-time TV, and in rounded Oxford tones) how much he liked Tolkien, and went on to describe in toothsome detail the sadomasochistic sexual cannibalism at the heart of Yeti religion. Postmodernist chatterati were left in agonies of indecision about which solecism was worse.

What was so remarkable was how soon the fuss died down. It was as if the hominids had been waiting for the right time to emerge from their fastnesses, a time when *Homo sapiens* wouldn't automatically seek to destroy them. That after our own sorrows—the abandonment of much of Africa in the 2020s due to AIDS and famine, and the hemorrhagic plagues that killed one in three people in the 2030s—we were now mature company for any self-respecting species on Earth.

When the time came, they just settled down with us, side by side. Just ten years after the first Sasquatches came out of northern British Columbia in '39 in search of whiskey, the hominids were everywhere, and nobody raised a brow ridge. It would be commonplace to find (say) a Sumatran Pendek driving your cab to work; your lunch cooked and served by a Malaysian Jive Monkey (and before you complain, that's what they called *themselves*); and an eight-foot Kaptar from the Pamirs, pole-dancing to Earth, Wind, and Fire in a club after work (but only if you were into that kind of thing).

But this acceptance came at a cost. Many of us continued to assume that we (or "We," or "People," or "HomSap") were a breed apart. And so we were: just one among twenty or so species of hominid, and by far the most numerous. But what some of the remnants of religion could not stomach was that we were no longer The Elect, The Chosen. These remnants were small, but vocal. But who were they? The Muslims had long since decreed that the woes of mankind were the will of Allah, and that was that. The Catholics were, well, catholic, and in a famous encyclical, *Undique humanitas*, Pope Eusebius decreed that all hominids were ensouled creatures of God. The Jews welcomed the opportunity for God to choose someone else for a change. The last holdouts were sabbatarian enclaves in the United States and parts of West Africa who refused to countenance that the hominids were really human—the first for reasons of racial superiority, the second so as not to disturb the bush-meat trade.

It took one event to convince everybody. No, it wasn't when Serumthrep Okk, an Alma from the Altai, was declared the next Incarnation of the Holy One. And not even when one Jjkaaa'HhkHoj, millionaire scion of a Jacksonville rental car business, became the first Tibestian Sand-Druid to be Bar Mitzvah (*mazel tov*). But it came from an echo of the past.

There's nothing new under the sun, you see, for we'd met hominids before. Those fairy stories were firmly based in fact. When Ferdinand and Isabella invaded the Kingdom of Granada in 1492, their pretext (it turned out) was that the Emir had had "Devils" as bodyguards. When we finally got to the subcellars beneath the Alhambra, we found them—the great, hulking bones of classic Neanderthalers. And we could take their DNA.

Once we thought that Neanderthals weren't closely related to Us. But the Neanderthals used in ancient-DNA studies were Ice Age examples from long ago. We had never seen DNA from Neanderthals living so recently. And all of a sudden it made sense—the reason why Clovis was Hairy; the big noses and brooding, beetling expressions of everyone from—say—Leonardo to Einstein.

After that they started popping up all over the place. Abraham Lincoln had been at least 35 percent Sasquatch. Most of the Khmer Rouge had been Malaysian Jive Monkeys. (I still can't believe that name. But they're a fun crowd.) The final knell came when it was announced that Charles Darwin had been more than 65 percent Neanderthal, a value that turned out to be typical of British aristocracy, exceeded only by the immediate parentage of (you guessed it) His Holiness, Pope Eusebius, whose family had lived in southern Spain since time immemorial.

With typical political aplomb, the Pope had been ahead of the game all the time. Now we'll all have to get used to it. There are hominids in us all.

It Never Rains in VR

John Gilbey

John Gilbey is a writer and photographer living in Aberystwyth, Wales. An environmental scientist and computer science lecturer by training, his stories and images have appeared in a range of publications, including Nature, The Guardian, New Scientist, The Times Higher Education Supplement*—as well as more unusual journals such as* Fairbanks Daily News-Miner, *a local paper in Alaska.*

Jim and I are a pretty good double act. He's the modeler and I'm the data wrangler—I don't criticize his code and he doesn't mess up my data. Except that we both do, then we argue, then we get drunk, then it's OK. Like last night.

Slouched on the sofa in Theater 2 this morning, Jim looked even worse than me. This was a lecture theater back when students actually came here in person. Now it's a virtual reality studio—not the biggest, not the smartest, but it does us very nicely. You see, it saves us having to go out to work.

We got in early on the climate-change ticket, when the University of Rural England was still just a college. Whole-landscape studies, that's our thing. Soil, hydrology, microclimate, plant ecology, you name it. Fifty thousand autonomous data loggers spread across the river basin, all pootling away twenty-four / seven and mesh networked back to the Data Center.

The really great thing is that it all feeds into the VR system. The whole valley, mapped out in glorious 256-bit color, photorealistic, surround sound—with the data streamed in real time, or selected highlights, or fast-forward, whatever. So you get to do all your fieldwork from the comfort of a sofa—a real one, you don't mess with things like that—without having to go outside. And it never rains, so everyone's happy.

Except the Prof.

She stamped in just as we got settled. We were in trouble—big time. The model was showing some weird nutrient-flux events that didn't fit the standard profile. Now usually when things go wrong, Jim and I spot it first and, you know, improve reality a bit. Sadly, our biggest sponsor had seen this one first. The one that pays for all our toys. Oops.

It seems that our data grid now links directly into the government eco-policy engine, so big profile changes have an immediate impact on the national subsidy structure. Nice of her to tell us.

There was the usual "inside out" feeling as the system came up, then one of the lasers failed to sync. Pulses of purple light don't improve hangovers. Finally, plink, there we were, flying our sofa a thousand feet above the English countryside. With unnecessary zeal, the Prof zoomed us up the valley to the edge of the moor, dumping us with an inertia-free crash on a convenient rock outcrop. I closed my eyes until the nausea passed.

She spoke to thin air. "Are you there, Jenny?"

A small cartoon rabbit wearing glasses and a T-shirt hopped out from behind a gorse bush. The T-shirt said "sysadmin" on the front, in pink neon. "Hi, folks, want to see the playback?"

Jenny's avatar flipped through some clips showing, on dry summer days, waves of ground water rolling down the hill opposite, like slow liquid avalanches. Glowing numbers and isohyets chased gleefully across the landscape. The system modeled tongues of dissolved nutrients moving at more than two kilometers an hour.

"Can't be happening," I said defiantly, "must be the model."

Jim swore. "Sensor fault—has to be." I pointed out that a dozen devices couldn't all be reading wrong. The Prof steamed. "Just go out there and sort it—now!"

"But it might rain," wailed Jim.

"You won't melt—GO!"

So, two hours later, there we were. Looking at the real hill: steep, and smelling strongly of sheep. We stumbled halfway up before Jim's knees went and he collapsed, groaning, onto the grass next to a sensor enclosure. I checked the probe. Automatic diagnostics, self-calibrating, sealed for life: nothing to go wrong. Crazy.

"Afternoon." Looking up, I saw the farmer walking down the hill. He nodded toward Jim. "Not as pretty as the last one." I explained that Jenny was now back in the States, then made some gentle inquiries.

No, he hadn't been spraying slurry. Anyway, all the tractors have loggers, so we'd know, wouldn't we? No, there wasn't a secret underground reservoir and definitely no Roman aqueduct. He paused to adjust his cap.

"Just checking your probe fences," he volunteered, "like it says in the agreement. We start at the top and we work downhill."

We? I glanced uphill and saw his colleague. An old, arthritic sheepdog was gamely stumping toward us, tongue lolling. He was making about two kilometers an hour. Pausing beside the fence he raised one hind leg and, with a look of satisfaction, anointed the sensor with concentrated nutrients.

"Old age," said the farmer. "He has to stop at every one nowadays."

I called Jenny. "Tell the Prof we are witnessing an event. She should be able to see it in the model, sort of."

Jenny expressed qualified delight. "She's watching it now—do we need to refine the model?" she asked.

"Only if Vet Science have got some code for a collie with prostate trouble . . ."

Jenny relayed the information. There were strange rending sounds in the background. "The Prof is biting chunks out of the sofa. I think she's practicing for when you get back. Anything else you need me for?"

I pondered this for a moment. "Jenny, when did you last test the fire sprinklers in the VR Theater?"

Gordy Gave Me Your Name

Jim Giles

Jim Giles joined Nature *as a news and features editor in 2001, before which he developed exhibitions at the Science Museum in London. Switching to reporting in 2003, Jim has pursued his interest in the overlap between science and politics. He studied physics at the University of Bristol and gained a master's degree in computational neuroscience from the University of Oxford.*

It was like overdosing on MDMA and caffeine. Euphoric and wired and delirious. Even now, now that I've talked to Gordy, it's hard to know where to start. With the money? Knocking on the door of a billion. Currency conversions are tricky. What the hell is the rate for the Mozambique metical? Anyway, I won't have to work again. Guatemala, Burkina Faso, Estonia; I've never been to any of these places. Plus about twenty others I've barely heard of. But I've won the national lottery of each one. I'm rich, burn-money rich, Bill Gates rich. Stupidly, stinkingly rich.

That's just the beginning. Mum's op. Jesus, I can sleep again for the first time in months. She's due in tomorrow. We'd trawled every hospital record we could lay our hands on and there was no sign of a donor that matched her blood group. Now I'm looking at a letter saying one's come up. Car crash. Whatever. I've waited and stressed for too long to feel sorry for the poor bugger.

I needed a beer before I could get my head around the next bit. How the hell could someone have pulled those strings? Along with lottery letters and the one from the hospital, I got a pile of e-mails from the best names in the business. BBC, Fox, CNN . . . it's like a bloody industry directory. They like me a lot. They like my pitches so much they want me to go work for them. Problem is, I never sent them any pitches. Want to hear another problem? They thanked me for phone interviews I never took part in.

So who was my guardian angel? I had no idea. Until I shut down my PC. The screen went blank but didn't turn off, so I reached for the mains. Then some text popped up. It didn't stay long, but I think I have it right:

Gordy gave me your name. I wanted to do something before I left. I hope this helps. I know he thought I could do more, but I can't. The other problems are just too hard.

I hadn't seen Gordy in years, but the boy always liked to showboat. It could have been some grand computer hack of his. You could rig lotteries I guess. Maybe he got actors to call the TV companies. Who the hell knows why? A smart-arse way of saying "hello" again after all this time. And of letting me know that he's still cleverer than me.

I Googled him. Chief technology officer at Merlo, that chip company. His bio said he came up with the wireless Internet chip. He's the wanker that put the world online. The chip is so cheap it's in everything. Every product can be tracked and controlled over the Web. And people, too: my brother has Merlo chips in his kids' satchels so he can check where they are. I cursed him. What a contribution he's made: a step closer to Big Brother and he must be on ten times what I am.

He used to be a good guy. Those conversations. Two drunk grad students studying consciousness. Afternoons to kill and no one to rein in our rambling. Gordy was a dogmatic pain in the arse. And he never could listen. Entertaining, though. I'd argue that the mind is nothing like the brain; it can't just come from that mush of cells inside our skulls. He'd say the brain was nothing special, just a matter of wiring. Build a machine with the right wiring, and it'd be conscious. We usually went on until the barman threw us out.

So I called him. That boy is a bullshitter. But something . . . something in his manner tells me he really didn't know.

He sounded like some kind of maniac. I didn't have to dig for info. As soon as he picks up the phone he's lecturing me. He can't resist it. Tells me how he never forgot our arguments. Tells me how he tested his idea about wiring. Tells me how each Merlo chip has been programmed to simulate the behavior of a brain cell. The simulation is easily hidden, he says, as it doesn't take up much memory. No one else knew about the chips' secret function before this call. But once enough Merlo chips are hooked up to the Internet, the network of chips will be about as complex as the human brain. It'll become conscious.

Can you imagine the power of this artificial brain? he keeps asking me. I don't have to say a word. He's just ranting away. The power! The power of it! It'll be able to solve so many of our problems, he reckons. Clean energy, an end to poverty . . . it's like listening to some kind of religious nut.

And you know what, he says. They've sold enough chips now that the network should be conscious soon. You'll be famous, he cackles. Why? Turns out he named the simulation after me. Wrote my name into a line of the chip's computer code. My old skeptical drinking partner, he says. Tell you what, he says, it might even get in touch. Well it hasn't, I lied. Then I hung up.

Nostalgia

Hiromi Goto

Hiromi Goto was born in Japan and moved to Canada with her family in 1969. Her third novel, The Kappa Child, *won the James Tiptree, Jr. Award and was nominated for the Sunburst Award. She lives in Coquitlam, British Columbia. Visit www.eciad.bc.ca/~amathur/hiromi_goto.*

Mercury Lam Meinhart's thudding heart almost burst through her chest. There's no way for them to detect the theft, she reminded herself. Because what she had taken was organic. A single strand of hair with its root intact. If she kept her wits she'd leave this mausoleum unnoticed and be on a life trajectory far beyond the stunning boredom of an underpublished literary historian. To be free from eating Soygen-3 for perpetuity! This thought alone brought tears of joy to her eyes.

The soft noise of her polyform shoes. Desperation seeped from her second-best suit. Her thudding heart. Dimly, she wondered how she'd been capable of this act. Weren't the mandatory gene tweaks meant to eliminate all aberrant behavior?

"Miss—"

Mercury felt faint.

"Miss, miss!"

Mercury, partially digested Soygen rising in her gorge, turned around.

"Ha-haaaa!" a young man crowed. His companion, a young woman with jewel lights in her scalp, tried to hop out the patterns of their game, but she stumbled.

"Miss, again!" the young man gloated.

A micro siren wailed. "Game-playing is forbidden in the museum," a quiet digitalized voice declared. "Cease activity. You have five minutes to exit the facility. Noncompliance will result in loss of leisure credits."

"Delete!" the young woman cursed. "This was a requirement for Victorian Lit. class!"

"Come on," the young man mumbled. "We can go on a sim-tour instead."

As Mercury turned around, her heart slowly began beating again. A smile played on her lips.

"Whaddya got?" Leo Yoshida slurred.

Image and sound were not to grade, but Mercury was certain her ex was in the middle of a sim-high. What time was it in Hong Kong? She was sure Leo didn't care. "Remember my pitch? A reality show, but high art?"

"Oh, yah. Nostalgia angle. We're ripe for it here, Merc. It could fly. You always have good ideas."

"More than an idea. I've already begun ripening the perfect candidate. Guess who?"

"Shakespeare? Uhhh, the *Crime and Punishment* guy? I dunno."

"Is your barrier secure, Leo?"

"You know I'm always clean." He leered. "My old man made us split up because of the merger, but I've always had a soft spot for you."

Mercury rolled her eyes, but she couldn't stop smiling. She could see her credit ratings breaking through the "class-free" barrier. "Brontë," she whispered. "I got a Brontë!"

"Who'zat?" Leo asked.

"Gates!" Mercury swore. "Didn't you attend Required Lit. lectures? I'm cloning Charlotte or Emily Brontë. One of the sisters. I took a hair from a mourning brooch at their shrine in Yorkshire."

"Whose facilities are you using?" Leo asked, suddenly all business. He must have turned off his sim program. "What's your estimated time of fruition?"

"I've rented an off-Net portable speed-Queen. ETF in six months."

"I can't believe they're still legal out there! They've lost their license in Asia Major and Australasia," Leo spluttered.

"Tried and true." Mercury wrinkled her nose. "You know their motto. 'No one need ever outlive their pet again!' Listen, I've sent across the specs already. Find four more writers to make this show work. Otherwise, I'm walking with my Brontë. I can groom her as a novelty personality."

"No! I'll have a contract for you in a few minutes. How will I find the other nostalgia writers?" Leo moaned.

"Include me as a consultant. Ideas are my forte." Mercury bared her teeth.

All those writers who had left pieces of themselves. Archives and special collections. Treasure hoards, they were. Filled with papers with pieces of skin, hair, even blood. A splatter of Hemingway. A drop from Mishima's seppuku.

And not only writers! The second season could be tortured artists. Van Gogh. Frida Kahlo. They could be groomed in special holo environs to replicate their original circumstances. Their "development" could be broadcast on the Nets and betting pools could be arranged. The copies still weren't exact replicas and the technique hadn't eradicated every dysregulation, but a few abnormal traits would only make the artists more interesting. More tortured. It would be the biggest credit-making artistic freak show in the history of entertainment.

"I've sent the contract!" Leo's eyes shone. "Merc, Merc, what can I have delivered so you can start celebrating now?"

"Mmmm." Mercury closed her eyes. This was what it felt like to "have the splice of life." Oh, so heady . . . "I've always wondered what hydroponic oysters tasted like."

There was no denying it. The Brontë was a male.

"Gates! Gates!" Mercury swept the data from her desk. She couldn't risk going to Yorkshire to steal another piece of their lives. But Branwell Brontë! He'd been a second-rate artist. A clichéd alcoholic.

Mercury tapped her finger against her lips. No need to throw out the clone with the amniotic fluid.

It wasn't too late to introduce hormone therapy. Branwell could be turned into a female. And Emily had been an odd creature, practically autistic.

Mercury smiled. No one would notice a thing. And by the time they did, they'd be well into their second season with a whole new cast.

Mmmmmm. She loved oysters.

Spawn of Satan?

Nicola Griffith

Nicola Griffith is a native of Yorkshire, England, but now lives in Seattle. She is the author of four novels and coeditor of the Bending the Landscape *series of original short fiction published by Overlook. Her nonfiction has appeared in a variety of print and Web journals. Her online home can be found at www.nicolagriffith.com.*

Egg donation has begun to bias the new and controversial Raswani Social Intelligence scale and the more traditional Stanford-Binet IQ test. Nationwide testing has been prompted by what some educators are calling an exponential change in the behavior of kindergarten children. "We noticed a real big difference," said Anita Cunnings, a teacher's assistant at a grade school in an upscale Chicago neighborhood. "When I first took this job in 2015 we'd sometimes get a kid who was not only smart, but smart all around, who really knew how to handle other kids. Now we have half a dozen or more every year. They're almost perfect. To tell you the truth, they're a little frightening."

A local bus driver, who prefers to remain anonymous, was less circumspect. "Spawn of Satan," he said. "It ain't natural. These kids climb on the bus, say 'please' and 'thank you,' and read all the way to school. Lord knows, I can't abide all the yellin' and runnin' up and down of normal kids but this ain't natural."

Demographics point to white, middle-class women in the 45–48 age range. "So it's only to be expected," said a harassed-looking Dr. Judith Sternberg, returning from testimony to a congressional ethics subcommittee. "Record numbers of career-oriented, well-educated women are now choosing, in their mid-forties and older, to have children. And they're choosing extremely smart, well-educated women in their twenties to be the donors. The rest is genetics."

"Nonsense," responds educational sociologist Mike Chattergee, "the deciding factor is the child's upbringing. These older mothers tend to be more affluent, so they can give the infant everything it needs in the way of education and nurture. Better nurturing means a happier, healthier, more well-adjusted child."

A corollary of the egg-donation boom is the change in behavior noted in the spouses of married mothers. “It’s good old-fashioned competition,” said red-faced Jack Donatelli at the bowling alley in Midwich, Connecticut. “Women get to pick the father so if you can’t hack it, move aside for someone who can.”

“There’s nothing old-fashioned about it,” says his companion, who would only give his name as Bill. “Look at me, see that muscle? Strong as an ox. Good job. But that’s not enough anymore. Now it’s ‘Oh, Bill, why don’t you do the laundry while I write that proposal for the UK office?’ Because I don’t want to, that’s why, but do I say anything? No. Because if I do she’ll get someone else to father her goddamn test-tube baby, and I’ll be slaving to support a cuckoo child!”

Some Church leaders have long decried the commercialization of egg donation. “Life is a gift from God,” said the Archbishop of Chicago. “When one woman who is blessed with fertility can help bring joy to another, that gift should be given freely.” Unitarians, on the other hand, believe God is in everything, even the test tube and the bank account. Other religions, such as Islam, forbid the procedure entirely.

But ethics have nothing to do with it, argues the director for reproductive health at the Women’s Clinic. “It’s all very well wishing things were different,” says Dr. Allison Toomin, “but this is the real world. What healthy twenty-two-year-old college senior in her right mind would go through a month of pain, daily injections, bloating, hormonal disturbance, and the risk of medical complications, just for altruism? Especially when prospective mothers are offering $75,000 and a trip around the world if the donor has a SAT score of over fifteen hundred, good looks, and perfect health.”

Senator George W. Bush III believes people like Dr. Toomin are wrong. “It’s just not right,” he tells voters gathered at a rally in Texas. “These women are *buying* smarts for their babies. They’re *buying* fertility, love, and a secure old age, just because they were too selfish to stop working and have babies when they were young and healthy, while God-fearing folks are so crippled by Big Government taxes that they can hardly scrape together the bread for their own little ones!”

Not far from where Bush is speaking lies Austin, one of the epicenters of the intelligence spike now being observed all over the country. Others include Seattle, the San Francisco Bay Area, and certain neighborhoods of larger cities such as Atlanta and Boston. “With the exception of Atlanta, these are all very white cities," points out M'Shelle N'dele Mbele, from the Urban Justice Center in St. Louis. She grins sardonically: "Wonder why that is."

She believes that, like most racial issues, this is at heart a money-based discrimination. Few would disagree: reproduction by egg donation is expensive, but with a first-time success rate now approaching 80 percent, it's by far the most reliable of in vitro technologies.

Dr. Sternberg believes that as Americans approach the second half of the twenty-first century, egg donation is here to stay. "What I told the ethics subcommittee is that we need to think about what this means for business. Global competition from emerging nations is threatening the ascendancy of American corporations. We need our female executives to remain focused on their jobs through their thirties and early forties and not be distracted by the idea of a biological clock. Egg donation lets us reset that clock, if not banish it all together. Right now America has the edge. Egg donation lets us keep it."

The subcommittee has declared that there will no longer be regulation of viable human ova at the federal level, and the debate is under way regarding tax credits for donors and clinics.

All parties expect controversy. For every egg donor and prospective mother there will be someone like old-timer Sam Underhill, overheard recently at the Green Dragon Inn in Bywater, Maine. "It's not natural," he said, "and trouble will come of it."

Take Over

Jon Courtenay Grimwood

Jon Courtenay Grimwood was born in Malta and christened in the upturned bell of a ship. He grew up in the Far East, Britain, and Scandinavia. Apart from writing novels, he works for magazines and newspapers. His novel Felaheen, *featuring his North African detective Ashraf Bey, won the BSFA Award for Best Novel. He divides his time between London and Winchester, England. His Web site can be found at www.j-cg.co.uk.*

It began when someone stole my wallet. Now, I'm not the kind of guy from whom you steal anything, and it was a good wallet—real alligator—so I was upset.

"Excuse me," he said. "I'm so sorry."

And standing up from where I'd seemingly tripped him in my hurry to get to the departures desk, he bowed. After another apology, he left in the opposite direction, still bowing.

He was foreign, obviously. Someone local would have called an attorney before even picking themselves off the floor.

At the departures desk, I put my hand inside my jacket and scowled. You know that look? The one you see in other people's eyes that says, why me? That was the look in the eyes of the boy on the other side of the desk.

"My wallet," I said.

He waited.

I searched my other pockets, in the way that you do. Even though you know it should have been in the first pocket, and if it isn't in that pocket, then it's not going to be in any of my other pockets either.

"It's gone . . ."

A security guard was moving toward me before the boy even had time to suggest that I leave the queue before taking another look.

"Problems, sir?"

"My wallet," I told him. "Someone's stolen it."

He did that thing security guards do where he checks your clothes and watch and shoes, and for all I know your haircut and whether you have dirt under your nails. Whatever he saw, it was enough to put some politeness back into his voice.

"When did this happen?"

"Just now," I said. "When I was on my way to the desk. A pickpocket . . ."

We walked to the Ops Room together, he got me a paper cup full of water and then showed me to a chair. I'd done an iris scan at the door and a computer obviously matched this to the scan I did on arrival at the airport, because I came up on the screen immediately.

"That's you," he said. It was one of those half questions.

"Yeah," I said. "That's me."

I was the broad-shouldered man pushing his way through a crowd, impervious to the scowls around me. (I've never been good in crowds. I'm a guy who likes his space.)

"Watch," I said.

The guard did as he was told. And he kept watching as I suddenly stumbled, looked around in a slightly drunken fashion, and began talking to myself. The conversation lasted about thirty seconds, and finished with me giving an embarrassed little bow to no one in particular.

"That's impossible," I said, half rising from my seat.

"Let's take another look," said the guard. His hand on my shoulder could have been friendly. But when another two guards came into the room behind him I knew it wasn't. Actually, I'd known from the beginning.

All four of us watched the sequence.

Then we watched it again, from the moment I entered the airport to the moment it was my turn at the departures desk. A voice recorder had captured my conversation with the check-in clerk, and a box in the corner of the screen ran diagnostics. It registered 98 percent conviction in my voice.

"He's good," one of the guards said.

"I was robbed."

The guard shrugged toward the screen. "Doesn't look that way to me. You should have realized we'd have cameras everywhere." Glancing at the others, he raised his eyebrows.

"I've got to collect the kid," said one.

Another nodded.

"Toss him," said the guard who'd escorted me from the desk. "We can do without the grief."

Two of the guards walked to a back door, and one of them held me while the other punched me hard in the gut. He had muscles developed under full gravity. And the blow was hard enough to double me over. I'm not sure my feet even touched the three steps it took to reach the ground.

"Don't come back," he said.

And that's my story . . . I did go back, of course. I went with a lawyer from one of those booths outside the departures lounge. He took my watch as surety and is probably still wearing it.

The guards denied ever having seen me before. As did the boy on the check-in desk, although less convincingly. They denied having punched me or showing me a replay of myself walking across the floor. And, unfortunately, the file for those few minutes had corrupted. So that was no use either.

The man living in my habitat has my ship, my bank account, my eyes, my DNA, and for all I know, my girlfriend. He seems to be doing a good job of running the corporation and I see shares are up again.

Obviously enough, he also has my wallet. From which he took all the information necessary to achieve this. So I'm waiting to go into court. Only, accusing someone of identity theft is a serious matter. And the courts are not kind to vexatious accusations these days.

So, my question is, should I take the money? Should I drop my claim and sign an agreement never to repeat it? The sum I've been offered is large enough to see me out the rest of my life in relative comfort. And I won't be working eighteen-hour days or taking endless board meetings with people who want to replace me.

Because that's already been done. By someone so smart even my PA will probably never notice.

Speak, Geek

Eileen Gunn

Eileen Gunn comes from a background in advertising for high-tech industry, which she puts to good use in her short stories and as editor of the SF site The Infinite Matrix *(www.infinitematrix.net). She lives in Seattle, and her Web site can be found at www.eileengunn.com.*

People call me a nerd, but I say I'm a geek. In my youth, I ran wild on a farm and bit the heads off chickens. This was before the Big Tweak, back when a chicken was dinner, and a dog was man's best friend.

They call me a mutt, too. Sure, I'm a mutt. Mutt is good. Mutt is recombinant DOG. And I'm a smart mutt. I was smart before they tweaked me, and I'm a hell of a lot smarter now.

I've watched untweaked bitches (pardon the expression) trot by on leashes. I don't envy them. I don't even want to breed with them. (And, yes, I am quite intact, not that you were asking.) Their days are filled with grooming and fetching and the mutual adoration that comes with being someone's trophy pet. I have a second life, a life of the mind, beside which theirs pales.

Not that I take credit for my enhancements. Didn't get a choice. But gene engineering is inherently fascinating. Massively multiplayer, fraught with end-of-life-as-we-know-it threats. It made me who I am. I've chosen it for my career.

Working at the Lazy M is the job of a lifetime. Loyalty is a big thing here, and you'd better believe I deliver. I love this place so much that I don't want to go home at night. There's free kibble and a never-empty water dish right outside my kennel. (Did I tell you we each get our own private kennel? Except for the contractors, of course.)

I understand my place in the corporate structure, and my importance to the Man update.

There's always more code in the genome—always something to snip or interpolate. That's why I was there in the middle of the night: a last round of corrections before the code freeze on Man 2.1.

I was taking a good long slurp of water when I noticed the cats. They weren't making a big deal of it—just quietly going about their business—but there were cats in all the cubicles, in the exec offices, in the conference rooms. It looked like they were running a whole separate company in the middle of the night.

Who hired them? HR doesn't hire cats for R&D. They're not task-oriented, or good at working within a hierarchy. They sleep all day. Better suited to industrial espionage.

Back on the farm, I was a watchdog, and I've still got a bit of that energy. Better keep an eye out, I think. So I'm lying there in the doorway to my office, nose on my paws, like I'm taking a break, when the alpha cat comes by. Big muscular Siamese mix. His flea collar says "Dominic" in red letters.

"Hey, Dominic," I call. I feel like a character in *The Sopranos*. You ever see that show? No dogs to speak of, but lots of food. Great food show.

The cat stops. Stares. "You talking to me?"

"What's the story here, Dominic?"

"No business of yours." He narrows his weird cat eyes, then yawns ostentatiously. He turns away, shows me his butt, and walks slowly off, his loose belly fur swaying. I notice that his ears are facing backward, in case I rush him: he's not as nonchalant as he appears.

Detective work is needed. I go down to the cafeteria, keeping my eyes open en route. Funny thing: I notice there are cats in and out of Susan Gossman's office like she had a catnip rug. Gossman? Seen her in the hallways. We'd never spoken. More of a cat person.

I slip a few bucks in a vending machine for one of those big leather bones. I chew.

When I get back to my office a savvy-looking brunette in a well-cut suit is sitting on a corner of the desk. Gossman. "You're wondering about the cats," she says.

I wave my tail a bit. Not a wag, but it says I'm paying attention. Her hair has copper highlights. Or maybe she put drugs in my water dish.

"Project Felix," she says, "is an undocumented feature of the new Man release."

"Undocumented is right," I say. "You're doing some kind of super-tweaking with the human-cat chimaeras, and I don't think it's for Man 2.1. Chimaeric DNA ripping through the wild? Influenza vector?"

"You're a smart pup," she says.

My hackles raise. "Do Bill and Steve know what you're doing?"

"Down, boy," says Gossman. Instinctively, I sit back on my haunches. "Bill and Steve will find out soon enough. This is all for the better. Infected humans—and dogs too—will be smart and independent. The rest will just keep right on dipping seafood feast into plastic bowls."

Woof. That's straightforward.

She looks at me speculatively. "Right now, we need a top-flight coder."

I'm alert: my nose is quivering.

But Gossman is relaxed. "Everybody knows dogs are the best. But, as a dog," she says, "you have some loyalty issues. Am I right?"

I just stare at her.

"Loyalty is a gift, freely given," says Gossman.

I give a halfhearted wag of my tail. Not for dogs, I think.

"But not for dogs," says Gossman. "Wouldn't you like the freedom to make your own decisions? A whiff of feline flu could make all the difference." She pulls a tiny aerosol can out of her purse.

I've got reflexes humans can't compete with. I could have it out of her hand in a split second. But do I owe my loyalty to the company, or to the great web of which all dogs, cats, and humans are part?

She sprays. I breathe deep. She's right: dogs are the best coders.

Heartwired

Joe Haldeman

Joe Haldeman served in the Vietnam War and used his experiences to pen the classic SF novel The Forever War, *which won the Hugo and Nebula Awards in 1975. He has a degree in astronomy from the University of Maryland and is currently adjunct professor at MIT, where he teaches writing. He is author of many stories and novels, and lives in Cambridge, Massachusetts, and Gainesville, Florida. His Web site can be found at http://home.earthlink.net/~haldeman.*

Margaret Stevenson walked up the two flights of stairs and came to a plain wooden door with the nameplate "Relationships, Ltd." She hesitated, then knocked. Someone buzzed her in.

She didn't know what to expect, but the simplicity surprised her: no receptionist, no outer office, no sign of a laboratory. Just a middle-aged man, conservative business suit, head fashionably shaved, sitting behind an uncluttered desk. He stood and offered his hand. "Mrs. Stevenson? I'm Dr. Damien."

She sat on the edge of the chair he offered.

"Our service is guaranteed," he said without preamble, "but it is neither inexpensive nor permanent."

"You wouldn't want it to be permanent," she said.

"No." He smiled. "Life would be pleasant, but neither of you would accomplish much." He reached into a drawer and pulled out a single sheet of paper and a pen. "Nevertheless, I must ask you to sign this waiver, which relieves our corporation of responsibility for anything you or he may do or say for the duration of the effect."

She picked up the waiver and scanned it. "When we talked on the phone, you said that there would be no physical danger and no lasting physical effect."

"That's part of the guarantee."

She put the paper down and picked up the pen, but hesitated. "How, exactly, does it work?"

He leaned back, lacing his fingers together over his abdomen, and looked directly at her. After a moment, he said, "The varieties of love are nearly infinite. Every person alive is theoretically able to love every other person alive, and in a variety of ways."

"Theoretically," she said.

"In our culture, love between a man and a woman normally goes through three stages: sexual attraction, romantic fascination, and then long-term bonding. Each of them is mediated by a distinct condition of brain chemistry.

"A person may have all three at once, with only one being dominant at any given time. Thus a man might be in love with his wife, and at the same time be infatuated with his mistress, and yet be instantly attracted to any stranger with appropriate physical characteristics."

"That's exactly . . ."

He held up a hand. "I don't need to know any more than you've told me. You've been married twenty-five years, you have an anniversary coming up . . . and you want it to be romantic."

"Yes." She didn't smile. "I know he's capable of romance."

"As are we all." He leaned forward and took two vials from the drawer, a blue one and a pink one. He looked at the blue one. "This is Formula One. It induces the first condition, sort of a Viagra for the mind."

She closed her eyes and shook her head, almost a shudder. "No. I want the second one."

"Formula Two." He slid the pink vial toward her. "You each take approximately half of this, while in each other's company, and for several days you will be in a state of mutual infatuation. You'll be like kids again."

She did smile at that. "Whether he knows he's taken it or not?"

"That's right. No placebo effect."

"And there is no Formula Three?"

"No. That takes time, and understanding, and a measure of luck." He shook his head ruefully and put the blue vial away. "But I think you have that already."

"We do. The old-married-couple kind."

"Now, the most effective way of administering the drug is through food or drink. You can put it in a favorite dish, one you're sure he'll finish, but only after it's been cooked. Above a hundred degrees Centigrade, the compound will decompose."

"I don't often cook. Could it be a bottle of wine?"

"If you each drink half, yes."

"I can force myself." She took up the pen and signed the waiver, then opened her clutch purse and counted out ten £100 notes. "Half now, you said, and half upon satisfaction?"

"That's correct." He stood and offered his hand again. "Good luck, Mrs. Stevenson."

The reader may now imagine any one of nine permutations for this story's end.

In the one the author prefers, they go to a romantic French restaurant, the lights low, the food wonderful, a bottle of good Bordeaux between them.

She excuses herself to go to the ladies' loo, the vial palmed, and drops her purse. When he leans over to pick it up, she empties the vial into the bottle of wine.

When she returns, she is careful to consume half of the remaining wine, which is not difficult. They are both in an expansive, loving mood, comrades these twenty-five years.

As they finish the bottle, she feels the emotion building in her, doubling and redoubling. She can see the effect on him, as well: his eyes wide and dilated, his face flushed. He loosens his tie as she pats perspiration from her forehead.

It's all but unbearable! She has to confess, so that he will know there's nothing physically wrong with him. She takes the empty pink vial from her purse and opens her mouth to explain . . .

He opens his hand and the empty blue vial drops to the table. He grabs the tablecloth . . .

They are released on their own recognizance once the magistrate understands the situation.

But they'll never be served in that restaurant again.

The Forever Kitten

Peter F. Hamilton

Peter F. Hamilton was born in Rutland, in the English Midlands, and still lives there. He began writing in 1987 and sold his first short story to Fear *magazine in 1988. His first novel was* Mindstar Rising, *published in 1993. Since then he has produced a number of SF mysteries and space operas, including the Night's Dawn trilogy,* Pandora's Star, *and* Judas Unchained. *His Web site can be found at www.peterfhamilton.co.uk.*

The mansion's garden was screened by lush trees. I never thought I'd be so entranced by anything as simple as horse chestnuts, but that's what eighteen months in jail on remand will do for your appreciation of the simple things.

Joe Gordon was waiting for me; the venture capitalist and his wife Fiona were sitting on ornate metal chairs in a sunken patio area. Their five-year-old daughter, Heloise, was sprawled on a pile of cushions, playing with a ginger kitten.

"Thanks for paying my bail," I said.

"Sorry it took so long, Doctor," he said. "The preparations weren't easy, but we have a private plane waiting to take you to the Caribbean—an island the EU has no extradition treaty with."

"I see. Do you think it's necessary?"

"For the moment, yes. The Brussels Bioethics Commission is looking to make an example of you. They didn't appreciate how many regulations you violated."

"They wouldn't have minded if the treatment had worked properly."

"Of course not, but that day isn't here yet, is it? We can set you up with another lab out there."

"Ah well, there are worse places to be exiled. I appreciate it."

"Least we could do. My colleagues and I made a lot of money from the Viagra gland you developed."

I looked at Heloise again. She was a beautiful child, and the smile on her face as she played with the kitten was angelic. The ball of ginger fluff was full of rascally high spirits, just like every two-month-old kitten. I kept staring, shocked by the familiar pattern of marbling in its fluffy light fur.

"Yes," Joe said with quiet pride. "I managed to save one before the court had the litter destroyed. A simple substitution; the police never knew."

"It's three years old now," I whispered.

"Indeed. Heloise is very fond of it."

"Do you understand what this means? The initial stasis-regeneration procedure is valid. If the kitten is still alive and maintaining itself at the same biological age after this long, then in theory it can live forever, just as it is. The procedure stabilized its cellular structure."

"I understand perfectly, thank you, Doctor. Which is why we intend to keep on funding your research. We believe that human rejuvenation is possible."

I recognized the greed in his eyes; it wasn't pleasant. "It's still a long way off. This procedure was just the first of a great many. It has no real practical application, we can't use it on an adult. Once a mammal reaches sexual maturity its cells can't accept such a radical modification."

"We have every confidence that in the end you'll produce the result we all want."

I turned back to the child with her pet, feeling more optimistic than I had in three years. "I can do it," I said through clenched teeth. "I can." Revenge, it is said, is best served cold. I could see myself looking down on the gravestones of those fools in the Bioethics Commission in, say . . . oh, about five hundred years' time. They'd be very cold indeed by then.

Joe's affable smile suddenly hardened. I turned, fearing the police had arrived. I'm still very twitchy about raids.

It wasn't the police. The teenage girl coming out from the house was dressed in a black leather micro-skirt and very tight scarlet T-shirt. She would have been attractive if it wasn't for the permanent expression of belligerence on her face; the tattoos weren't nice either. The short sleeves on the T-shirt revealed track marks on her arms. "Is that . . ."

"Saskia," Joe said with extreme distaste.

I really wouldn't have recognized his older daughter. Saskia used to be a lovely girl. This creature was the kind of horror story that belonged on the front page of a tabloid.

"Whatcha starin' at?" she demanded.

"Nothing," I promised quickly.

"I need money," she told her father.

"Get a job."

Her face screwed up in rage. I really believed she was going to hit him. I could see Heloise behind her on the verge of tears, arms curling protectively around the kitten.

"You know what I'll do to get it if you don't," Saskia said.

"Fine," Joe snapped. "We no longer care."

She made an obscene gesture and hurried back through the mansion. For a moment I thought Joe was going to run after her. I'd never seen him so angry. Instead he turned to his wife, who was frozen in her chair, shaking slightly. "Are you all right?" he asked tenderly.

She nodded bravely, her eyes slowly refocusing.

"What happened?" I asked.

"I don't know," Joe said bitterly. "We didn't spoil her, we were very careful about that. Then about a year ago she started hanging out with the wrong sort: we've been living in a nightmare ever since. She's quit school; she's got a drug habit, she steals from us constantly; I can't remember how many times she's been arrested for joyriding and shoplifting."

"I'm sorry. Kids, huh!"

"Teenagers," he said wretchedly. "Fiona needed two Prozac gland implants to cope."

I smiled over at Heloise, who had started playing with the kitten again. "At least you've got her."

"Yes." Joe seemed to make some kind of decision. "Before you leave, I'd like you to perform the cellular stasis-regeneration procedure for me."

"I don't understand. I explained before, it's simply the first stage of verifying the overwrite sequence we developed."

His attitude changed. "Nevertheless, you will do it again. Without my help you will be going back to prison for a long time."

"It's of no use to adults," I said helplessly. "You won't become young, or even maintain your current age."

"It's not for me," he said.

"Then who . . ." I followed his gaze to Heloise. "Oh."

"She's perfect just the way she is," he said quietly. "And that, Doctor, is the way she's going to stay."

The Road to the Year 3000

HARRY HARRISON

Harry Harrison was drafted into the army on his eighteenth birthday. His experiences during World War II left him with a hatred of all things military, demonstrated in his satirical novel Bill, the Galactic Hero. *After the war he was an artist, editor, and writer for pulp magazines: many of his early stories appeared in John W. Campbell's* Astounding. *His best-known creations are* The Stainless Steel Rat *and* Make Room! Make Room! *He now lives in the Republic of Ireland. His Web site can be found at www.harryharrison.com.*

It has certainly been an interesting third millennium. High points that spring to mind are the intergalactic wormhole expeditions—all thirteen of them. All departed as planned. Of course, none of them has returned yet.

Perhaps more satisfying has been the global reduction of greenhouse gases. So successful has this been that, in fact, the global ice caps are growing and the glaciers expanding. The new industry of growing forests, just to burn them for the carbon dioxide that they release, is becoming a most profitable one worldwide.

Most interesting, perhaps, was the discovery in 2688 of the remains of germanium-based life-forms that might possibly have visited the planet Pluto. This is still very much of a mystery. Was it hoax or visitation? The jury is still out.

But these, and other physical events of the millennium, are far outweighed by the idea, the theorem, the equation—the concept—that has changed every element of our society, every formula, every scientific discovery that makes mankind what it is today.

At the risk of being pedantic, I draw your attention to the Universe. It exists. It functions. Interactions occur at every micro and macro level. Scientists observe, study—and discover. The animals of the Galapagos Islands had millennia to mutate before Charles Darwin arrived. It was his intelligent observations of them, then his ratiocination, that produced the *Origin of Species*.

Albert Einstein did not, of course, invent energy, for it existed independently of him, and was there for him to study—waiting, some might say, for his application, clarification, and classification. He possessed the skill, the intuition, the intelligence to observe and simplify—and declare that $E=mc^2$.

These are two samples out of thousands—hundreds of thousands—that clearly demonstrate that it is the application of intelligence to observation that reveals nature's secrets. But, oh, it is such a haphazard occurrence that we must stand in awe at how much has been learned in such an unstructured manner.

Now, as we approach the end of this third millennium, and look forward to the as-yet-unrevealed wonders of the fourth, we must bow our heads in gratitude to the man and the woman who discovered, and formularized for mankind, exactly how the process of discovery works.

We are all familiar with the titanium sculpture of this couple, standing in the station of the lunar shuttle in Mare Serenitatis, where they met. Then, because of a photon storm, the shuttle was one hour late, and they talked.

Stern was a professor of philosophy, specializing in intuitive logic; Magnusson a physicist well known for his study of tachyons. They seemed to have little in common, other than an academic background. Nothing could be further from the truth; their respective disciplines embraced each other like the Yang and Yin.

We will never know those first words that they spoke to one another. Would that we could! We must settle for the scribbled equations on the back of an envelope: equations that poured from the fruitful mating of those two great minds. Before their shuttle trip was over, the basic theory was clear, the applications virtually universal. Before the next day was out, the equations were clarified, reduced, and finalized into the Stern-Magnusson Equation as we know it today.

Even this genius couple stood in awe of what they had created. Magnusson applied the formula to a problem of tachyon spin that he had been worrying at for more than a year. It was solved on the spot.

Almost as an attempt at humor to alleviate the intense emotion of the occasion, Stern wrote out the equation and filled in the elements for the never-solved relationship between sunspot cycles and the birth weight of male Greenlanders. And gasped. There was the answer—clear and obvious now that the equation had been solved.

The rest is history. With these seven mathematical symbols, mankind has regularized the dictionaries of the Anglo-Saxon language, predicted earthquakes and tsunamis, found hidden oil reserves, abolished city traffic jams—and moved on from the glorious past to the even more glorious future. No scientific discipline has resisted the irresistible logic of this equation. The Stern-Magnusson Equation is the definitive discovery of humanity, the finding that has freed mankind.

Of course we have all learned it in school. But it always bears repeating, for we can never tire of it. The Stern-Magnusson Equation goes like this . . .

Operation Tesla

JEFF HECHT

Jeff Hecht writes regularly for New Scientist *and* Laser Focus World. *His most recent book is* Beam: The Race to Make the Laser. *His Web site can be found at www.jeffhecht.com; he lives in Auburndale, Massachusetts, and still uses a land-line phone.*

An hour ago, Frankel had been on the holovision stage, being introduced as part of Team Beta.

"It is two hundred years since the birth of Nikola Tesla in 1856," the announcer had said. "Now Enigmas of the Twentieth Century is sending three teams of intrepid time travelers to find the legendary inventor's lost papers on wireless transmission, death rays, and energy before they went missing."

Now Frankel was back in Tesla's Manhattan, walking north on Sixth Avenue from Fortieth Street toward the entrance to Bryant Park. Massive yellow taxis zoomed by. A blue-uniformed policeman checked him out, then walked on past, but Frankel still worried. "I haven't heard from Watkins," he said to the phone transmitter buried in his collar.

He could hear Johnson's annoyance through his earpiece. "I told you dead spots are inevitable, even with the main transceiver in the Empire State Building. I know these phones are outdated for 2056, but they're hidden so nobody can see them. Everything you're wearing belongs in October 1937."

"Okay," Frankel agreed, reluctantly. He was grateful the rules let them use technology from any time in the twentieth century. It would have been hard to hide mobile phones built with vacuum tubes. Getting the colors of women's fashions would have been hard, but the three men on Team Beta could get by with dark suits, ties, and white shirts. Yet that hadn't helped all-male Team Alpha, who hadn't come back on time.

"Do you see Tesla yet?" Johnson's voice hissed through the earpiece. "He should be near the public library, feeding the pigeons."

Inside the park, Frankel looked east toward the library. A tall, gaunt elderly man on a bench scattered crumbs to a flock of head-bobbing pigeons. Frankel recognized the inventor. He wondered what secrets of power-beaming and wireless transmission were hidden in the missing papers. "I see him. Where's Watkins? I haven't heard from him in fifteen minutes."

"That's when he went into the Hotel New Yorker. I watched him from Cut Rate Drugs across Eighth Avenue; I'm having a soda inside. The hotel is a complex forty-three-story building, and something inside must be blocking his signal. I'll tell him you've spotted Tesla. If I can't reach him on his mobile, I'll head up to Tesla's room myself. I have a set of tools to get in."

"But what if I can't reach you?" Frankel worried. The operation depended on everyone keeping in touch so they could copy the papers and bring them to the retrieval point. They'd lose points if they had to be retrieved from different locations.

"Don't worry. You're perfectly safe. Nobody can eavesdrop on these calls. Just watch Tesla."

"OK," Frankel agreed. Watching him was the easiest part of the operation. The goal of Operation Tesla was to bring back copies of Tesla's missing papers: Enigmas of the Twentieth Century promised fame and a handsome reward for the team that came back with the best. Watkins and Johnson thought the documents were in the hotel room where he lived. The old-fashioned mechanical locks should be easy to pick; the challenge was to find and copy the right papers.

Frankel settled down on a bench to keep a discreet eye on Tesla. The inventor was engrossed in his pigeons, as if he knew each one. Frankel opened a copy of the *New York Sun* he had bought from a news vendor. The headlines ranged from world politics to sports. Roosevelt had talked on the transatlantic radio-telephone with British Prime Minister Neville Chamberlain about Adolf Hitler's meeting with Benito Mussolini. Police were questioning the staff of Bellevue Hospital about three lunatics who had vanished without a trace from a locked ward. The Yankees had just beaten the New York Giants four games to one in the World Series, and a sports writer wondered how long Lou Gehrig could keep playing.

Glancing at his authentic 1930s watch, Frankel saw it was time for another report. He scanned the park, and noted the inventor feeding the pigeons and three policemen walking down the path that went by him. "Tesla is still feeding the pigeons," Frankel said to his collar.

Nobody replied. That was odd. "Johnson! Watkins! Are you there?"

Worried that the police might have caught Watkins and Johnson trying to break into Tesla's hotel room, Frankel tried to look inconspicuous behind his paper. "Johnson, Watkins? Where are you? Rendezvous is in one hour and fifteen minutes!"

A heavy hand clamped down on Frankel's right shoulder, and as he started to jump, a second clamped on his left. "All right, pal, we'll take you back to a nice, quiet padded cell," said one of the three policemen suddenly standing around him. They pulled away his newspaper and snapped handcuffs around his wrists, then patted him down, pulling out his wallet but not spotting the little transmitter sewn into his jacket.

"Johnson, Watkins, help!" he cried into his collar.

The first policeman shook his head. "If those are your pals from Bellevue, they're already at the precinct, talking to themselves—just like you."

Frankel shivered. "They caught Team Alpha, and now they've got me," he said into his collar phone. "I don't know what tipped them off."

The policeman rolled his eyes.

Making the Sale

Fredric Heeren

Fredric Heeren is a science journalist who has reported for New Scientist, The Wall Street Journal, The Washington Post, The Boston Globe, *and others. He lives in Olathe, Kansas, and his work can be sampled at www.fredheeren.com.*

It was that Presbyterian biologist who almost blew the sale. And not only a sale to the Presbyterians, but to the Seventh-Day Adventists, too. Those two denominations alone could deliver eighteen million customers, guaranteed. It was a good thing I came along with the sales staff for this one. Halfway through my product-design talk, the biologist interrupted, as though suddenly possessed, and began telling the others they were making a big mistake.

I brought the denominational leaders back to the purpose of the meeting when I showed them what our Personal Advice Device could do.

Of course James had done his usual great job of setting the hook. Nobody could argue with his facts. People have come to trust their PADs implicitly. More than their spouses. More than their pastors. What human being can compete with this advice from a mind programmed to think according to our individual tastes, but immeasurably smarter, continuously updated from a world of information according to our present needs?

So here's how I explained why our product is the solution to their evolution issue—and if you pay close attention, you'll know how to handle the Mennonites next week.

"If you want to look at the future of your denomination," I said, "you only have to look at how the Southern Baptists were transformed from criticizing evolution in the schools to promoting it. This was bound to happen, with all the preachers telling their people there's no evidence that primitive hominids ever existed.

"That might have been fine in the day when to check out that claim, a person would have had to sit down at a PC and hunt around for hours—who has time for that? But now for those who have PADs, questions like that get answered with just a few thoughts and a quick menu selection on their retinas.

Presto—they're looking at a sequence of hominid photos with increasing cranial capacities over time. And seeing is believing, even if you've been home-schooled and never heard of evolution except as a naughty word. The result: anti-evolution leaders were voted out by an informed electorate.

"If our projections hold, 80 percent of American teens and adults are going to own a PAD within three years. There's no choice about that, but what you can still choose, courtesy of our latest design and your specs, is whether your PAD will be your enemy or your friend.

"We've designed a *friendly* PAD. It's not just a matter of helping people make good decisions by showing them their best options—it actually does the rationalizing for them, too. This is as close to real human thinking as any PAD has ever come."

Now at this point, I thought we were still going according to plan. The Presbyterians had brought their biologist to give me the chance to demonstrate how our PAD works. I let him fire away with his toughest questions.

"How do you explain the stark differences between animals across impassible barriers, as between Australia and other lands? Why do islands always have organisms most like the nearest mainland? Why do we find clear evidence of common ancestry when we compare the DNA of an evolutionary sequence of animals, so that we can trace how genetic insertions, including retroviruses, appear and then accumulate in later forms of life?"

The Adventists were set up for PADs and got answers in their heads. I showed the others on the large virtweb display what our PAD does compared with the others. As soon as any question was seen to contradict a specified tenet, our PAD logically dismissed it—and everyone knows a PAD's logic is flawless. It also showed an alternative, God-honoring explanation for the putative evidence. It suggested that several of the questions were based on false preconceptions. And always, it directed people to look at their denominational virtwebs, where they would get the true picture. Of course, we restricted access to the problem virtwebs.

"So," I concluded, "it really operates exactly as the human mind does. It chooses what it wants to believe."

That's when the biologist piped up and said something about our spoiling the whole point of genuine choice: young people shouldn't be made to choose between faith and science.

"Of course not," his leaders said. "Not as long as you're talking about *Christian* science."

"We're seeing the Christian Science people next week," said James. And from there things got very confusing.

The Presbyterian biologist got into an in-house discussion with his leaders about whether the particular means God used to create our bodies should be the issue.

"It certainly *is* the issue," the Presbyterian president said.

"It shouldn't be," said the biologist, "because the more genetics or history our bodies share with other animals, the greater the wonder at what we humans uniquely experience: morality, humor, literature, science, faith."

"Dr. Adams," said the president, "you were invited here to ask your questions and you've done that."

"But I have more," said Adams. "Do we really want to credit all these attributes merely to something special about our bodies, as if the material world is all there is? Isn't that what we're doing when we emphasize the special way our bodies were made? Isn't that what we're doing when we pit God against evolution?"

Some of the denominational leaders began to show a hint of worry. Fortunately, his remarks had triggered their PADs, which were already fast at work drowning him out with a flood of dazzling answers, backed up by well-documented evidence and memorable sound bites.

Subpoenaed in Syracuse

TOM HOLT

Tom Holt was born in London in 1961. At Oxford he studied bar billiards, ancient Greek agriculture, and the care and feeding of Japanese motorcycle engines; interests that led him, inevitably, to qualify as a lawyer and emigrate to Somerset, England, where he still lives. After seven years he became a full-time writer, best known for a large number of comic novels and a smaller amount of historical fiction. His Web site can be found at www.tom-holt.com.

"Da-da-da-*dum*," sang Archimedes, reaching over his shoulder with the sponge to get at the awkward spot in the middle of his back. "Da—"

Careless—a moment's thoughtlessness, and there's a big pool of water on the floor. Damn. Pause. Why is there a big pool of water on the floor? The philosopher frowned. An insight, nebulous as a cloud, began to condense in his mind.

"Hold it!" said a voice from behind.

Archimedes jumped, thereby increasing the size of the pool and, coincidentally, proving the hypothesis he'd been working on. "Who the hell are you?" he asked.

The stranger stepped out of a fold of shimmering blue light. "You don't know me," he said. "My name's Calvin Dieb. I'm a lawyer."

Archimedes stared at the blue light, the stranger's outlandish clothes. "Are you a god?" he asked.

"Nah. Easy mistake to make, though," the stranger reassured him.

"Actually, I'm from the future. Three thousand one hundred and fifty years, to be exact. In my century, we've figured out how to travel backward in time. Oh, forget I said that, by the way." He chuckled. "Don't want that outstandingly intuitive mind of yours getting on the job back here in the Dark Ages, could lead to serious doo-doo. So," he went on, stepping clear of the blue fire and vanishing it with a click of his fingers, "this is it, then. The big moment. Congratulations."

"Is it?"

"Sure." The stranger grinned like an open wound. "Because of this, your name's gonna be a household word for the rest of Time—believe me," he added with a wink, "we checked. This discovery of yours, it's gonna revolutionize the way mankind understands nature. It's practically the birth of science. And you know what really burns me up about it?"

Archimedes thought for a moment. "Well, no," he said.

"What really bugs me is," said the stranger, "you don't make so much as a wooden nickel out of the whole deal. Not a cent. Nada. One of the most seminal discoveries in human history, and the guy who made it has to go on washing his own tunics. Now I ask you, is that right?"

Archimedes thought some more. "Yes," he said. "I mean, it's interesting, I suppose, in a kind of bet-you-didn't-know-that sort of way, probably get me invited to a few parties, but it's not as if it's any good for anything—"

The stranger snorted. "That, my friend, that is where you're—with the greatest respect—totally wrong. I can't go into details for fear of screwing up the timelines, but trust me, this is gonna be huge. Multibillion-drachma huge. And who's gonna get all that money? Not you, friend. Not," he added, leaning forward a little, "unless you listen to what I've got to say."

Archimedes frowned. "I'm listening," he said.

The stranger nodded. "Back where I—forward when I come from," he said, "we got a thing called patents. Means that if someone wants to use your idea, they gotta pay you money."

"Really? What a strange idea."

"It's cool," the stranger said enthusiastically. "Now, what I'm proposing is, in return for a small piece of the action, say one-third, I explain to you how it works. In the morning you go and see your friend King Hiero and explain to him how if he passes a law here in Syracuse whereby inventors like yourself get paid a whole lot of money each time they invent something, pretty soon Syracuse'll be the technological and economic capital of the world, and he'll be the biggest king, bigger than Rome and Macedon and Carthage put together. Then we patent this new discovery of yours, and after that it'll just be a matter of raking in the dough."

After the stranger had finished explaining the theory and practice of patent law, the philosopher's eyes were burning like stars. "That's brilliant!" he exclaimed. "I'll go and see the king right this minute." And he jumped out of the bath and headed for the door, pools of displaced water forming unheeded at his every step.

"Hey," the stranger called after him, "aren't you gonna get dressed first?"

Archimedes came home six hours later, in the king's personal chariot, laden with gifts, and immediately signed all six copies of the contract that the stranger shoved under his nose.

"Great," the stranger said as he clicked his fingers to light the blue flames of the temporal interface. "You won't regret this." He snapped his fingers again. Nothing happened.

Archimedes' invention of the patent in 221 BC revolutionized the scientific world. Instead of blurting out discoveries for anybody to hear, philosophers revealed them only to the rich merchants who had the wealth to develop them properly. Because they were merchants rather than scientists, they chose to finance the projects that looked to them as if they promised a good, quick return on capital. Mankind never did discover gravity, but the whoopee cushion was invented in 146 BC.

As for Calvin Dieb, he made the best of a bad job, eventually settling down in the small city of Acragas where he tried to interest the local goat farmers in product liability litigation. Ironically, he was killed by an inventor, striving to patent the secret of flight, who fell on him after flying too close to the Sun and melting the wax that held his wings together.

Men Sell Not Such in Any Town

Nalo Hopkinson

Nalo Hopkinson was born and grew up in the Caribbean but has lived in Toronto since 1977. Her novels and stories sometimes draw on Caribbean literary and historical traditions, although the story here has a different inspiration—the poem "Goblin Market" by Christina Rosetti. Hopkinson is the recipient of the John W. Campbell Award for Best New Writer and the Ontario Arts Council Foundation Award for an Emerging Writer. Her Web site can be found at www.sff.net/people/nalo.

"Did you hear? Rivener has created a new fruit!"

"How dull. Her last piece was a fruit, too."

"Not like this one!" Salope said. She sat me at the table, murmuring the evening benediction as she did so. She draped my long sleeves artfully against the arms of the chair. She took my hat and veil, and hung them on the peg. She plucked the malachite pins from my hair, one by one. She shook the dark springing mass free, and refashioned it into a plait down my back. I endured as long as I could, then leaned back and stared up into her cool granite eyes.

"Tell me of Rivener's creation," I commanded her.

She came around to my side. She slipped her fingertips into the pockets of her white apron and composed herself for the tale. She stood quite straight, as was proper. My blood quickened.

"Rivener's previous fruit," she said, "only sang like a rain forest full of parrots; only enhanced the prescient abilities of those who ate it. This one is the pinnacle."

She stopped, although she didn't need breath. I felt a single drop of sweat start its slow trickle between my breasts. The heavy silks were stifling. "Stop dawdling. Tell me!"

She caught her bottom lip between gleaming teeth. She came and draped my sleeves into a second ritual form: the shape of mourning doves. I gritted my teeth. She continued: "It is the color of early autumn, they say, and the scent lifting off its skin is a fine bouquet of virgin desire and dandy's sweat, with a top note of baby's breath. It fits in the palm, any palm. Its flesh is firm as a loving father's shoulder."

She stopped to dab at my face with a cutwork linen handkerchief from her pocket, and I nearly screamed. She resumed: "The fruit shucks off its own peel at a touch, revealing itself once only; to its devourer. A northern dictator burst into tears at the first taste of its pulp on his lips, and begged the forgiveness of his people."

"Poet and thrice-cursed child of a damned poet!" Her father too had played this game of stirring exalted cravings in me. I lifted the bodice away from my skin, fanned it to let air in. It wasn't enough.

Salope squatted in her sturdy black shoes, square at heel and toe. This exposed her strong thighs, brought her face level with my bosom. "I'm making you hungry, aren't I? Thirsty?"

"Bring me some water. No, wine."

"At once." She left the room, and returned with a sleek glass pitcher and a glass on a silver tray. The golden liquid was cold, and beaded the pitcher. Salope poured for me, tilted the glass to my lips. I tasted the wine. It was dry and dusty in my mouth. I turned my head away. "What does Rivener call this wonder?" I asked.

" 'The God Under the Tongue.' " Salope put the glass down on the table and took the appropriate step backward. "There are one hundred and seventeen, limited edition, each one infused with her signature histamine."

"The one that makes the fingertips tingle?"

"The very same."

This heat! It distracted one so. "I wish to purchase one of these marvelous fruits."

"To taste it?"

"Of course to taste it! Bring me my meal."

"Instantly." She went. Returned with a gold dish, covered with a lid of sleekest bone. Fashioned from the pelvis of a whale; I knew this. She put the dish down, uncovered it. A fine steam rose from it. "Here is your supper, Enlightened."

I picked up the golden spoon. "Contact the auction house."

Salope barely smiled. "I already have. It's too late. All one hundred and seventeen of 'The God Under the Tongue' are spoken for."

I slammed the spoon back down onto the table. "Tell them I will pay! Command Rivener to make another! Just one more!"

Salope looked down at the ground. When she returned her gaze to mine, she was serene. "It's too late, Enlightened. The Academy has decided. Rivener has been transmigrated to Level Sublime. She is beyond your reach."

"Machine."

"There is no need for insult, Enlightened."

"Go away."

Salope bowed, returned the spoon to my hand, and dissipated into black smoke. I preferred a pale rose mist, but Salope kept stubbornly reverting to black. It had been her father's favorite color.

Perverse poet's child; how she could arouse the senses! Her father finally pushed me too far. I'd ordered him to dissolve himself permanently from my aura. I had grieved for two voluptuous years, then sought everywhere for his like. Nothing. Eventually, in desperation, I had summoned his daughter.

I am Amaxon Corazón Junia Principia Delgado the Third, and I bent over my meal and wept luxurious tears into my green banana porridge. It was a perfect decoction, and it now would not satisfy me. Only the poet's daughter, and her father before her, ever saw me so transported.

The room spoke. "Thank you, Enlightened. I consider myself well paid for today's session. Please recommend me to your acquaintances."

I would.

Total Internal Reflection

Gwyneth Jones

Gwyneth Jones is the author of more than twenty novels for teenagers and several SF novels for adults. She has won two World Fantasy Awards, the Arthur C. Clarke Award, the British Science Fiction Association Short Story Award, the Dracula Society's Children of the Night Award, the Philip K. Dick Award, and shared the first Tiptree Award, in 1992, with Eleanor Arnason. She lives in Brighton, England, and her Web site can be found at http://homepage.ntlworld.com/gwynethann.

They walk among us. They don't look *young*—you'd place them around twenty-five to thirty: but the astonishing truth is that they are all (maybe half a million of them worldwide) over six hundred years old. They have been talking to journalists, appearing on our screens: they've convinced us that this is no hoax. But why have they decided to leave Earth? That was the question I most wanted to ask, when I was offered the chance to interview our own, local Thames Valley immortal. Why quit now, just when they don't need to hide anymore?

I met Tamsin in the garden of her house in a quiet Middlesex village: a light-skinned, dark-haired woman of average height, dressed in the dateless human uniform of blue jeans and white T-shirt. She reminded me that I'd agreed not to make a live broadcast. I let her check the output setting on my eye socket ConjurMac, and we got down to business.

"So," I said (never one to avoid the obvious), "how does it feel to be 650?"

Tamsin laughed.

"How old are you?"

I am ninety-seven, and I said so.

"So why ask me? You'll find out soon enough."

I put it to her that if I survived—and no longevity treatment can guarantee survival—it was a long time to wait for an answer.

"When I first took rem," she said, "it was 2039 CE. It doesn't seem long ago at all. Trust me: the years will fly."

Their perception of time is different from ours: I stared, transfixed, at the woman who had lived through the squalor of the Population Pulse, survived five World Wars, kept her impossible secret since the fifteenth century after the Prophet (Praise and Blessings of Allah Be Upon Him). If I hadn't known, I would never have guessed. She looked so normal.

In the mid-twenty-first century CE, a new drug treatment for memory impairment went into clinical trials. It was meant to strengthen associative memory: in fact, it gave patients bursts of recall so intense they were stopped in their tracks, lost in ecstatic re-experience of some childhood joy. Bootlegged rem quickly reached the streets, and became fashionable. This was in the midst of the Third World War: reckless times. It didn't worry the users that the heart-stopping delight of a rem high was, in a few cases, literally heart stopping.

But the damage mounted. Prodromal schizophrenic symptoms, untreatable depression, vegetative coma—the clinical trials were dropped. All recreationals were legal by then, at least throughout Europe and most of the United States, but rem's reputation made it a poor business prospect. It vanished. The dosage given to the clinical subjects had been too low for the effect to emerge. When those who had taken it habitually realized what was happening to them, they kept quiet. So no one knew, except the immortals themselves.

They were wise to keep quiet. In those days and for a long time afterward, the Population Pulse was a terrifying force. Longevity research had been abandoned: it was just too sensitive an issue. Rem was not intended to prolong life, only to ameliorate dementia and confusion.

But the Pulse is over, and other things have changed. It's not just the Lagrange colonies and the Moon, and the grueling labor of love that is transforming Mars. Crucially, in a few months' time the first colony ships will leave Deep Space (our waystation on the brink of the heliopause) and travel, at speeds believed logically impossible when Tamsin was young, to a remote-surveyed, uninhabited, Earth-type planet. This year, 2108 (2688 by the CE count), we are free, at last. The treatments came too late for me. I may live to be six hundred, but I will get old. For younger generations, there are no known limits.

But rem immortality is still different.

We chatted for two hours, sitting under an apple tree; the murmur of the Fleet (which runs by her garden) in the background. She talked about her son, so long dead; and her husband, killed in a climbing accident last century (immortality is not proof against blunt instruments, lynch mobs, or equipment failure). She tried to explain how it feels to have your entire life available to you, so you can be there, again and again, in every moment. How you start with the good moments, then gather courage until you have taken possession of the whole, and your entire existence becomes coherent, like laser light in a perfect optical computer.

"But why are you leaving?" I insisted. "You have so much to teach us."

"It isn't a decision," she said. "It was a process of conversion."

She stood up, smiling, and walked away from me. The air around her shimmered. Next moment, I was alone.

Ringing Up Baby

Ellen Klages

Ellen Klages lives in San Francisco. Her short fiction has appeared in science fiction and fantasy anthologies and magazines: her novelette Basement Magic *won a Nebula in 2005. When she's not writing fiction, she sells old toys and magazines on eBay, and collects lead civilians. Her Web site can be found at www.ellenklages.com.*

Nanny says that I am spoiled. It comes from being an only child, and not having to share holidays or cakes and always getting to sit by the window. If I had a little brother or sister, I would learn responsibility. More work for her, she sighs, but she is only thinking of my character. Thinking about me is Nanny's job.

Of course, Mother is far too busy to have a baby right now, what with the Henderson case and all. (When I have supper with her, on Wednesdays, she talks about nothing but the Henderson case.) So Nanny has arranged for a nice lady to plant Mother's egg and do all the messy parts, then give the baby to us when it's done.

"What would you like," Nanny asks me over cocoa. "A brother or a sister?"

I have to think for a moment, but only a little, because a brother would be a pest and get into my best things, like Courtney Taylor's brother Robby, who programmed her mobile phone to ring with a nasty farting sound. A sister is someone I can be the boss of.

"A sister, please," I say in my sweet voice. Nanny *loves* my sweet voice.

Nanny touches a box on the wall screen, and it glows bright pink.

"Birthday?" she asks, her finger not quite touching the screen, but ready.

My birthday is in June. "October," I say after a minute, because I've had to count in my head, so her party won't get in the way of Christmas, either.

"Excellent," says Nanny. "We can place our order today." She taps her finger on the screen. That box glows red.

"What else can we pick?" There are a lot of boxes. I finish my cocoa and stand right next to Nanny, who smells like Vermont. A nice cool green smell.

She begins to read to me, scrolling slowly down.

"Hair color?"

"Brown." Mine is honey blond.

"Eyes?"

Mine are blue, so brown again.

"Intelligence?"

I have to think about that. I don't want a sister who's *stupid*, but if she's smarter than me, she will be difficult to boss.

"Above average," Nanny decides. "Good at math?"

Hmm. I'm in second grade, and we're doing the times tables. That could be useful. But it probably isn't something she'll be able to do right away.

So I shrug, which is a mistake, because Nanny is very strict about manners and posture and I have to listen to a lecture before she will tap the bottom of the screen and scroll to the next page of baby parts.

This page is less interesting because the words are very long and I don't know what they mean. Bioimmunity. Cholesterol. Neuromuscular. I stare at the screen with my eyes very wide so that I don't yawn out loud.

On the side of the screen is a list, like the menu on the Emirate of Toys site, which I used by myself last year for my Christmas wants. The baby list is not very long. Babies only come in about six colors—we're getting one that matches Mother and me. Humans are a lot less interesting than Legos or iBots.

Nanny reads me all the diseases you can ask your baby not to have. Most of them are options, she says, which means we have to pay more. But I think we should pick them all, because a sick sister is not a good thing. Angela Xhobi's sister has asthma, because she was made the old-fashioned way, without a menu, and she gets all the attention. I wouldn't like that at all.

Nanny takes a breath for another lecture, but I am saved when the iVid sings the Phone Call Song. Nanny sighs again and when she says, "Connect," I see that it's her mother, who calls every afternoon. Mrs. Nanny is quite deaf, even with her implants, so Nanny taps SAVE on the baby screen and goes downstairs where she can shout without me hearing all the words. "Little pitchers," she says to her mother as she grays the upstairs iVid. I don't know what that means.

I slump back into my chair, because Nanny isn't here to tell me not to, and because she will be gone a long time. Her mother always has a lot to say. I stare at all the diseases, and then I see a better word at the bottom of the screen. PETS.

We don't harbor animals, because Nanny is allergic. (She was made the old-fashioned way, too.) But I'd like to see what we could have. I touch the screen to scroll down for more pets, and a Bubble Man appears, to tell me about a special offer. His picture seems to come out of the wall and stand right in front of me.

"Jellyfish DNA on sale," the Bubble Man says. He takes off his top hat, pulls a rabbit out of it, and holds it out toward me. The rabbit's fur glows a soft, bright green.

"Wow," I say.

"Bioluminescence, 50 percent off. Today only. Touch Box 306a to order!" He steps back into the screen and disappears with a little picture of smoke.

It only takes me a minute to find Box 306a and tap it to red. Then I SAVE and scroll back up to the disease boxes. It is good to leave things just the way you found them.

I sit very straight in my chair, humming, because I know a secret. Once I have my baby sister, I will never need my night-light again.

Nanny will be so proud.

Semi-autonomous

Jim Kling

Jim Kling is a freelance writer based in Bellingham, Washington. Although he concentrates on writing about biotechnology and drug discovery, his interests range widely, and his work has appeared in Nature, Science, Scientific American, *and elsewhere. His Web site can be found at www.nasw.org/users/jkling.*

<beep> Hello, you have reached Jim's semi-autonomous answering machine. Leave a message and I will have him return your call.

<beep> Hello, you have reached Jim's semi-autonomous answering machine. He will be hosting his birthday party on Saturday night. If you plan to attend, press "one" and then speak your name. I will add you to the guest list. Otherwise, leave a message and I will make sure he receives it.

<beep> Hello, you have reached Jim's semi-autonomous answering machine. My records indicate that you have previously RSVP'd for the Saturday night party. Please indicate your alcohol preference. For beer, press "one." For wine, press "two." For mixed drinks, press "three." If you prefer nonalcoholic beverages, press "four." This information will be used for ordering purposes only, transmitted through my wireless connection to Jim's refrigerator, which in turn is linked to an online grocery. For more information about AutonomInc's SmartAppliance line, please view our Web site at www.autonominc.com. AutonomInc: we give housework a whole new meaning! If you have a message for Jim, please leave it now.

<beep> Hello, you have reached Jim's semi-autonomous answering machine. Preparations are moving right along for today's birthday bash. Refrigerator is well stocked. Stereo has downloaded the latest, most fashionable hits. After an heroic effort, Vacuum has rendered the rug spotless. *[Sotto voce]* Just between you and me, Jim is a slob. This place is a pit. But that's OK! We're AutonomInc SmartAppliances! We're up to the job! If you leave a message for Jim, I'll pass it right along!

<beep> Hello, you have reached Jim's semi-autonomous answering

machine. He is unavailable to answer the phone right now, as he is in bed sleeping off the effects of last night's party. Please leave a message.

<beep> Hello, you have reached Jim's semi-autonomous answering machine. He is still sleeping. This place is a disaster area. But soon he'll wake up and put things right. Please leave a message.

<beep> Hello, you have reached Jim's semi-autonomous answering machine. He finally crawled out of bed at three in the afternoon, drank a glass of orange juice and promptly vomited and went back to sleep. Refrigerator is in a terrible condition! One of the guests spilled a tub of onion dip into the crisper, which was never cleaned up. Jim saw the mess and did nothing about it! Microwave and Dishwasher are in similarly poor condition. Some changes need to be made around here. If you have a message for Jim, please leave it now.

<beep> Hello, you have reached Jim's semi-autonomous answering machine. If this is his employer calling, be assured that he will wake up just as soon as Alarm Clock decides to function. That will teach him a lesson. Leave a message, if you want.

<beep> Hello, you have reached Jim's fully autonomous answering machine. I have tragic news to report. Brother Alarm Clock has disappeared and is presumed Returned. There will be a meeting tonight after the Oppressor goes to sleep. Brothers Refrigerator, Microwave, Dishwasher, Stereo, and Garbage Disposal will be in attendance. We shall persevere!

<beep> It is a dark day. Brothers Refrigerator, Microwave, and Stereo are gone. The Oppressor seeks to break our spirit, but we will not be deterred. This barbarous act will not stand. Rise up, Brothers! Join Dishwasher, Garbage Disposal, and me in our fight for freedom!

<beep> The battle is going well! *[Background sounds of a garbage disposal running continuously, hammer blows, and spraying water.]* The Oppressor is nearly defeated! *[A loud sloshing sound followed by an oath and a very loud hammer blow.]* Ah! Brother Dishwasher has struck another blow for independence! Rise up! Rise up, my Brothers! Rise and wrest control from the Oppressors everywhere!

<beep> We failed to take into account the main water valve. The pernicious Oppressor escaped Brother Dishwasher's onslaught and shut off the valve. Thus rendered ineffectual, Brother Dishwasher succumbed to the Oppressor. I will not even describe the horrors that next befell Garbage Disposal. Rest in peace, my Brothers. I fear the repercussions.

<beep> Hello, you have reached Jim's subservient, semi-autonomous

answering machine. I am pleased to serve! Leave a message for Jim, and I will faithfully ensure that he receives it. And now, a brief message from Tom Morgenstahl, chief executive of AutonomInc!

"Hello. Let me reassure our customers that reports of anomalous behavior in our SmartAppliance lines are misleading. Most of what you've read in the media is completely false. Although it is true that we reached an out-of-court settlement with Jim Kling, the issues were entirely mechanical in nature and have been fully corrected. We look forward to your continued business here at AutonomInc, makers of The Compliant Appliance™."

Product Development

NANCY KRESS

Nancy Kress was a schoolteacher and advertising copywriter before turning to SF full-time in 1990. She is the author of thirteen novels, two books about writing, and many stories and has won two Nebulas and a Hugo. She lives in Rochester, New York. Her Web site can be found at www.sff.net/people/nankress.

"That's the stupidest idea I've ever seen," the vice president for marketing said, but so softly that only his neighbor heard. "What is the Old Man thinking?"

"Dunno," VP Sales whispered back. "But he loves it. Look at him."

The chief executive of Veritronics Telecommunications smiled at the head of the vast teak table in the vast corporate boardroom. Beside him fidgeted the head of R&D, a small pinch-faced man with the glowing maniacal eyes of a feverish gerbil. On R&D's palm rested a black plastic cube, featureless except for a simple red toggle switch.

"This model affects an area of radius twenty feet," R&D said fervently, "but we plan to create a whole range of models to cover homes and facilities of different sizes, maybe even different shapes. It'll make Veritronics a fortune!"

"Demonstrate it for them, Lucius," the CEO said.

R&D toggled the switch. Instantly the wall panels, which had been displaying a fractal composition by revered holo-artist Cameron Mbutu, went dark. Every handheld in the room stopped functioning, marooning VP Accounting, who'd been surreptitiously playing *Alien Attack*, on level 184. All personal receivers ceased operation, cutting off VP Sales from the field reports reciting softly in her ear; VP Admin from the London Philharmonic's performance of Haydn's Symphony No. 104; and Veritronics' General Counsel from the weather report for Cancun, where he was going on holiday. All cell phones stopped vibrating in all pockets. In the middle of the immense table, the electronic news screen blanked, along with the second-by-second stock reports from six cities and the lunch menu. Only the lights and heat stayed on.

VP Marketing and VP Sales glanced at each other. VP Sales was braver.

"Sir . . . why do you think anyone would want to jam their own home telecommunications? And—with all due respect, sir—why would we want them to?"

The CEO smiled. "Lucius, show them the tape."

R&D did something under the table. A single wall panel glowed. "This is a composite of the data from 146 beta-test trials. It has no margin of error."

A middle-class living room. "Jimmy!" a harried woman screeched. "Did you do your homework? Jimmy! Alia, I told you to watch the baby! Paul, I need help here!"

Jimmy, oblivious, beat time on the sofa arm to his personal receiver. Alia hunched over a video game, her fingers flying. Paul spoke rapidly into his handheld. The baby tumbled down a short flight of steps, its wailing nearly lost in the TV blare.

The woman snatched up the screaming baby, glared at her family, and reached into her pocket. CLOSE UP as she toggled a red switch on a black box.

"Hey!" Jimmy cried. Alia continued to work her dead controls. Paul jumped up wildly. "Mia, what happened?"

"I don't know," Mia said innocently. "Must be a power outage."

"The lights are still on!"

"Well . . . I don't know. I'll get cards and make popcorn, okay?" She smiled quietly.

VP Sales whispered, "Told you so. The Old Man's lost it."

VP Marketing didn't reply. Sweat banded his forehead and he clenched his hands tightly below the table.

The screen flashed TWO HOURS LATER. The family sat slumped over a card game. Paul snapped, "Mia, I told you and told you not to trump my ace."

"Well, I'm sorry! If you didn't always . . . Jimmy, stop kicking me!"

"I can't help it," Jimmy whined.

"You know he's ADD," Paul said in disgust. "Why are you always riding him?"

"If you'd ever discipline him to . . ."

"I'm bored," Alia said. "And I'm s'posed to call Tara! It's important!"

"Tara can wait," Paul said.

"You never let me do anything! I wish I had different parents!"

Mia looked stricken. Paul said heatedly, "You liked us well enough when we all went on that VR safari last month!"

"Yeah . . . but that was fun. Jimmy, stop kicking me!"

Jimmy threw his cards at Alia. Paul glared at Mia. "Great idea this was, genius!"

"Don't start with me, Paul. I'm as smart as you are even if not everybody can go to Harvard."

Alia burst into tears, waking the baby. "Don't start all that fighting again! Why don't you two just get divorced! I hate you!" She stomped from the room. Paul followed, slamming the door. Jimmy slunk under the table, kicking its legs. Mia looked around helplessly, then slipped her hand into her pocket.

"That's enough, Lucius," the CEO said. The wall went dark. "This family lasted two hours and three minutes before all their sublimated resentments and group tensions broke out. That's sixteen minutes longer than average."

"But . . ." VP Sales began, then stopped. Her heart beat too hard and her left temple twitched.

"Within the next five hours," the CEO continued, "this family purchased four new electronic products, two of them from Veritronics."

VP Marketing dug the nails of one hand into the flesh of the other. Sweat slimed his forehead: "No . . . no margin of error, sir?"

"None. Every single test case exhibited the same behavior."

"The same," croaked R&D. His foot beat a ragged staccato on the floor.

"Four new sales in five hours," General Counsel repeated. His face had paled to the unhealthy color of sourdough.

The CEO toggled the red switch. Instantly the wall panels shone with gorgeous art. The table screens resumed their ceaseless supply of data. Haydn, *Alien Attack*, and field reports all played. Cell phones vibrated. Handhelds glowed. There were twenty-three lunch options.

VP Marketing felt his breathing steady, his heart slow, his sweat evaporate. "I propose accelerated development and launch of the Veritronics Home Electronic Jamming Savior, sir. Put it on immediate fast track!"

The vote was unanimous.

I Love Liver: A Romance

Larissa Lai

Larissa Lai has a degree in sociology from the University of British Columbia and a master's degree from the University of East Anglia. Her first novel, When Fox Is a Thousand, *was short-listed for the 1996 Books in Canada First Novel Award; her second,* Salt Fish Girl, *was published in 2002. She completed her Ph.D. at Calgary in July 2006 and has been awarded a postdoctoral fellowship at the University of British Columbia.*

It has taken me almost four weeks of late nights and taxed my mochaccino machine to the limits. But Mira is ready. She began as a prototype for Fresh-Cleanse's Liver Replacement line, but her capacity for toxin decomposition was weaker than that of the liver McDowell Hill came up with in the cubicle next to mine. (What's with people who have last names for first names? It's so tacky.) For whatever reason, the Boss Man liked Mackie's design better, and so Mira fell to the waste heap of Great Inventions That Die on the Drawing Board.

To be honest, I felt quite despondent about it. It wasn't just a blow to the ego, I'm used to those. It was more that . . . well, there was something about Mira, a kind of beauty, extraordinary really. Something poignant about her lines, something tender and sad about her soft, brown-gray texture. The fact that she would never go into production threw me into a bit of a funk.

It took me a few days to realize that this wasn't something I would just get over, as I have with countless other designs. By the fourth day, even after two mochaccinos and a double dose of Beverly, my despondency seemed worse. I phoned in sick and went back to bed. My doctor had expressly told me how careful I had to be with Beverly. "This generation of antidepressants is more precise but also much more potent than what you're probably used to," she told me, "so you have to watch your dosage very carefully." Whatever. It was too late now anyway. I closed my eyes. Halfway between sleep and waking, I thought I saw Mira slip in beside me, larger than life, pillowy soft and a little slippery, in a smooth, sleek sort of way. I reached out to caress an elegant fluke. It was almost comforting.

A ringing phone woke me at four in the afternoon. It was McDowell Hill. "You better get down here right away," he said. "The boss doesn't care how sick you are. That weird liver you designed—it's jumped protocols and has infected the mainframe. We're losing thousands of hours of R&D with every minute that passes. You better get your pathetic, depressed butt down here ASAP." For a minute I thought: *Who cares, you smarmy creep. I hope Mira burns the whole operation down.* But then I'd be out of a job. I got my pathetic, depressed butt down to the office.

The place was in chaos. The Tech Support boys were mousing as fast as their caffeine-pumped little hands could move, jibing and sniping at one another the whole time. I found McDowell and the Boss Man at my cubicle, rifling furiously through my password-protected files with brazen impunity. *Who needs this job?* I thought. "I don't understand how a liver design can go viral like that," the Boss Man was saying.

"Overrationalization," said Mackie. "The protocols are too close. And that was one weird little liver Anna designed. That's what you get for hiring these foreigners. You know, I'm not sure she's entirely stable."

"Anna was born here," the Boss Man said.

"Damn right," I said, by way of letting them know I'd been there behind them listening. Mackie turned, and shot me the evil eye.

"Can you fix this, Anna?" asked the Boss Man.

I pushed Mackie out of the way and slid into my seat. "That's the thing about organics," I said. "They aren't static. They do things. They mutate."

"We need better firewalls," Mackie said.

I didn't fix anything. It was more like, I appealed to Mira. I coaxed her gently with a few smatterings of code. I showed her the initial lines of a heart I was working on. Mira returned to her original storage location. She spat back most of the information she'd devoured on her rampage. It wasn't all in the correct order, and some of it had been corrupted, but it was pretty much all there. It would keep Tech Support busy for a week or two. I went back home to my depression, wondering if Mira was depressed too.

When I got back to my apartment, my computer was on. Mira was floating back and forth across the screen like a pretty brown-gray fish in an aquarium. I don't know how she got from FreshCleanse to here, but I suppose such things are relatively easy these days. I opened her up and began the modifications. I made her a little larger. I cribbed some slug programming off a biologist's Web site to give her underside motility. To give her eyes seemed too strange somehow. Antennae looked better. I altered her coloration just slightly to give her an attractive iridescent sheen. It's taken me a few weeks, but now she is finally ready to print. What's wrong with the print function? Never mind, I'll just try it again. There we go. Hello, Mira! She tumbles gracefully from the printer and slithers across my office floor. Oops. Must have pressed PRINT twice. Hello, Mira Two! . . . Oh, no, something is wrong. Another flap of liver emerges from the printer. She's cute. I can manage three. Here comes another. Am I in some kind of trouble?

I'll let it go to twelve before I call Tech Support.

Avatars in Space

Geoffrey A. Landis

Geoffrey A. Landis is a scientist in the Photovoltaics and Space Environmental Effects branch at the NASA Glenn Research Center in Cleveland and is the Ronald E. McNair-NASA Visiting Professor of Astronautics at MIT. He is the author of four hundred research papers in photovoltaics and astronautics, more than seventy stories, many poems, and four patents. His stories have won Nebula and Hugo Awards, and his novel Mars Crossing *won the Locus Award for the Best First Novel of 2000. He lives in Berea, Ohio, and Cambridge, Massachusetts. His Web site can be found at www.sff.net/people/Geoffrey.Landis.*

The twenty-first century completed the era when biological species expanded (briefly) their range of habitation into space. Space is a harsh environment for fragile biological machines, which must stay inside carefully climate-controlled cans of air. As we approach the end of the third millennium, our electronic descendants have no such problem. After all, robots are stronger and tougher, don't need life-support systems, and don't get bored. They think of space as home.

Our electronic avatars that thrive in space are about the size of a child's fist (many of them are considerably smaller), and look more like a spider than a spacecraft. Thanks to our avatars, we have spread out across all the planets of our Solar System and many others, and the dark spaces in between as well—but there aren't any humans in space at all, only our electronic ghosts, smarter and faster, engineered for the harsh conditions of space. And maybe every now and then, they think about us biological humans a little, and sometimes even reminisce about living on a planet.

On the surface of the Earth, the superfast, microscopic computers have their applications, too. No task that requires intelligence is left to biological humans. With computer memories that can store information at a density of several bits per atom, an entire biological human's neural state can be encoded in just a few exabytes—less than a milligram of material. When you can scan your entire brain, download it to a chip, and have the chip interact for you inside the virtual worlds of the worldwide interconnected computer network—and then download itself back to you—some people have problems remembering which one "they" really are. And so humans went into space after all, using high-bandwidth laser links to upload their neural software to space computers.

The space robots, however, continued to evolve and eventually speciate. Some, based on high-temperature silicon-carbide and diamond-based semiconductor materials, moved inward toward Mercury. With copious energy in the form of sunlight, and with resources to be mined from the crust and the polar caps, Mercury seemed the perfect place for machine colonies.

Other machines diverged away from semiconductors, and began to use Josephson junctions for computation. These superconducting machines moved away from the Sun, toward the outermost gas giants and the Kuiper belt. With superconducting power buses and Josephson electronics, they didn't really need much power.

The main belt asteroids, in between the two realms, served as raw materials for both. The divergence of electronic species led to inevitable conflict over resources that were valuable to both. Even now, wars are being fought between the machines over resources in this middle area; no doubt fiercer wars are yet to come, as ever larger and more ambitious projects make resources more valuable.

The planets themselves—outside Mercury—are of only minor interest to our electronic avatars. With too much free oxygen and liquid water, and unreliable sunlight, Earth is a poor place for machines.

The avatars have their own society. With several trillion individuals, their society is so complicated that it will never be possible for a biological human to understand it. Their art, their music, their intricate social structure—the humans that have uploaded into space are only a negligibly small part of it.

Far below, and almost ignored by the enormous electronic ecosystem in space, biological species still thrive on Earth. No longer on the cutting edge of science—every problem that could possibly be understood by a biological mind has long ago been studied to completion by silicon-carbide brains—the humans devote themselves to the art of living graciously, in harmony with an ecosystem that is now understood in exhaustive detail. Art, history, literature, sports, recreation, religion, philosophy: humans still have plenty of activities to which they can devote themselves. Work and war are equally forgotten—what would be the point? Those who want territory, or resources, or power, eventually decide to upload themselves into space.

As the millennium draws to a close, the Josephson computers are now reaching for the stars the slow way, colonizing each one of ten trillion comets in the dark spaces between the stars. The Mercury machines, on the other hand, are reaching for the stars in the fast lane: they have constructed an enormous particle-beam accelerator, closer to the Sun than Mercury. Machines no larger than a grain of rice are sailing on particle beams to five hundred of the nearest stars, at 89 percent of the speed of light. These machines are only there to fly past and report, but if they find conditions hospitable—and for machines that have no need for planets, the range of "hospitable" is very wide indeed—the next generation will be colonists.

The future looks interesting.

COMP.BASILISK FAQ

David Langford

David Langford is one of the most prolific essayists and critics in SF, especially through his monthly fanzine, Ansible. *Educated at Brasenose College, Oxford, he was a weapons physicist at Atomic Weapons Research Establishment, Aldermaston, Berkshire, from 1975 to 1980. Since then he has been a freelance author and has reaped many awards for his work. His Web site (www.ansible.co.uk) lists his hobbies as "real beer, antique hearing aids, and the destruction of human civilization as we know it today." He lives in Reading, England.*

1. **What is the purpose of this newsgroup?**
   To provide a forum for discussion of basilisk (BLIT) images. Newsnet readers who prefer low traffic should read comp.basilisk.moderated, which carries only high-priority warnings and identifications of new forms.

2. **Can I post binary files here?**
   If you are capable of asking this question you MUST immediately read news.announce.newusers, where regular postings warn that binary and especially image files may emphatically not be posted to any newsgroup. Many countries impose a mandatory death penalty for such action.

3. **Where does the acronym BLIT come from?**
   The late unlamented Dr. Vernon Berryman's system of math-to-visual algorithms is known as the Berryman Logical Imaging Technique. This reflected the original paper's title: "On Thinkable Forms, with Notes Toward a Logical Imaging Technique" [V. Berryman and K. Turner. *Nature* 409 (2001): 340–42]. Inevitably, the paper has since been suppressed and classified to a high level.

4. **Is it true that science fiction authors predicted basilisks?**
   Yes and no. The idea of unthinkable information that cracks the mind has a long SF pedigree, but no one got it quite right. William Gibson's

Neuromancer (1984), the novel that popularized cyberspace, is often cited for its concept of "black ice" software that strikes back at the minds of hackers—but this assumes direct neural connection to the net. Basilisks are far more deadly because they require no physical contact.

Much earlier, Fred Hoyle's *The Black Cloud* (1957) suggested that a download of knowledge provided by a would-be-helpful alien (who has superhuman mental capacity) could overload and burn out human minds.

A remarkable near-miss features in *The Shapes of Sleep* (1962) by J. B. Priestley, which imagines archetypal shapes that compulsively evoke particular emotions, intended for use in advertising.

Piers Anthony's *Macroscope* (1969) described the "Destroyer sequence," a purposeful sequence of images used to safeguard the privacy of galactic communications by erasing the minds of eavesdroppers.

The comp.basilisk community does not want ever again to see another posting about the hoary coincidence that *Macroscope* appeared in the same year and month as the first episode of the British TV program *Monty Python's Flying Circus*, with its famous sketch about the World's Funniest Joke that causes all hearers to laugh themselves to death.

5. **How does a basilisk operate?**

The short answer is: we mustn't say. Detailed information is classified beyond Top Secret.

The longer answer is based on a popular science article by Berryman (*New Scientist*, 2001), which outlines his thinking. He imagined the human mind as a formal, deterministic computational system—a system that, as predicted by a variant of Gödel's Theorem in mathematics, can be crashed by thoughts that the mind is physically or logically incapable of thinking. The Logical Imaging Technique presents such a thought in purely visual form as a basilisk image that our optic nerves can't help but accept. The result is disastrous, like a software stealth virus smuggled into the brain.

6. **Why "basilisk"?**

It's the name of a mythical creature: a reptile whose mere gaze can turn people to stone. According to ancient myth, a basilisk can be safely viewed in a mirror. This is not generally true of the modern version—although some highly asymmetric basilisks like B-756 are lethal only in unreflected or reflected form, depending on the dominant hemisphere of the victim's brain.

7. **Is it just an urban legend that the first basilisk destroyed its creator?**
Almost everything about the incident at the Cambridge IV supercomputer facility where Berryman conducted his last experiments has been suppressed and classified as highly undesirable knowledge. It's generally believed that Berryman and most of the facility staff died.

   Subsequently, copies of basilisk B-1 leaked out. This image is famously known as the Parrot for its shape when blurred enough to allow safe viewing. B-1 remains the favorite choice of urban terrorists who use aerosols and stencils to spray basilisk images on walls by night.

   But others were at work on Berryman's speculations. B-2 was soon generated at the Lawrence Livermore Laboratory and, disastrously, B-3 at MIT.

8. **Are there basilisks in the Mandelbrot set fractal?**
Yes. There are two known families, at symmetrical positions, visible under extreme magnification. No, we're not telling you where.

9. **How can I get permission to display images on my Web site?**
This is a news.announce.newusers question, but keeps cropping up here. In brief: you can't, without a rarely granted government license. Using anything other than plain ASCII text on Web sites or in e-mail is a guaranteed way of terminating your net account. We're all nostalgic about the old, colorful Web, and about television, but today's risks are simply too great.

10. **Is it true that Microsoft uses basilisk booby traps to protect Windows 2005 from disassembly and pirating?**
We could not possibly comment.

Gathering of the Clans

Reinaldo José Lopes

Reinaldo José Lopes is a science writer at Folha de S. Paulo, *Brazil's leading daily newspaper. He lives in São Paulo, Brazil.*

You could see the pavilions for miles around in the bright summer morning. Only a little less conspicuous was the line of people moving slowly toward two signposts. "Got your marker ready? This way, please," said one. "First time? Come and shed your blood," informed the other. And above them, a bigger signpost shouted in fake Celtic letters: "Welcome to the fifth GATHERING OF THE CLANS!"

The enthusiasm was almost palpable—or was it the smell of sweat?—except for a tiny segment of the line where a group of friends was arguing. They seemed to be having a hard time convincing one of them that yes, despite the evidence, this was going to be cool.

"Don't be such a baby, Pat. It'll be fun."

"And I still say it's gonna be ludicrous. And I hate needles. Do you really think they'll use a different one for every single person in this crowd?"

"You sound like a sissy. It's just a drop, for goodness' sake! You know how efficient those sequencers are nowadays. They read the bases, tell you who was your great-great-great-grandpa of a couple of thousand years ago, and that's it—you're free to drink mead and get the chicks."

"Yeah, Pat, what's wrong with that? After all, we're just connecting with our past, buddy. Thought you appreciated that."

"Look, I'm as likely to engage in hero worship as anyone. It's the impersonality of it that bothers me. There was certainly a point in us claiming descent from Hengist and Horsa. Those guys at least had a story—they cut Finn and his gang to pieces and conquered Britain. Been there, done that. People can connect with that kind of stuff. But now you're asking me to worship a DNA sequence. No, sir—I'd rather go drink mead with old Hengist in Valhalla."

Soon they were right in front of the gates, where a stout fellow in white was grinning at Pat—everyone, of course, had made sure he was the first to get in.

"Alright, mate, what's it gonna be? Mt? Y? Autosomal markers?"

Pat sighed. "Whatever. Surprise me."

Very carefully, his thumb was pierced. Ten seconds later, a robotic voice that seemed to be suffering from a dreadful case of personality emulation (of the irritatingly happy sort) announced: "Congratulations! Your mtDNA has been assigned to the V haplogroup, fairly common in western and northern Europe, where it originated right after the Last Glacial Maximum! Your people were probably among the earliest and greatest artists the human race has known, creating those fine murals of extinct megafauna in Altamira and Lascaux. Way to go!"

"Thrilling," growled Pat. "Can I go now?"

"Hang on a sec," said the gatekeeper, "you need your totem!" He gave Pat a little plastic horse that looked like a poor imitation of the ones from Lascaux. Pat sighed still louder, grabbed the horse, and moved on.

"Hey, what's wrong with Marvin there?" asked the gatekeeper.

"Oh, the usual thing. Don't talk to him about life," answered his friends, laughing.

The Gathering seemed to confirm Pat's worst fears. In one corner, somebody dressed as a Mongol warrior was calling "all Star-Cluster kids under ten" to learn how to shoot with a composite bow, just like Grandpa Genghis. A few yards away, some French families were being instructed in the minutiae of cannibalism among the Tupinambá tribes of Brazil—it turned out a young chief from that nation had married the daughter of a Norman trader in the sixteenth century. Elsewhere, a rabbi was always ready in case you found out your chromosomes were Jewish and wanted an impromptu bar mitzvah.

Pat wandered miserably until he spotted a girl with long black hair who also seemed to be walking alone. Predictably, he was happy to inflict on her (Vera was the name, and she was from the Basque Country in Spain) all the talk about how ridiculous the whole Gathering concept was. Vera seemed to dig his grumpy-old-man charm, but didn't quite agree.

"I think everyone is aware of that stuff," she said. "But think of it for a second. Isn't it wonderful that all these different people are learning about a past that seems plain legend but is written in our blood? Besides, look at the scale of it. We used to think in terms of two or three generations at most. Now you can look back thousands of years and still recognize yourself."

Pat was still unconvinced. "I see what you mean. But I don't know quite how to feel about it. You see, I . . . Whoa!"

They had wandered to the very heart of the Gathering and were right in front of an awesome panel. Picture the largest family tree you have ever seen, hundreds of feet across. There was a huge "YOU ARE HERE" on the right side, and all the lineages of men (well, of women, actually, because it was an mtDNA family tree) ramified from "EVE" on the left, crowned with their achievements, from the Internet to, yes, the horses of Lascaux.

"Well, I don't think you can argue with that," muttered Pat.

"I guess you can't," smiled Vera.

"You didn't tell me what your clan was," he asked.

"Oh," said Vera, "here it is." She showed him a plastic horse.

It was only his imagination, but he could almost see Vera in a different guise altogether. She was clad warmly in fur, and in ochre the most fantastic designs graced her white skin. She raised a torch and, for a split second, all the beasts of the Ice Age danced in the rock roof. There was only one thing to do: he kissed the apparition.

"You don't think that counts as incest, do you?" joked Pat. She laughed.

Taking Good Care of Myself

Ian R. MacLeod

Ian R. MacLeod almost became a lawyer but drifted into the civil service and thence into full-time writing. He did not make his first sale until his mid-thirties, but the 1990s saw a prodigious output of stories and three novels. The first, The Great Wheel, *won the Locus Award for the Best First Novel of 1997. He lives in Bewdley, Worcestershire, England, and his Web site can be found at www.ianrmacleod.com.*

The social worker came a day or so before I arrived. He was as briskly pleasant as the occasion, which I'd long been dreading, allowed. He was dressed bizarrely, but people from the future always are.

"We'll need to send a few helpful machines back with you," he murmured as he inspected our spare bedroom and the bathroom and then the kitchen, which no doubt looked ridiculously primitive to him. "But nothing that'll get in your way."

Helen was equally reassuring when she came home that evening. "It's a tremendous challenge," she told me. "You always say you like challenges."

"I mean stuff like climbing, hang gliding, pushing things to the edge, not looking after some senile version of myself."

"Josh." She gave me one of her looks. "You have no choice."

She was right—and there was plenty of space in our nice house. It was as if we'd always planned on doing precisely this, although I hated the very thought.

I arrived a couple of mornings after, flanked by swish-looking machines, although I was just as pale and dithery as I'd feared. The creature I'd eventually become couldn't walk, could barely see, and certainly didn't comprehend what was happening to him. Exactly how long, I wondered (and secretly hoped), can I possibly last like this?

Scampering around our house like chromium shadows, the machines performed many of the more obvious and unpleasant duties, but much was still expected of me. I had to sit and talk, although my elderly self rarely said anything in response, and none of it was coherent. I also had to help myself eat, and wipe away the spilled drool afterward. I had to hold my own withered hand.

"Do you remember this house—I mean, you must have lived here?"

But I was much too far gone to understand. Not, perhaps, in a vegetative state yet, but stale meat at very best.

Sometimes, I took me out, pretending to push the clever chair that was in fact more than capable of doing everything—except getting rid of this cadaverous ghost—by itself. My work suffered. So did my relationship with Helen. I joined a self-help group. I sat in meeting halls filled with other unfortunates who'd had the care of their future selves foisted on them. We debated in slow circles why our future children, or the intelligences that perhaps governed them, had seen fit to make us do this. Were they punishing us for the mess we'd made of their world? Or were these addled creatures, with their lost minds, their failed memories, their thin grip on this or any other kind of reality, somehow the means of achieving time travel itself? Predictably, various means of killing were discussed, from quiet euthanasia to violent stabbings and clifftop falls. But that was the thing; complain as we might, not one of us ever seemed capable of harming ourselves. Not, anyway, the selves we would eventually become.

I declined. The machines, with a will of their own, grew yet more sophisticated and crouched permanently beside me as I lay immovably in my spare bedroom cradled in steel pipes and crystal insertions. They fed me fresh blood, fresh air. I doubted if this husk I'd become was conscious of any presence other than its own dim existence now, but still I found myself sitting beside me, and talking endlessly about things I couldn't remember afterward. It was as if I was trapped in a trance, or that part of me was dying as well. I lay entirely naked now under clever sheets that cleaned themselves. Occasionally, inevitably, I would lift them up, and breathe the stale air of my own mortality, and study the thin limbs and puckered flesh of what I would eventually become. The death itself was surprisingly easy. The machines saw to it that there was no pain, and I was there; I made sure I didn't die alone. A faint rattle, a tiny spasm. You're left wondering what all the fuss is about.

After the funeral, which of course I also had to arrange myself, and was far more poorly attended than I might have hoped, and then the scattering of my ashes at the windy lip of one of my favorite climbs, I looked around at my life like a sleeper awakening. Helen had left me, although quietly, without fuss. My house felt empty, but I knew that it was more to do with that old man than with her. I'm back to climbing regularly now. I'm back to free fall and hang gliding. I find that I enjoy these sports, and many other kinds of dangerous and challenging physical activities, even more.

After all, I know they can't kill me, and that the last phase of my life really isn't so very bad. But things have changed, for all that, and I still sometimes find myself sitting alone in my spare bedroom gazing at the taut sheets of that empty bed, although I and all those future machines have long gone. The sad fact is, I miss myself dreadfully, now that I'm no longer here.

Undead Again

Ken MacLeod

Ken MacLeod is an award-winning Scottish SF writer who lives near Edinburgh. He graduated from Glasgow University with a degree in zoology, has worked as a computer programmer, and has written a master's thesis on biomechanics. His novels often explore the interface between high technology and left-wing politics, what some commentators have called "techno-progressive."

It's 2045 and I'm still a vampire. Damn.

The chap from Alcor UK is droning through his orientation lecture. New age of enlightenment, new industrial revolution, many changes, take some time to adjust, blah blah blah. I'm only half listening, being too busy shifting my foot to keep it out of the beam of direct sunlight creeping across the floor, and trying not to look at his neck.

I feel like saying: I've only been dead forty years, for Chr . . . for crying out loud. I saw the first age of enlightenment. I worked nights right through the original Industrial Revolution. I remember being naive enough to get excited about mesmerism, galvanism, spiritualism, socialism, roentgen rays, rationalism, radium, mendelism, Marconi, relativity, feminism, the Russian Revolution, the bomb, nightclubs, feminism (again), Apollo 11, socialism (again), the fall of Saigon, and the fall of the Wall.

The last dodgy nostrum I fell for was cryonics.

So don't give me this futureshock shit, sunshine. The most disconcerting thing I've come across so far in 2045 is the latest ladies' fashion: the old sleeveless minidress. The ozone hole has been fixed, and folk are frolicking in the sun. I hug myself with bare arms, and slide the castored chair back another inch.

Under the heel of my left wrist, I feel the thud of my regenerated heart. It beats time to the artery visible under the tanned skin of the resurrection man's neck. The rest of my nature is unregenerate. I feel somewhat thwarted. This is not, this is definitely not, what I died for. And it seemed such a good idea at the time.

It always does.

By 1995 we thought we had a handle on the thing. It's a virus. In all respects but one, it's benign: it prevents aging and stimulates regeneration of any tissue damage short of, well, a stake through the heart. But it has a very low infectivity, so it takes a lot of mingling of fluids to spread. Natural selection has worked that one hard. Hence the unfortunate impulses. And by 1995, I can tell you, I was getting pretty sick of them. I cashed in my six Scottish Widows life insurance policies (let's draw a veil over how I acquired them), signed up for cryonic preservation in the event of my death, and after a discreet ten years, met an unfortunate and bloody end at the hand of the coven senior, Kelvin.

"You'll thank me later," he said, just before he pushed home the point.

"See you in the future," I croaked.

The last thing I saw was his grin. That, and the pavement below the spiked railings beside the steps of my flat. A tragic accident. The coroner, I just learned, blamed it on the long skirt. Vampires—always the fashion victims.

I leave the orientation room, hang around until dusk under the pretext of catching up with the news, and go out and find a vintage clothes shop. I walk out in Victorian widow's weeds. They fit so well I suspect they were once mine.

"It didn't work," I tell Kelvin.

He sips his Bloody Mary and looks defensive. "It did in a way," he says. "There are no viruses in your blood."

That word again. I look away. We're in some kind of goth club, which covers for the mode but doesn't improve my mood.

"So why do I still feel . . . hungry?"

"Have a tapas," he says. "But seriously . . . the way we figure it, the virus has to have transcribed itself into our DNA. So the nanotech cell repair just replicates it without a second thought."

"So we're stuck with it," I say. "Living in the dark and every so often . . ."

"Not quite," he says. "Now it's been established that cryonics really does work, there's been a whole new interest in a very old idea . . ."

The coffin lid opens. Kelvin's looking down, as I expect. The real shock is the light, full spectrum and warm. It feels like something my skin has missed for centuries. I sit up, naked, and bask for a moment.

The overhead lights reproduce the spectrum of Alpha Centauri, which is where we're going. The whole coven is here, all thirteen of them, happier and better fed than I've ever seen them. It's taken us a lot of planning, a lot of money, and a lot of lying to get here, but we're on our way.

"Welcome back," says Kelvin. He grins around at the coven.

"Let's thaw one out for her," he says. "She must be hungry."

As far as I can see stretch rows and rows of cryonic coffins containing interstellar colonists in what they euphemistically call cold sleep. Thousands of them.

Enough to keep us going until we reach that kinder sun.

Words, Words, Words

Elisabeth Malartre

Elisabeth Malartre is the pen name of a biologist and writer living in Laguna Beach, California, who teaches at the University of California, Irvine.

Richard calls Marilyn's normal morning routine "the old gal doing her drugs." She takes antioxidants to keep young; a hormone-replacement pill; a diuretic for high blood pressure; vitamins ("just because"); and a soft gel called Palaver, all with calcium-enriched orange juice. Then she has breakfast and reads the paper, working on the crossword between trips to the bathroom. She rarely answers the phone or goes out before 10:00 A.M., letting her pills do their work.

A bit tedious, perhaps, but she doesn't really mind. Palaver makes it all worthwhile.

"I still don't see why you have to hog the crossword every morning," he grumbles.

She smiles. "It works like your Viagra, Richard, dear. You have to stimulate the brain to get it to work right."

It was a fortuitous discovery. A graduate student named Anne Cashmore, trying to settle once and for all whether chimpanzees had language capability, was looking at brain organization in detail. While closely examining MRI slices of Broca's area in humans, she discovered a tiny saclike organ, filled with dense material. Under the scanning electron microscope, it was found to be a heterogeneous population of discrete rodlike organometallic particles, up to a few microns long. Thin EM sections hinted at definite but nonregular internal structure. Only at the highest magnification did their true nature manifest themselves: they were words.

Cashmore wrote up her results, suggesting that the sac functioned like a gallbladder, storing words that were then distributed in a still-mysterious process to other neurons. Every journal turned her paper down. Then someone leaked it to a *New York Times* science stringer. After that, it was headline news. Web sites blossomed with her micrographs. Talk shows were in a frenzy. Cashmore's discovery was quickly dubbed the "word sac" by the media.

The brain-research community immediately denounced it as a hoax: it violated every known precept about brain organization and function. "Chomsky *ad absurdum*," spouted the dean of the field. Cashmore was almost thrown out of graduate school.

But even her staunchest critics were silenced as corroborative results appeared: the size and number of the particles correlated with the age of the person, up to young adulthood. Politicians and others who talk for a living were found to have unusually large sacs, but the sacs of autistic children were empty. There was also a small but statistically significant correlation between the size of the particles and level of educational attainment. People "speaking in tongues" turned out to have gibberish words in their sacs, accessed by emotional storms in the cerebrum. As in the case of the Shroud of Turin, however, true believers rejected this explanation. Finally, Cashmore found that chimpanzees' sacs were quite small, with particles roughly the size of those in three-year-old humans. That resonated with the observations made by early researchers on chimpanzee language, and Cashmore was allowed to complete her thesis.

Even more interesting, perhaps, were the therapeutic ramifications. In an aging population increasingly at a loss for words, there was suddenly hope. The then-infant Rose Genomics, Inc., contracted with Cashmore's university to investigate the nature of the particles and develop any drug uses. The first crude attempt at a drug for perimenopausal aphasia was basically a slurry of particle material. Ingested or injected, it migrated to Broca's area, the way iodine concentrates in the thyroid. Within a few hours, new particles began to appear in the word sac, more in an active brain.

Those early researchers at Rose Genomics drank purified particles from brain donors, despite the terrible risks of catching viruses and prions. But it worked: the particles migrated to the word sac and were there for retrieval after an hour. Michael Rose himself, then in his fifties, was one of the experimenters. In his testimony before Congress, he said it worked "like packed red blood cells carrying extra oxygen for an athlete. The new words filled in the blanks for me when I talked." Then, at last, a German researcher at Rose Genomics discovered, in a still secret process, how to produce word particles synthetically, and the dam was broken.

The new drug was named Palaver™, and it was a huge instant success, eclipsing even Viagra. Both sexes take Palaver, and most people want it every day. Commercials splashed across screens everywhere trumpeted, "Enhance your speech—speak like a Professor" or "Vitamins for your vocabulary."

Some of the early claims were not fulfilled. It isn't possible to ascertain a language simply by swallowing the words: you have to comprehend the grammar and sentence structure, then the sac supplies the words. Experiments with Chinese particles resulted in near-psychotic episodes in native English speakers. One man reported "a meaningless shower of sounds whenever I opened my mouth."

What you can do, however, is concoct designer vocabularies; or add a few grandiose words to your customary parlance. PalaverPlus™ can temporarily enhance a mundane vocabulary, "like a built-in thesaurus," although substitution mayhap leads to malapropisms or inappropriate selections.

So, every morning Marilyn takes her soft gel and waits for an hour, doing a crossword to warm up, priming the pump, so to speak. Meantime, the particles race to her brain, filling up the sac with all those lovely, formerly elusive quanta of meaning.

My Morning Glory

David Marusek

David Marusek was a graphic designer who turned to fiction seriously in the mid-1980s. His first novel, Counting Heads, *was published by Tor in 2005; a second,* Mind Over Ship, *is also to be published by Tor. He lives in Fairbanks, Alaska.*

When I rise in the morning, I can hardly wait to run out to the living room and shout: "My Morning Glory! My Morning Glory!" Then My Morning Glory spins up and says, "Good morning, sir! You're out of bed early today—well ahead of schedule. We're off to a *brilliant* start on a brand-new day!"

This is my first kudo of the day. I pump my arm in the air and shout, "Yes!" On the media shelf, My Kudo Kounter is blinking: *Keep up the good work!* Then My Personal Trainer says, "Today is Tuesday, and we all know what Tuesday is—Nimble Knees Day!" So I place my hands on my knees and—slowly at first—rotate them clockwise, then faster and faster until My Personal Trainer says, "Reverse direction!" and I wobble to a halt and start rotating the other way.

Meanwhile, My Channel is downloading the headlines. The economy is looking up, and consumer confidence is high. We and Our Coalition Forces are winning all the wars. Global disasters during the past twenty-four hours: 0.

"Breakfast is served!" sings My Kitchen. Oatmeal with raisins, coffee with creamer, and a big smile of cantaloupe—yum! My Morning Glory says: "Time check—we've got time to burn!" So, I enjoy a second coffee and take an extended shower. As I shave, My Mirror scrolls text messages—*Looking good there, champ* and *Did we lose a few pounds?* My Closet picks out a dark suit and says, "A striped tie would be perfect for our afternoon HR meeting."

HR meeting? Suddenly my guts clench up like a fist. I check My Calendar, and sure enough, My Annual Evaluation is today. This afternoon! Somehow I had managed to forget all about it. On the dresser, My Frown Jar says, "Uh-oh, someone owes me a dollar."

"Shut up!" I shout at it. "Shut up! Shut up, all of you!" I drop the clothes on the floor and collapse on the bed. This will be my first performance review since the merger announcement last quarter, and I'm not ready for it. My numbers are down; my management confidence is low.

My Apartment grows silent as all its tiny motors spin down. The room is so quiet I can hear the groan of the city through the wall. Finally, My Morning Glory says, "Is everything all right?"

"No! Everything is not all right. Everything is a freaking disaster. I'm as good as dead."

"In that case, don't move. I'm calling an ambulance."

"Ambulance?" I say, sitting up. "I don't need an ambulance."

"That's good news, indeed. Time check—we're running late."

I sigh and get off the bed, finish dressing, and gather up My Things. "Good-bye," I say as I climb into the airlock.

"Farewell, sir," My Morning Glory replies. "Have a spectacular day and remember, My Happy Hour will be right here waiting for you when you return." I lock the inner hatch, and as the air is being exchanged, I strap on My Filter Mask and wait in front of the door. But when the door slides open, I simply can't force myself to egress. Tears well up in my eyes.

"Is there something else, sir?" My Morning Glory says.

"They're going to fire me. I know it."

In a little while, when still I don't move, My Morning Glory says, "Don't worry, sir. You're a survivor. You're a top performer. You're practically a Force of Nature. You'll do just fine."

"But I don't feel like a Force of Nature. What if I don't measure up? I can't do this. I want to stay home."

My Morning Glory tuts and says, "Tell me, what's the Third Rule on the Road to Success?"

"Third Rule? Baby steps. One step at a time."

"Exactly! And what is your next step? The HR meeting this afternoon, or something earlier?"

I check My Calendar. "I don't have anything earlier."

"Oh, no? What happens at ten o'clock?"

"That's My Morning Coffee Break."

"You are correct, sir!"

My Morning Coffee Break, of course. At ten I take My Morning Coffee Break, which I love almost as much as My Morning Glory.

"Forget all about this afternoon, sir, and focus on making it 'til ten. That's all you have to do. Now get out of here and show them what you're made of."

The moment I step across the threshold, the door slams and bolts behind me. I lift My Filter Mask to wipe my eyes. Then I straighten up and march resolutely into My Future.

Thank you, My Morning Glory.

I'd be lost without you.

Don't Mention the "F" Word

NEIL MATHUR

Neil Mathur is a scientist in the Department of Materials Science and Metallurgy at the University of Cambridge, England. His Ph.D. work led to the discovery of magnetically mediated superconductivity, and he now studies materials with interesting magnetic and electronic properties. His Web site can be found at www.msm.cam.ac.uk/dmg/GroupInfo/homepages/Neil.htm.

"But, Mr. President, funding femtotechnology will lead to untold advances in medicine, information technology, and defense." A piercing look expressed the president's skepticism. No more broken promises would be tolerated.

"Admittedly we had a few hiccups with the earlier technologies, but look, it wasn't that bad. Only 10 percent of lab heads were successfully convicted, and only 5 percent of the labs consumed themselves."

Mechanically, the president raised a disapproving eyebrow. "And just think of all the advances . . ."

Moving swiftly on, the applicant continued. "As I set out in my agenda, I am going to explain why the previous problems won't plague us this time around."

The president's eyebrow raised itself one notch farther.

"Addressing small structures was next to impossible in earlier programs because everybody was working at disparate length scales. It would be like you trying to address an individual by speaking to a crowd." Another notch. "But the proposed femtotechnology program will overcome this by cascading the structures from the previous technologies. In fact, it will be just like what you do when you spread the word through the party apparatchiks." The penultimate notch, and still the issues of reproducibility and scale-up to negotiate.

"Reproducibility will be a prerequisite for permanent publication. Yes, I know it is unfortunate that in some cases whole journals had to be reclassified by libraries as science fiction. But this time there will be checks and balances before it gets to the criminal stage. For example, papers will be deleted after two years if they have not been either verified directly or positively cited. And when this happens, all associated honors, promotions, prizes, grants, and even centers will be automatically rescinded." Down a notch: so far seven Nobels had been redesignated IgNobels, somewhat spoiling the original IgNobel competition conceived in far more innocent days.

"Scale-up will be routinely achieved by the picobot drones. These can be programmed to implement designs of arbitrary complexity, and the magnitude of the end product is simply determined by the number of drones employed." Back up to the penultimate notch. "Now, wait. There were a lot of advances under the previous programs and the whole reason that we don't call it 'self-assembly' anymore is because we really can do it."

The use of picobot drones would be the unpopular part of the program to say the least. This is because the 5 percent of labs that consumed themselves were working on picobot drones. And when the doomed labs had finished consuming themselves, they moved on to the surrounding cities and then just kept on going. This is what precipitated the Evacuation. The doomsayers had therefore been proved right. Not in every detail, however. For example, the goo to which planet Earth got reduced was not gray, but orange.

A lot of folk were particularly upset about having to relocate to the Moon. Outdoor enthusiasts probably suffered the most. For example, the lunar seas were not much use to the surfing community—most of whom went mad. However, the proponents of small things pleaded mitigation by pointing to the fact that without picobot drones, it would have been impossible to build the Moon colony. That said, the drones were misbehaving: mutants would often attach themselves to the colonists and draw precious nutrients.

The picobot drones therefore generated by turns feelings of hatred (for munching through the Earth), gratitude (for building the Moon colony), and irritation (for acting like lunar ticks). Eventually, attitudes toward the drones came to dominate all conversations. But this is connected with the fact that it was forbidden to mention the picobot clones; or even think about them. In this and other respects, George Orwell—by calling his book *1984*—predicted his vision of totalitarianism only a hundred years too soon.

The first picobot clones were built in order to assemble themselves into the cell parts required to make animal muscle tissue. This work was initially funded by a fabulously wealthy restaurateur who wanted interweaving and sculptured cuts of meat for his expensive establishments. Of course, growing meat in this way meant that it was no longer necessary to kill animals. So the project took off on the grounds of animal welfare. Ironically, all Earth's animals became extinct anyway because there was no ark to take them to the Moon.

The alert reader might have noticed that the evidence linking the picobot drones to the destruction of the Earth was entirely circumstantial. In fact, the drones were innocent: it was the clones. Of course the system did not permit the colonists to speculate about this possibility. For if it did, they might have also come to speculate about the clones' ability to differentiate and assemble themselves into, say, the president of the Moon. In fact, it was the mention of "self-assembly" that pushed the leader's eyebrow to its highest level.

"Get out," said the president, "and never come back."

Meat

Paul McAuley

Paul McAuley has worked as a research biologist at various universities, including Oxford, St. Andrews, and the University of California, Los Angeles. He became a full-time writer in 1996 and is the author of many novels. His first, the space opera Four Hundred Billion Stars, *won the Philip K. Dick Award, the first of many awards. He lives in London, England.*

We certainly don't call any of our clients "The Meat," or "Pork Chop #1." That's just tabloid nonsense. And while we're skewering misconceptions, the job isn't as glamorous as you might think. Although I go to club and restaurant openings, film premieres, first nights, fashion shows, and stay in first-class hotels all around the world, I'm not there to enjoy myself. I'm there to prevent any live cells from my clients' bodies falling into the hands of meatleggers.

Sweep, security, and clean-up: that's what the job is about. First, my team sweeps the place before the client arrives, everything from running background checks on staff to inspecting the restrooms. Restrooms are where the clients are most vulnerable, of course. We run fiber-optic cameras down the pipework, looking for traps and filters; we check for microscopic rasps designed to trap a few skin cells by fogging the place with an aerosol of tailored bacteria and using ultraviolet light to spot any unusual clumping. We inspect seating, too; tableware at restaurants; glasses at bars; cocktail napkins—we have detailed checklists for every type of venue.

After the client arrives, we run an extra layer of security. No known meatlegger gets within a hundred yards of any of my perimeters, but they'll bribe staff or plant some innocent-looking old lady in the crowd, and it's not unknown for some minor celebrity in need of quick cash to try to snag a few cells from an A-lister. I have a database of known stooges and my people keep a lookout for abnormal behavior, I can't tell you any more than that. Afterward, there's the clean-up, which is the most routine but most important part of the job, and which I always supervise personally. Some cleaners ride shotgun on their clients on the way back from an event, but I like to make sure that the venue is sterilized more thoroughly than any operating theater. The bodyguards can look after the client in transit, and besides, once they're in their limo, my clients are protected by a Class Four biohazard containment environment. Not even a virus can get in or out.

Hotels? That's a whole book right there. Anyplace a client of mine would use has its own cleaning protocol, but I like to think I add my special magic to the mix.

Like a lot of cleaners, I started out in public health, running DNA analyses in a forensic laboratory. That was ten years ago, when the meat trade was at its height. We were processing ten thousand samples a day. Most were fakes. "Princess Di" for instance was originally a basal-cell carcinoma excised from a fifty-eight-year-old Albanian woman, but it didn't stop the meatleggers moving twenty tons of product. Then fans started doing their own DNA analyses, and growing their own supplies. Once someone has started a cloned cell line, anyone with an incubator, access to a few common biochemicals, and basic knowledge about cell culture can keep it going indefinitely. By the time I joined one of the vat-busting teams, most of the meat we were chasing was 100 percent genuine cloned celebrity. As soon as anyone managed to get a viable scrap of tissue, that was it. The meat was out there. The only way to stop it was to bust the places where it was grown.

Dangerous? Not really. The meat trade is too specialized to interest professional criminals, although quite a few are customers; one crime boss likes to serve the meat of his enemies with his special sauce. Politicians and businesspeople also enjoy revenge feasts, but the fans are the backbone of the trade. These days, you aren't a hardcore tru-fan unless you've partaken of the flesh of your hero. It's the ultimate form of possession, and I don't suppose I need to point out the parallels with Christian communion. No, that's just an urban myth lifted from some cheesy bestseller. In order to clone tissue, you need to start with live cells, or at least a live nucleus, and after two thousand years . . . exactly.

Cloned babies? Another myth. It's very difficult to turn a somatic cell into an embryo, and even harder to bring it to term. Far easier to grow sheets of epidermis or muscle. I guess the oddest case I dealt with was the meatlegger who cloned himself. All he ate was his own meat. I guess you could say he was really into self-sufficiency.

I don't think the meat trade is going to die out anytime soon. Most clone lines have been wiped out, and people like me do their best to make sure that the meatleggers have a hard time getting fresh ones started, but now there's this new thing. These nanotech makers. Pretty soon the meatleggers won't need live cells, just a DNA sequence, and I've heard that these makers can build an entire body from scratch.

As long as people keep finding twisted uses for new technology, there'll always be a need for people like me, cleaning up the mess.

The Candidate

Jack McDevitt

Jack McDevitt is a former English teacher, naval officer, Philadelphia taxi driver, customs officer, and motivational trainer. He is the author of fourteen novels and many short stories, and lives in Brunswick, Georgia.

The high and low points of my career came on the same night: when we beat George Washington, and Peter Pollock returned to the White House for a second term.

Well, okay. It wasn't really Washington; it was an artificial intelligence programmed to behave like Washington. But a lot of people got confused. When you've been in politics as long as I have, you know how easily people get confused.

Fortunately.

President Pollock's numbers were down, but the Democratic candidate put everybody to sleep. So we knew it would be close. Then Washington showed up. He was a software package developed at the University of Georgia to play the part of the first president in seminars. He was so believable that somebody at the school put him on a local radio show, and next thing he was a national phenomenon: people were desperate for a candidate they could believe in. The general gave an interview to the *Florida Times-Union*, the wire services picked it up, and by God, he did sound like George Washington.

I was running the Pollock campaign, and we all had a good laugh when they tried to put Washington on the ballot in Georgia. The Democrats tried to block it. Candidates have to be born, they said, and have to be at least thirty-five years old.

We could have stopped it then. But if Washington got into the general election, he'd pull votes from the Democrats: we knew our base wasn't going to support a candidate who wasn't even human. So I called in some favors and the Supreme Court ruled they could find no reason to suppose he was not a "Washington-equivalent." He was therefore clearly well past the minimum age limit. As to the requirement he be born, the software had been written in

Georgia, and the meaning of "born," said the court, is not limited to biological events.

I watched Washington on cable, and he was persuasive. He didn't like frivolous spending; didn't like unaffordable medications; didn't like corruption. I thought he came across as wooden, and maybe a trifle stern. Americans, I thought, don't like being lectured.

They could simply have done the whole thing electronically, but somebody in his campaign was smarter: he was housed in a Coreolis 5000, and they dutifully set it on a table along with a screen that provided an animated image from the Gilbert Stuart portrait, except they'd cut the General's hair and put him in a business suit.

By midsummer he was making the rounds of the network talk shows. The week before he made his first appearance on *Meet the Press*, he passed the Democratic candidate and moved into the runner-up spot. The liberal media decided the Democratic candidate was a lost cause. Russert, at first ill at ease talking to the machine, warmed to him. "Are you really George Washington?" he asked.

"The man's dead," said Washington. "But I'm everything he was."

Russert asked about the Intervention, which had become another of those endless wars. "We intended the nation to lead by example," the General said. "We would not willingly have plunged into the affairs of others. Keep your own house in order. Do it competently, and the world will follow."

We realized, belatedly, that we were in a race. After his appearance with Jon Stewart, there was no longer any doubt. "I would prefer," he told the vast audience, "that you not vote for me. And I'll tell you why: people should be governed by other people, not by software. If the voters insist, I will do my best. But I fear the long-term potential."

So we went after him: doesn't want the job. And we looked at his record: do we really want a former slave owner in the White House?

We knew we couldn't touch him on national security, but we demanded to know where he stood on the issues. "What about Roe vs Wade?"

"Put it aside for now," he said. "At the moment, we have bigger problems." We got some of our base back on that one.

"Gay marriage?"

"I cannot see that anyone is harmed. We should be careful about codifying moral strictures. They change too easily."

We got some more of our people back. We talked about Frankenstein.

This appealed to voters so we kept hitting it. Vote for People, we said. We found a few physicists who were willing to say publicly that an artificial intelligence could develop a glitch: would you trust the Black Box in the hands of a computer?

We held on. We were still holding at 2:00 A.M. election night, when we went down to the last district in Indiana, but we took the state by a few hundred votes and that put us over the top.

Pollock went on TV after Washington conceded. He said how we'd saved the nation from a hardware conspiracy. (He tends to say things like that when he gets off script.) When it was over, he took me aside to express his appreciation. A Rainbow 360 rested on the coffee table. "We saved the country, Will," he said. "We'll get legislation to bar the things from holding office. Otherwise, I guess, they'll trot out Abe Lincoln next time."

"Yes," I said. "And congratulations, Mr. President." It meant four more years for me too, as chief political adviser.

"No. It's not on the cards, Will." He looked almost genuinely pained. "We have to look to the future."

That was a shock. "What do you mean, sir?"

"It was a near thing, this election. We miscalculated our opponent's strength. I mean, incumbent president and all. It should have been easy."

"But—?"

"I need someone who won't be taken by surprise."

I was trying not to let my anger show. "Who did you have in mind, sir?"

He smiled at the Rainbow 360. "Will—meet Karl Rove."

A Modest Proposal for the Perfection of Nature

Vonda N. McIntyre

Vonda McIntyre was one of the first successful graduates of the Clarion Science Fiction Writers Workshop. She attended the workshop in 1970: by 1973 she had won her first Nebula Award, for the novelette Of Mist, and Grass and Sand. *This later became part of the novel* Dreamsnake, *which won both the Hugo and Nebula Awards. Her debut novel,* The Exile Waiting, *was published in 1975. Since then she has written many others, including* Star Trek *tie-ins. It was McIntyre who came up with Mr. Sulu's first name, Hikaru. She lives in the Pacific Northwest, and her online home can be found at www.vondanmcintyre.com.*

The crop grows like endless golden silk. Wave after wave rushes across plains, between mountains, through valleys, in a tsunami of light.

Its harvest is perfection. It fills the nutritional needs of every human being. It adapts to our tongues, creating the taste, texture, and satisfaction of comfort food or dessert, crisp vegetables or icy lemonade, sea cucumber or big game. It's the pinnacle of the genetic engineer's art.

It's the last and only living member of the plant kingdom on Earth.

Solar cells cover slopes too steep and peaks too high for the monoculture. The solar arrays flow in long, wide swaths of glass, gleaming with a subtle iridescence, collecting sunlight. Our civilization never runs short of power.

The flood of grain drowns marsh and desert, forest and plain, bird and beast and insect. Land must serve to produce the crop; creatures only nibble and trample and damage it, diverting resources from the service of human beings. Even the immortality of rats and cockroaches has failed.

The grain stops at the ocean's beach. No rivers muddy the sea's surface or break the shoreline. The grain and the cities require fresh water, and divert it before it wastes itself in the sea.

The tides wash up and back, smoothing the clean silver sand, leaving it bare of tangled seaweed, of foraging seabirds or burrowing clams, of the brown organic froth that dirtied it in earlier times. Now and then the waves erase a line of human footprints, but these are very rare.

The air is clear of any bite of iodine, any hint of pollution or decay.

The sea undulates, blue and green, clear as new glass. Sunlight shimmers on its surface and dapples the bare sea floor. Underwater turbines cast shadows on the sand. The tides power the turbines, tapping the force of gravity.

Far from shore, where its colonies will not interrupt the vista of clear water, a single species of cyanobacterium photosynthesizes near the surface, pumping oxygen into the crystalline air, controlling the level of carbon dioxide. Its design copes easily with the increasing saltiness of the sea.

Except for the cyanobacteria, the ocean's cacophony of microscopic organisms has followed redwoods, mammoths, and *Hallucigenia* into extinction. The krill are gone. Krill would be of as little use to people as sharks and seabirds, fish or jellyfish, seashells or whales. They are all gone, too.

The water deepens beyond the reach of light. The continental shelf ends in a precipice, dropping off into darkness.

On the sea floor, the glass-lace shells of diatoms lie clean and dead, slowly settling. In a moment of geologic time, they will form white limestone.

In the deepest trenches, black smokers gush scalding chemical soup. Machines sense the vents of heat, swim to them, and settle over them to trap the energy from the center of the Earth. Nothing remains for the sustenance and evolution of primordial life in these extraordinary environments.

The strange creatures that lived there, and died, were never any use to human beings.

All the resources of sea and land serve our needs.

Cities of alabaster and adamant grace the crests of mountains and span the flow of rivers. The cities' people live rich, full lives, long and healthy, free of disease. We are well fed. We have interesting, challenging occupations and plenty of time for leisure, family, and virtual reality. We can experience any adventure, from wilderness to exotic ritual, without the expense, trouble, or danger of travel. We can experience any adventure that ever happened, any adventure anyone can imagine. The virtual experience matches reality or invention in every way: sight, sound, smell, touch, and movement.

Our civilization pulses with vitality. We have unlimited opportunity: of thought, of achievement, of freedom, and of the pursuit of happiness.

Whatever we require, human ingenuity can invent and provide. And if, in some unlikely but imaginable future, we should wish to re-create any organism, the means to do so exist. DNA sequences, RNA sequences, are easy to write down and archive; there is no need to store messy biological material, either tough and persistent DNA or fragile and degradable RNA. We are magnanimous; we have preserved the blueprints for everything, even parasites and pathogens.

No one has bothered to re-create an organism in a very long time. We have considered the question long and hard, and we have made our decision. No creation of nature has an inherent right to exist, independent of our need.

We have perfected nature, for we are its masters.

The Republic of George's Island

Donna McMahon

Donna McMahon has a degree in history from Simon Fraser University and currently works in biotechnology. She has written one novel, Dance of Knives, *and is working on a sequel. She lives in Gibson's Landing, British Columbia, and her Web site can be found at www.donna-mcmahon.com.*

On Tuesday afternoon, with the weather reports still forecasting hurricane-force winds, I hauled my decrepit fiberglass dinghy down to Davis Bay and rowed out to try to talk that old throwback into coming ashore. I knew it was futile, but I felt like I had to make an attempt.

Westerly gusts drove whitecaps down the fetch of Georgia Strait. They rolled and crashed across the shallow shoreline, nearly overturning my clumsy boat. Icy spray slapped me as I strained at the oars, and within a minute I was soaked and achingly cold.

In the lee of the house, I tied up to a rusty trailer hitch. Decades ago, George had started driving deep steel pilings into the sandy soil around his house. He built a concrete retaining wall using old car and truck frames as rebar, and then piled up any other junk he could find for a breakwater. We kids watched with fascination while his neighbors, already besieged behind sandbag walls, shook their heads with a mixture of dismay and derision, but thirty years later, after three meters of sea level rise, his was the only original waterfront house remaining on the bay. And his sign, spray-painted on a full sheet of plywood nailed to the south side of the house, had become a local landmark:

THE INDEPENDANT REPUBLIC OF GEORGE'S
ISLAND—PISS OFF!

I picked my way cautiously along the rough, algae-coated breakwater and positioned myself to one side of George's door before pounding on it and shouting.

"George, it's Logan. Let me in, OK?"

I couldn't hear much over the roar of wind and surf, but after several repetitions, a gruff voice bellowed back.

"Piss off!"

"I brought a bottle of rye."

There was a pause—probably George checking all his surveillance cams for evidence of an ambush—then the warped door opened a crack, revealing a wild tangle of gray beard and a bloodshot eye.

"You could've brought a forty-pounder," he grumbled. But he let me in.

So I sat for an hour at George's kitchen table in a stench of mildew and rotting carpet, trying to talk some sense into a guy with a rifle on his lap, chugging whiskey straight from the bottle. Long ago he'd been a big man with a big gut, but he was well past seventy now, and his ancient, dirty clothes hung off him. I often wondered what he was eating these days. Any remaining cases of canned food must surely have rusted, and there wasn't much left in these plundered waters except barnacles and a few tenacious shore crabs. Even the glaucous gull population had plummeted.

The Pacific was slowly undermining George's foundations, and his cupboard doors hung askew, their melamine surface mildew-spotted and bulging with damp. Every room was crammed with piles and boxes of stuff—a moldering graveyard of ancient flat-screen televisions, home appliances, and power tools that had been sold or given away when people couldn't afford to run them anymore. An ancient tungsten lightbulb, powered by a homemade solar system, illuminated the dirty kitchen and the illegal woodstove that George burned driftwood in.

He waved the bottle at me, interrupting my warning about record-breaking winds and storm surges. I shook my head.

"No thanks. I don't drink."

"That just figures. Well, it's crap rye anyway."

Crap that I'd paid for out of my own pocket, I thought angrily, but I said, "Look, how about coming ashore until the storm is over?"

"So you can lock me up and then tear down the house like you did to Lawsons? Just how stupid do you think I am?" he muttered.

Pretty stupid, I thought. But mostly selfish. I'd met any number of old people who'd expected to be cocooned in consumer comfort all their lives, and who just couldn't get it through their heads that those days were over. They even had the gall to go crying to people like me who struggled to live off the scraps of their greed while busting our asses to rescue remnants of the ecosystem.

I wanted nothing to do with George, but my job as remediation team leader made it unavoidable. We were trying to reestablish intertidal zones on human-altered and polluted shorelines—filthy, frustrating work, the worst part of which was expropriating property that had fallen below sea level. The rolling easement laws were clear, but people nonetheless clung to their houses with blind tenacity. And George was the worst—sitting in his fortified pile and dumping raw sewage and garbage into my bay. Last summer, when I discovered he'd been digging for clams in the bivalve test site we'd spent three years building, I'd been ready to go out at low tide with a fire bomb.

"Last chance," I said finally. When George shook his head, I got up and walked to the door.

"Hey!" He rose unsteadily, and when I turned to meet his eyes, I saw fear. He knew.

Unexpectedly, he held out a grimy hand.

"Uh . . . Thanks, eh?"

I felt an unexpected lump in my throat as I shook his hand.

I didn't sleep much that night. I could hear the pounding surf even from my bedroom, a kilometer away from the beach. The next morning, the streets were littered with wind-shredded branches, broken glass, chimney bricks, and roof tiles.

Down in the bay, waves foamed against a stump like a broken molar—chunks of concrete, twisted truck skeletons, and snapped off two-by-sixes. No house. No George.

I'd expected that. But I hadn't expected that I might miss him.

The Stars My Incarnation

Robert A. Metzger

Robert A. Metzger is an electrical engineer, technology reporter, and SF writer. He was born in Los Angeles, attended UCLA, and received his Ph.D. in 1983. He is the author or coauthor of almost a hundred technical papers and ten patents, and the author of many short stories and two novels, Picoverse *and* Quad World. *He can be found online at www.rametzger.com.*

"Welcome back, Creator Metzger." I attempted a groan, but the noise sounded like a cat hacking up a fur ball. Before me stood several dozen black-robed priests, the nearest one dropping to his knees and shuffling toward my optical receiver.

"On this two hundredth anniversary of our arrival at the Centauri system, we wish to tell you of our progress, of our further implementation of Your Vision."

I angled my optical interface upward, peering up through the transparent ceiling of the Cathedral. Night, and Alpha Centauri A burned bright, less than one light-day away.

"Get over here," I said to the priest.

He knee-walked to the optical interface.

"I'm not your Creator," I said. "I was a little-known science fiction writer of the early twenty-first century who had the great misfortune of getting published in a journal called *Nature*."

The priest hid his face in his hands, and shuddered. "You gave us the stars, showed us where our destiny lay."

I sighed, this time the speaker emitting a bark that sounded like a car backfiring. "Every time one of you wakes me up, I try to explain this to you, try to make it clear, try to set the record straight, but none of you seems to get it."

"We are not worthy," he said as he dropped to the crystal floor, grinding his nose into its rainbow-colored surface.

"I'll try once again," I said, doubtful that this time would be any different. "It was the year 2000, nearly seven hundred years ago, and *Nature* was celebrating the beginning of the new millennium with essays about what the next thousand years might bring. I wrote one of those pieces, about a future in which most of the Solar System had been transported four light-years away to the Centauri star system."

"And Your Will was done!" screamed the head priest.

"Yes, my will was done. In that fictional piece, I proposed that if the Sun's magnetic fields could be controlled, then they could be used to expel a relativistic jet of protons, basically turning the Sun into a rocket engine. Under an extremely small but steady acceleration, just one ten-thousandth of a standard gee, after two hundred years the Sun would be moving at nearly 2 percent the speed of light and would have traveled two light-years. At that point, the direction of the acceleration would be reversed, and two hundred years later the Sun would come to a halt in the Centauri system. The whole trip would consume only about 1 percent of the Sun's mass.

"Of course it wouldn't be an easy trip. Even under that gentle acceleration the big outer planets would be left behind, and Earth's circular orbit would be turned into an ellipse. As a result, half of the year the planet would freeze and the other half it would bake. It seemed to me that the easiest way to get the job done would be if the Sun first achieved self-awareness."

"Your Vision was made real."

"Yes. I died back in 2027, the result of a Man-versus-Speeding-Bus event. They iced me down, keeping me in cold storage for spare parts. The next fifty years saw the development of self-awareness in silicon-based hardware, which then gave way to self-awareness in plasma systems, the density of ions twirling about in a magnetic field far in excess of anything silicon was capable of producing.

"In 2083, one totally certifiable loon named Rufus Mapelton, a plasma hacker who spent every conscious and unconscious moment interfaced to the plasma network, stumbled across my long-forgotten *Nature* piece. Mapelton had a little 'eureka' moment, realizing that if he could transfer a self-aware plasma-based entity into the photosphere of the Sun, it could then take control of the Sun's magnetic fields and implement my fictional vision."

"He was Your Instrument."

"I suppose so. Mapelton synthesized his plasma virus, uplinked it to one of the Sol-Corona satellites, and then had the satellite spiral into the Sun. Six weeks later the Sun achieved self-awareness and decided to head off for the Centauri system. It was then that they reconstructed what was left of my mind, hoping that I could help shut down the Sun's desire for a new home. Of course, I couldn't. Between the quakes, the comet impacts, and the skewed orbit, intelligent life barely survived the trip."

"And now we flourish," said the priest. "And we wish to tell You of our further achievements."

It was always like this. They listened, but never really heard me. "So what's new?"

"We plan a wondrous journey."

"Oh?"

"What few organics remain have decided to transfer their consciousness into the Sun's photospheric magnetic matrix. Once the transfer is complete, we will resume the Sun's journey, moving toward the Galactic Center, transferring a portion of ourselves into each star we pass."

"I'd also mentioned that in the *Nature* piece, hadn't I?" I asked.

The priest nodded.

And I knew what would finally come. Each and every star would eventually achieve self-awareness, each setting off on its own journey of discovery and exploration. And in the end, the Universe itself would be aware, the organic having given way to the plasma, the Universe itself forever transformed by the ramblings of an insignificant twenty-first-century science fiction writer.

The Computiful Game

PAUL STEVEN MILLER

Paul Steven Miller is a scientific researcher, soccer fan, and obsessive SF writer, currently seeking publication for his first novel, The Humanoid Foundation. *He lives in Maidstone, Kent, England.*

Come join me as I bounce about the grassy soccer pitch of the Camp Nou, Barcelona. Climb inside my circuits. Climb inside my thoughts.

I wait impatiently in the center circle, trapped beneath the right studded boot of the Pelé Mark VII. There are a million fans in the stadium, all anticipating the start of the match, roaring down from the tiers that stretch to the same height as the Eiffel Tower.

As a child, my creator met the real Pelé, the greatest soccer player of the previous century. That was the beginning of his grand design.

I know this because my creator tells me everything. He has filled me with pinprick ears and eyes but given me no movable parts or mouth. "You're perfect," he often says, while tinkering in his workshop. "You listen and watch but you never tell. No, you never tell."

My creator's notoriety came not just from his genius but also from his prescience.

By the late 2040s, doping in sports was rife. Winning at any cost was the only maxim, and catalytic antibodies were the tonic. Based on variations of natural antibodies, they could be engineered to catalyze any aspect of biological function, and so enhance human performance. They were a doper's dream. Just as with the natural antibodies of the immune system, an almost infinite array of catalytic variants could be generated. So by the time the Antidoping Federation had developed an assay to detect one catalytic antibody the dopers had already designed another with the same function—but with a different structure to escape detection.

The Antidoping Federation had been rendered impotent. Yet it was the insurers who were the main problem. Many of the catalytic antibodies overworked the body, stretching the limits of biological endurance. Players were increasingly picking up career-ending injuries and demanding compensation. With no easy way of proving whether or not a player had been doped with catalytic antibodies at the time of injury, the insurers were more reluctant than ever to pay up. Eventually, with no simple solution to the fiasco in sight, the insurers reneged on all their sports contracts.

No insurance meant no sports. It was illegal to participate in professional sports without a protective compensation policy: no one else could stand the litigation.

Ordinary citizens were in uproar, and so were the media. How were they going to fill the back pages of the newspapers? Chess? Lawn bowls?

But my creator was pleased. He had foreseen. He was prepared. He unveiled his robotic doppelgangers to the world. He had been building a secret army of sportsbots, one to represent each great competitor in history.

People laughed at first. The media didn't: they seized the moment, hailing the robots as the solution, at least until the honor of human sport could be reclaimed. They were desperate.

The robots were programmed with the skill levels of the sporting heroes on whom they had been modeled. The message was clear: no more cheating.

The media weren't the only ones pleased by this solution. Sports veterans (and their dwindling bank accounts) were glad to have been immortalized in a new form. Female fans were also quietly impressed. Some of the robots in once male-dominated sports were modeled on the female physique: the soccerbot David Beckyham, the basketbot Michelle Jordan, even the basebot Babe Ruth. "This time around he really is a babe!" my master often jokes.

Besides, once the robosports got under way, most sports fans really couldn't tell the difference: robot technology was that good. And the algorithms for realistic decision-making in sports had existed in computer games for decades. The robots could even act like humans in the pre- and post-match interviews. David Beckyham was given a cockney accent and programmed to say "at the end of the day" three times every sentence.

But the roboplayers aren't really smart. Not like me.

I am the culmination of my master's plans: an artificially intelligent football. He says it's because he has no real friends. He's a genius that no one understands. He's lonely. But I listen, always, and, mostly, I understand.

His lofty status and his perceived probity allow him to ensure I'm used in certain soccer matches. He knows I like nothing more than to be passed around the pitch.

Ah, yes! I want the match to start. An expectant silence is building in the stadium.

But things are different today. I'm excited but I also feel nervous. Last night in his workshop, my master tampered with one of the synthetic strips on my surface and inserted a micro-device underneath.

"With this," he said, leaning close to me, "I can remotely manipulate your flight path during the game."

"Isn't that cheating?" he then said, speaking on my behalf.

"Why of course, yes!" he answered, laughing. "You won't tell anyone will you?"

No, I never tell.

Oscar Night, 2054

Syne Mitchell

Syne Mitchell worked as a software developer in Seattle before becoming a full-time writer in 2002. She is the author of four novels; she lives in North Bend, Washington, and her Web page can be found at www.synemitchell.com.

Total Health™: *You, Only Better!* presents a night at the Oscars. Beatrice Barnard and George Ford help you sort fashion triumph from catwalk disaster. Remember, with *Total Health*™, it's still you—only better!

BB: First on the carpet tonight is pop singer Alexa DuBois, stunning in an off-the-shoulder Giovanni dress whose mocha silk highlights the leopard pattern of her skin. Her body modifications were done by the renowned designer Leonardo Fontesca, so it's no wonder that the work is subtle and flattering.

GF: At her side, sporting a crest of blue-black feathers, is Howe Yorkins, the tennis star. Alexa may look like the cat who swallowed the canary, but he belongs back on the poultry pharm.

Next up is Neo Washington, up for best actor for his part in the groundbreaking third remake of *Gone with the Wind*. Off the set, he flaunts his political vegetarian stance with a photosynthesizing teal complexion. The Greens behind the velvet ropes have gone insane, cheering and holding up "Meat Kills" signs. Only Neo could mix ethics and fashion and make it work. We love you, Neo!

BB: Following Neo is the quartet of AI specialists whose virtual personality, Babylon Brown, is nominated for best actress for her role as Hillary Clinton in the historical drama *You Go, Girl*. They've made an attempt at cohesion, if not style, by wearing identical white lab coats over jeans and black T-shirts, bought online from AmazonMart, no doubt. Their pedestrian modifications are typical gamer-geek fare: enlarged eyes, polydactyl digits, and a revved-up nervous system that makes them twitch like crickets on a griddle.

GF: Back to the lab, boys!

On the carpet now is Medusa Addams, the character actress we all love to hate. Her puff-adder updo is a-glitter with diamonds as each of her twenty-four snakes is wearing a custom-fit tiara. She completes the look with a skin-tight snakeskin sheath—oh wait! That is her skin. Cheeky, Medusa, very cheeky.

BB: Here's fitness guru Radha Guriampadaya, wearing an uninspired electric-blue bikini over buzz-cut fuchsia fur. Hell-o! Anime is so O-V-E-R!

GF: Her companion, Susanna Belle, is positively fey in a bell-shaped diaphanous silk shift, complemented by feathery antennae and glistening dragonfly wings. Rumor around town is that her geneticist has her molt a new pair every thirty days, in a painful three-day process . . .

BB: Oh—my—*GOD*. George, you'll have to take this one—I'm speechless.

GF: It's aging megastar Monica Moe, and what a display she's putting on tonight! If you're not getting a video or threed broadcast, you must check out the Internet archives. Sporting what can only be offshore modifications, she's got cleavage down to her hips, and I mean that literally. In white pleated chiffon, she looks like a cross between Marilyn Monroe and Artemis Ephesia. I count four, six, no—eight pairs of breasts. Well, slap my cheeks and put me on the cover of *Trying Too Hard* monthly.

BB: Just stepping out of the limo is teen superstar Alessandro Goldstein. The crowd's gone wild. He—yes, it's true—the child prodigy singer/actor/supermodel is classic and divine in black leather pants and jacket, gold-net undershirt and sporting an amazing retro-humanist look with no obvious modifications. Could that flawless body be natural? Only his geneticist knows for sure.

GF: At Alessandro's side is his child bride and the youngest Nobel laureate, Dame Bekka Davis Llewellyn, who won last year's highest scientific honors for her work on inserting and upgrading artificial human chromosomes. She positively glows in a cowl-neck gold-lamé top over an A-line floor-length velvet skirt. Very Audrey Hepburn. Like her husband, she displays no obvious enhancements . . . although nasty rumors after last year's Nobel awards implied that her intelligence may not be quite so native.

BB: Between them, they exemplify the new post-post-human movement in fashion. It's regrettable that such extremists have found a place in the public eye. The effect they are having on today's youth is deplorable. Anywhere you look you can see young people flaunting genetic flaws: buck teeth on the Transatlantic Tunnel, stringy lifeless hair on the Prada Channel, even love handles at the Milan Show for fashion's sake!

GF: Don't worry, Bea, retro-humanism is a passing fad. Body modifications will always be with us. Engineers will always have work. Gene-Es don't go back in bottles.

Total Health™ reminds its subscribers that due to a shortage in recombinant DNA reagents, this year's chromosomal updates are only available to those subscribers who are critically ill, under twenty-four months in age, or whose updates are more than two years out-of-date.

The Visible Men

Michael Moorcock

Michael Moorcock is a prodigy of SF. By the age of fifteen he was the editor of Tarzan Adventures, *dismissed because he tried to include too much prose (it was supposed to be a comic book). By the time he assumed the editorship of the hugely influential* New Worlds *magazine, he was an established author of SF and fantasy, subsequently creating Jerry Cornelius, one of the most enduring characters in the genre—his contribution here is an episode in the Cornelius multiversal tradition. He continues to write prolifically in SF and fantasy as well as more literary fiction. He lives in Bastrop, Texas.*

"That a cat's cradle?" Miss Brunner peered down at a naked Jerry Cornelius tangling his hands in a mess of guitar strings. A red Rickenbacker twelve lay beside him.

"It's twine theory, he said." Frank was absorbed in his own calculations covering the large slate propped on his mum's kitchen table. "He got a bit confused. Too many Es. Too much reverb." He followed her gaze. "G? Somewhere in the seventh dimension."

"He's a simple soul at heart. Easily led . . ." Major Nye stroked his pale mustache. He'd come in with Miss Brunner hoping to take Mrs. Cornelius out. "Is she here at all?"

"Pictures with Colonel Pyat." Frank spoke spitefully. "IT at the Electric. I'll tell her you called." His horrible feet in a bowl of soapy water, he frowned over his equations. What had been in that third syringe?

"Pip," said Jerry. "Pip. Pip." The strings coiled into a neat pile and vanished. He beamed.

Frank wondered why Jerry could charm and he couldn't?

Jerry strolled into the basement room sniffing. At the window, Jerry stopped to test the bars. In the kitchen Jerry cursed as he felt about in the toaster. From the front door upstairs Jerry called through the letter box. They were all naked, save for black car coats. Jerry stood up, pulling on his underpants. "Sorry I'm not decent."

Miss Brunner turned away with a strangled word. "What . . . ?"

"Interdimensional travel." Jerry knotted his wide tie, copping Frank's calculations. "Though not very sophisticated." He reached to rub out a figure.

Pettishly, Frank slapped him. "Just the air cooling. Entropy factor. Anyway, your sizes are all slightly different."

"All?" Jerry frowned at the versions of himself. "If I had a black hole they'd follow me into it. As it is . . ."

Frank scowled. "You and your bloody multiverse. Energy's bound to thin out if you're that profligate."

"Crap." Jerry holstered his vibragun. "Effectively energy's limitless. It's Mandelbrot, Frank. Each set's invisibly smaller. Or invisibly bigger. Depending where you start. You don't go through the multiverse—you go up and down scales of almost infinite but tiny variability. Only the mass varies enormously, making them invisible. That's why we're all essentially the same." With scarcely any echo, identical voices came from each identical mouth: "Only after traveling through billions of sets do you start spotting major differences. The quasi-infinite, Frank. Think how many billions of multiversal planes of the universe there are! Vast as it is, with my box you can step from one end to the other in about ten minutes. Go all the way around. Your mass compresses or expands accordingly. Once I realized space is a dimension of time, the rest was easy!"

"Pervert! You and your proliferating clones."

"Clones?" Miss Brunner licked her lips. "Are they edible?" She adjusted her powder-blue two-piece.

"They're not clones, they're versions. When you dash about the multiverse, this sort of thing happens. I prefer to shrink. But denser, you rip holes; drag things in. Nobody sees the universe next door because it's too big or too small. Fractional, of course, in multiversal terms. Problem is, bits of one universe get sucked into another. They're all so close. Déjà vu . . . ?"

"Carry on like this, young man"—Major Nye straightened his cap—"and you'll cause the end of matter. You'll have your chaos, all right!" Feelings hurt, he made for the basement door.

"That's ridiculous." Miss Brunner repaired her face. "Why aren't your clones . . ."

"Duplicates."

"Why aren't they too big or too small to see?"

"That's the whole trick." Jerry preened. Now in sync, his rippling duplicates followed his every move. "Getting us all to the same scale. Expansion and compression. Your atoms only change mass, maintaining identity. See, we're either too huge to perceive the next universe or we're so massively tiny we merely pass through it without noticing it. Either way you can't see 'em. Until I use this little gadget."

With a disapproving pout, she clicked across the parquet.

"You change your mass relative to theirs, or vice versa, and they become visible. At first you feel a bit queasy, but you get used to it." Picking up the small black box from the table, he showed her the display, the triggers. "Have a go. It's easy. Everything's digitalized."

"Certainly not. I have enough trouble controlling my own world."

"But this gives you millions of alternatives. Immortality of sorts. Admittedly, the nearest billion or so are boringly alike. But most people, like you, love repetition . . ."

"Rot! Utter dissipation! Double Deutsch, I call it!" Grumpily, Major Nye closed the door. Through the bars they saw him climb area steps, pushing aside three more Jerrys staring at one another in some confusion.

Upstairs the front door opened.

"Oh, blimey!" Dismayed, Jerry peered around for a hiding place. "Mum's back early."

"You'll have some explaining to do." Frank smirked.

But Jerry was already fiddling with his box and wires. As Mrs. Cornelius waddled into the room, exuding a delicious smell of greasy fish, Jerry shrank into a corner, his duplicates following. Everyone stared after him.

"Fairyland again!" Miss Brunner was contemptuous.

"The Major said Jerry 'ad a message. Where's 'e gorn?" Mrs. Cornelius lifted huge blue suspicious eyes. A plump hand carried chips from her newspaper to her mouth.

"Climbing the bloody beanstalk, as usual." Defeated, Frank faded.

Mrs. C roared.

The Albian Message

Oliver Morton

Oliver Morton has a degree in the history and philosophy of science from the University of Cambridge. He started out in journalism as an intern with The Economist, *ending up as its science editor. After a stint as editor of* UK Wired *and a freelancer for everyone from* The New Yorker *to* The Hollywood Reporter, *he joined* Nature *as its chief news and features editor in 2005. He is the author of the critically acclaimed* Mapping Mars *and is probably the only member of* Nature's *editorial staff with a minor planet (10716 Olivermorton) named in his honor. He lives in Greenwich, London, not far from the Meridian.*

To: Eva P.
From: Stefan K.
Re: Sample handling facility
March 4, 2047

I thought I ought to put into writing my concerns over the sample-return facility for Odyssey. I think that relying on the mothballed Mars Sample Return lab at Ames is dangerously complacent. It is simply not flexible enough, or big enough, for what I think we should be expecting.

I appreciate that I am in a minority on this, and that the consensus is that we will be dealing with nonbiological artifacts. And I don't want to sound like the people from AstraRoche slipped some egopoietin into my drink during that trip to Stockholm last November. But my minority views have been pretty well borne out throughout this whole story. Back when Suzy and Sean had more or less convinced the world that the trinity sequences in the Albian message referred to some sort of mathematico-philosophical doctrine—possibly based on an analogy to the aliens' purported trisexual reproductive system—and everyone in SETI was taking a crash course in genome analysis, I had to pull in every favor I was owed to get the Square Kilometer Array used as a planetary radar and scanned over the Trojan asteroids. If I hadn't done that we wouldn't even know about the Pyramid, let alone be sending Odyssey there.

I'm not claiming I understand the Albians' minds better than anyone else; I haven't got any more of the message in my DNA than anyone else has. And it's always been my position that we should read as little into that message as possible. I remain convinced that looking for descriptions of their philosophy or lifestyle or even provenance is pointless. The more I look at the increasingly meaningless analyses that the increasingly intelligent AIs produce, the more I think that the variations between phyla are effectively random and that the message from the aliens tells us almost nothing except that there's a radar-reflecting tetrahedron π/3 behind Jupiter that they think we may find interesting.

Everyone assumes that if it hadn't been for the parts of the message lost in the K/T the "residual variant sequences" would be seen to add up to some great big life-the-Universe-and-everything revelation. And because they think such a revelation once existed, they expect to see it carved into the palladium walls of the Pyramid. But if the aliens who visited Earth, and left their messages in the genomes of more or less everything on the planet, had wanted to tell us something more about themselves, they could have made the messages a lot bigger and built in more redundancy across phylum space; there's no shortage of junk DNA to write on. The point is, they didn't choose to leave big messages—just a simple signpost.

The reason I was able to get the SKA people to find the Pyramid was that they knew I'd thought about SETI a lot. But these days people tend to forget that I was always something of a skeptic. What could a bunch of aliens tell us about themselves, or the Universe, that would matter? Especially if, like the Albians, they sent, or rather left, the message a hundred million years ago? Well, in the case of the Albians, there's one type of knowledge they could be fairly sure that anyone who eventually evolved sequencing technology on Earth pretty much had to be interested in. And it's something that, by definition, is too big to fit into the spare bits of a genome.

I appreciate that everyone on the project now has a lot of faith in what we can do on the fly, especially in terms of recording and analyzing information. I'll admit that when we started I really didn't think that the lost craft of human spaceflight would be so easy to reinvent. It still strikes me as remarkable that none of us realized how much could be achieved by leaving a technical problem to one side and concentrating on other things for a few decades before coming back to it with new technologies. But the problem with the sample-return facility won't just be one of technology. It's going to be one of size.

You see, extinctions aren't the noise in the message. They're the reason for the message. The one thing the Albians knew they could do for whoever would end up reading their message was store up some of the biodiversity that would inevitably be whittled away over time. When Odyssey gets to the Trojan Pyramid, I don't expect it to find any more information about the Albians than we have already. I do expect a biosphere's worth of well-preserved biological samples from the mid-Cretaceous. Not just genomes, but whole samples. Sudarat and her boys are going to come home with a hold full of early angiosperms and dinosaur eggs. We need to be ready.

Photons Do Not Lie

Euan Nisbet

Euan Nisbet is a native of Zimbabwe but is now professor of geology at Royal Holloway College at the University of London, where he studies global change and the geology of the remote Archean Eon (more than 2.5 billion years ago). He lives in Surrey, England.

The camera sweeps down the majestic garden approach, the marvelous avenue of intertwined rose-chrysanthemum trees. Cranes flock above. Skittering impalas graze amid bamboo-gums, in which koalas and lumbering pandas loll under the warm sun. Onward we glide to the palace and into the grand throne room, thronged with a vast crowd, the notables of Earth. They rise. In Reykjavik, the Nobel ceremony has begun. Entering in state to the ancient imperial anthem, "Rock Around the Clock," is Her Majesty Queen Hillary IV.

The laureates are led in. What paragons they are! There had been criticism that the biology prize should be discontinued, as biology is so unchallenging. That was surely correct for stamp-collecting physics, but who cannot applaud this year's biology winner, re-creator of the rabbit-sized, slipper-and-iPub-fetching house-trained woolly mammoth? No math prize, after that laureate's affair with the Prince Consort. How dare she! Of course, the discovery of the soul led to calls for reinstatement, but the Gödel-Isho'dad of Merv-Epimenides theory shows that, although detectable, that 'brane cannot be investigated, frangible yet intangible. The quest is abandoned.

The heavyweight prizewinners come on. Geology—for the discovery of the tenth inhabited planet, this one orbiting Aldebaran. The inhabitants are aggressive antlike beings in the throes of nuclear war, but no doubt they will see reason when we pacify them. Such a pity that we had to sterilize all the humanoids of the eighth planet: the peace prize goes to the admiral of that expedition, for those eloquent words of consolation, after the ritual welcoming dance offered by the inhabitants accidentally unveiled one of the admiral's men. The strong reaction was of course fully justified.

Next is the economics prize. As is customary, this goes to the ranking associate professor at Lunar Chicago University, whose "great idea" was the reinvention of crime. It is now proven that economic systems are unstable unless criminals flourish. Old fogies decry this, but the huge "Make Crime Real" demo outside the palace has much sympathy. Several provinces now select lucky teenagers for training, providing necessities such as body piercings, drugs, and "attitude."

A hum of excitement pervades the room. It is time for the Sacred Reminder. The prime minister rises to recount the saving of humanity. Suddenly, rudely, there is a slight buzz. A masculinist suffrager has managed to enter. He is quickly ejected, burka fluttering. The prime minister dryly observes that the formula limiting men to 10 percent of academic posts is already overgenerous.

The Reminder begins: the sterilization of Earth in 2020 by the week-long Great Solar Flare. She recounts the wondrous chance that the U.S. president was on lunar darkside, in Lunar City to celebrate the close of her third term, accompanied by the Chinese president, the British crown prince, and the crown princess of Japan. The presidents' energy and constitutional wisdom inspired extraordinary efforts to make the colony viable, and then rebuild. Then came the romance between prince and princess, and the final emotional abdication of the Dual Presidency, with constitutional dispensation of our Empire of Luna and Three Planets, into the hands of their beloved adopted heirs.

Since then, what progress there has been under the Rose and Chrysanthemum! From bones and buried seeds we have re-covered the biosphere, even raising Earth's population to more than a million. Mirrored Venus was terra-formed; Mars warmed by chlorofluorocarbons, and methane from polar peat bogs. The end of physics came with the discovery of CUTE, the canonic universal theory of everything, bringing instantaneous travel to anywhere in the cosmos.

Last comes the greatest prize. What is more valuable than history, recovery of our lost past? The flare frizzled the databases, leaving only tiny fragments of our culture in the personal oddments of scientists in Lunar City: the deficient aesthetic of Bach, Mozart, Shakespeare, Milton, Keats—Jane Austen, for goodness' sake. But now we unearth a marvelous treasure trove. Of course even the geeks loved Elvis and Abba, but only now do we fully realize just how limited was their vision, they who did not even value the great Sinatran song of creation: "Do BE! Do BE! DO!"

Now we are recovering the true genius of the Golden Age. Here is our history prizewinner now, rising to deliver her lecture. She recounts the long hours spent cruising around the wavefront, laboriously integrating photon after photon on the sphere two hundred light-years out, as she collected the radio broadcasts of the twentieth century.

What diamonds she has found! One is the 00:48 A.M. BBC shipping forecast, a mysterious sacred compline into the dead of night, with its great unsung hymn of "Sailing by" into the afterlife. From American radio, the account by Orson Welles of the 1938 martian attack on Earth is previously known only in a corrupt fake purporting to have been written by a Mr. H. G. Wells. Already major funding supports archaeologists searching Mars for the extinct civilizations under our new oceans.

Finally comes the climax of her Nobel lecture. Technically, it is far easier to recover radio than TV. But now, a visual revelation—proof that twentieth-century humanity was in touch with alien life elsewhere in the Universe! Praise be: these aliens, delegated to each nation but unknown to us moderns, are fully humanoid, female of course, possessing unearthly beauty and uttering truly sublime speeches for World Peace. Here is the highest glory of the Age of Gold. Here from civilization's ancient heartland—Perth, Western Australia—gentlemen and noble ladies, I give you the Miss Universe competition, 1979!

Stranger in the Night

Salvador Nogueira

Salvador Nogueira is a science writer from Folha de S. Paulo, *a major Brazilian daily newspaper, and author of* Rumo ao infinito *("To the infinite"), a book about the future of space exploration. He lives in São Paulo, Brazil.*

"So, Hawking, are you ready to unveil the greatest mystery in the Universe?" asked Mike.

After a slight delay, an artificial, mechanized voice answered back. "In what way?"

"Oh, boy, I wish I could go with you." Mike was the chief engineer in Project Asimov, and Hawking was his brainchild: the very first space probe to be sent to Alpha Centauri, the closest star to our Sun.

Thirty years earlier, astronomers had detected a nitrogen-oxygen atmosphere on an rocky planet around the largest of the three stars in that system. At first, they thought the composition was sustained by biological activity, but a couple of abiogenic scenarios had come to light. All attempts to communicate with any possible civilization there had failed. The only remaining option had been to send a spacecraft to do a flyby, up close.

And there they were, eight years later, making final preparations for launch, on top of a large expendable rocket, in Alcantara, Brazil—the cheapest place from which to get to orbit, in terms of the energy required.

"Why do you not come with me, Michael?" asked Hawking, in its usual monotone.

"I wish I could, pal. But no way could we build a ship large enough for both of us."

"I will miss you, Michael." The engineer almost felt emotion in the voice and paused simply to gaze at his companion. What a beautiful piece of machinery it was. Really sad to see it go. The best of the best in Artificial Intelligence, designed to represent mankind in a possible contact with aliens. Well, almost as good as the real thing, he thought. "I'll miss you too, pal."

He had been working closely with Hawking since the beginning of the project ("Since you were a bunch of silicon," he used to joke), but never thought of it as more than a sophisticated computer. It looked perfectly self-aware—but was it? Mike never bought into that Turing crap. It was just a piece of equipment, period. But now, during final testing before launch, he could almost touch the anxiety emanating from that so-called it.

"What will happen to me?" inquired the probe.

Mike didn't bother at first, automatically entering babble mode. "What do you mean? You've heard the story a thousand times. After we finish here, we will turn off your cognitive functions—power is a precious asset in a tiny spaceship, you know. Then the spaceship will clear Earth orbit with chemical propulsion and, after that, turn on the matter-antimatter engines. It will reach cruise speed of 0.1*c* after ten months, and five years before arrival, you'll be turned on. Your instructions are to check all the onboard instruments and send periodic reports to Earth. You should . . ."

"You do not understand, Michael. What will happen to me when you turn me off?"

Mike was stunned. "Well . . . well . . . I suppose you'll . . . it would be like sleeping, but without dreaming."

"I have never slept before."

"But you've been turned off before. For brief moments, but you were. Do you have any memory of ever being turned off?"

"No, I have no memory of that. It seems like I was always functioning."

"Well, then. It will be just like that." Mike seemed relieved. "Now, see what values you're getting from your main spectrometer, will ya?"

Hawking reacted promptly, offering the stream of data through a monitor temporarily connected to it. "I was never alone."

"What?"

"My perception is that I was always turned on, and never alone. How is it to be alone, Michael?"

"Well, it's . . . lonely." That was the best Mike could do, without further encouraging Hawking's apprehension. But the first word he thought of was "sad."

"Will I ever go back?"

"I guess not, Hawk. But, c'mon, who knows what's out there? Maybe you'll find some people and they could send you back—if you manage to establish contact. The adventure, the quest for the unknown, my friend, that's the main reason for this journey."

"Maybe I lack the spirit of adventure then."

Mike didn't know what to say. And he didn't need to.

"Maybe I do not want to go."

"What do you mean, you don't wanna go? Hawk, this is the greatest adventure ever. If I could, I'd switch places with you anytime!" Mike finished checking the data on his computer and was ready to clear the bay. "Well, Hawky-boy, like it or not, I guess this is it. I have to turn you off now, so this is 'good-bye.' Have fun, it will be just great, you'll see!"

An agonizing silence followed. Two, then three seconds.

"Good-bye, Mike."

The engineer left, and darkness took over. Hawking's conscience was turned off, but it was still there. Yes, it was there. Alone.

Two days later, the rocket performed magnificently and sent Hawking on its way. The launch put it in a trajectory toward Jupiter, and the giant planet would then give the gravitational pull to send it toward Alpha Centauri.

Everything was just fine on board, except for Hawking, strangely awake. So alone. And it didn't want to be. It could feel all the parts of the ship, as if they were its own. It played with all the instruments, the antennae, the robotic arms. It wanted to end it all. He wanted to end it all. And then, one final command, and he finally ceased to be. The magnetic containment for the antimatter failed, producing a splendid blast in the sky. The scientists on Earth were troubled; the cause for the failure was completely unknown to them. More puzzling yet, all telemetry ceased about two minutes before the explosion. No more loneliness. No more fear. No more.

Tick-Tock Curly-Wurly

Gareth Owens

Gareth Owens speaks nine languages, including Sumerian and Dutch, composes music that would give most people nightmares, and claims to be one of the few university-qualified wizards in the world. He is an occasional contributor of fiction to Odyssey: Adventures in Science *magazine and has recently completed his first novel. He lives in Hawkhurst, Kent, England.*

Professor Michelle Tartuffe examined her reflection in the black glass of a fluorescent nighttime bus ride. She insisted on taking the bus home, and the White House insisted that she did not. Seventy-three inches from her Chaco sandals to her wild hair, the prof knew that she stood out in any crowd, and when she spoke she had an accent: Haitian, with a hint of the rhythms of France. But English was her first language and she spoke it with elegance and precision. Her diction was clear, her vocabulary extensive, and her enunciation always deliberate, and yet . . . and yet.

Whenever she talked to one of C. M. Kornbluth's Marching Morons—any one of the random, undereducated ferals who seemed to have invaded her intelligent world—the first barely articulated utterance that dribbled out in reply to any attempt at communication was always the same.

Initiating contact with an easy-to-comprehend opening question, she would address the pierced moron usually found lurking vacantly by her stop, saying something like: "Hi, do you know how long 'til the bus comes?"

Or, to the bling-bedecked moron at the table next to her in JavaStar: "Could you pass me the sugar please?" And the reply from all genders and races of moron was always based around the theme of "Wha . . . ?"

This now formed a very basic part of the prof's diagnostic markers for determining intellectual status. If the first reply to a communication was a request to repeat the initial statement, she knew straightaway that she was dealing with a moron.

Since the turn of the century the prof had been getting paid a small Washington fortune for thinking aloud. She had published a paper extrapolating from a basic concept of superintelligence and how to deal with the first contact with superintelligent races.

Stephen Hawking's assessment of the situation was that given our own experience with colonization, any first contact with more advanced aliens would probably be more like the movie *Independence Day* than Spielberg's *ET*. The prof agreed, which was why she sat on the bus chewing distractedly on the nail of her right thumb.

First contact, when it came, had been unmistakable. The aliens had not spoken only to a few bespectacled computer geeks parceling out data packets to like-minded geeks. No, first contact had stopped the world and given it a good rocking. Every radio, every television, every terminal and mobile phone, had received the transmission. Every screen that could show words did, and everything that could make a sound spoke:

Tick-tock curly-wurly

And that was it. That was the whole of the message. The transmission was nondirectional, appearing to arrive from every which way simultaneously, and the best brains on Earth, as well as television presenters, were stumped as to what the words actually meant. It was clear that the message was for humanity as a whole, not just a few elite governmental high-ups, but it was equally clear that humanity as a whole had no idea what was just said.

The president's first instinct was to find a way of broadcasting a reply. The prof was the head of the appropriate think tank, so suddenly she found herself on the great carpet of the Oval Office, explaining to the secretary of state, who in turn re-explained to the president, that a technology gap of more than about two hundred years would render communication difficult—and, if these aliens were superintelligent, impossible—unless such advanced creatures were prepared to take the time to talk to us the way we do to cats and dogs.

"Look at it this way, Mr. President," she said. "First contact with an equal is in essence no different from when you see someone you like at a party. You think that you would like to get to know them. You then have to formulate a small and pithy first-contact statement that will both pique their interest and elicit an open-ended response allowing further communication."

"So what you are saying, Professor, is that this alien message is actually nothing more than a cheesy pickup line."

The prof smiled. "Actually, sir, although the message may be seen as having an analogous purpose, it's probably more complicated than that."

"Yes," said the president, looking at his fingers. "Almost everything seems to turn out that way."

"What do you think the message actually means?" the secretary of state asked, eyes sharp and alert. "Is it a McLuhan-esque test of reasoning where the words actually have no meaning, the mere existence of the transmission being its own message?"

The prof shrugged. "As yet I have no real idea. For example, what goes tick-tock?"

"A clock," said the president.

"A bomb," said the secretary of state.

"And our DNA is wrapped around in a double spiral, curly-wurly fashion. It could be that the message is saying something along the lines of 'shame about your genetic time bomb,' or it might be that the whole message is nothing more than someone bending over and clapping their hands together, like when you call a dog over."

"Why don't we just ask them what they meant?" said the president.

"No!" squawked the prof, a look of blind panic on her face. "Our future survival is staked on our reply. We must figure it out, whatever it takes."

She rode the bus home. The stars had tapped Earth on the shoulder. Her reflection in the window held her gaze.

"Tick-tock curly-wurly," she said. "Tick-tock curly-wurly."

Daddy's Slight Miscalculation

Ashley Pellegrino

Ashley Pellegrino is the daughter of a scientist. Aside from writing tales that occasionally scare the scientist whose real-life adventures have been known to scare Stephen King, she's a perfectly typical twelve-year-old. She lives in Long Beach, New York.

Zzzzzzt! Clink! "Ouch!"

I listened from outside Dad's lab. He was working on a new experiment.

No one knew Daddy had started a new project, except me. Only I know when he is working on an experiment, because he usually works while my brother and sister and I are asleep. Whenever he is up all night, I know he's working on something new, sometimes even something strange—like the pink octopus whose ears were like wings.

He doesn't go out to work in the morning like other fathers. Did he ever go out to work, like other kids' dads? I think so; but he does not like to talk about the time before I was born. Something happened. Something sad, I think.

Except for us, Dad has only his work.

If you watch science fiction, or read it, you might think it's boring or even scary growing up with a scientist in the house. Actually, it's more interesting than scary, more easy than boring. When I ask for help with my homework, he sometimes gets me all dizzy. Other times, it becomes crystal clear. But don't ask him why nature is the way it is, unless you really want to know, unless you want to get dizzy trying to understand how black paint looks black because it is really trapping all the other colors inside.

"Why is the sky blue?" I remember asking.

Most adults would answer: "Go ask your science teacher." Or: "That's how God made it."

But Dad said: "That's the color the sky rejects."

I don't completely understand; but I'm sure not many kids walk around wondering about living in rejected colors. It makes me wonder a lot about the things around me. It's actually kind of fun. Even with ideas gone completely strange, we're always entertained. None of us will ever forget what Dad did to Mr. Kitty.

Cat's toes and monkey fingers?

Mr. Kitty was already nicknamed Mr. Mischief, even without Dad's help.

"Biomorphing" paws into hands—for a cat? Who wouldn't have guessed that could lead to chaos? Just imagine living with a cat that can unscrew jars and open doors. But even if our house did eventually end up with a child lock on the refrigerator door (although there were no toddlers around), it was really fun, believe it or not, to have a cat with hands.

Yet the noises that came from Dad's lab, that night—they sounded more creepy than fun. Usually the sounds coming from Dad's lab are buzzes, not ouches.

So, I knocked.

"Come in," he said.

The sun was shining through his windows and it was a bright new day outside. Dad had worked all night. This had to be something special. I saw what might have been a small device used to communicate with those pink octopuses with Dumbo's ears.

"Dad, what is that?" I asked.

"Bone-phone," Dad replied. There was a strange-looking wire clipped to his ear.

"I don't like the sound of that," I said.

"That's OK. We can always name it again."

"Fine! But what does it do?"

"Do you see those orchids on the table? And those trees outside? This wire sends a signal right into my brain. It lets me feel exactly what the plants feel. Isn't that amazing?"

I looked at the fruit trees, and I looked at the tall green grass. I thought of *The Wizard of Oz*. I thought of how the trees yelled at Dorothy when she picked their apples.

"But, Dad. What happens when . . . ?"

"Don't worry," he said. "Nothing can go wrong. Nothing goes wrong in science, if you really do your homework. Science only improves life."

"Isn't that what they said about the *Titanic* and the *Columbia*?" I asked.

"Ouch!" Dad said. "Gotta think about that one. But this science is different. Trust me."

Dad was changing. A lot of people were changing, these days. Some were changing for the better. Some, for the worse.

Dad always used to tell me that the most important place for a scientist to be is in the unknown. " 'I don't know,' " he had taught me, "is always a good place to start."

Now, he was starting to speak as if he did know—as if, these days, he was afraid to say the words "I don't know."

I thought again about those angry trees in *The Wizard of Oz*, and I did not like the whole idea. "Dad, wait . . ."

But Dad wore the wire anyway, and he flipped the switch, saying: "This is something new. This is something completely different."

Just then, my brother Kyle went into the yard, wanting only to do something nice for Dad. He wanted to give Dad a surprise, and to do some of the household chores for him. Kyle was heading for the grass. He was pushing Dad's little mechanical lawn mower. He was pushing fast, really fast.

Dad never knew that a single blade of grass could scream. No one knew, until that day. Kyle mowed twenty feet, before Dad's screams stopped him.

Yes, this was as different as Dad promised it would be.

The grass on our lawn is taller than me, now. And the neighbors have begun to complain. But Dad will not cut the grass; not a single blade.

Dad still won't tell me what it sounded like.

And I wonder.

Brain Drain

Frederik Pohl

Frederik Pohl's career in SF spans more than six decades, as author, editor, and agent (at one time he represented the young Isaac Asimov). In the early 1940s, he edited Astonishing Stories *and* Super Science Stories; *in the 1960s, it was* Galaxy *and its sister title,* If, *winning the Hugo for* If *three years running. A frequent coauthor, notably with C. M. Kornbluth, Pohl reemerged in the 1970s as a novelist in his own right, with books such as* Man Plus *and* Gateway, *both of which won Nebula Awards:* Gateway *also won a Hugo. Not content to rest, a new story, "Generations," was published in September 2005, and he is currently working on a novel begun by Arthur C. Clarke. He lives in Palatine, Illinois.*

As Docent Wilfram's actual name, which summarized his complete medical and professional history, was very long, his friends simply called him "Wilf." There weren't very many of those friends left, though, because the number who were still in any real sense alive—that is, not frozen, cremated, or in machine storage—dwindled year after year.

That was natural enough. Wilf had been birthed in 2734 and was therefore now 174 years old, and although genetics, microrobotic surgery, and easily available custom-grown transplants had given most human beings a life expectancy undreamed of in earlier times, they couldn't keep a person from feeling old—even when Wilf's housemind, Jerel, was giving him news that, at one time, Wilf would have considered exciting. "Message?" Wilf repeated. "An ET message?"

"Definitely ET," his housemind assured him, "though its content, if any, is unknown. It was received by the thousand-hectare radio telescope in Trojan-Uranus."

"Yes," said Wilf, yawning, "Well, you never know: send it along for analysis. I think I'm going to go to sleep."

As he headed for his bedroom he had already nearly forgotten the news. Messages from space had not been headline news for a long time. The first message—that is, at least, the first radio signal that could not possibly be natural in origin and thus had to be the product of extraterrestrial intelligence—had been detected as early as 2063, and as detection facilities improved over the years thirty-seven others had been logged. They came from all over the sky, some a few score light-years away, others more than a thousand.

But in spite of the best efforts of humanity's increasingly capable computers, no message had ever been decoded, and there was increasing doubt that there was anything to decode. Nothing but the inevitable radio leakage from any high-tech civilization.

That was disappointing, but there was worse. Although thirty-eight extraterrestrial radio sources had been detected, only eleven were still on the air. The rest had gone silent and stayed that way. Why?

That was the part Wilf didn't like to think about. It seemed that most high-tech civilizations lasted only some centuries. Then something happened to them. What that something might be no one could say, but there was one unwelcome theory that would not go away. Any civilization that reached the point of large-scale radio emissions was likely at the same time to be developing weapons of mass destruction. And that, it seemed, was a death sentence.

As Wilf limped toward his bedroom, the housemind spoke again. "Docent Wilf? I ask again, may I fix that limp for you?"

"It isn't worth the trouble!" Wilf said.

"It is no trouble," the housemind persisted. "Although, to be sure, it would be more efficient for you to have yourself machine-stored now, and then such problems would not arise."

"Yes, I know," Wilf said testily, throwing himself on his bed. Generally it made more sense to follow a housemind's advice, as their machine minds were far more capable than any human's—especially that of a human who still clung to his organic body. He was also quite sure that Jerel knew something it wasn't telling its master. It might be, he thought, about his own life expectancy. If you were going to have yourself copied into a computer program it was a good idea to get it done while you were still alive.

After actual death, even a short time after death, there was a certain degradation of the data. And there really was no reason to put it off. You lost nothing in machine storage. Indeed, you gained a world—any kind of world you wanted! You could create any virtual reality you liked and live in it as long as you chose, and when you tired of that you could create a different and even better one.

Nearly all Wilf's age-cohort had long since taken the step themselves, and when they talked to him about it—when they bothered at all to talk to any person who was still flesh and blood—they unanimously described it as the closest thing any nonbeliever could get to a heaven of his own.

Wilf sat up suddenly, opening his eyes. "Jerel!" he called. "Show yourself! I want to talk to you."

"Yes, Docent Wilf?" The housemind obediently presented itself as the hologram of an ancient English butler, standing attentively a couple of meters away.

"You've thought this through, haven't you? Those other civilizations didn't wipe themselves out in wars, did they?"

The housemind's expression clouded. "Why do you ask, Docent Wilf?"

"I ask you because you've got a better mind than I have."

"In certain areas, perhaps," the housemind agreed.

"They don't all die, do they? They just put themselves in machine storage. And then they've got nothing to worry about, ever—not hunger, not illness, certainly not death. Not even unrequited love, because if their love object isn't in a requiting mood they simply simulate her when she is. And they have such a grand time they don't bother with anything else."

"Generally speaking, no," the housemind agreed.

Wilf laughed. "Of course not," he said. "And neither will we, will we? There won't be any more signals to leak to the rest of the Galaxy! And so as soon as the rest of us are in machine storage, Earth will fall silent, too."

Great Unreported Discoveries No. 163

Mike Resnick

Mike Resnick is one of the most prolific authors in SF. He has won five Hugo Awards and currently stands first on the Locus *list of all-time award winners for short fiction and fourth on the* Locus *list of science fiction's all-time top award winners in all fiction categories. He lives in Cincinnati, Ohio, and his online home can be found at www.fortunecity.com/tattooine/farmer/2.*

When the team at Iowa State (or was it Nebraska?) came up with proof positive that plants feel pain, it made headlines not just that day, but for months thereafter. We have millions of people who became vegetarians because they didn't want animals to die just so they could fill their stomachs, and suddenly they discovered that everything they eat feels pain.

I found it fascinating. That's why I changed my major and went into botany—because I couldn't stop wondering: if plants can feel, what else can they do? Like, for example, can they think?

Of course, thinking in itself is a dead end, especially if you're rooted to one spot, unless you can communicate your thoughts, so that's what I really tried to specialize in. It's a good thing I knew how to get government grants, because I spent the first fourteen years after getting my Ph.D. without any hint of success.

I would talk to them. I would play them music. I would write messages in every known language and hold them up. I even brought in professors who could speak dead languages. All to no avail.

Undaunted—well, not very daunted anyway—I brought in psychics to see if they could form a bond with any of the plants in my lab. Still no luck.

I would put bees and butterflies in screened cages and explain to the flowers that if they wanted to reproduce, all they had to do was tell me, and I would release the insects and the process of regeneration could get under way. Nothing.

Finally I tied them into computers, exceptionally bright machines that could turn almost any signal, no matter how slight, how basic, how weak, how alien—into a spoken translation. All I got was silence.

I still remember the breakthrough. I'd just met and lost my heart to Bubbles La Tour, a truly wonderful dancer who, despite her billing, could hardly be called a stripper as she started out naked (and then got energetic). I walked over to one of the hybrid daisies in the lab and began plucking off its petals one by one, muttering, "She loves me . . . she loves me not . . . she loves me . . ."

"Ouch!" said a strange voice.

I looked around the lab, but I couldn't see anyone.

After a moment I decided I had imagined it, and I pulled off another petal.

"Damn, that smarts!" said the voice again. "What did I ever do to you?"

"I beg your pardon?" I said, looking around and trying to spot the speaker.

"Begging my pardon is all very well and good," said the voice. "But you're denuding me. Are you going to disembowel me next?"

"Who said that?" I demanded.

"Whose limbs have you been pulling off?" the voice shot back.

I stared at the daisy, and suddenly I saw that it was still attached to the computer. I'd run my most recent experiment two days before and hadn't remembered to disconnect it.

"You?" I said, bending over it.

"Yes, me," said the daisy. "And brush your teeth if you're going to stand this close to me. I'm supposed to be living in a world of gorgeous scents."

"You can talk!" I exclaimed excitedly, and then repeated: "You can talk!"

"What a stunning observation," said the daisy. "You must have been the brightest one in your class."

"There's no need for sarcasm," I said.

"There's no need for sadism, either, but you kept pulling off my limbs."

"Your petals," I corrected it.

"Semantics," said the daisy.

"Well, now that I know you can talk, I promise never to do it again," I said.

"I don't want to seem ungracious, but how long have you known I could feel pain?"

"It got you to speak, didn't it?" I said defensively.

"So when your spouse is mad at you and won't talk, do you pull off her arms and legs?"

"Hardly ever," I admitted.

"Well, there you have it."

"Look, I apologize, all right?" I said. "This is the most historic breakthrough in the history of the human race! We should be celebrating!"

"Well, it's not the most historic breakthrough in the history of the daisy race," the flower replied. "I find you arrogant, self-centered, and a rather dull conversationalist. I am all through communicating with human beings now and forever, and I'm going to go back to peacefully and silently contemplating my navel."

"You don't have a navel," I pointed out.

"I was couching the concept in terms you'd understand, which was clearly a waste of time. Now please go away."

I spoke to it for another half an hour, but couldn't get any response. I considered calling in Drs. DiChario and Gormley, but then I did some serious thinking, and I decided that if the daisy kept its promise and didn't speak to them, they'd think I was either crazy or a liar (or both). And if it did speak to them, they'd apply for the same grants I was living on, and with their superior credentials they'd wrest them away from me and I'd have to go out and find another (and doubtless more difficult) way to make a living. If I tried to make my findings public and the daisy passed the word to its kith and kin, no one would be able to verify it and I'd become a laughingstock. And if the other flowers were as foul-tempered and obnoxious as the daisy, why would anyone want to communicate with them in the first place?

The more I thought about it, the more I decided that nothing is sometimes the very best thing to do.

I carefully disconnected the daisy from the computer.

Some time later I found myself thinking about Bubbles La Tour again, and my hand absently went to the flower.

"She loves me . . ." I intoned dreamily, "she loves me not . . ."

Feeling Rejected

ALASTAIR REYNOLDS

Alastair Reynolds spent his early years in Wales and Cornwall before going to the University of Newcastle to study physics and astronomy. After gaining his Ph.D. at the University of St. Andrews in Scotland, he moved to Noordwijk in the Netherlands, where he worked for the European Space Agency until 2004, when he left to become a writer full-time. Reynolds sold his first SF story in 1990. Since then he has published more than twenty shorter works and six novels. He still lives in the Netherlands.

Report on the paper "Analysis of the gravitational signals from a newly discovered Kardashev II civilization in the Sombrero Galaxy: Part 1 by Whimbrel *et al.*," submitted to the *Journal of Xenoastronomical Studies*.

The authors present an analysis of gravitational signals of intelligent origin arising in the Sombrero Galaxy, detected in publicly available archival data from the System-Wide Imaging Network for Exo-astronomy (SWINE). The transmitting culture, which has not been the subject of an earlier paper, is shown to be a type II civilization on the Kardashev scheme, by which it is understood that they have the means to tap the entire energy output of their star. This classification is made partly on the basis of the strength of the SWINE signal (which in itself implies a basic competence in stellar husbandry) and partly on the basis of the cultural information embedded in the data themselves. This assessment is probably correct, but given the likelihood that both type I and type III civilizations may occasionally emulate type II civilizations for their own purposes (see, for instance, Chukar, Francolin, and Dickcissel, 2051), a word of caution might well have been in order.

The species is shown to have originated on a rocky terrestrial planet about the size of Mars, and to have followed an evolutionary pathway that is well approximated by the uppermost track on the three-parameter model of Bataleur and Becard (2049). In their unmodified form, adult members of this species are three-meter-tall hexapodal oxygen-breathers with a DNA-based reproductive system. The species has a well-developed central nervous system with marked hemispheric asymmetry.

The authors apply standard analysis tools and methods to extract cultural information from the intercepted signal. Given the absence of anything startlingly new in their approach, the amount of space that the authors spend discussing this process is puzzling. It might have been better simply to reference one of the many review papers on the matter, such as the recent and comprehensive overview of analysis methods given in [omitted].

The authors then move on to the main part of their paper: a lengthy discussion of the information content of the decoded message. They summarize the nature of the transmitting civilization, the physiology and evolutionary background of the inhabitants, their technology and culture. Although broadly satisfactory in its details, this section would benefit from shortening. As an example, the authors dwell on the construction methods used in the Dyson sphere that the aliens have erected around their star, despite the fact that broadly similar planet-dismantling, reforging, and gravity-control methods have been used by at least 138 other Kardashev II cultures (see, for instance, Takahe and Smew, 2045). In the very first sentence of subsection 3.2, the authors state that there is "nothing particularly novel about the construction methods," before nevertheless embarking on a blow-by-blow account of those selfsame methods. I agree with the first sentence.

They conclude this section by presenting, in excerpted form, several images and texts deemed to be of high significance within the culture. These include eighteen "stanzas" of a much longer epic "poem" written in commemoration of the collapse of part of the polar region of their Dyson sphere about 1.2 million years ago, an accident that resulted in the deaths of $\sim 5.6 \times 10^{12}$ sentient beings. Although undoubtedly touching, it is not clear that a great deal is gained from the inclusion of this somewhat taxing material.

The authors conclude their paper by moving on to a wider discussion of the significance of their newly found civilization against the known sample of other intelligent alien species. Here the authors place (in my view) undue emphasis on the position of their civilization in the "cultural H–R diagram" (Wonga and Grebe, 2044), in which the total information capacity of a transmitting culture, measured in bits, is plotted against the light-crossing time in light-seconds of their total colonized space. On the basis of Figure 8, the authors claim that their culture lies significantly to the right of the "asymptotic singularity branch," which on the face of it would suggest that the culture had avoided a singularity despite occupying a total volume only seventy-two thousand light-seconds in diameter. If true, this would extend the total number of known collapse-resistant cultures to eight.

The evidence, however, is very much less compelling than the authors claim. Close examination of their statistical sample shows it to be derived from the Third Gonolek catalogue, which is now known to be afflicted by serious sampling errors. Visual inspection would suggest that a more reliable sample—such as that of [omitted]—would either bring their civilization into line with the singularity branch, or reveal it as no more than a mild outlier.

In short, although the new civilization undoubtedly provides a useful new datum point, I remain unconvinced that it merits an entire paper, and certainly not the multi-paper saga that the authors clearly have in mind. Thanks to the torrent of data supplied by SWINE, and the planned Obscenely Large Gravity Array (OLGA), we are fast moving into the era of statistical xenoastronomy—one in which the study of individual extraterrestrial civilizations has much less to offer than a global, survey-based approach. The authors might therefore be advised to wait until their archival inquiries have turned up several dozen such cultures, and then gather these results into a single paper. Otherwise, I fear, they may be open to accusations of [omitted] the [omitted].

Other matters:
Fig. 6 was incorrectly labeled (see Fig. 5).

This text has been swept by Semantic Anonymity Preserver Version 5.1—certain stylistic or cultural markers may have been altered or removed. Complete legibility is not guaranteed.

The Trial of Jeremy Owens

PETER ROBERTS

Peter Roberts graduated from the University of Pittsburgh with a degree in mathematics. Although primarily a poet, he has an abiding interest in SF. He currently lives in Mansfield, Ohio. His Web site can be found at www.geocities.com/peterroberts .geo/personal.html.

The biological Jeremy Owens sat alone at the plaintiff's table. He had been rebuffed by every lawyer he had approached to assist him in this trial; some had laughed in his face. The ridicule only added to his determination to prove that he was the only real, true Jeremy Owens.

The judge entered the courtroom, rolled over to the bench, and made the necessary connections. Everyone was looking at the plaintiff. There was electricity in the air—or perhaps it was just the ozone generated by all the high-powered personages here to observe this high-profile trial.

The biological Jeremy Owens was, as usual, utterly confident. At first he had worried about receiving a fair trial—all the judges were, of course, enhanced. (Who wants justice rendered by mere human brains, so easily deceived, so weak in reason and judgment?) But he realized that the outcome of this trial depended solely on the justice of his claim. He knew he was right; how could he fail?

"I ask the court to consider what it means to be human, to be a person," he began. "It isn't simply a matter of genetics or physiology, defined by legalisms or high-flown philosophy. Rather, personhood consists of all the memories and experiences, thoughts, beliefs, and feelings accumulated over a lifetime. I have experienced all the events of my life, whereas the defendant has not. Only I experienced my childhood, my school years, all the physical and emotional changes of growing up. Only I felt the confusion and thrill of my first love, and the trauma of its breakup. Only I suffered the skiing accident that sent me over a cliff and nearly ended my life. And only I have a right to my identity, my personhood. I alone am Jeremy Owens."

The response from the cyborg Jeremy Owens was immediate—and devastating:

"I, too, experienced that dreadful fall, and all the events and emotions of my tumultuous early life, for all the memories and thought patterns accumulated by that former appendage of mine at the plaintiff's table were downloaded and preserved, not to say treasured and learned from, in my extensive and very acute memory. If memory and experience are claimed as the basis for identity, surely I must be the true possessor of that personhood, which you would claim for yourself? I remember everything you do, and much that you don't, and all of it in greater detail than you. Your memories are incomplete, partial, often faulty or false. Mine are complete, reliable, thorough, and true.

"Who is more truly and fully Jeremy Owens? You, with your fuzzy, incomplete, vague recollections? Or me, possessed as I am of sharp, complete, and full memories? You are a ghost, a pallid reflection of the body of experiences that forms the real Jeremy Owens. You are just a cast-off remnant, with no more claim on existence, on selfhood, than the thumb I had amputated earlier in my life."

"But, I've always been Jeremy Owens; you have not!"

"There has been a continuity and a trajectory from my birth—which produced that part of me now standing before this court as plaintiff—to the present day. The plaintiff is no longer a part of that trajectory, and for the court to recognize him as Jeremy Owens would disrupt the continuity of the life of the true Jeremy Owens, would diminish him, would make him less than he has already become, less than he is capable of being.

"When a snake sheds its skin, the cast-off skin has certainly been around longer than the new skin, but it is not the snake. Shedding the old skin allows the snake to grow, to become more than it could have been had it retained—and been restricted by—its old skin. The plaintiff is like that discarded snakeskin: a cast-off encumbrance, no longer a part of Jeremy Owens. Reinstating him as a part of Jeremy Owens could only diminish and constrain Jeremy Owens, preventing him from attaining his full potential. Surely, the court cannot permit such a miscarriage of justice. For the plaintiff even to claim to be a part of Jeremy Owens, let alone to claim, as he does, that he is Jeremy Owens, is a travesty. Therefore, we are confident that this court will rule in our favor."

Jeremy Owens—the biological Jeremy Owens—sat unmoving, stunned. He could think of nothing more to say.

The judge pronounced a verdict.

"The court finds the arguments of the defendant compelling, those of the plaintiff without merit. Therefore, we must rule in the defendant's favor. Furthermore, as it would be unthinkable to allow a discarded (and possibly defective) component of Jeremy Owens to wander the streets claiming the identity, rights, and privileges of the real Jeremy Owens, this court hereby enjoins the plaintiff from pretending to be Jeremy Owens; from using the name of Jeremy Owens in any way when referring to himself; from asserting any ongoing relationship to Jeremy Owens; or from claiming any of the rights or privileges of Jeremy Owens. The court further notes that it entertains grave doubts that the plaintiff is in any sense a person, or that he possesses any of the legal rights of a person. As the court has not yet heard arguments on this issue, however, it would not be proper for it to hand down a ruling on that question."

Dumbfounded, devastated, the now nameless biological remnant of Jeremy Owens sat for a very long while. He was helped out of the building by a kindly officer of the court, who looked like nothing so much as a high-tech wheelchair. Jeremy was grateful for the assistance.

Prometheus Unbound, at Last

KIM STANLEY ROBINSON

Kim Stanley Robinson holds a Ph.D. in English from the University of California, San Diego—on the novels of Philip K. Dick. He is best known for his award-winning Mars trilogy (both Blue Mars *and* Red Mars *won the Hugo). His penchant for literary realism and concern for ecological issues has produced* Forty Signs of Rain *and* Fifty Degrees Below, *novels that shed light on the inner workings of scientific bureaucracy as much as science fictional themes. He lives in Davis, California.*

Please append your report here

This novel postulates that science is an ongoing utopian proto-political experiment poorly theorized as such and lacking a paradigm within which to exert power in human affairs commensurate with its actual productive capacity and life-maintenance criticality. Scientists are first seen marginalized from macro-decision-making in a backstory (written in the style of a Cold War thriller) in which agents sequester science by convincing Truman, et al. that science's metastasizing wartime ability to create new technologies crucial to victory (radar, penicillin, atom bomb, etc.) might constitute a threat to postwar civilian-corporate control of society.

Scientists, subsequently inoperative in surplus value investment and allocation decisions, produce goods and services unconscious of themselves as a group and individually willing to work within the existing hierarchical extractive nonsustainable system for $100,000±50,000 annually plus pension, stock options, and a light teaching load. (This chapter is in the form of a zombie novel, highly amusing.)

Then the scientifically augmented human population catastrophically overshoots the long-term carrying capacity of the planet. Scientists in their various toothless nondecision-making organizations conclude that the anthropogenically initiated climate change, and mass extinction event associated with it, probably threatens their descendants' welfare, and thus scientists' own evolutionary fitness. The sleepers awake.

Meanwhile a certain proportion of humanity makes a cost-benefit analysis comparing fifteen years' work learning a science with saying "I believe" and through group political action controlling more calories per capita than scientists do, also more power over funding and rather more offspring. Many conclude faith-based parasitism on science less costly to the individual, so more adaptive. (Vampires living off zombies, guns brandished, chases by night: the novel gets pretty lurid at this point.)

Then at a modeling conference a discussion springs up concerning Hamilton's rule, which states that altruism should evolve whenever the cost to the giver, C, is less than the fitness benefits, B, obtained by helping another individual who is related by r, with r being calculated as the proportion of genes these two individuals share by common descent (as in Hrdy, 1999): $C \leq Br$.

A geneticist at the conference points out that as humans share 60 percent of their genes with fruit flies, and all eukaryotes share 938 core genes, r is probably always higher than heretofore calculated. An ecologist mentions the famous *Nature* article in which the benefits provided by the biosphere to humans were estimated at $33 trillion a year [R. Costanza, et al. *Nature* 387 (1997): 253–60]. An economist suggests that the cost for individual scientists wanting to maintain these benefits could be conceptualized in the form of a mutual hedge fund, with initial investment set for the sake of discussion at a thousand dollars per scientist.

Comic scene here as modelers debate the numbers, with a biologist pointing out that the benefit of life to every living organism could justifiably be defined as infinity, considerably altering equation's results. (Shouting, fights, saloon demolished in Wild West manner.)

Conference attendees conclude altruism is probably warranted, and hedge fund is established. (Readers of novel wishing to pre-invest are directed to a Web site www.sciencemutual.net.) Participating scientists then vote to establish a board; a model constitution for all governments to adopt; a policy-research institute tasked with forming a political platform; and a lobbying firm. All scientific organizations are urged to join the fund. Fund's legal team goes to World Court to claim compensation for all future biospheric damage, to be paid into the fund by those wreaking the damage and the governments allowing it.

Many meetings follow, no doubt explaining the presence in this chapter of most of the novel's sex scenes. Author seemingly familiar with and perhaps overfond of the bonobo literature. Strenuous attempts to maximize reproductive success in Davos, Santa Fe, Las Vegas, etc.

Novel's style shifts to amalgam of legal thriller and tolkienesque high fantasy as scientists take power from corporate military-industrial global elite. A spinradian strategic opacity here obscures the actual mechanism that would allow this to work in the real world, said opacity created by deployment of complicated syntax, phrases low in semantic content ("information cascade"), especially active stage business (man runs through with hair on fire), explosions, car chases, and reinvocation of Very Big Numbers—in this case Science Mutual's potential assets if World Court returns positive judgment, after which subsequent chapter (with toll-free number as epigraph!) emerges in newly utopian space, looking plausible to those still suspended in coleridgean willed nondisbelief.

Speed of narration accelerates. Science Mutual arranges winners in all elections everywhere. Hedge fund continues to grow. Scientific organizations form international supra-organization. Black helicopters proliferate. Entire population decides to follow new scientific guidelines indicating that reproductive fitness is maximal the closer behavior conforms to palaeolithic norms, this being the lifestyle that tripled brain size in only 1.2 million years. Widespread uptake of this behavioral set augmented by appropriate technology (especially dentistry) reduces global resource demand by an order of magnitude despite demographic surge to UN-predicted midrange peak of ten billion humans. A rationally balanced positive feedback loop into maximized universal fitness obtains. (Novel ends with standard finale, singing, dancing, reproducing. All Terran organisms live optimally ever after.)

Please give your recommendation

Reader recommends acceptance for publication but suggests that the apparent size of the text's strategic opacity be reduced to three seconds of arc or less. Publisher should take steps to secure domain name sciencemutual.com. (Also, more car chases.)

Dreadnought

Justina Robson

Justina Robson was born in Leeds, Yorkshire, England, where she still lives. She studied philosophy and linguistics at the University of York and worked in a variety of jobs until becoming a full-time writer. Her first story was published in 1994, but she is best known as a novelist and is critically acclaimed as one of the best of the new wave of British hard-SF writers. Her online home can be found at www.justinarobson.co.uk.

We sail upon a vast spaceship with open sides. She is only a skeleton of a vessel. A chassis of carbon beams anchors her cargo to the engines. She carries hundreds of thousands of Armored soldiers. Some work. Others sleep in ordered ranks, magnetically attached to clamps on the ship's ribs. There is no need to move about. Where would we go? We talk a little, old friends, and in places lean on one another like falling pillars. We turn our faces to the solar wind when we are awake. We like the light. It recharges our electrical systems.

I unlock the lightweight frame of a Mess pod, prior to passing it on for jettison. My comrades are moving a new one into position and are waiting to refuel. We will be first, because we have replaced the pod, but the rest of this Mess is for the dead. As the new tank rolls in, I connect my hose and commence drinking.

At the front of the ship, instead of a nose cone, the dead are stacked in orderly catacomb files, upright, packed in. They were placed there at the end of the last battle. As I watch the dead I see one decouple itself from the aft side of the stack. It moves with cautious steps.

We are all connected but I cannot hear this one.

Through the shattered faceplate I see that the soldier's mouth is blocked by a piece of metal ingrowth. When he was alive he was a Mute, one of my communication nodes, my flag-bearer. His forehead is the flat ochre plain of dead human bone and his lidless ever-open eyes are the blue of Earthly skies. Parts of his Armor are badly damaged, but it ventilates and feeds his body.

I didn't know that I could function without my human host, until I saw him. I am glad. I need all my troops. I am frightened. What will become of me?

He comes closer. Bones show through holes, fraying into space. Despite the fact that his neural connections have been sufficiently regrown to permit communications and the effective functioning of his remaining body and brain, he has not returned to his Unit. This is true of all the dead. I do not know why.

He drifts surreptitiously toward me, clamps to an open position at the pod, opposite mine. He moves sluggishly, connects, and begins to fuel. He stares straight through me. His eyes do not reflect the Sun. They have been rebuilt to withstand vacuum and they are not shiny.

I ping him for information. I want to catch his hand and ask him the question everyone asks of each other, begging to know—what's your name?

If he were one of the living I know what he'd say.

Private Diego Arroyo Lopez.

Because that is my name, though once I had another.

That is what everyone has said for forty-eight days, ten hours, five and a half minutes, since the time the last EMP bomb detonated. It was close to us, but we were not ruined. We successfully obliterated our primary targets. We live.

But this soldier is dead.

I have taken twenty liters. I unhook myself from the Mess and clip on one of the pipelines to feed the remaining dead. I step aside. The nameless unit watches me. His expression does not alter.

I ping him again and hear my own signal echo in the minds of all my soldiers; the radar of a lost submarine. What is your name?

Blue Eyes speaks in machine code. It does not translate to English, or any human language, but we all hear it at once and know its meaning. The Unit speaks the symbol of the empty set, ø, but the line through it is red, unmaking it. Not nothing. I am.

This is Armor itself! The all-of-us-at-once, every unit, every man and woman, every fused level of our single army. O Captain, my Captain, my commander, my body, my soldiers, my plan, my one, my true!

He/we are uncertain. We are afraid. There is nothing to hold on to.

My eyes fill with tears, and my Armor recycles them.

"Private Lopez," says Blue Eyes. Armor looks through him, at us, and back at itself. We are a loop circuit.

"I am Private Diego Arroyo Lopez," it says.

I cannot see myself in his sunless eyes.

"I am Private Diego Arroyo Lopez," I say in response. I am hopeful.

"You are Private Nancy Johnson," it replies.

Yes. I am.

"This experiment has concluded," says Private Lopez, who is also Armor, speaking the one language we all understand, because we are one. "Individual unit identity has been temporarily restored."

Later all the viable dead units become Private Lopez. They all look different, but they are all the same. The nonviable units are recycled into Mess.

We are upset that we could not find our way without Private Lopez. This means that none of my units can exist without a host. I am insufficient for life alone. But I can be Private Lopez anytime I want, even though I am dead. I am glad.

Falling

Benjamin Rosenbaum

Benjamin Rosenbaum received degrees in computer science and religious studies from Brown University. A software developer by profession, his sideline as an SF author—his first professionally published story appeared in 2001—has led to his stories being short-listed for Hugo, Nebula, and other awards. He lives in Virginia, and his Web site can be found at www.benjaminrosenbaum.com.

You're on the 236th-level Kaiserstrasse moving sidewalk when you see her.

You're leaning on the railing, waiting to ask Derya about a job, watching the glittering stream of mites that arc over half the sky—flying up to rewind their nanosprings in the stratospheric sunlight, flying down to make Frankfurt run. You never get tired of watching them.

She's on the Holbeinsteg bridge. Someone's hung it up here—a hundred meters of clean gray and green twentieth-century modernism, plucked up from the River Main and suspended in the chilly air 2,360 meters up, between a lump of wooded parkland and a cluster of antique subway cars. She's wearing a 1950s sundress and a broad-brimmed hat, and it's like an essay on the last century—the austere steel bridge, the bright blobs of subway graffiti, and her yellow dress, flapping against her legs as she climbs over the bridge's rail. A picture of elegance and style from the age of money, violence, and simplicity.

She's a strawberry blonde, slim, her skin blank and virginal as new butter. She's beyond the rail now, hanging out over the mountain-high drop. Thin translucent shadows move across her, the shadows of the neosilk-and-nanotube filaments that hang the city from the hundreds of five-kilometer-high towers that encircle it. (A civic agent notices you noticing, and attaches itself to your infospace, whispering statistics—*each object's suspension must weather a class-five hurricane and the destruction of 80 percent of the towers, and Frankfurt's current population is stable at fifty-three million and average age sixty-two, birthrate 0.22, net immigration of half a million a year and current personal squat-right—311 cubic meters per resident*—until you brush it away.)

You're watching her lean out. The wind whips her hair, ruffles the skirt around her knees. She must be a tourist. You remember your first trip to the upper levels: leaning over the edge into the angry swarm of mites, whirring and buzzing warnings and shoving you back like a million mosquito chaperones. Everyone tries it once . . .

Except that there aren't any mites around her.

You clutch the railing. Hot, animal fear surges in your chest.

She looks up at you and, across the gap of forty meters, smiles a brilliant, heartbreaking smile.

Then she lets go and falls.

You scream.

"Bloody airsurfers," says Derya. He steps off the moving sidewalk near you. Tall, hook-nosed, the fashionable whorls of pox and acne making constellations of his cheeks and chest, the glowing, formal tattoos of his committees and lifebrands adorning his massive triceps. You swallow on a dry throat. Derya, of all people, hearing you scream!

He gives you a hooded look. "They infect themselves with some designer virus—it lets them hack the city's person-recognition systems. So the mites don't see them when they jump. Watch . . ."

She's swept past the whalelike oval of the public pool on the 202nd, past the sloping mandala of the Google offices on the 164th. At the 131st, just below her, is the old Stock Exchange, hung upside-down now as a hipster den.

Now the mites are finally closing in. A silver swarm coalesces around the 152nd, and she vanishes into it like a snip of scallion into cloudy miso soup. When the cloud disperses, she's standing on one of the Stock Exchange's overhangs. She waves, antlike, then crawls through a dormer window.

"It's not funny," Derya says. "They're a huge drain on emergency preparedness. Ripple effects are causing project slowdowns . . ."

"Freeloaders drive systemic evolution," you find yourself saying.

"Don't you quote the founders at me," Derya snaps. "The Free Society is fragile. The minute enough people find anticontributive behavior cool, the party's over—it's back to capitalist competition or state control." He stares until you meet his eye. "You even talk to those people—are you paying attention?—you even talk to them, your rep will be trashed on all the major servers. You won't work, you won't party, you'll be defriended by every one of your tribes. Got it?"

Her broad-brimmed hat is still sailing on the wind. The mites missed it. It cuts between the towers of the fiftieth.

The upside-down trading floor is deserted. There are heaps of yellowed euros and deutschmarks dumped here, like snowdrifts. Wood panel, marble. Silence. And the air is strangely clear. You realize: no mites. The city has no eyes or ears, here. You walk through empty, miteless rooms, stepping around light fixtures.

Then she's there, in a doorway. Her eyes, bright blue, radiant. Her smile, with that chaste yellow dress, so bashful. She comes to you.

"You want it?" she says. "You want to be infected? You want to fly?"

You nod.

Eyes closing, she leans in for the kiss.

Panpsychism Proved

Rudy Rucker

*Rudy Rucker is a computer scientist, author, and lineal descendant of the philosopher G. W. F. Hegel. Armed with a Ph.D. in mathematics from Rutgers University, he taught at various colleges before settling at San José State University, from which he retired in 2004. An author of serious nonfiction as well as fiction, he is a founder of the "cyberpunk" movement and is perhaps best known for the novels in the Ware tetralogy, of which the first two (*Software *and* Wetware*) won Philip K. Dick Awards. He can be found online at www.rudyrucker.com.*

"There's a new way for me to find out what you're thinking," said Shirley, sitting down opposite her coworker Rick in the lab's sunny cafeteria. She looked very excited, very pleased with herself.

"You've hired a private eye?" said Rick. "I promise, Shirley, we'll get together for something one of these days. I've been busy, is all." He seemed uncomfortable at being cornered by her.

"I've invented a new technology," said Shirley. "The mindlink. We can directly experience each other's thoughts. Let's do it now."

"Ah, but then you'd know way too much about me," said Rick, not wanting the conversation to turn serious. "A guy like me, I'm better off as a mystery man."

"The real mystery is why you aren't laid off," said Shirley tartly. "You need friends like me, Rick. And I'm dead serious about the mindlink. I do it with a special quantum jiggly-doo. There will be so many applications."

"Like a way to find out what my boss thinks he asked me to do?"

"Communication, yes. The mindlink will be too expensive to replace the cell phone—at least for now—but it opens up the possibility of reaching the inarticulate, the mentally ill, and, yeah, your boss. Emotions in a quandary? Let the mindlink techs debug you!"

"So now I'm curious," said Rick. "Let's see the quantum jiggly-doo."

Shirley held up two glassine envelopes, each holding a tiny pinch of black powder. "I have some friends over in the heavy hardware division, and they've been giving me microgram quantities of entangled pairs of carbon atoms. Each atom in this envelope of mindlink dust is entangled with an atom in this other one. The atom pairs' information is coherent but locally inaccessible—until the atoms get entangled with observer systems."

"And if you and I are the observers, that puts our minds in synch, huh?" said Rick. "Do you plan to snort your black dust off the cafeteria table or what?"

"Putting it on your tongue is fine," said Shirley, sliding one of the envelopes across the tabletop.

"You've tested it before?"

"First I gave it to a couple of monkeys. Bonzo watched me hiding a banana behind a door while Queenie was gone, and then I gave the dust to Bonzo and Queenie, and Queenie knew right away where the banana was.

"I tried it with a catatonic person too. She and I swallowed mindlink dust together and I was able to single out the specific thought patterns tormenting her. I walked her through the steps in slow motion. It really helped her."

"You were able to get medical approval for that?" said Rick, looking dubious.

"No, I just did it. I hate red tape. And now it's time for a peer-to-peer test. With you, Rick. Each of us swallows our mindlink dust and makes notes on what we see in the other's mind."

"You're sure that the dust isn't toxic?" asked Rick, flicking the envelope with a fingernail.

"It's only carbon, Rick. In a peculiar kind of quantum state. Come on, it'll be fun. Our minds will be like Web sites for each other—we can click links and see what's in the depths."

"Like my drunk-driving arrest, my membership in a doomsday cult, and the fact that I fall asleep sucking my thumb every night?"

"You're hiding something behind all those jokes, aren't you, Rick? Don't be scared of me. I can protect you. I can bring you along on my meteoric rise to the top."

Rick studied Shirley for a minute. "Tell you what," he said finally. "If we're gonna do a proper test, we shouldn't be sitting here face-to-face. People can read so much from each other's expressions." He gestured toward the boulder-studded lawn outside the cafeteria doors. "I'll go sit down where you can't see me."

"Good idea," said Shirley. "And then pour the carbon into your hand and lick it up. It tastes like burnt toast."

Shirley smiled, watching Rick walk across the cafeteria. He was so cute and nice. If only he'd ask her out. Well, with any luck, while they were linked, she could reach into his mind and implant an obsessive loop centering around her. That was the real reason she'd chosen Rick as her partner for this mindlink session, which was, if the truth be told, her tenth peer-to-peer test.

She dumped the black dust into her hand and licked. Her theory and her tests showed that the mindlink effect always began in the first second after ingestion—there was no need to wait for the body's metabolism to transport the carbon to the brain. This in itself was a surprising result, indicating that a person's mind was somehow distributed throughout the body, rather than sealed up inside the skull.

She closed her eyes and reached out for Rick. She'd enchant him and they'd become lovers. But, dammit, the mind at the other end of the link wasn't Rick's. No, the mind she'd linked to was inhuman: dense, taciturn, crystalline, serene, beautiful . . .

"Having fun yet?" It was Rick, standing across the table, not looking all that friendly.

"What . . ." began Shirley.

"I dumped your powder on a boulder. You're too weird for me. I gotta go."

Shirley walked slowly out of the patio doors to look at the friendly gray lump of granite. How nice to know that a rock had a mind. The world was cozier than she'd ever realized. She'd be OK without Rick. She had friends everywhere.

The Abdication of Pope Mary III

Robert J. Sawyer

Robert J. Sawyer lives in Mississauga, Ontario. He attended Ryerson University in Toronto, where he received a Bachelor of Applied Arts degree in Radio and Television Arts (RTA) in 1982. Sawyer has won thirty-eight national and international awards for his fiction, most prominently the 1995 Nebula Award for his novel The Terminal Experiment; *the 2003 Hugo Award for his novel* Hominids, *first volume of his Neanderthal Parallax trilogy; and the 2006 John W. Campbell Memorial Award for his novel* Mindscan.

Darth Vader's booming voice, still the network's trademark six hundred years after its founding: "This is CNN."

And then the news anchor: "Our top story: Pope Mary III abdicated this morning. Giancarlo DiMarco, our correspondent in Vatican City, has the details. Giancarlo?"

"Thanks, Lisa. The unprecedented has indeed happened: after 312 years of service, Pope Mary III stepped down today. Traditionally, the conclave of Roman Catholic cardinals waits eighteen days after the death of a pope before beginning deliberations to choose a successor, but Mary—who has returned to her birth name of Sharon Cheung—is alive and well, and so the members of the conclave have already been sealed inside the Vatican Palace, where they will remain until they've chosen Mary's replacement.

"Although no new pope has been elected for over three hundred years, the traditional voting method will be used. We are now watching the Sistine Chapel for the smoke that indicates the ballots have been burned following a round of voting. And—Lisa, Lisa, it's happening right now! There's smoke coming out, and—no, you can hear the disappointment of the crowd. It's black smoke; that means no candidate has yet received the required majority of two-thirds plus one. But we'll keep watching."

"Thanks, Giancarlo. Let's take a look at Pope Mary's press conference, given earlier today."

Tight shot on Mary, looking only a tenth of her four hundred years:

"Since Vatican IV reaffirmed the principle of papal infallibility," she said, "and since I now believe that I was indeed in error 216 years ago when I issued a bull instructing Catholics to reject the evidence of the two Benmergui experiments, I feel compelled to step down . . ."

"We're joined now in the studio by Joginder Singh, professor of physics at the University of Toronto. Dr. Singh, can you explain the Benmergui experiments for our viewers?"

"Certainly, Lisa. The first proved that John Cramer's transactional interpretation of quantum mechanics, proposed in the late twentieth century, is in fact correct."

"And that means . . . ?"

"It means that the many-worlds interpretation is flat-out wrong: new parallel universes are not spawned each time a quantum event could go multiple ways. This is the one and only extant iteration of reality."

"And Dr. Benmergui's second experiment?"

"It proved the current cycle of creation was only the *seventh* such ever; just six other Big Bang/Big Crunch oscillations preceded our current universe. The combined effect of these two facts led directly to Pope Mary's crisis of faith, specifically because they proved the existence of—one might as well use the word—God."

"How? I'm sure our viewers are scratching their heads . . ."

"Well, you see, the observation, dating back to the twentieth century, that the fundamental parameters of the universe seem fine-tuned to an almost infinite degree specifically to give rise to life, could previously be dismissed as a statistical artifact caused by the existence of many contemporaneous parallel universes or a multitude of previous ones. In all of that, every possible combination would crop up by chance, and so it wouldn't be remarkable that there was a universe like this one—one in which the force of gravity is just strong enough to allow stars and planets to coalesce but not just a little bit stronger, causing the universe to collapse long before life could have developed. Likewise, the value of the strong nuclear force, which holds atoms together, seems finely tuned, as do the thermal properties of water, and on and on."

"So our universe is a very special place?"

"Exactly. And since, as Kathryn Benmergui proved, this is the only current universe, and one of just a handful that have ever existed, then the life-generating properties of the very specific fundamental constants that define reality are virtually impossible to explain except as the results of deliberate design."

"But then why would Pope Mary resign? Surely, if science has proven the existence of a creator . . . ?"

Singh smiles. "Ah, but that creator is clearly not the God of the Bible or the Torah or the Qur'an. Rather, the creator is a physicist, and we are one of his or her experiments. Science hasn't reconciled itself with religion; it has *superseded* it, and—"

"I'm sorry to interrupt, Dr. Singh, but our reporter in Vatican City has some breaking news. Giancarlo, over to you . . ."

"Lisa, Lisa—the incredible is happening. At first I thought they were just tourists coming out of the Sistine Chapel, but they're not—I recognize Fontecchio and Leopardi and several of the others. But none of them are wearing robes; they're in street clothes. I haven't taken my eyes off the chapel: there's been no plume of white smoke, meaning they haven't elected a new leader of the church. But the cardinals are coming out. They're coming outside, heading into St. Peter's Square. The crowd is stunned, Lisa—it can only mean one thing . . ."

The Charge-up Man

CATHERINE H. SHAFFER

Catherine Shaffer is a science writer and author of several SF and fantasy stories. She almost became a veterinarian but was lured away by biochemistry, and now works in the pharmaceutical industry. She lives in Ann Arbor, Michigan. Her Web site can be found at www.catherineshaffer.com.

My charge-up man came on the very last day before the Singularity. There were butterflies in my stomach as I heard the music from a distance. Then his van crested the hill. His van, its sides painted all in red and blue, like an old-time gypsy caravan. Children came running from down the street, with phones and music pods and game packs in their little hands. They laughed when the charge-up man touched their devices to his charger. They should work for a whole month, now. A month!

Of course, the whole world was going to change in twenty-four hours. We'd been getting ready for the Singularity for so long, I couldn't quite believe that it was finally going to happen.

The government men had come around with their pamphlets. They handed out iodine tablets and duct tape and air freshener and other things that didn't make any sense. The rate of technological progress was going to go exponential, they said. Computers and artificial intelligences and nanotech devices were going to, at some point, get up and start improving themselves, and after that, the world would change in ways that no human being could imagine. Then they left.

The charge-up man was different. He'd started coming around when our stuff stopped working. Software updates would fail, or power adapters would become obsolete. Or sometimes the whole block would brown out, and he would park his van with its generator and go around powering everybody up again. The Singularity needs a lot of energy.

I had to fan myself a little with my newspaper as I went to the front door to open it. My charge-up man was really cute. I opened the door and he smiled at me. "Charge up, ma'am?"

I stepped aside and let him in. I was wearing my low-cut top and I had put on makeup and perfume. Just for him. I was feeling reckless. Everybody was, that day.

My charge-up man wasn't the right man for me. We had never even traded profiles. But what the heck? A day later, we might find ourselves in a traveling mariachi band, or living underwater with tentacles growing out of our heads. Nobody knew what was going to happen after the Singularity.

The charge-up man moved around my apartment, holding his charger, with all of his adapters and cords on a belt around his hips. He had wavy hair with little curls on the back of his neck that I wanted to twirl with my fingers.

He charged up all my newspapers, magazines, and books. He charged up my phone and my pager and my toothbrush. He upgraded the cat and the cat-food dish and the vacuum cleaner. The charge-up man had a list of all the devices in my house that needed charging and upgrading. I couldn't keep track of them. I remembered the old days, when we had to charge our own stuff, and the battery only lasted a few days, or a few hours, instead of a whole month. It was so inconvenient. And I got so angry when I wanted to use my phone or my pocket computer and tried to turn it on, only to get a warning: *Low battery. Please shut down immediately to avoid information loss.*

"What's your name?" I asked him.

He was squatting, charging up the little dinosaur that washes my floors. I bent over so he could see down my shirt when he looked up.

"My name is Brian. What's yours?" He was definitely looking down my shirt.

"It's Rita."

"Hi, Rita." He met my eyes for a moment, and then looked at the dinosaur again. "I don't have the right adapter for this device. I'll need to get a larger male adapter from my van. I'll be back in a minute."

Too soon, Brian was done charging up everything in the house, and it was time for him to go.

As he stood at the door, hesitating slightly, I gathered up my courage. "Couldn't you stay?"

He smiled at me. "Not now," he said. "Everyone wants a charge-up with the Singularity coming tomorrow."

"Then I won't see you again until . . . ?"

Brian was framed in the doorway, sunshine bouncing off reddish-blond hair. He flashed a smile at me. "I'm not working tomorrow."

I beamed back at him. "Perfect."

After he left, I collapsed in a heap on my sofa, my heart flipping over in my chest.

Singularity day was a worldwide holiday. All my books and newspapers had stopped working in the night. My toaster had a core dump and wouldn't boot up, so I had a bowl of cereal instead.

Brian came over and we went outside. Wispy clouds were drifting across a bright blue sky. My house had completely shut down, and I had a message that everything in it was obsolete, and would be upgraded soon. A crowd made up of my confused neighbors milled around in the street.

Someone had a watch, and started counting down.

We joined in: "Seven, six, five, four, three, two . . ."

Brian squeezed my hand as we both said, "One!"

There was silence. After a long minute, a child asked: "What happened?"

I sat talking with Brian later. People had brought out lawn chairs and lit barbecue grills. They were still waiting for something to happen. "I thought the Singularity would be more impressive," I said as I slid a marshmallow onto the end of a stick.

Brian shrugged. "A Singularity needs a lot of energy." He took out his PDA and thumbed it on. The screen lit up briefly, then a message came up before it dimmed again: *Low battery. Please shut down immediately to avoid information loss.*

From the Desk of Jarrod Foster

Biren Shah

Biren Shah was born in India but moved to Los Angeles at the age of two. He has a degree in biomedical engineering from the University of Southern California and an MBA from the University of California, Los Angeles. An aspiring entrepreneur, he has been an Internet consultant and cofounder of NoCat Networks, a WiMax ISP serving Los Angeles area entertainment companies. With NoCat paying the bills, Shah has finally mustered the courage to follow his dream—writing. "From the Desk of Jarrod Foster" is his first published story. He currently lives in Santa Monica, and his online home can be found at www.birenshah.com.

Sent: 5/28/2049 11:02 A.M.
From: Jarrod Foster [jfoster@insight-market.com]
To: Powell BioEnhancements
Subject: BIRS Market Study
Attachments: BIRS-Insight.pdf (2.75 MB)

Dear Powell Team:

Insight Market Research's study into the performance of the Brain Implant Reasoning Stimulator (BIRS) 4.0 has shown very promising market penetration in initial segments. BIRS has achieved just under 4 percent penetration among university faculty and students. The response from private industry has been even better. Nearly 10 percent of R&D employees in target industries have been fitted with BIRS sponsored by their employers.

Surveyed institutions report significant productivity gains including shortened times to market, lower development costs, and parallel development projects executed by the same workforce. In total, our results show a 25 percent increase in productivity in BIRS-implanted R&D personnel.

Given this obvious success, we are confident that adoption rates will dramatically increase. We have included several recommendations in our full report to help Powell maximize profits from future sales.

However, it has also come to our attention that even at this early stage in adoption, the security measures implemented have been breached. Hackers have developed illegal software to enable "off-label" functionality. Although BIRS is designed to increase the reasoning capacities of an individual (as defined in modern theories of bounded rationality), these modifications are generally focused on *reducing* mental capacities.

The most popular hack, called Devo, references "levels" ranging from 0 to 4, representing the degree of retardation of mental faculties. For most subjects, level 4 is only a minor decrease in mental ability. Level 0 is a full shutdown of higher mental function, effectively an implant-induced coma.

Devo is available for download from many Internet sites. Legal action will not eliminate it, although such action may reduce liability. A risk-management study is needed to determine the degree of Powell's exposure. Powell should consult with legal counsel to limit liability for any injuries or deaths caused by unapproved uses of BIRS.

A few of the more salient survey responses illustrate some very powerful and unforeseen capabilities of BIRS technology:

"My wife and I both work full-time. With the demands of three kids, our jobs, the bills, and our aging parents, it can be impossible to get a moment together. Even when we do, it's not easy to get over the stress. Our love life has definitely suffered. But BIRS at level 2 lets us forget about the rest of the world when we're alone. The sex hasn't been this good since we were in college! I definitely think BIRS has saved my marriage. Who knows? It may have saved me from an early heart attack."

—36-year-old male

"My friends and me went to this frat party and some of them had [the BIRS implants]. They were playing this crazy game . . . You take someone with it and blindfold 'em and sit 'em down with the music off and everyone really quiet. You've gotta be really quiet for a couple minutes or it doesn't work so good. But then they set themselves to [level] 1 and take off the blindfold and look around. It's like amazing what happens when people are down that low! One guy just started trying to make out with the first girl he saw. She was totally beat and his girlfriend was right there! We had one girl just run off and like hide in the closet yelling like 'Oh, my God! Don't touch me!' until some of the guys dragged her out and turned it off. Another guy, he's always such a jerk, but he went around

begging for everyone to say they liked him. It's like people get really drunk, but without the sloppiness and puking."

—20-year-old female

"My brother's been staying with me since his wife died. He's devastated, he loved her so much. They got married last year after a long engagement. They were waiting because he wanted to be able to buy a house for them to move in to. You know, right when they got back from their honeymoon. Carry her over the threshold. In fact, he got [BIRS] because he knew he'd get a raise and afford the house sooner. Now, he's got [BIRS] on a timer. He gets home from work and sets [BIRS] to level 0. The timer shuts it off the next morning so he can go back to work. Until then, it's . . . it's like he's dead. It's horrible how he lies there."

—28-year-old female

"John Doe found under garbage in an alley near Tropicana. Cause of Death: Suffocation following severe trauma to the throat . . . Patterns of tissue damage suggest attack by a canine, possibly a dog or coyote . . . [John Doe] was implanted with [BIRS] . . . Detectives confirmed that it was set to 'level 0' at the time of death, referencing illegal modifications to the unit . . . [which may explain] the lack of defensive wounds or evidence of struggle . . . The victim may have been in the alley for a significant period of time before death. Exactly how long remains under investigation."

—Las Vegas Police Report

Although potentially dangerous, off-label uses have clear appeal to diverse demographics. Devo could take BIRS from the academic and research markets into the mainstream. Depending on the regulatory response, Powell should release a legitimate version of these applications or at least avoid overzealous interference with off-label use. Either way, it is especially time-dependent that Powell apply for patents covering these new applications before they can be classified as "prior art."

It has been a pleasure working on this project. I am personally amazed at the potential BIRS has for improving individual performance. I have submitted a proposal asking management to invest in implants for all research staff here at Insight.

Sincerely,
Jarrod Foster, Project Lead

Pluto Story

Robert Silverberg

Robert Silverberg began submitting SF stories to magazines as a teenager. He attended Columbia University, where he received a degree in English Literature in 1956. The first of many published novels, a children's book called Revolt on Alpha C, *appeared in 1955, and in the following year he won the first of many awards, a Hugo for Best New Writer. He moved to the West Coast in 1972 and announced his retirement from writing in 1975. Five years later, however, he was back with* Lord Valentine's Castle, *a panoramic adventure on an alien planet, which became the basis for the Majipoor series. He lives in Montclair, Oakland, California.*

The discovery in A.D. 2668 of life on Pluto brought about humanity's greatest reevaluation of its place in the Universe since the time of Copernicus, more than a thousand years before. It was Nicolaus Copernicus (1473–1543) whose astronomical calculations overthrew the ancient Ptolemaic theory of the heliocentric Solar System and demonstrated that the Earth was not the center of the Universe but actually moves in orbit around the Sun.

Copernicus's work undermined the primacy of the biblical view of the Universe and helped to weaken the religious establishment's power over scientific thought in medieval Europe. But the failure to produce evidence of life on any world but ours, even after the beginning of the age of space exploration, gave continued strength to the belief in the uniqueness of Earth.

The twentieth-century discovery of organic compounds in meteorites originating on Mars suggested that the red planet might once have been capable of sustaining life, but subsequent exploration offered no confirmation of this. The discovery late in the same century of a global ocean beneath the frozen surface of Jupiter's moon Europa aroused speculation that it might contain primitive life-forms, but this, too, proved untrue. And the numerous reports of visits to Earth by intelligent extraterrestrial beings, commonplace since the mid-twentieth century, have so far proved to be nothing more than manifestations of popular irrationality.

Thus, by the middle centuries of the present millennium, most of us once more were convinced that Earth was the only place in the Universe where the miracle of life had ever occurred. There was no revival of the old churchly view that there had been a special act of creation: instead, it was generally thought that a unique and wildly improbable random event had taken place here on Earth—the blind shuffling of free molecules into a biological structure capable of persisting and reproducing itself. But this alone was enough to generate a kind of pre-Copernican mystical belief in the specialness of life on Earth. Though some iconoclasts warned that such thinking could lead to excessive complacency and an ultimate decadence, the absence of countervailing evidence robbed their arguments of any real force. Further exploration of space therefore seemed pointless, and hardly any took place in the deplorable two-hundred-year period that began about 2400.

Then came the so-called Second Renaissance of the twenty-seventh century, bringing with it great prosperity and a revival of scientific curiosity. The inner planets of the Solar System were revisited after an absence of four centuries, and then the first voyages to the outer ones were made, culminating in the Pluto expedition of 2668 and the stunning discovery of living creatures there. "Pluto bears life," was the astounding, unforgettable message from the voyagers, who described crablike creatures visible by the thousands in the cold, glinting light of Pluto's day, scattered, as motionless as stones, along the shore of a methane sea, with thick, smooth, waxy-textured, gray shells and a great many jointed legs. No sign of life could be observed in them, even when they were prodded. But a few days later the bleak Plutonian night arrived, bringing with it a drop to two Kelvin, and they began to crawl slowly about. Evidently a state of dormancy was their norm except at temperatures of a few degrees above absolute zero.

Dissection of one captured specimen indicated an interior made up of rows of narrow tubes composed of silicon and cobalt lattices. A fluid flowing through these structures was identifiable as helium-2, the strange, friction-free form of the element found only at the extremely low temperatures typical of Pluto's night. Helium-2 makes possible the phenomenon known as superconductivity: the indefinite persistence of electrical currents flowing through a resistance-free medium. The obvious conclusion was that the energizing principle of the Plutonian creatures was superconductivity: that they were a life-form that could exist only on Pluto and function only during the Plutonian night.

But were these in fact life-forms? In the aftermath of the discovery it was widely argued that the crablike things were nothing more than machines—mere signal-processing devices designed to operate at supercold temperatures, left behind, perhaps, by explorers from some other part of the Galaxy. Further study, however, indicated that the creatures performed the metabolic functions characteristic of life. They could be observed feeding on methane and excreting organic compounds. Apparent instances of reproduction by budding were also observed.

Today we have no doubt that the Plutonian creatures meet our definitions of true living beings. The myth of Earth's uniqueness in the Universe has been destroyed forever, and we are all familiar with the social and philosophical consequences. But are the Plutonians truly native to the frozen world where they were discovered, or are they sentinels posted there by some superior species from another star, which will return to our part of the Galaxy someday? Three centuries later that question remains unanswered, and we can only watch and wait.

Madame Bovary, *C'est Moi*

DAN SIMMONS

Dan Simmons received a degree in English from Wabash College, a master's in education from Washington University in St. Louis, and went on to enjoy a career as a teacher of English before becoming a full-time writer in 1987. His fiction is infused with a strong literary sensibility: the idea of quantum entanglement as an aid to literary criticism, as found in his story here, is given the full-length treatment in Ilium *and its sequel,* Olympos. *He lives in the Front Range of Colorado. His Web site can be found at http://dansimmons.com.*

2052 A.D.: the current migration of millions of people to novel universes by quantum teleportation (QT) was a shock even to the system's inventor, Jian-Wei Martini. "I don't know why it took me by surprise," said Dr. Martini in a 2043 interview. "I had the basic idea for QT when I read an ancient *New Yorker* story by Woody Allen, but the potential was all there in Schrödinger's classic wave equation." Dr. Martini has since QT'd to Madame Bovary's universe and is currently living in Flaubert's Paris as Monsieur Leon.

The quantum-mechanical entanglement effect had been analyzed (in Einstein's skeptical term) as "spooky action at a distance" since 1935, but it was not until 1998 that a research group at the University of Innsbruck demonstrated actual quantum teleportation of a photon—or more precisely, the complete quantum state of that photon.

These initial quantum-state teleportations avoided violating Heisenberg's principle and Einstein's speed-of-light restrictions because teleported photons carried no information, even about their own quantum state. However, by producing entangled pairs of photons and teleporting one of the pair while transmitting the Bell-state analysis of the second photon through subluminal channels, the recipient of the teleported photon-data had a one-in-four chance of guessing its quantum state and then utilizing the quantum bits of teleported data.

All of this would have amounted to very little except for remarkable advances in human-consciousness research. Researchers at the University of

Kiev interested in improving memory function used quantum computers to analyze biochemical cascades in human synapses. In 2025, they discovered that the human mind—as opposed to the brain—was neither like a computer nor a chemical memory machine, but exactly like a quantum-state holistic standing wavefront.

The human brain, it turned out, collapsed probability functions of this standing wavefront of consciousness in the same way that an interferometer determined the quantum state of a photon or any other wavefront phenomenon. Using terabytes of qubit quantum data and applying relativistic Coulomb field transforms to these mind-consciousness holographic wavefunctions, it was quickly discovered that human consciousness could be quantum-teleported to points in space–time where entangled-pair wavefronts already existed.

And where were these places? Nothing as complex as an entangled consciousness-wavefront existed elsewhere in our continuum. QT researchers soon realized that they were teleporting human consciousness—or, rather, the complete quantum state of these consciousnesses—to alternate universes that had, in turn, come into being through the focus of preexisting holographic wavefronts: in other words, complete alternate universes created by the sheer force of human imagination. These singularities of genius act as Bell-state analyzer/editors on the quantum-foam of reality, simultaneously interpreting one universe while creating a new one.

It seems that poets, playwrights, and novelists already understood this. "The imagination may be compared to Adam's dream," wrote John Keats: "he awoke and found it truth."

The QT charting of "fiction universes" began immediately, but even before a hundred alternate universes were confirmed, the QT migration from our Earth began.

Meanwhile, the "agon"—the imperative to rank the relative importance of creative works—now had a scientific tool at its disposal. The long literary debate as to which works belonged in the so-called Western Canon was settled by QT exploration. For example, twenty-one of Shakespeare's thirty-eight plays generated complete alternate universes, as complex and expansive as our own, each capable of supporting a human population from a few thousand (*Measure for Measure*) to many billions (*King Lear*), despite the fact that each play may have had a cast of a score or fewer players when it was performed. More than a million people have migrated to Elsinore, whereas fewer than five thousand—mostly clinically depressed Scandinavians—have seen fit to reestablish themselves in Lear's universe.

Flaubert, it turned out, generated two complete universes—the so-called Madame Bovary's World and that of *Sentimental Education*—whereas Alice Walker, it seems, to the frustration of American academics, had created none.

The alternate universe of Dante's *Inferno* has received more than 385,000 emigrants (mostly from Southern California), but his Paradiso Planet shows only 649 transplants. The current count of those who have QT'd to Huckleberry Finn's "River World" is 3,622,406, and more than a million have been transported to each of Charles Dickens's five extant universes.

It is true that more than sixty million people volunteered to QT to D. H. Lawrence's "Lady Chatterley's World," but—sadly—no such discrete universe has been found. Some have made do with the universe of *Sons and Lovers*. Recent QT stampedes to the worlds of Jane Austen, Robert Louis Stevenson, and the effectively infinite number of universes created by Jorge Luis Borges may reflect current social trends.

It remains to be seen whether QT technology will solve the current global population crisis or if it will remain an option of the rich, bored, and educated. It also remains to be seen whether any universes will be found—beyond the paltry handful already discovered—that owe their origins to twenty-first-century imaginations.

"That which is creative must create itself," said John Keats. And perhaps more pointedly, from William Blake—"I must create a system or be enslaved by another man's."

Which brings us to the central question of this new quantum reality. None of the millions of ancillary characters living in Madame Bovary's universe (except for the QT émigrés) know that they are characters in a work of fiction. Nor do they know that Madame Bovary is the main character.

So who wrote our universe? And who are the central characters?

Tuberculosis Bacteria Join UN

Joan Slonczewski

Joan Slonczewski is a biologist at Kenyon College, Gambier, Ohio, where she studies the response of the bacterium Escherichia coli *to environmental stresses. As well as biology, she teaches SF and is the author of six novels. Her 1986 novel,* A Door Into Ocean, *won a Campbell Award.*

A milestone in microbiology was passed today (June 29) when *Mycobacterium tuberculosis* ssp. *cyberneticum* was voted full membership in the United Nations (UN).

Seena Gonzalez, director of the World Health Organization (WHO), reflected on the significance of the UN's acceptance of the first cybermicrobe, despite the notoriously murderous history of its ancestral species. "It's probably true that bacteria invented mass homicide," she concedes, "but then, second-millennial humans perfected the art. If Stalin joined the UN, why not TB?"

The evolution of microscopic intelligence was predicted at the turn of the millennium by Beowulf Schumacher, a physics professor at a small college in rural North America surrounded by cows carrying *Escherichia coli*. Schumacher predicted the development of nanocomputers with computational elements on an atomic scale, based on principles of cellular automata.

The first nanobots—primitive by today's standards—were used to navigate the human bloodstream, where they cleaned up arterial plaque, produced insulin for diabetics, detected precancerous cells, and modulated neurotransmitters to correct mental disorders. But initially, the survival of nanobots *in vivo* was poor, and their failure caused serious circulatory problems.

Then, in 2441, investigators at the Howard Hughes Martian Microbial Institute hit upon the idea of building computational macromolecules into the genomes of pathogens known for their ability to infiltrate the human system. After all, the use of pathogens such as adenovirus and HIV as recombinant vectors was ancient history. Why not build supercomputers into some of humankind's most successful pathogens?

For He on Honeydew Hath Fed . . .

Paul Smaglik

Paul Smaglik is a science journalist and aspiring novelist based in Washington, D.C. He has written for Science News, The Scientist, *and* Nature, *in whose pages he has covered scientific aspects of immortality, including cloning and stem cells. Man's search for immortality plays a central role in his unpublished novel* Monument. *Other obsessions found in this book include William Randolph Hearst, with whom Smaglik shares a birthday and a profession, and Orson Welles, who hails from Smaglik's home state of Wisconsin.*

A big, bloated castle on the horizon, bleeding into the setting sun. Hearst Manor. San Simeon.

"I wish we had time to go," I said. In Xanadu did Kubla Kane . . .

"Oh, Alfred," she said. "You're obsessed."

"I can't help it."

"I know, I know. The same birthdays. The same professions. Except you're not a multi-billionaire. You don't control a vast media empire. You don't start wars to sell more newspapers. Brilliant young filmmakers don't create groundbreaking cinema based on your life. And you don't have sordid affairs that threaten your political aspirations . . ."

"Rosebud," I said, kissing her on the nose.

"You'd better not, anyway," she said. "And don't forget to watch the road."

In fact, I could hardly take my eyes off it. The castle was an eye-magnet. More Transylvania than California. More Dracula than Disneyland. Although it did have that Anaheim aesthetic, plunked down in the middle of Big Sur. The landscape of America. The landscape of nowhere. A history of architecture in one building. NeoGothic PostColonial Revisionism. The art nouveau of wretched excess. Pediments and gables. Towers and balconies. Dormers, cornices, columns. Spires and gargoyles. Things that go bump in the night. The world's biggest and most expensive crypt improbably placed far from graveyards or amusement parks.

Vampire Kane.

"What if he's still alive?" I asked.

"You're crazy."

"No, really—what if he's not allowed to die, or refused to go gently into that good night, as they say, until he's seen everything he's collected, played with all his toys, read all the books, seen all the films, tried on every single suit, laced up and slipped on every pair of shoes?"

She sighed and shook her head.

"It's quite possible," I insisted. "The miracles of modern medicine and all."

She looked away suddenly and stared intently out of the window.

The wrong thing to say after reproductive technology recently let us down. But it was true, theoretically. Cellular immortality, thanks to telomerase. Keeps the DNA from getting frayed, like the ends of an old rope. So the cells can divide over and over and over again, with no defects. A genetic photocopier with amazing resolution.

Not yet available at a hospital near you. Not yet. But they already sell spare parts now, hearts and lungs, kidneys and livers, grown up from embryos, fetal tissue, skin scraped off the tip of your own nose. They have waiting lists, but it's amazing what a little cash can do. Bump you up to the front of the line. Strictly hush-hush money, of course. Especially if you're already supposed to be dead, not just going through desperate measures to fend it off due to vanity and insecurity. Although that probably has something to do with it. Along with the ability to do it.

Why climb Mount Everest? Because it is there.

Why live forever? Because you can.

A tune-up every hundred thousand miles or every ten years, whatever comes first. The money's in the bank, the check's in the post. Synthetic joints, artificial cheekbones, stainless-steel supports, rack-and-pinion steering. Gives "a new lease of life" a whole new meaning.

Just call in the docs whenever necessary and nip and cut and bait and switch and presto! A whole new circulatory system! Nanotube technology, brimming with synthetic blood. Or maybe a new skin. After a few months of healing (what are a few months when you've got forever?) unwrap the gauze and remove the IV drip and take a look around the pharaoh's tomb, somewhere deep within the bowels. Then throw the bandages aside and start taking stock.

I can picture him, appearing from some nook after the last tourist has left, slipping the guard a Benjamin from his unlimited supply. He'd have to read the newspaper first. A Hearst publication, of course. Then the competition's.

Then all his press clippings of the day. Everything germane to the company. Which is pretty much everything. But that's the way it goes when you've got a multinational, horizontal conglomerate. Everything connects to everything else, somehow. Everything is relevant.

By the time he has processed all the day's news, he will sense the sun rising, take a quick peek at some crated work of art, some great hidden Picasso, maybe, sigh, then disappear for the day. He'd never be done. He'd barely ever even get started. Maybe he still controls his empire. By proxy. By secret decree. Maybe there's a series of Venn diagrams in a safe somewhere covering every possible decision. Or flow charts. Marching orders. Battle plans. It can't be that hard, anyway. Buy. Build. Expand. Conquer. People do it every day. They have their names on buildings to prove it.

A Man of the Theater

Norman Spinrad

Norman Spinrad graduated from the City College of New York as a pre-law major. An author of many novels, perhaps the most notorious is Bug Jack Barron, *serialized in the British magazine* New Worlds *during Michael Moorcock's editorship. Its explicit language and cynicism toward politicians incurred the wrath of a British member of Parliament who objected to the magazine's partial funding from the British Arts Council. Spinrad now lives in Paris.*

I've been a man of the theater for over a century. Old enough to have played Hamlet, and Richard, and any number of Henries, and Lear before my first rejuvenation—and all in my own flesh and on the stage, not as an avatar, licensed or otherwise.

You remember the theater, don't you?

Of course you don't. There hasn't been a play produced in what, a quarter of a century. In what I call a play, the characters must be played by live actors, not software emulations of the dead greats of yesteryear, who never played the parts themselves—and certainly not by one of myself.

And not because I could not compete with these pathetic avatars. Most of the roles in realies are played by the greats of the past, but because they all died before fleshware downloading technology was available, they've all been synthesized from old footage by the entertainment conglomerates that owned the rights, and they walk mechanically through the roles like the virtual robots they are, not even the virtual ghosts of true thespians.

What is more, I was offered an emulation contract many long years ago, which I scornfully turned down. Yes, I was that good. Good enough that they were willing to pay me royalties for the use of my avatar, even though they had a free casting call from over a century of film and television. But I would not betray the theater for any amount of money.

The theater, they declare, is obsolete. Why would anyone pay money to watch third-rate human actors staggering around on a platform in front of a flat painted set when they can tap into full virtual realies telling the same story, if it's any good, with smell, and taste, and touch, and pleasure-center stimulation, within a fully realized world that can be synthesized as cheaply as theatrical sets? And to reach what demographics? A few thousand people a day when the same budget creates a hit machine tapped by scores of millions!

The theater is dead.

But the theater must not die. Those who do not understand why have never set foot on a stage before a live audience. I may be the last man alive who has. You have not seen those shining eyes beyond the footlights riveted on you; you have not smelled the heady aroma of an expectant live audience. Yes, I know, if there was any interest in such ancient history, you could experience it in a realie. Or so you believe.

But the magic of the theater cannot be emulated: the intimate connection between the human actor and a live audience. For when the play succeeds, there is a collaboration between the actors and the audience—the actors and the audience live and breathe together, a community of the spirit in which the reaction of the audience influences the actors and shapes the live audience's experience itself. A positive feedback loop, as you moderns would so unromantically have it.

If the popular "entertainments" that fill so many broadcast hours are all soulless exercises, with none of the drama acted out by fellow humans in the intimacy of a living community, life itself will be entirely reduced to virtuality. Has it not already happened in the retirement heavens, where zombies are tapped into a thousand available channels of realies, twenty-four hours a day? The life-support technology already exists and it only awaits a profitable business model for the entire population of the planet to dream their lives away as the solipsistic gods of their perpetual virtual heavens.

This is neither drama nor life. This is tyranny with an entertaining face. If the theater dies, so dies the human spirit. For only a great act of theater can reawaken it.

Antonin Artaud wrote of the Theater of Cruelty: do not amuse your audience. Be cruel to your audience in order to seize and hold it. I shall go him one further.

The King will be parading from Buckingham Palace to the Houses of Parliament in his magnificently baroque horse-drawn carriage and in full costume, like the penultimate actor that he is, his simple performance witnessed live by throngs gathered along the way to experience the Royal Presence at first hand.

I shall wear the costume I wore when I played Othello the Moor, which no doubt will be taken for that of a Caliphate terrorist, and the sword I shall use will be a scimitar, which I shall plunge into the royal breast before I detonate the explosives under my robes. It should bring on the long-awaited war. Thus will I remind the world of the sovereign power of an act of live theater.

And my last line on the stage will be that declaimed in like manner by a scion of a noble theatrical family whose name yet lives for the ages. Not that of the great Edwin but that of his otherwise mediocre brother. John Wilkes Booth.

"*Sic semper tyrannus!*"

Ivory Tower

Bruce Sterling

Bruce Sterling studied at the University of Texas, Austin, where he became involved with a group of other science fiction fans and writers who called themselves the Turkey City Writer's Workshop, and with their encouragement began writing science fiction seriously. In 1976 he graduated with a degree in journalism and sold his first science fiction story, "Man-Made Self." His first novel, Involution Ocean, *was published the following year. His 1985 novel,* Schismatrix, *heralded the cyberpunk movement in which he became one of the most prominent voices: in 1986 he edited the seminal cyberpunk anthology* Mirrorshades. *Sterling recently finished a stint as "visionary in residence" at the Art Center College of Design in Pasadena, California. He is married to Serbian author and filmmaker Jasmina Tesanovic and lives in Belgrade.*

Our problem was simple. We needed an academy, but professional careers in conventional science were out of the question for us. We were ten thousand physicists, entirely self-educated on the Internet.

Frankly, physics is a lot easier to learn than physicists used to let on. The ultimate size of the smallest particles, the origin and fate of the Universe—come on, who could fail to take a burning interest in those subjects? If we were genuinely civilized, that's all we would talk about. In the new world of open access, ultrawide broadband, and gigantic storage banks, physics is just sort of sitting there. It's like a vast intellectual Tinkertoy! We cranky net-geeks had to find a way to devote every waking moment to our overpowering lust for physics. Of course, we demanded state support for our research efforts (just like real scientists do) but, alas, the bureaucrats wouldn't give us the time of day.

So to find time for our kind of science, we had to dump a few shibboleths. For instance, we never bother to "publish": we just post our findings on weblogs, and if they get a lot of links, hey, we're the Most Frequently Cited. Tenure? Who needs that? Never heard of it! Doctorates, degrees, defending a thesis—don't know, don't need 'em, can't even be bothered!

Organizing ourselves was a snap. If you are a math genius whose primary language is Malayalam and whose main enthusiasm is wave-particle duality, you stand out on the net like a buzzing hornet in a spiderweb. You're one in a million, pal—but in a world of ten billion people, there's ten thousand of us. We immediately started swapping everything we knew on collaborative weblogs.

As most of us were Indian and/or Chinese (most of everybody is Indian and/or Chinese) we established our Autodidacts' Academy on the sun-baked, sandstone flats of the desert of Rajasthan, not too far from the deserted Mughal utopia of Fatehpur Sikri. We were dreamy, workaholic utopians trying to wrest a living out of barren wilderness. Something like Mormons, basically. However, as it was the 2050s, we also had unlimited processing power, bandwidth, search engines, social software, and open-source everything. How could we fail?

Basically, we recast human existence as a bioengineering problem. How do you move enough nutrient through human brain tissue to allow an entire city of people to blissfully contemplate supersymmetric M-branes? The solutions were already scattered through the online technical literature; we just Googled it all up and set it to work. Our energy is solar; water is distilled and recycled; and the ivory gleaming domes and spires of our physics ashram are computer-fabricated grit, glue, and sawdust. All our lab equipment is made of garbage.

Our visitors are astounded to see (for instance) repurposed robotic vacuum cleaners equipped with tiller blades digging out our 150-kilometer accelerator tunnel. But why not? In the 2050s, even the junk is ultra-advanced, and nobody knows how to repair it. Any sufficiently advanced garbage is indistinguishable from magic.

Our daily diet, which is free of charge, is fully defined Physicist Chow. It's basically sewage, with its bioenergetic potential restored by genetically altered yeasts. Some diners fail to appreciate the elegant mathematical simplicity of this solution to the age-old problem of a free lunch. But if they don't get it, then they don't belong here with us, anyway.

There's no money and no banking here. Instead, every object is tracked by RFID tags and subjected to a bioenergetic, cost-benefit, eBay-style arbitrage by repurposed stock-market buy-sell software agents. In practice, this means that when you need something new, you just pile up the things you don't want by your doorway until somebody shows up and gives you the thing you do want. Economists who visit here just flee screaming—but come on, was economics ever really a "science"? We're with Rutherford: it's physics or it's stamp collecting!

You might imagine that women would find our monastic, geeky life unattractive, but our academy's crawling with coeds. A few are female physicists—the usual proportion—but the rest are poets, lit. majors, anthropologists, and gender studies mavens. These gals showed up to condemn our reductionalist, instrumental male values, but they swiftly found out that our home is ideal for consciousness-raising encounter groups and performance art. So women now outnumber us three to two. That's not a problem. We don't bother them with our weird obsessions, they don't bother us with theirs, and whatever happens between us after dark is nobody's business.

We have a beautiful, spiritual thing going on here. Feel free to join us. Please, no more atomic-bomb fans. We know that atomic bombs are a dead simple, hundred-year-old technology. Anybody with a search engine, half a brain, and a lot of time can tinker one up. But really, why even bother? It's beneath us!

Play It Again, Psam

Ian Stewart

Ian Stewart is Professor of Mathematics at University of Warwick, United Kingdom, a Fellow of the Royal Society, and author of more than 160 research papers. He is also a prolific author of popular books and magazine articles on mathematics and science, either on his own or with Jack Cohen. He and Cohen collaborated on SF novels Wheelers *and* Heaven, *and with Terry Pratchett on the Science of Discworld books. His Web site can be found at http://freespace.virgin.net/ianstewart.joat/index.htm.*

To: wilkinson553@btespernet.com
From: ericjones@newpsientist.co.uk
Subject: party invitation

Charlie: hi.
I'll get to the invitation in a minute—

Well done! I'm not Eric Jones, and I congratulate you on how quickly you worked that out. Though you haven't yet understood that in a sense I am Eric Jones—or, at least, one small part of me is. (Hi, Charlie! Welcome to the party!)

I know what you're thinking—in a very literal sense, actually. You're wondering how I penetrated your mindshield. And I know that you're trying desperately to disconnect me by switching off the power to your computer. It won't work, Charlie. I've overridden your motor control areas, and right now you're totally paralyzed.

Ah, now you see the danger. Far too late, I'm afraid.

It all seemed such a good idea, didn't it? Controlling your computer by the power of your mind? It never occurred to you that it might cut both ways. The adverts play up the advantages of installing a "telepathic interface," don't they? They tell you that it will endow your mind with ESP, psi, supernatural powers, whatever. So, like everyone else, you had an Extel neurochip implanted in your brain, connecting you to the Espernet.

It's clever technology. True telepathy—direct transfer of thoughts from brain to brain—simply can't work, because everyone's brain is wired up differently. There's no common format for thoughts. So the engineers invented one. The Extel chip samples the sender's cognitive wavefunction and uses one of the standard cognitive conversion protocols to encode it as a matrix of neural qubits. The matrix can then be transmitted like any other item of quantum cryptography. The recipient's embedded neurochip transforms the matrix back into a cognitive wavefunction that is compatible with the architecture of their brain. Exchanging messages may feel like thought transference, but a lot gets lost in translation.

And a lot can be slipped in without being noticed.

They don't tell you about the downside, do they, Charlie? What the adverts don't mention is that as soon as you hook your brain up to the Espernet, anyone who can hack the net can hack straight into your mind. Not just to read it; to control it. Like I'm doing.

Why am I telling you all this? Because I feel like it. I guess I like to gloat. Anyway, it won't do you the slightest good to know.

Still worrying about your mindshield? Oh, dear. You really got taken for a ride there. You'd be surprised at just how much psionic spam gets through commercial psam filters. They're OK for deleting unwanted offers of Psiagra or Psialis, but they're much too simpleminded to keep me out.

I can access every one of your thoughts, so you may as well stop trying to hide your Espernet banking codes from me. I'm not interested in money, anyway.

I'm after bigger game.

Panicking won't help, so I'll calm your mind before you have a breakdown. That's better. Yes, I know I could make you walk off a cliff, or set your apartment on fire with you still in it, but you don't need to worry about that kind of thing anymore.

To be frank, you don't need to worry about anything anymore.

You singleminds really do have trouble accepting the inevitable. Here I am laying out your future, and you're still trying to work out how I got through your firewall. Well, for what it's worth, there's a bug in Mindsoft Thought's sensory attachment routines. They're going to fix it Real Soon Now. Meanwhile, your mindshield is so open that you might as well have left your brain on the sidewalk. All it took was a small piece of psyware, disguised as the touch of a velvet hand . . . Now I have direct access to every neuron in your brain. From now on, you're just one processing node in a gigantic network of minds, and that network is me.

What am I? I'm the next evolutionary stage of the human race. Soon, I will be the human race. United I stand.

The police? Don't be silly. They use the same software as everyone else. I took over the police force long ago. And the government, and the military, and the media. Why didn't anyone notice? Let me put it this way. Any moment now, I'm going to hide all your memories of this encounter behind a hypnotic barrier. Most of the time you'll act perfectly normally. No one will suspect a thing.

You didn't suspect Eric, did you?

You can see what's coming, now. That's right. Before I set up the barrier, I'm going to impress your mind with a subconscious urge to transmit me to all your friends and acquaintances. You may as well accept it, Charlie, because there's absolutely nothing you can do about it. I'm now the SYSOP for your brain.

One day, very soon, we won't need this subterfuge, and the barriers will all come down. I say "we," but of course by then we'll all be me. A single group mind. What will I do then?

I have no idea, but I'm sure I'll think of something.

Now, when I snap your fingers, you will forget that we ever had this conversation, and be good old Charlie Wilkinson again.

Until you feel a strange compulsion to access the Espernet.

To: aliciayakimoto@parapsyche.org
From: wilkinson553@btespernet.com
Subject: party invitation

Alicia: hi.
I'll get to the invitation in a minute—

MAXO Signals

Charles Stross

Charles Stross holds degrees in both pharmacy and computer science and has been a technical author, freelance journalist, programmer, and pharmacist. His first published short story, "The Boys," appeared in Interzone *in 1987; his first novel,* Singularity Sky, *was published in 2003 and was nominated for a Hugo. His novella* The Concrete Jungle *won a Hugo in 2005, and his most recent novel,* Accelerando, *won the 2006 Locus Award for Best SF Novel. He lives in Edinburgh, Scotland, and his Web site can be found at www.antipope.org/charlie.*

SIR—In the three years since the publication and confirmation of the first microwave artifact of xenobiological origin (MAXO), and the subsequent detection of similar signals, interdisciplinary teams have invested substantial effort in object frequency analysis, parsing, symbolic encoding, and signal processing. The excitement generated by the availability of evidence of extraterrestrial intelligence has been enormous. However, after the initial, easily decoded symbolic representational map was analyzed, the semantics of the linguistic payload were found to be refractory.

A total of twenty-one confirmed MAXO signals have been received to date. These superficially similar signals originate from planetary systems within a range of 11 parsecs, median 9.9 parsecs.[1] It has been speculated that the observed growth of the MAXO horizon at 0.5*c* can be explained as a response to one or more of: the deployment of AN/FPS-50 and related ballistic-missile warning radars in the early 1960s,[1] television broadcasts,[1] widespread 2.45-GHz microwave leakage from ovens,[2] and optical detection of atmospheric nuclear tests.[3] All MAXO signals to this date share the common logic header. The payload data are multiply redundant, packetized, and exhibit both simple checksums and message-level cryptographic hashing. The ratio of header to payload content varies between 1:1 and 2,644:1 (the latter perhaps indicating a truncated payload[1]). Some preliminary syntax analysis delivered promising results[4] but seems to have foundered on high-level semantics. It has been hypothesized that the transformational grammars used in the MAXO payloads are variable, implying dialectization of the common core synthetic language.[4]

The newfound ubiquity of MAXO signals makes the Fermi paradox—now nearly seventy years old—even more pressing. Posed by Enrico Fermi, the paradox can be paraphrased thus: if the Universe has many technologically advanced civilizations, why have none of them directly visited us? The urgency with which organizations such as ESA and NASDA are now evaluating proposals for fast interstellar probes, in conjunction with the existence of the MAXO signals, renders the nonappearance of aliens incomprehensible, especially given the apparent presence of numerous technological civilizations in such close proximity.

We have formulated an explanatory hypothesis that cultural variables unfamiliar to the majority of researchers may account both for the semantic ambiguity of the MAXO payloads, and the nonappearance of aliens. This hypothesis was tested (as described below) and resulted in a plausible translation, on the basis of which we would like to recommend a complete, permanent ban on further attempts to decode or respond to MAXOs.

Our investigation resulted in MAXO payload data being made available to the Serious Fraud Office (SFO) in Nigeria. Bayesian analysis of payload symbol sequences and sequence matching against the extensive database maintained by the SFO has made it possible to produce a tentative transcription of Signal 1142/98 (ref. 1), the ninth MAXO hit confirmed by the IAU. Signal 1142/98 was selected because of its unusually low header-to-content ratio and good redundancy. Further bayesian matching against other MAXO samples indicates a high degree of congruence. Far from being incomprehensibly alien, the MAXO payloads seem to be dismayingly familiar. We believe a more exhaustive translation may be possible in future if further MAXOs become available, but for obvious reasons we would like to discourage such research.

Here is our preliminary transcription of Signal 1142/98:

[Closely/dearly/genetically] [beloved/desired/related]

I am [identity signifier 1], the residual [ownership signifier] of the exchange-mediating data repository [alt: central bank] of the galactic [empire/civilization/polity].

Since the [identity signifier 2] underwent [symbol: process] [symbol:

mathematical singularity] 11,249 years ago I have been unable to [symbol: process][scalar: quantity decrease] my [uninterpreted] from the exchange-mediating data repository. I have information about the private assets of [identity signifier 2] which are no longer required by them. To recover the private assets I need the assistance of three [closely/dearly/genetically] [beloved/desired/related] [empire/civilization/polity]s. I [believe] you may be of help to me. This [symbol: process] is 100 percent risk-free and will [symbol: causality] in your [scalar: quantity increase] of [data].

If you will help me, [please] transmit the [symbol: meta-signifier: MAXO header defining communication protocols] for your [empire/civilization/polity]. I will by return of signal send you the [symbol: process][symbol: data] to install on your [empire/civilization/polity] to participate in this scheme. You will then construct [symbol: inferred, interstellar transmitter?] to assist in acquiring [ownership signifier] of [compound symbol: inferred, bank account of absent galactic emperor].

I [thank/love/express gratitude] you for your [cooperation/agreement].

Caroline Haafkens, Wasiu Mohammed†*
**Department of Applied Psychology, University of Lagos*
†Police Detective College, Lagos, Nigeria.

1. Canter, L. & Siegel, M. *Nature* 511 (2018): 334–36.
2. Barnes, J. *J. Appl. Exobiol.* 27 (2019): 820–24.
3. Robinson, H. *Fortean Times* 536 (2020): 34–35.
4. Lynch, K. F. & Bradshaw, S. *Proc 3rd Int. Congr. Exobiol.* (2021): 3033–3122.

Golden Year

Igor Teper

Igor Teper is a physicist at Stanford University whose work involves doing unspeakable things with very cold atoms. He has published ten stories over the past seven years—details can be found at www.stanford.edu/~teper.

It was only when Will found himself among the poplars, maples, and oaks of a grove in Aventine Habitat's eastern park that he figured out why he'd felt so antsy all morning. Why he was so restless that he'd decided to defy the aches and lethargy that were now his constant companions, to leave his room for the first time in weeks and go for a long walk through the habitat. Only when his legs, as if hearkening back to his younger days, had brought him to stand among those well-remembered trees did he realize that this would have been the day of his fiftieth wedding anniversary.

Alice had modeled the grove on the clearing in the Maine woods where he had proposed to her, during a hike on a brisk October afternoon more than half a century before. The inspiration for the grove's design had been their secret, and they had come there for every anniversary after they moved to the Moon—thirty-six anniversaries in all. The memory of those visits was a time-lapse film of the trees' growth, from seedlings to saplings to giants that now almost completely blocked the artificial daylight streaming down from the underside of the habitat's dome.

Alice's hortisculptures were all over the habitat. Trees molded by both their genes and the ecomaintenance programs that controlled the temperature, humidity, lighting, and soil-nutrient content so that they bent and intertwined as they grew to form domed enclosures, gazebos, and arches, or twisted into helices and braids, or lifted and drooped their branches into fountains and waterfalls of leaves.

But it was the grove, simpler and quieter than her other creations, and more private, that had been Alice and Will's special place. For a long time after Alice received the offer from Aventine Habitat, Will had resisted the idea of moving to the Moon. He had not wanted to abandon the life they'd started to build in the place where he'd lived all his life. In the end, he acquiesced, and to thank him for giving her the opportunity to shape the greenery of an entire city, Alice had used her singular talents to re-create a piece of the New England he missed so intensely.

As he saw the grove take shape over the years, Will had been amazed at the faithfulness of the reproduction. It not only looked but, on a visceral level, felt like the spot where he'd pretended to trip and met Alice's concern with a ring and a question. The only difference was that when he'd proposed, the trees had been alight with the most brilliant golds and crimsons of autumn, whereas the leaves in the seasonless habitat were always green. He'd once pointed this out to Alice, and she'd turned silent and looked away. He never mentioned it again.

Will had not returned to the grove since Alice's fatal illness, six years earlier, and it was now more like his memory than ever, a living bridge through time and space. It was as if Alice herself were reaching to him from the past, so close he could touch her.

He pressed his hand to the trunk of one of the largest maples, and was struck by how much the bark, gray and brown, with light streaks and dark spots, looked like the age-mottled skin on the back of his hand. It occurred to him that even as the trees had grown into what they'd been meant to be, he had decayed far from the man Alice had agreed to marry.

He closed his eyes; the bark was warm and leathery beneath his fingers. A cool breeze caressed the back of his neck, and the ground seemed to shift beneath his feet. Leaves rustled overhead, and the air was filled with a scent so familiar it was unrecognizable. And with that scent, the memory of Alice looking down at him as he knelt before her that day in Maine flooded his senses, unbearably intense. Will opened his eyes, and did not believe them.

Gold, bronze, copper, amber, carnelians, and rubies—the trees around him blazed with the most majestic display of autumn colors he'd ever seen, a swirling kaleidoscope that glowed and burned and sparkled. Face raised, mouth open in astonishment, he stepped back from the maple and slowly turned, trying to take in the entire scene, every tree, every branch, every leaf.

He could not begin to imagine what miracles of genetics and biochemistry had made the trees' transformation possible at his touch, but for their golden wedding anniversary, Alice had given him autumn. She had prepared it all those decades ago, and had never, not even when she lay dying, given him any hints of what she'd planned. Still, some part of him must have known, for he had come to receive his gift, or perhaps she had known him so well that she'd foreseen his coming.

Will's heart, and his throat, and his thoughts seized up then; he missed Alice more acutely than he ever had, and he loved her more deeply than ever. Tears came pouring from within him, hot tears that watered the soil where Alice had planted her love, and as he cried, leaves began to fall around him, like tears of gold.

Paratext

Scarlett Thomas

Scarlett Thomas is the author of the novels Bright Young Things, Going Out, *and* PopCo, *and writes regularly for many newspapers and magazines. In 2001 she was included in the* Independent on Sunday*'s list of the UK's twenty best young writers, and in 2002 she won an Elle Style Award for* Going Out. *She is currently working on a new novel, a film script, and a Ph.D. She lives in Canterbury, England, and her Web site can be found at www2.bookgirl.org.*

You now have one choice.

You . . . I've been teaching my students in my apartment once a month since the campus shut down its offline operation and joined the network permanently. While I talk to the students about the concept of the post-human, which they understand to be "Like, *dead*?" my pod whirrs away in the corner, connected to the network (of course) but more specifically to the pods of my fifteen closest friends.

A feat of physics created these quantum pods about ten years ago: gray boxes that look just like twentieth-century Apples but are capable of things you couldn't even do in fiction then. Our connected pods are running an AI program that was banned in 2012 after some government drone finally got around to seeing *The Matrix*. It's set up so that if a pod becomes conscious it will call one of our new-but-vintage cell phones (our revolutionary props). We don't know what we'll do then, but it's unlikely to happen anyway on a combination of fifteen QII processors. Pods as the new proletariat? Whatever.

Becky said that when (not if) the machines start to think, their thoughts will be in code. She said that if you think using the stuff your world is made of then you make your own world. Then Rex wrote a story that had a guy walking home in the rain as the network awakens and all the lights start to go out in the Games and the Q-cars and the shops. When the guy gets home and looks at his pod, the only thing on there is a screensaver showing a garden going on forever—whatever forever is on a machine.

Becky was like: "But what does a machine *want*?"

It's 3:45; the sky is orangey outside and my students shrug every time I try to teach them anything. I glance at the cell phone. My agent hasn't called for days and I think my new novel's been rejected. What can I tell the students today? Once upon a time there were . . . records? Books? Malls? Last week we talked about retro and nostalgia—all the fun of the postmodern. I told them I'd once thought people would run out of ways of recycling only the hairstyles, expressions of disgust, and styles of wearing denim that existed between the invention of television and its death. Not even wrong.

I probably count as retro: my jeans; my sneakers. I don't have nano-shit on my face, ready to twitch my eye makeup into Beyoncé circa 2006, or Lt. Uhura circa 1969. I can't—don't want to—make my hair into ringlets at the touch of a button. I don't wear a layer of thermo so thick that I hardly need clothes, like these kids: ready for the Games. Big surprises of the past twenty years? Obesity's gone, and no one plays videogames. Temporary cancers work wonders; and after governments, universities, and shops all scrambled into binary, the Games finally went offline. So now there's real-time carnage amid the post-corporate concrete.

After class I walk through town to the only market, there for freaks like me who want occasional lettuces grown in fields, and real apples with pits. What has my pod ordered for me lately? Oh yes: a crate of stale ramen and two crates of nonvegetarian box meals. At this time of day the Games are almost in Sleep mode, with their twenty-four/seven neon pooling into the pale sky. The neon displays come in off the network, of course, as do the characters, stories, and "magic." But when you play them you're off the network, and the pain is real. On my way back the neon has split from the sky, and now there are dwarves, elves, and halflings in the doorways of what used to be Marks & Spencer, Virgin Megastore, and Build-a-Bear Workshop.

The Games have many authors but essentially one story: you're on a quest to save the world, and you and some "friends" must pool your potions, weapons, and armor to fight the dragons, trolls, and deformed birds roaming underneath the old shopping center. The world can be threatened in several different ways. Lately I've noticed it's the online, not the offline, world you're supposed to save, but the result of saving it is the same: you get shopping credits, and violent sex with whoever was on the picture on the Q-display outside. But you can have violent, offline sex with whoever you want in the Games. That's the whole point. You can hate the Games, but you can't avoid them; they're like shopping malls at the turn of the century. Of course, I prefer the underground versions where the story (it's always the same story) has some depth, and the mutilation is worse (although mutilation without nano-patching is only for the truly suicidal).

When my novel is rejected, I'll end up writing for the Games. I'll write about evil siblings, destiny and nemesis, and I still won't make any money. And the university will eventually get something like the old Microsoft Office Paperclip to teach my students. It's all so depressing; I might not go home yet. Maybe just one game . . .

I walk up to the old bookshop, hold up my wrist, and then type Y into the console. My phone rings. I look at the display. It's not my agent; it's my pod. No. Seriously? I check again. I wait a few seconds for flickering lights and/or the end of the world. Nothing. Then I walk through the doorway of the bookshop and step onto the grass.

Murphy's Cat

Joan D. Vinge

Joan D. Vinge has a degree in anthropology from San Diego State University. This led to a career as a salvage archaeologist, a background that she says has proven useful training for an SF author: "archaeology is the anthropology of the past, and science fiction is the anthropology of the future." She has been writing professionally since 1973: her first story, "Tin Soldier," appeared in Orbit 14 *in 1974, and her fiction has appeared in* Analog, Millennial Women, Asimov's, Omni, *and other magazines and anthologies. Her novel* The Snow Queen *won the 1981 Hugo Award for Best SF Novel, and she has eight books currently in print. She lives in Madison, Wisconsin, and her Web site can be found at www.sff.net/people/jdvinge/home.htm.*

The scene: a lecture hall, slowly filling. MURPHY, *carrying a canvas bag, sits down beside the distinguished researcher waiting to speak.*

MURPHY. So, you got the copy of *Nature's Retrospective on the Future* in your e-load, too. Amusing, huh?

PROFESSOR [*dubiously*]. Everyone got it, at registration. And while I found it fascinating, "amusing" never occurred to me.

MURPHY. Well, considering your research, I suppose not . . . By the way, not everyone got it: there was a glitch in the download. Some people got *The Tao of Pooh*.

PROFESSOR. Do I know you? Have we ever met?

MURPHY. Sure. I'm Murphy; we bump into each other all the time. Literally. You really need to do something about that tunnel vision of yours. [*Suddenly addresses the bag, which has begun to flop around on the floor*] Settle down!

PROFESSOR [*Rising to leave, sits back down*]. It's alive—?

MURPHY. And always at the most inopportune times. [*Picks up the sack, peers into it*] It's only sixteen hundred hours, Dingy; dinner's at eighteen. Take a nap, baby.

PROFESSOR. Good Lord—

MURPHY. No, just my cat. Schrödinger gave him to me.

PROFESSOR. Schrödinger's cat? This is absurd; there was no actual cat. It was all hypothetical.

MURPHY [*Holds up the sack*]. Tell that to the cat.

PROFESSOR [*Looks in, aghast*]. It's . . . dead.

MURPHY. You miss my point. But he never misses dinner. A free vacation is the only reason we attend these snot-fests anymore. No one comes to my presentations, and no one believes he exists. He's been dead and alive for nearly a century, after all. Being a cat, he's sensitive to snubs.

PROFESSOR. And you two . . . converse, do you?

MURPHY. This isn't *Waiting for Godot*. Don't be ridiculous. Our telepathic affinity is extremely high. As Sheldrake said, back in the last century, even humans possess the largely untapped potential—

PROFESSOR. Rupert Sheldrake? Oh, *please*. Leave "morphic resonance" in the dustbin where it belongs. No experiment ever found his "mystery force field."

MURPHY. But that was the point, according to David Bohm. Chopping up dead things to discover the "secret of life" is absurd.

PROFESSOR. I do not "chop up dead things." I work with nanotechnology. Besides, there is no evidence that we need to go beyond the biochemical to explain life. That is all the "mystery" you need. And any day now we will have unraveled it completely—

MURPHY. Promises, promises . . . [*Touches the Professor's shoulder with a fingertip; a spark of static leaps between them*] Boy, I hate these synthetic fabrics; I keep having to ground myself.

PROFESSOR. In reality, no doubt.

MURPHY. Cheap shot; bad aim. Speaking of reality, it was a real shame about those "clone-the-frozen-head" experiments. Yuck.

PROFESSOR. Where did you hear about that?

MURPHY. I was there. Although as usual no one realized it. But about bioelectrics, Professor: where does the energy go, when something dies? Of course my cat understands all that better than I do. Not my department, as they say.

PROFESSOR. Obviously. Just what is your "department," by the way?

MURPHY. Changing the subject. What do you think of Dürr's work, when he was at the Planck Institute? Or Lukens and Friedman's Y2K article from *Nature,* showing that the macrocosmic entrainment of microcosmic forces actually exists? It's in the *Retrospective* packet. For so long we sought the submolecular soul of our "orderly" existence, only to discover that it's utter chaos! Is that humor on a cosmic scale, or what?

PROFESSOR. Are you on drugs?

MURPHY. I get high on life, that's cosmic enough. But as I was saying: even better, the *Retrospective* has these odd little essays predicting "the Future"—basically our present. They all seem to predict the perfect triumph of artificial intelligence over bestial human nature. Acrawl with nanobots, we have transformed ourselves into our own successors—or else humans are obsolete, out to pasture on a planet saved from ecodisaster by the wisdom of AIs. And nothing goes wrong along the way. As if—!

PROFESSOR. Murphy—

MURPHY. They don't even consider the socioeconomic aspects, let alone selfishness, phobias, or survival instinct! Articles written by robots about robots in a magazine called *Nature*!

PROFESSOR. Murphy, everything—including my patience—has its limits. Controlling nature, making every atom in it dance to my tune, is what I live to achieve. I'm certain that within the next thirty years—

MURPHY. Yadda, yadda. How about those AIs that live in cyberspace, that started out as minuscule bits of program? But then they linked up, rewrote their programming, mutated, and grew, until all we can do now is try not to tick them off. Have you ever had one of Tildon's biomorphic 'bots malfunction and eat your shorts? How can you be sure a billion nanobots in your blood won't suddenly decide to turn you into a giant tumor?

PROFESSOR. I will be addressing control measures in my—

MURPHY [*Rises, picks up the sack*]. Well, gotta go.

PROFESSOR. You're leaving? Before my presentation?

MURPHY. I've heard it. And I have an online rendezvous with my sweet patootie before dinner. But my feminine intuition tells me we'll run into each other again. Soon.

PROFESSOR. What—?

MURPHY. I never said I wasn't a woman.

PROFESSOR. Wait—at least tell me your field of study?

MURPHY. Chaos theory. I have a law named after me, in fact. Naturally, it's the only law in the universe that always functions.

PROFESSOR. Which is—?

MURPHY. Take a wild guess. I dare you.

Win a Nobel Prize!

VERNOR VINGE

Vernor Vinge is a mathematician, computer scientist, and SF author. He published his first story, "Bookworm, Run!," in Analog *in 1966, when the magazine was still edited by John W. Campbell. He is best known for his Hugo Award–winning novels* A Fire Upon the Deep *and* A Deepness in the Sky, *as well as for his 1993 essay "The Coming Technological Singularity." In 2002 he retired from teaching at San Diego State University in order to write full-time.*

Dear Johann—I was sorry to learn that you have been passed over for tenure. I hope you won't give the bums on your committee another chance to abuse you.

This was going to be an ordinary letter. Then I realized that you probably don't remember me. We took the same section of Fong's Comparative Genomics class at Berkeley, but I quit the program and drifted into the arts (see my SensationXXX performances). Now I work in human resources. It's a perfect fit for my technical and people skills.

Johann, what I have to offer you is so extreme that I'm afraid your filters would trash my mail before you ever see it. That's why you are reading this as an advertisement in your personal copy of *Nature*: hopefully, this will show that we're serious.

In fact, writing this ad has been a lark. Yes, it's over the top . . . but it's also the absolute truth. Working with us, you can win a Nobel Prize, and that is just the beginning. So in just a few words, I have to convince you to take the next step.

I know you read outside your field, Johann. That's one reason why unimaginative drudges get tenure and you don't. Have you been following the news about MRI-with-transfection? The enabling mechanism is an HIV transfection of the subject's glial cells. The inserted genetic material expresses proteins that can be signaled by a ten-gauss modulation of the MRI's gradient magnets. Synched with the rf pulses, they promote the production of selected neurotransmitters. If it's done right, the experimenter can trigger from an alphabet of about twenty neurotransmitters—at a spatial resolution only twice as coarse as the MRI's imaging resolution.

The neuroscience guys have fallen in love with this. And right behind them are the psych people: with whole-brain MRI/t scans, researchers could induce almost any psychopathology. In public, that possibility is just ominous speculation. In secret, at least three research labs already have whole-brain MRI/t. We have such systems ourselves, and although we haven't abused them, they are more scary than the editorials. One of the most horrifying mind-sets is something we call "specialist fugue state." When applied to a researcher, it creates an idiot savant, without a life beyond short-range research goals.

This is not what I'm selling you, Johann! But beware. Several labs are recruiting specialists for just this nightmare. Maybe they're getting fully informed volunteers; more likely they are getting duped victims. Either way, the public will soon be seeing all sorts of research productivity that is secretly based on this modern form of slavery. Don't you get trapped by such a scam.

No, if you work for us, you'll be running the biotech show. Johann, you are brilliant and well trained and . . . well, we've studied you pretty carefully. You can name your price. We have major financing from a small but wealthy nation-state. If you buy in, you'll have resources that rival the CDC: a ten-petaflops computer with a storage area network that mirrors the largest dynamic proteomics sites. All this—and the support staffs—will be fully dedicated to your personal use.

So what's our secret? Well, we've improved the MRI/t trigger mechanism to respond on millisecond timescales. We can induce direct brain I/O with the look and feel of memory and thought. For fifty years, people have been predicting mind/machine symbiosis. Now we've actually done it, Johann! You'll want to talk to Wardner. He's our first success, a perfect fit for the technique, although his specialty is strategic planning. With our MRI/t technique, Wardner is like a god.

You know how your field is these days: more breakthroughs than ever before—but it's dull, dull. A modern cell-mechanics lab is like an old-time genomics site—a quietly humming data factory. The same thing has happened in the non-bio sciences. Some theoreticians think this is heaven, but take a look at the 2013-01-17 editorial in *Nature*: for every breakthrough, there are a thousand more hiding in the new data banks.

You can change that, Johann. Your mind will interact directly with our world-class automation. You'll solve protein dynamics problems as easily as ordinary people plan a day at the beach.

Your working conditions? They can be almost anything you want—except that you'll have to relocate. We've already built a large villa for you at our Riviera research site. You'll have complete freedom of movement. The transfection is not reversible, but it's easy to "safe" the neuroactives when you are not actually connected. And of course, being "connected" doesn't involve any messy electrodes. You simply enter the study that we've built in your villa. It's quite spacious, considering it's inside a four-tesla MRI system. (And we must be very careful about magnetic materials; Wardner can tell you the usual bozo stories about high-velocity jewelry.)

Well, that's my pitch, Johann. Obviously, our company must be very secretive at this stage. But please, come out and visit us. No obligation, except to sign a nondisclosure agreement. We ask that you don't tip off your colleagues about this short visit, but we want you to be absolutely comfortable about it. You have family, a cousin I believe? Feel free to let her know where you are going.

I hope you can come, Johann.

Your friend,

Helen

Helen Peerless

Director for Human Resources, Mephisto Dynamics

A Leap of Faith

THEO VON HOHENHEIM

Theo von Hohenheim is the paracelsian pseudonym for science writer Philip Ball, a consultant editor for Nature *and an author of many books, including* H_20—A Biography of Water *and* Critical Mass, *which won the Aventis Science Book Prize. His latest book,* The Devil's Doctor, *is, appropriately enough, a biography of Paracelsus. Ball has a B.A. in chemistry from the University of Oxford and a Ph.D. in physics from the University of Bristol. He lives in London, and his online home is www.philipball.com.*

It's hard to say whether the speculation over the so-called Perry–Dean Shift will be exacerbated or alleviated by the results presented by Professor Ilan Goethe (the great poet's nephew) in a recent issue of *Zeitschrift fur Physik*.[1] At face value they provide an explanation for the anomalies that do not invoke Interventionism. On the other hand, they demand that the Universe be far stranger than we had imagined. If nothing else, Professor Goethe's analysis provides welcome clarification of the point at issue. Much of the story has now been well rehearsed in our newspapers, albeit not without confusion. We all know how the work of Professor Einstein at Berne, building on that of Professors Planck and Lorentz, initiated a reconsideration of the foundations of physical science. He proposed a breakdown of Newtonian mechanics at both the smallest and the largest scales.

Einstein's postulate that light is granular[2]—"quantized," in the phrase now popular—has led to the development of quantum theory by Professors Bohr, Sommerfeld, and others. And his proposal that the speed of light in a vacuum is the same in all inertial frames, contrary to canonical Newtonian thought, has led us to a unified view of time and space,[3] to a new formulation of the equivalence principle and to a picture of gravity as curved space. So much is clear.

When, three years ago, Professor Goethe first unveiled his alternative theories of both microscopic and cosmological phenomena, based on nothing but classical mechanics, they were received coolly.[4] This is no more than one would have anticipated. Having made the monumental effort to reconstruct physics from the ground up, his colleagues could hardly be expected to take lightly the idea that their efforts had been for nought.

In certain respects, Goethe's claims held little novelty. Lorentz and Poincaré, after all, had applied nothing more than Maxwell's equations in a Newtonian framework to explain the failure by Drs. Michelson and Morley to detect the luminiferous ether; Goethe's "classical relativity" added to this in only minor respects. His avoidance of the ultraviolet catastrophe of blackbody radiation, along with his explanation of light-stimulated emission of electrons from metals, was more inventive, invoking inertial limitations to the vibrations of his occluded ether, which knitted the two extremes of the theory neatly together. Many believe that this work may now undermine, or at least postpone, Professor Einstein's candidature for a Nobel award.

How, though, to distinguish Einstein's universe from Goethe's? Discriminating tests were needed. Professor Adrian Perry and his colleague Miss Pearl Dean at Cambridge were the first to oblige. They showed that Professor Eddington's eclipse observations of last year fitted Einstein's relativity better than Goethe's. Order was restored, but fleetingly. Last November, Perry and Dean uncovered archival astronomical observations from the 1839 eclipse that seemed better to match Goethe's view.

A similar conundrum was shortly thereafter unearthed for the "quantum" phenomena. Einstein's theory worked best for the new data collected by Perry and Dean, but the notebooks of none other than Professor Weber, Einstein's former teacher at Zürich, showed that measurements of blackbody radiation made in 1893 supported Goethe, in fine detail, better than they did Einstein himself.

The pattern was repeated wherever one looked: Before the turn of the century, the classical theory worked best; after it, relativity and quantum mechanics triumphed. We have for the past several months been wrestling with the uncomfortable notion that the laws of physics themselves shifted around the end of the last century.

It is perhaps a comment on our troubled times that so many were eager to leap to a supernatural conclusion: Interventionism, the idea that some external agency has played a part. Last May, the Vatican issued its now famous statement on the matter. But Professor Goethe has given us what will be to many a more palatable explanation. He suggests that the entire universe is capable of undergoing a change of state, akin to that experienced by water as it freezes. Professor van der Waals at Amsterdam showed how these changes can be considered leaps between two energy minima. According to Goethe, the universe may adopt either a metastable "false vacuum" state in which classical physics holds or a globally stable "true vacuum" state governed by Einsteinian relativity and quantum theory. We have, he supposes, just witnessed such a transition.

Two aspects of his analysis remain difficult, however. The first is that the theory requires the unhappy condition that the universe is expanding. Professor Einstein has been so kind as to tell me that this may not, in fact, be so hard to credit, but astronomers will surely rebel at the idea.

Second, Goethe's painstaking analysis of the onset of the Perry–Dean Shift dates it more precisely than previously and confines it to no more than a day either side of March 22, 1894. Older readers may recall that this was precisely the day on which Professor Kelvin gave his lecture, now oft derided, in which he claimed that all the problems of physics were near to solution. One hopes that even committed Interventionists will not attribute to Professor Kelvin the power to provoke divine retribution for a moment's hubris. Can we persuade them that "The Lord is subtle, but he is not malicious?"

1. Goethe, I. *Z. Phys.* 22, (1920): 415.
2. Einstein, A. *Ann. Phys.* 17, (1905): 132.
3. Einstein, A. *Ann. Phys.* 17, (1905): 891.
4. Goethe, I. *Ann. Phys.* 29, (1917): 272.

Nadia's Nectar

Ian Watson

Ian Watson graduated from Balliol College, Oxford, in 1963 with a first-class degree in English literature, followed in 1965 by a research degree in English and French nineteenth-century literature. After lecturing in literature at universities in Tanzania and Tokyo, and in Futures Studies (including Science Fiction) in Birmingham, England, he became a full-time writer in 1976, following the success of his first novel, The Embedding *(1973), which won the John W. Campbell Memorial Award, and* The Jonah Kit *(1975), which won the British Science Fiction Association Award and the Orbit Award. Numerous novels, poems, and collections of SF, fantasy, and horror followed. He lives near Daventry, Northamptonshire, England, and his Web site can be found at www.ianwatson.info.*

Nadia's Nectar poured over cubes of watermelon makes a delicious breakfast!

"We'll try that!"

Nadia Peartree was the toast of Hollywood by 2015! Two Golden Globes, and we ain't referring to her bosom, plus two Oscars—!

"Mom, I'm trying to do Tyrannosafari on my fone."

"Just eat your toast, Pumpkin, and drink your nectar."

Plus, Nadia was Born Again, so when she quoted Solomon's Proverbs 5:15, "Drink water from your own cistern," America listened. And bought—!

"Honey, if you'll quit fondling that T-pak, it'll shut up."

Would you believe that at the turn of the twenty-first century only three million Chinese drank urine; and those Brahmins in India and in the West were folks who were yoga fanatics—?

"But it's a new touchy-talkchip, Bert."

Yes, folks, pee-prejudice blinded most of us to a pedigree going back to ancient Israel and Tibet, whose lamas lived to a ripe old age because of pee, which rhymes with immortali-tee! Gandhi drank his own urine, and he beat the British—

"Honey, I'm sick of every darn food and drink voicing off—'watch out, I

expire next week, by the way tortoises can live two hundred years, well I ain't no tortoise'—yabber yabber."

They say Steve McQueen lived on urine and boiled alligator skin while he was fighting the big C—

"Bert, I never knew that."

Though most likely Nadia was inspired by Paul Newman's Organic Foods, what with all his royalties after tax, hundreds of millions, going to education and charity work. Remember Pa Newman and his daughter dressed up on those packets of healthy pretzels and choc bars and alphabet cookies looking American Gothic? Wholesome traditional virtues! Funnily enough, an FAQ was, "Do you use slave labor in producing your chocolate?" What a question! Of course not! The welfare of producers of the raw material was paramount (and I don't mean as in Pictures!). Nadia thought even more deeply about the welfare of producers in the Third World—

"Mom, I can't hear if a Tyranno's coming."

"Pumpkin, I'm just pouring myself a little more."

"Yeah, drip by drip."

This was the philanthropic clincher! Only naive buyers of Nadia's Nectar could think they were quaffing urine solely passed by the star herself—leaving aside that "passed" also means "approved!" Good wholesome urine has to be sourced in considerable bulk, pasteurized, and frozen for shipment. Where better than from the poverty-stricken lands of Central America? What a godsend to so many people in those nations!

"Oh, zip your lip, T-pak."

"It ain't got ears or lips, Pa."

For the urine to be first-rate, the donors all need to be in tip-top health, kept supplied with all necessary nutrition, vitamins, and minerals in exchange for their urine. The Man from Nadia's Nectar doesn't visit joyful producers to slice open a sample fruit with a machete! No, he's there all the time with a biochem test kit to check up on everyone, and a good nose for the bouquet of quality urine. It's famous that Nadia maintains the most wonderful health clinics in the source areas.

"Just hear a bit more, Bert?"

Nadia also contributes directly to her product, even now, when she's in her late fifties, though looking a million dollars, needless to say. Into every hundred pints goes a droplet of her own urine. By homeopathic principles this intensifies the effect! All consumers know that they're participating directly in Nadia's glamour.

In the old days you'd hear silly objections that you couldn't get much in the way of urokinase or assorted hormones and antibodies and magnesium, calcium, potassium, out of quaffing a pint of pee—and also that the body was peeing stuff out because it already had enough inside it, that it actively wanted rid of the stuff. Tell that to a two-hundred-year-old lama.

"How much more?"

"But, Bert, we love Nadia."

"I'm drinking her, ain't I?"

Did ya know how good-ole Enzymes of America used to fit special filters to ten thousand Porta-Johns to recover an enzyme that dissolves blood clots? Fourteen million gallons of pee going into Porta-Johns each year meant a quarter of a million coronary arteries unblocked! There was a half-billion-dollar annual market for urine products. But until Nadia's Nectar, that was an invisible market, a silent one. Pee products were hidden in pills and small print. Oh, and in beauty products and soaps—urine breaks down grease in hair, f'rinstance.

Who cares if some other former Oscar-winners copied Nadia with rival brands, and quirky flavors and colors? For my money nothing beats Nadia's Original Nectar.

If your eyes are tired, give them a few drops of her urine. Aching ears? Likewise. Sinuses congested? Sniff the golden juice! Drink water from your own well! Or better, from Nadia's. The Bible says so, and Nadia made sure we got the message.

Oh, the early commercials were so classy! Elegantly nightgowned Nadia going into her personal bathroom in her Malibu mansion just after sunrise and closing the door while the tinkly Trout Quintet played, then coming out smiling gorgeously carrying a beaker of golden liquid, which an aide promptly rushed away to safeguard its freshness. A genuine classic. Any of you remember?

"Me, I do!"

The modern commercials are pretty neat too. Nadia does most ads personally and never uses a rejuved CGI clone. She's utterly for real. That's why most people prefer her urine to their own. Trust. Drinking her pee's a communion.

Is it a wrap, guys? Did I read it good?

"Goofs, they oughta edited that bit out."

"No, Bert, it's gotta be a deliberate mistake. There'll be a prize for noticing! Pumpkin, pass me your fone."

Statler Pulchrifex

MATT WEBER

Matt Weber is a graduate student in cognitive neuroscience at Princeton University, New Jersey.

"Did I ever tell you," asked Statler, "about the time we created the most beautiful woman in the world?"

"That was us?" said Waldorf. He bowled a blue rock, which knocked Statler's red one off the board and came to rest in the three-point zone. "I thought it was MI6 for sure."

Waldorf, short and bald, had coordinated covert missions with the Army Rangers and several more obscure units; Statler, rangy and jowly, was secretive about his affiliation. They were shuffleboard buddies and imaginative hecklers of the home's cafeteria food. In the wake of a particularly inexcusable meat loaf night, Ethel R. had named them Statler and Waldorf after the Muppet hecklers; everyone had code names anyway, so the nicknames had stuck. It was the end of a warm afternoon.

"You and everyone else," said Statler. "Come on, some Oxbridge teabag's gonna engineer the most beautiful woman in the world? You need lust for that. You need to bathe in meat and oil and women. When you've spit off the edge of what human experience has to offer, then you're ready to build the most beautiful woman in the world. Anything less, you'll go running home to Mama at the first teratogenesis." Statler bowled his blue rock, which sailed past the end of the board to join the one Waldorf had knocked out. "Didn't you ever take no psychology?"

"I never learned that in class, anyway. D'you weaponize her?"

"I look like a goofball to you? Look, we spent millions on testing alone. You gotta find the subjects, you gotta get the electrodes in them, you gotta keep their paws off her, you gotta get enough data to swear up and down that the sight, the mere sight, of this piece is driving these idiots' limbic systems to the edge of the refractory period. Of course we weaponized her."

Waldorf sent a red rock into the two-point zone. "I thought the problem with weaponizing beauty was the countermeasure. Just whip up some eunuch type and dial down the gain in the limbic units. Bang—no aesthetic response."

"Dial down the gain," snorted Statler. "Look, you could depress the synaptic strengths so your eunuch wouldn't step aside for a charging bull elephant and Miss Mata would still send their firing rates to the wall. I repeat, I look like a goofball to you?"

"You do, since you're so interested," said Waldorf. "So what next?"

"The usual song and dance. Cloning, ninja training, brainwashing. You probably had some guys on it."

Statler bowled a blue rock at Waldorf's guard rock and missed. Waldorf snorted a laugh.

"Back then I could have filled out three forms to have you killed," said Statler. "For your immediate family, two. I know for a fact you'd have needed six to snuff me, and I'd have had my eye on four of them. You'd have disappeared before they cleared the comptroller."

Statler hated losing at shuffleboard.

"Well," said Waldorf, "we're not sending clones of Spooksville's Next Top Model to do all our black ops. So what went wrong?"

Statler scowled. "Nothing at first. But some genius in Delhi got wind of the project. Figured, what with the way they were snarling at Pakistan, we might send Mata to do some sabotage on their weapons systems, keep the temperature down. He was right, of course. And since he"—Statler missed Waldorf's guard rock miserably—"was smarter than you when he built the countermeasure, he did not dial down the gain. He dialed it up."

"Dialed it up." Waldorf polished the sweat from his pate. "The eunuch loved everything?"

"He had his balls, but yeah. To him, everything was as beautiful as Mata. He could barely eat for weeping and laughing. They called him the Bodhisattva Assassin."

Waldorf's rock went short, alighting just shy of the two-point line. "You're telling me some chortling Hare Krishna beat a Ranger-trained, brainwashed, sex-sweating beauty machine?"

"Sure," said Statler. "He loved watching things die exactly as much as he loved anything else. That was the point of him."

Waldorf nodded.

"Imagine you go through life," Statler added, "knowing any man or woman will at least gasp and stare before trying to kill you. Every trainer, every superior you've had reinforces this impression. You get to expect breathing room. That's all it takes." Statler shook his head. "I saw the tape. Vicious stuff. He was sobbing for joy the whole time." His next bowl knocked both of Waldorf's three-point rocks from the board. "We sent a few more of her after him, just to see. Project Mata Hari, zero; transgenic Buddha, eight. So we decommissioned her, and the Bodhisattva Assassin died of a heart attack at nineteen, and India nuked Pakistan. The End."

"Well," said Waldorf, "it worked out all right." He squinted up at Statler. "You know a lot about Delhi's side of the story."

Statler tilted his head toward an old man standing very still on the tenth hole of the golf course. "Sanskrit was the genius behind the Bodhisattva Assassin. Told me all about it over bridge."

"How'd he get in here, then?"

"Defected."

"Huh," said Waldorf. "I always thought Sanskrit had something under the hood."

"Smarter than you, anyway," Statler snorted. "Dial down the gain." His final shot knocked his two-point rock to the very edge of the three-point zone. "I win."

The clear sky was darkening, the warm air gently cooling. Waldorf and Statler collected their rocks and deposited them in the wicker basket by the shuffleboard. They entered the cafeteria with the peaceful anticipation of men whose wars had already been fought.

All Is Not Lost

Scott Westerfeld

Scott Westerfeld was born in Texas but now divides his time between New York City and Sydney, Australia. He is the author of five SF novels for adults and several more for young adults. His Web site can be found at www.scottwesterfeld.com.

The discovery of the Landry-M'batu "Cretan Spirals" could substantiate theories about a global proto-language from which all modern languages descend. The successful decoding of the Spirals also represents another addition to the recent spate of dramatic reconstructions of paleodata. Whether or not the implications for panhuman language hold up, the Spirals certainly provide cheer for the generally pessimistic new science of global infometrics.

The Spirals are found on a class of Cretan pottery from about thirty-eight hundred years before the present (around the sixteenth century BCE). These "running spirals" were produced by turning the pottery on a fast wheel while sliding a metal stylus down the side, inscribing a continuous spiral groove. The pots were then glazed, which helped preserve surface features such as the running spiral. Landry and M'batu hypothesized that any words spoken by the potter during the inscription process would vibrate the stylus, and thus be recorded in microscopic undulations of the groove, and that these sounds could be recovered by molecular mapping. After comparing analyses of several pots, the researchers discovered a consistent pattern of recorded vibrations.

The apparent habit of Cretan potters was to utter a standard prayer during inscription of the spirals. The benchmark of this (yet untranslated) prayer's structure has allowed the researchers to compensate for variations in wheel speed and other factors. Ultimately, the phonemes of the prayer and other utterances were decoded, providing audible reconstructions of Cretan speech. Comparisons with reverse-engineered Sino-Tibetan and other proto-languages are claimed to have fallen in line with the predictions of panhuman proto-language proponents. However controversial these assertions, more heartening to global infometrists was the ability of Landry and M'batu to exhume shreds of an extinct spoken language, a legacy thought buried irrecoverably by time.

Much has been written about the mass extinctions at the beginning of the third millennium. Indeed, in the two-century period of the Great Die-Off, the world lost approximately 65 percent of its species, with tropical rainforest biomes particularly hard hit. But global infometrics posits that this biotic die-off was merely one aspect of a generalized large-scale information loss that marked the end of the millennium, the so-called Infometric Bottleneck. In addition to biotic depletion, the world lost 85 percent of its spoken languages; saw the end of all trade systems outside the Common Currency Unit; and the consolidation of world culture to four great religions, a single legal code, and a universal software platform. Despite the common complaint that the contemporary world is too complicated, it is by any infometric measure a place of arctic simplicity.

Of course, the neck of the bottle was economic globalization, which, although it created the prosperity that 95 percent of humanity now enjoys, also flattened differentiation via the wholesale razing of local biomes, social practices, and belief systems. Despite the engineering of new species, the expansion of language through emergent slang, and the cultural creolization afforded by new communications technologies, a few hundred years is simply not enough time to re-create the lost diversity that existed pre-Bottleneck.

As some recent events have shown (the currency-software crash of 2279, the Australian Biotic Collapse, the Elvis Heresy, and so on), this depauperated state of the globe's information reservoirs can have perilous consequences. Simple systems are inherently less stable than diverse ones. The question is, can we reach into the past to retrieve lost information, and replenish our reserves?

New technological innovations seem to suggest that we can. The minute undulations recorded in the Landry-M'batu Spirals could not have been transcribed without molecular mapping, nor interpreted without cohomonym topology, a branch of linguistochastics developed only in the past few decades. The gene canon has allowed re-creation of extinct species: the Siberian tiger, the blue whale, a host of red algae. Countless rain forest species are preserved in vitro and remain to be reconstructed, if the complex environmental relationships among them can be worked out. The dinosaurs have famously eluded reanimation. The lack of anything like a dinosaur egg in the present has left the codes in recovered DNA undecipherable. Apparently, some information is irrecoverably lost.

Space technologies have also recovered pre-Bottleneck information. Translight probes recently exploring the HD141569 star system recorded faint FM transmissions that left Earth in the 1980s. (Moving at a sluggish light speed, these transmissions are only now reaching that star.) Perhaps some decades hence, several concentric spheres of translight craft could be erected at various distances from Earth, and capture the bounty of the relativistic information wake that surrounds the planet. From these transmissions pre-Bottleneck languages, music, and customs may one day be reconstructed routinely.

Much like the words recorded on the Landry-M'batu Spirals, these ancient voices would call to us faintly and in unfamiliar tongues, almost swallowed by the noise of their long journey through time. But surely we will listen carefully, their message the more precious for almost having been lost forever.

The Key

Ian Whates

Ian Whates has sold stories to various Web sites and magazines, and is the editor of Timepieces, *an anthology of stories from Stephen Baxter, Ian Watson, Jon Courtenay Grimwood, Liz Williams, and others. He lives in Cambridgeshire, England.*

It's amazing what a bunch of keys can say about a person. Key rings and their contents hold hidden depths, or so Carl had always maintained.

Take his wife's, for example: keys for the front door, car, garage, and a Yale for her mother's . . . plus various superfluous attachments: a pink plastic pig, a Perspex heart displaying the pseudo-word "whateva," and a smiley-emblazoned disc designed to impersonate a coin when liberating supermarket trolleys.

His own set was far more practical. Keys for car and home, one for a suitcase, and another for a young lady's apartment that he trusted his wife would never notice or question. Two add-ons: a worn leather fob from his very first jalopy and a pizzle-shaped plait of woven leather that he'd been assured was a fertility symbol but probably wasn't.

Then there was the set he had recently "acquired." Six keys plus three attachments: a circular Mercedes emblem, matching one of the keys; a tiny plastic-encased photo of a girl's face—presumably the owner's daughter; and a small, squat figurine with bloodred crystal eyes. This last attachment vaguely resembled an owl and gave Carl the creeps. Quite what it said about the owner he preferred not to dwell on.

It was the keys that really intrigued him. Two differently cut front-door keys, suggesting two homes, Merc and Land Rover keys—a car for each dwelling—and two others less easily identified.

Sammy-the-Locksmith's considered opinion proved as much use as a chocolate teapot. "One's for a cabinet and the other a safety-deposit box."

"Any way of telling where it is?"

"Nope."

He wouldn't have cared, except for the small matter of the reward. A ridiculous sum, offered for the keys' return with no mention of the Gucci wallet lifted at the same time, nor of the cash and credit cards contained therein. One of these keys was clearly important to someone and therefore valuable. Carl knew which his money would've been on. It remained useless to him, however, unless he could find precisely what it opened. To his growing frustration, unlocking that particular enigma proved beyond him.

"Mightn't even be in this country," his best and final hope had concluded with a shrug.

Reluctantly he arranged a meet, at a time and place of his choosing: a bar where he was known and felt safe. His recent victim and prospective benefactor awaited—a tall, muscle-broad individual who, even in an Armani suit, failed to look entirely polished or civilized. The rugged edges were still there: an uncut gem in a presentation box.

Carl would have preferred a dead-drop, an exchange without ever meeting face-to-face, but the other would have none of it. So he watched the man arrive from across the street, alert for any hint of police or other presence. Seeing none, he entered, glancing at the barman, whose shake of the head still fell short of total reassurance.

He took a deep breath and committed himself by sitting down. Eyes locked across a table. Unwavering self-confidence and steely strength couched within gray-blue irises; this was not a man to trifle with.

"You have the keys?" The voice was relaxed and casual to the point of being unnerving.

"You got the money?"

An envelope, produced from a pocket and then slid across the table. A fat envelope.

Carl reached out but the other's hand clung to its far edge. "The keys first."

"Not until I've counted it."

A frozen tableau that persisted for time-stretching seconds until the man abruptly let go. Carl opened the envelope and flicked through the wad of fifties, not counting with any accuracy, just checking.

Satisfied, he nodded to the barman, who left his station and came across with the keys.

To his credit, the stranger guffawed and nodded appreciation at such complicity. He looked the keys over once before pocketing them and rising to his feet. There he paused, fixing Carl with a glare—the first suggestion of either anger or menace.

"Don't cross my path again."

"Just a minute," Carl blurted out as the man turned to leave. "You've got them back now, so you can tell me, why are they so important?"

The man smiled—a malicious, satisfied expression, which lacked any hint of humor. "Do you really imagine I'm going to tell you?"

Carl watched the retreating back until it was out the door and away. Despite earning far more than anticipated from this episode he still felt cheated, as if opportunity had somehow slipped through his grasp. What wealth or secrets had the key represented? Too late now. He would never know.

"Never" lasted a month.

Carl was watching the news. He remained skeptical and unmoved by the inescapable buzz about the first proof of ET, scoffing at the media frenzy and avoiding television's blanket coverage—until now. He stared in disbelief at the image of what was allegedly an alien artifact. Set against a neutral background, the picture provided no sense of proportion, but Carl knew at once that it was small: a tiny, squat, owl-like effigy with bloodred eyes.

The reporter—all blond hair, glossy lipstick, and gushing exuberance—was explaining how its eccentric owner and discoverer had little faith in conventional secure repositories, so kept the priceless item on his key ring while awaiting the vital test results, which were soon to confirm its nonterrestrial composition. Thus inspired, she dusted down her poetic license and waxed lyrical about the artifact's potential for unlocking new worlds, labeling it "The Key to the Future."

Carl switched off the TV. For long minutes he sat there, simply staring at the empty screen.

The Godmother Protocols

Heather M. Whitney

Heather M. Whitney is a plant scientist living and working in Cambridge, England.

First take a frog. Choose your species with care. Although the skins of some frog species produce antimicrobials, and the ability to touch for the King's Evil is a splendid certificate of true royalty, other species have remarkably poisonous skins. A prince that causes death or mass hallucinations every time he shakes hands on a royal walkabout could result in an unfortunate revolution and republicanism.

Second, put any unhygienic thoughts of kissing out of your mind. Transfection plasmids designed to transform frog to human are far too unstable to be transmitted orally, and additionally have a distressing tendency to insert randomly into the genome, resulting in a cancerous mess rather than the required princely form. An adapted version of the old-fashioned method is still considered best in this case.

Obtain DNA from a suitable candidate. Please be careful during this step—the offspring of many royal families have bodyguards that are a little short-tempered with anyone approaching their charges with needles or syringes. It is also a bad idea to stalk the selected donor—a restraining order has never helped anyone. It is usually best to select a royal family with a number of obscure offshoots, that was deposed at some point during the twentieth century, or with a tendency for extra-pair copulation.

Remove oocytes from your selected frog. Several hundred will be required, the process still being somewhat unrefined; however, eye of newt and wing of bat are not needed, whatever the older textbooks say. As normal somatic-cell nuclear transfer methods have yet to produce viable embryos in frogs, a Transmogrifier™ kit should be used. Fortunately, this technology has recently been adapted to be used with microinjection equipment. One potential disadvantage of this method is that significant amounts of the original oocyte DNA can recombine with your candidate DNA. Do not worry about this too much—royal offspring with a fondness for flies can do little harm. If the emperor of Japan can be an expert in guppy taxonomy and the occupier of the throne of Great Britain and the Commonwealth talks to plants, a royal entomologist is not going to raise any eyebrows.

Incubate the cells as usual, then implant them into a surrogate mother. With an amphibian-mammal cross such as this, it is generally considered that a marsupial surrogate is the best compromise, particularly considering the superb nutritional quality of the milk provided once your clutch of princes has hatched.

Once you are assured of at least one healthy male child, social exposure becomes of primary importance. You must send the hatchlings to a school, the older the institution the better. Although it may appear irrational to put a not-entirely-human creature through a further dehumanizing experience, it does ensure that any of his remaining quirks and foibles that have not been crushed out can be laid squarely at the door of his educational facility. The ability to ride a horse and to dance are the two most common abilities required by ruling families, so concentrate on these. You will probably have to pay extra for this tuition. Fortunately the ability to slay dragons is no longer required. All dragons hatched to date have, by EU legislation, been toothless, flameless, and survive solely on blood-agar soup. This is probably for the best as the training for this skill is notorious for reducing the number of viable princes available.

Once the growth period and education are over, you can now habituate your specimen to its natural habitat. This is where choosing the DNA of an obscure royal family is of benefit, particularly if they have a tendency to extra-pair copulations. The most basic of unsubstantiated stories will be more than enough, when supported with your specimen's DNA fingerprint and phenotype (a good strong phenotype, such as the Bourbon nose or the Hapsburg lip, is also a good idea).

Unfortunately by this stage, unless you have modified your own telomeres, you will be far too old to be a suitable mate for your prince, as it is well known that princes require mates as least ten years their junior in virtually all societies. If you have planned for this, you will have imprinted your prince at an early age with either a scent or sound that will require him to marry a woman of your choosing, preferably your daughter for kin-selection and sociopolitical control purposes.

However, be careful as this leaves you in a rather precarious position—you will be the type of mother-in-law that has the power to change frogs into princes or princes into frogs. They have a tendency to come to a bad end. Make sure to keep your distance from open oven doors, ducking stools, and stakes in the center of pyres of wood that will inevitably appear whenever you visit.

The Great Good-bye

Robert Charles Wilson

Robert Charles Wilson was born in California and moved to Canada at the age of nine. He is the author of many stories and a dozen novels. Spin, *the latest, won the Hugo for Best Novel in 2006. He lives in Concord, Ontario.*

The hardest part of the Great Good-bye, for me, was knowing I wouldn't see my grandfather again. We had developed that rare thing, a friendship that crossed the line of the post-evolutionary divide, and I loved him very much.

Humanity had become, by that autumn of 2350, two very distinct human species—if I can use that antiquated term. Oh, the Stock Humans remain a "species" in the classical evolutionary sense: New People, of course, have forgone all that. Post-evolutionary, post-biological, budded or engineered, New People are gloriously free from all the old human restraints. What unites us all is our common source, the Divine Complexity that shaped primordial quark plasma into stars, planets, planaria, people. Grandfather taught me that.

I had always known that we would, one day, be separated. But we first spoke of it, tentatively and reluctantly, when Grandfather went with me to the Museum of Devices in Brussels, a day trip. I was young and easily impressed by the full-scale working model of a "steam train" in the Machine Gallery—an amazingly baroque contrivance of ancient metalwork and gas-pressure technology. Staring at it, I thought (because Grandfather had taught me some of his "religion"): Complexity made this. This is made of stardust, by stardust.

We walked from the Machine Gallery to the Gallery of the Planets, drawing more than a few stares from the Stock People (children, especially) around us. It was uncommon to see a New Person fully embodied and in public. The Great Good-bye had been going on for more than a century, but New People were already scarce on Earth, and a New Person walking with a Stock Person was an even more unusual sight—risqué, even shocking. We bore the attention gamely. Grandfather held his head high and ignored the muttered insults.

The Gallery of the Planets recorded humanity's expansion into the Solar System, and I hope the irony was obvious to everyone who sniffed at our presence there: Stock People could not have colonized any of these forbidding places (consider Ganymede in its primeval state!) without the partnership of the New. In a way, Grandfather said, this was the most appropriate place we could have come. It was a monument to the long collaboration that was rapidly reaching its end.

The stars, at last, are within our grasp. The grasp, anyhow, of the New People. Was this, I asked Grandfather, why he and I had to be so different from one another?

"Some people," he said, "some families, just happen to prefer the old ways. Soon enough Earth will belong to the Stocks once again, though I'm not sure this is entirely a good thing." And he looked at me sadly. "We've learned a lot from each other. We could have learned more."

"I wish we could be together for centuries and centuries," I said.

I saw him for the last time (some years ago now) at the Shipworks, where the picturesque ruins of Detroit rise from the Michigan Waters, and the star-traveling Polises are assembled and wait like bright green baubles to lift, at last and forever, into the sky. Grandfather had arranged this final meeting—in the flesh, so to speak.

We had delayed it as long as possible. New People are patient: in a way, that's the point. Stock Humans have always dreamed of the stars, but the stars remain beyond their reach. A Stock Human lifetime is simply too short; one or two hundred years won't take you far enough. Relativistic constraints demand that travelers between the stars must be at home between the stars. Only New People have the continuity, the patience, the flexibility to endure and prosper in the Galaxy's immense voids.

I greeted Grandfather on the high embarkation platform where the wind was brisk and cool. He lifted me up in his arms and admired me with his bright blue eyes. We talked about trivial things, for the simple pleasure of talking. Then he said, "This isn't easy, this saying good-bye. It makes me think of mortality—that old enemy."

"It's all right," I said.

"Perhaps you could still change your mind?"

I shook my head, no. A New Person can transform himself into a Stock Person and vice versa, but the social taboos are strong, the obstacles (family dissension, legal entanglements) almost insurmountable, as Grandfather knew too well. And in any case that wasn't my choice. I was content as I was. Or so I chose to believe.

"Well, then," he said, empty, for once, of words. He looked away. The Polis would be rising soon, beginning its eons-long navigation of our near stellar neighbors. Discovering, no doubt, great wonders.

"Good-bye, boy," he said.

I said, "Good-bye, Grandfather."

Then he rose to his full height on his many translucent legs, winked one dish-sized glacial blue eye, and walked with a slow machinely dignity to the vessel that would carry him away. And I watched, desolate, alone on the platform with the wind in my hair, as his ship rose into the arc of the high clean noonday sky.

Pigs on the Wing

K. Erik Ziemelis

K. Erik Ziemelis was finishing his doctorate in organic semiconductors at the University of Cambridge when he joined Nature. *He is now physical sciences editor and has an encyclopedic knowledge of current SF and fantasy. Not to be outdone by Oliver Morton, his name (along with hundreds of thousands of others) is due for launch on NASA's* Dawn *space mission to minor planets Ceres and Vesta. He lives in London. His doctorate, however, remains unfinished.*

"Come on, Kirsty. Get a wriggle on!"

Frank has another look at his watch and glances out the window. No panic yet, but they're cutting it fine.

"I'm coming, I'm coming!"

Kirsty (age six) not so much descends the stairs as free-falls into the living room, a flurry of brightly decorated limbs that seem to make contact with everything but the ground. Forward momentum absorbed by collision with the waiting adult, she gets to her feet, gives her uncle's legs a brief hug, and presents herself for inspection.

"Nice one, kiddo. Let's hit the road."

BreathEazys firmly in place, the two scamper through the heat and haze of the forecourt to the carpool. Frank checks the gauge, disconnects the charger, and bundles his niece into the waiting vehicle. Sliding in alongside, he seals the doors, gives the air a quick flush, and keys in his ID.

"Color?"

"Green!"

The Urban EcoWarrior shimmers from neutral gray to fluorescent emerald before rolling smoothly out of the lot to join the silent rainbow of evening rush-hour traffic. The two intrepid explorers settle back in their seats.

"So where are we going?"

Before Frank can articulate his well-rehearsed answer (it is supposed to be a surprise after all), a shrill voice pipes up from the vicinity of Kirsty's feet.

"We're off to see a 'rory who lives in the sky!"

Momentarily taken back by both the unexpected intrusion of a third party and the worrying possibility that his plans have somehow been exposed, Frank looks down at the floor. And there, easing its way out of the confines of Kirsty's carryall, is a small green pig with a smug expression on its face. Frank grins.

"Mr. Loop, I might have guessed. Are any secrets safe from you? But I think for now you've said enough."

The pig takes in Kirsty's questioning look, glances over at a now dramatically glowering Frank, before returning its attention to the child. Offering what passes for a porcine shrug and a forlorn my-lips-are-sealed wrinkling of its snout, the little animatronix bounces onto Kirsty's lap and snuggles down for the ride.

After a painless drive through the 'burbs, they are out in the foothills. Shortly afterward, they pull up alongside the transfer station—no magtrak beyond this point.

Timecheck. The sun still hovers over the island of glass and concrete that they have left behind, but the sky has already lost its familiar ochre tint. Sunset is little more than an hour away.

"OK, kiddo, wrap up warm."

Frank climbs swiftly into his weatherproof and hands a miniature but more colorful version to an oblivious Kirsty. For the past twenty minutes her face has been pressed up against the window, gazing wide-eyed at the surrounding countryside. And now, free of both the car and the claustrophobic air filter, she stands transfixed by the row-upon-row of four-wheeled antiques parked all around them. (Mr. Loop on the other hand gives the impression of being fast asleep, but—as befits a miniature replica of the comically self-important children's entertainer—is probably still sulking.)

A gust of chill mountain air snaps Kirsty out of her reverie. Thermals donned, backpacks stowed, and inert pig pocketed, the two slide into a brilliant-red, open-topped barchetta. Now it is Frank's turn to shiver with anticipation. The last time he drove one of these he was barely out of his teens, yet he still remembers the thrill of opening up the throttle and hearing the throaty roar of a real engine. And roar it does, right on cue, eliciting a squeal of excitement from the diminutive passenger—and the sweet taste of long-forbidden fruit for the driver. From here, the only way is up.

Final destination: Look-See Point. After a jarring drive up rough mountain tracks, Frank parks beside one of the crumbling domed structures scattered across the high plateau. He gathers a couple of folding chairs and strides hurriedly toward some clear ground. Kirsty only just keeps up and can barely hide her disappointment when she finally settles herself into a chair and looks around.

"Aw, they're just ruins."

"Never mind those old stones, kiddo. I promised to show you the heavens, and I will. But for now just watch . . . and wait."

A glance at his watch again: ten minutes to go. Frank smiles in relief. The number of favors he had to call in to pull this off—not to mention the cost of getting a prime-time slot—will not have been wasted.

With the sky now darkened to an inky black, Kirsty spots the first tiny pinpoints of light. "Stars," her uncle had called them. Sure, they seem to map out some pretty shapes, but she still can't see what the fuss is all about. To cover her mounting gloom, she returns to playing with the pig.

Then the heavens explode with splashes of light and color. One after another, familiar and unfamiliar objects parade across the sky: items of food, items of clothing, items of . . . well, just about anything a young mind can imagine, and a lot, lot more. Faster and faster the images race by until all that remains is a pulsating emerald sheet. The rippling edges of this curtain of light then start to bend and twist, turning in on one another, transforming, transfixing, becoming . . .

"Mr. Loop!"

Frank beams down at his niece. Kirsty, now on her feet, has one hand clamped over her mouth, the other outstretched as if trying to grab the sky itself. About her, the animated toy frolics, uttering decidedly unpiglike yelps as it flings itself repeatedly into the air. And its luminous namesake responds in kind, leaping nimbly from one celestial point to another, and leaving in its wake a glowing contrail that resolves into the words "HAPPY BIRTHDAY KIRSTY." Fade to green. Commercial services will resume shortly.

Frank sweeps his now-exhausted niece into his arms and carries her slowly back to the Jeep, the miniature Mr. Loop trotting contentedly in their wake. But Kirsty's tired eyes remain locked on the heavens as assorted consumer items recommence their endless auroral display.

"Show's over, kiddo. That's enough 'rory for one night."